COMES
THE BLACK MARIAH

H.L. ANDERSON

APEIRON

GRANTSVILLE, UTAH

Apeiron Books
An imprint of Immortal Works LLC
Grantsville, Utah

Cover Art by Ashley Literski
http://strangedevotion.wixsite.com/strangedesigns

ISBN 978-1-953491-89-3 (Paperback)
ASIN B0DJZJTW2L (Kindle Edition)

To the millions of people who have suffered and died—are still suffering and dying—under the tyrannical boot of Socialist utopianism.
And to those who have not yet learned—may your eyes be opened to the horrors this ideology rains down on people, before it's too late. Before they come for you.

AUTHOR'S NOTE

I first became interested in Russian history while listening to a Dr. Jordan Peterson lecture in which he referenced Aleksandr Solzhenitsyn and The Gulag Archipelago. I realized I knew next to nothing about the USSR and how it came to be, Lenin, Stalin, labor/re-education/prison camps, and the alarming number of people who lost their freedom and all too often their lives during this time period. The Russian Revolution (at least the one that preceded the events described in this book) began in 1917—there were actually two revolutions only months apart that ended centuries of imperial rule and ushered in an even darker period of rule led by self-declared Marxist, Vladimir Lenin. And if you think things couldn't get worse —after Lenin's death, Joseph Stalin, Lenin's successor, would prove you wrong in ways that would make the devil himself laugh with delight.

Everything that happens to the people in this work of fiction, happened in real life to someone—millions of someones—during the dark reign of Stalin from 1929 to 1953. I've pulled specific incidents from works such as The Gulag Archipelago (all three volumes); Gulag A History, by Anne Applebaum; The Whisperers: Private

Life in Stalin's Russia by Orlando Figes; and Varlam Shalamov's Kolyma Tales.

As I see increasing numbers of young people gravitate toward Marxism, socialism, and communism, I feel impressed to, in some small way, reveal to them the horrors and atrocities that have been borne of such ideologies. Writing fiction is part of who I am, so this work of fiction based on true events is my contribution in revealing the evils men and women commit when obsessed with political ideologies—leaving no room for dissenting opinions or freedom of thought.

~H.L. Anderson

Picture to yourself that the island environment differs so sharply from the normal human one and so cruelly confronts a man with the choice of immediate adaptation or immediate death that it grinds and masticates his character much more thoroughly than could a foreign national or a foreign social environment. And the only thing it can be compared with is a transmutation into the animal world.

~Aleksandr Solzhenitsyn

PART I

Late Summer-Fall 1938

1

They came at night, the Black Mariahs, and stole away the public enemies, politicals, the undesirables—the *Fifty-eights*—under the cover of darkness. But Anna Levitskaya didn't need to worry. Did she? She always chose her words with caution, never spoke without first considering the implications of her remarks. *Any* possible implications. Asking herself, "Could this thought be construed in any way as anti-government? Anti-Communist? Is it something a good Comrade would say? Something I could say in the presence of the Supreme Leader?" Even when sitting alone with her fiancé, Nikolai, on the couch of her family's apartment, they whispered. They whispered not because they had anything to hide, but because the walls were thin, and they sometimes weren't as careful with each other as they were around others. Not that Anna's mother would denunciate them, nor would her sister, Anna was sure. But the neighbors...one could never trust the neighbors.

Everyone knew someone who had been taken—and not always at night. One of Nikolai's professors had been arrested right from his office in the middle of the day. The *intelligentsia* were prime targets... No, Anna shook her head. That wasn't the right way to think about it. The *intelligentsia* were full of wreckers and traitors to the Motherland. That had to be the reason so many had been taken.

"What are you thinking about, Anna?" Nadya asked.

Anna jumped a little at her sister's voice. She'd been lost in thought again. But what else was there to do while waiting in line for bread? They'd come early, hoping to get something besides the heavy rye that was usually the only thing available. "Oh, lots of things. Mostly how grateful I am not to be using ration stamps anymore."

Nadya glanced quickly around, then frowned at her. "Comrade Stalin's second five-year plan has brought about great prosperity. This year's crop yield is set to be the best yet."

"I know!" Anna rushed to agree, nodding so hard her tight bun loosened on top of her head. Her overzealous head-nod was at least partially to keep from rolling her eyes. The Soviet Union did not know what prosperity was. Standing in line for hours to buy overpriced, low-quality bread even without having to use ration stamps wasn't much of an improvement. Of course, she'd only been a baby during the Revolution. She didn't remember what things were like under the Czars. But her grandmother, in a defiant whisper, had told her once that things only got worse when the Bolsheviks took over. People starving by the millions. Families forced from their homes and land—into exile or compelled to join the collective farms, the *kolkhoz*. Anna looked around as if someone near her could hear her thoughts, and she vowed silently that she would never repeat her grandmother's traitorous words. She pulled her sweater closed in front. Even though it was still August, the mornings were getting colder in Moscow.

The door to the market swung open, and the line surged forward, sweeping Anna and her sister along with it. They'd come early enough that the initial push saw them through the doors, within sight of the bread piled on tables. When Anna and Nadya reached the table nearest them, Anna clapped her hands together and smiled. "We'll take a small loaf of wheat bread."

The gruff man standing behind the table picked one up and plopped it onto the scale. "That will be one-half ruble," he barked.

Anna frowned but unzipped her purse.

Nadya took hold of her arm and whispered, "Anna, no. Just get the black bread. That is too much."

Her sister was right. She shouldn't spend that much money when she could get the rye bread for so much less. She shook her head and reached into her small purse. "Just this once, I want to splurge. Nikolai can come over tomorrow and bring the sausage he bought yesterday, and the five of us can have a nice dinner for Mama's birthday." She dug out five kopeks and dropped them in the man's outstretched hand.

Nadya scowled and muttered, "Mikhail prefers black bread. He says that is what *real* Russian men eat."

Watching the man wrap the small loaf in a sheet of paper, Anna said, "Well, your husband can buy his own bread for dinner tomorrow, then." She smiled as the store worker shoved the package into her hands. "I'm having this."

"Anna!" Nadya scolded her as they made their way back out to the street. She leaned in close so she could talk in a low voice. "That is no way to treat the man who makes it possible for us and Mama to live in a decent apartment. Without Mikhail's Party membership, we'd be assigned housing in one of the dormitories. Forget about living in a shared apartment!"

"I'm sorry." Anna sighed. "I am grateful for Mikhail." Her sister was right. After their father died, they were set to be moved to the dormitories on the other side of the city. Her mama wouldn't have done well in that setting, not to mention that Anna would have had a forty-five-minute walk to and from work every day. Her sister's marriage saved the day.

They walked along in silence, Anna's gaze flicking from people—mostly kids—curled up in doorways or lying on benches, to the government posters lining the street touting the wonders of socialism and decrying capitalism, encouraging exercise, and threatening shirkers with slogans such as "We smite the lazy workers!" Interspersed among them, of course, were larger images of the Supreme Leader, Comrade Stalin, dressed in his sharp military uniform and staring off into the distance. Anna wondered what that resolute expression meant. What was he thinking? She turned and looked up at the studded spires rising from behind the wall of the Kremlin.

Did he really care about them? His citizens? Did he truly believe his "five-year plans" were successful, even as people were starving in the streets? Were his Comrades feeding him lies about the state of things down here while he hid away in his palace?

Anna sighed and looked away from the compound just in time to avoid tripping over the bare feet of a sleeping—or passed out—street urchin. So many orphans...

That had to be it. Comrade Stalin wouldn't allow these things to happen if he knew... Would he? She shook her head and quickened her steps to catch up to her sister. All of those thoughts were treasonous, and she must push them from her mind. The Motherland was thriving, all thanks to the genius of the Supreme Leader.

Her pasted-on smile was a lie—an appropriate façade in this country full of deception. But as her thoughts turned to Nikolai and the tender kisses they'd shared hidden in the shadows of a deserted doorway as he walked her home last night, a genuine smile crept onto her lips.

"What are you smiling about?" Nadya scowled. She seemed to do that an awful lot lately.

"Just thinking about Nikolai." Anna wouldn't let her ill-tempered sister ruin her daydreams.

"Pfft. You'd be better off dumping that scholarly fiancé of yours and finding yourself a Party man like my Mikhail." Her scowl deepened, and she shook her head. "I don't know how you let yourself get tangled up with a devotee of the *intelligentsia*—you know they are nothing but loafers and wreckers."

"Nadya!" Anna's indignant voice whooshed out in a gruff

whisper. "You know Nikolai isn't like that. His sole reason for seeking acceptance into the school of engineering is to use his knowledge to help build up the Motherland. He is a dedicated citizen, loyal to the Supreme Leader." Of course he was. To be anything else would be considered *anti-Soviet agitation* or *treason to the Motherland.*

Nadya's face softened, and she sighed. "I know, little sister. You are right. Nikolai is a good man and will be a good husband to you. I just wish he showed more interest in joining the Communist Party."

Anna pursed her lips. She was glad Nikolai wasn't interested. Ever since Nadya had married a Party member, she'd become increasingly sanctimonious.

He didn't need to join the Party, anyway. Nikolai would soon complete his studies at the Industrial Academy and be assigned a position fitting of his genius. They would marry. He'd already found an Orthodox priest to perform the ceremony—no small feat, since most of them had been arrested, tried, and either executed or sent to the Gulags. Her mother had been thrilled at the news.

The sisters entered their apartment building, and Anna smiled again, thinking about Nikolai and those kisses...and when, on their wedding night, the lovers would finally be able to surrender to the stirrings they created.

2

Boots clomping up the stairs roused Anna from her troubled sleep. Her heart ricocheted inside her chest as the echoes of pounding fists came from the hallway outside their apartment. Her legs shook, and the cabbage soup she'd eaten for dinner nearly made a reappearance as her stomach churned. She crept to the door, soon joined by Nadya and Mikhail, then her mother.

A timorous sigh of relief eked past Anna's paralyzed vocal cords as it became evident that the hammering was not at their door, but at the neighbors'.

The three women pressed their ears against the thin wall separating the two apartments.

"Boris Narokov!" a booming voice shouted, eliciting cries of terror from several of the apartment's occupants. "You are under arrest. Get dressed!"

"Me?" came the gravelly voice of the man who, until moments ago, had likely been sleeping. "What for?"

"You'll find out soon enough. Come on now, let's go."

A woman's voice, high-pitched and broken, begged, "Let me pack him some things. It'll only take a moment. Please."

Through the insubstantial wall, Anna listened to the woman's footsteps and mumblings as she opened and closed drawers. "You'll need some underwear. Soap, I'll break a piece off for you. Some potatoes and a sausage. Your pea jacket. What...what else?"

"Hurry up, citizen. He doesn't need anything. They'll feed him, keep him warm. He'll get what he needs at the Lubyanka."

"Boris!" The fear in the woman's voice chilled Anna clean through. That slight tremor, the high pitch, revealed that she knew the likelihood she'd see her husband again was slim. "Here. Take this."

"Fine, fine," the NKVD officer said. "Take the bag and say goodbye to your kids."

"Daddy!"

The child's cry nearly caused sympathy to overtake Anna's tremendous relief that it wasn't *her* door the Secret Police had pounded on.

"It's okay, sweetie." The man was more awake now, his tone less raspy. Barely contained fear lurked beneath the brave front he tried to present to his daughter. "There's been a mistake. Just a mistake. It'll get figured out and set straight. You'll see. I'll probably be back by breakfast."

"Let's go," the officer barked. "You two stay here and search the place."

The door slammed, and several sets of boots stomped through the hallway and down the stairs. The wall between the two apartments shook as the brutal sounds of the "search" drowned out the crying of the children. Crashes, heavy items being thrown around, drawers being dumped on the floor, and the crunch of broken glass and dishes under the jackboots of the Secret Police.

Nadya sniffed indifferently and stood. But her gait was unsteady as she made her way to the table and pulled out a chair to sit.

Anna, Mama, and Mikhail joined her. There was no sense in hurrying back to bed; the noisy "search" would likely go on for hours.

Mama's eyes bulged, and she whispered, "That poor family."

They didn't know each other more than just an occasional nod in the hallway or on the stairs, though they'd lived next door for over a year. Letting anyone besides family into your circle was dangerous—you never knew who might be an informant.

Anna glanced at her brother-in-law. Even letting family know your thoughts could be dangerous.

Nadya folded her arms, stared at their mother, and hissed, "He is an *Enemy of the People*, Mama. The whole family probably is. They deserve it."

"You don't know that, Nadya," Mama whispered, barely audible across the small table. "They take so many people. Every night. Even in the daytime." She wiped her eyes with a shaky hand. "They can't all be Enemies of the People."

Mikhail stiffened. "I hope you aren't suggesting that our Leaders are wrong, Mother. Their vigilance in rooting out the anti-Soviet agitators is what allows the Motherland to prosper." He leaned toward the aging woman. "You'd do well to follow Nadya's lead in recognizing that arrests are not made without cause."

Anna hated seeing the fear flash in her mama's eyes just before she looked down at her shaking hands and murmured, "Yes, of course you're right, Mikhail."

Patting her mother's hand, Anna said, "We have nothing to worry about, Mama. We are loyal citizens who are doing our part to accomplish the Supreme Leader's plan." She hid her concern from Mama and Mikhail. She used to truly believe that, but lately... Mama was right; the Black Mariahs were filled to bursting every night. It almost seemed people were taken at random.

Anna smoothed the worried crease from her brow and turned her mouth up into a slight smile as she looked Nadya and her husband in the eye. "I'm going to try to get some sleep before I have to head to the factory for my shift." She scooted her chair back, wincing as a loud crash came from next door. She knew she wouldn't sleep anymore this night, but she needed to get away from the reproving glare of her brother-in-law.

She hugged her mother from behind and kissed her cheek, then ducked under the clothesline stretched across the small kitchen, draped with yesterday's laundry, and held her breath until she lowered herself to the thin mattress that lay inches from her mother's in the tiny room they shared. Lying on her back with her eyes open, she stared at the stained ceiling, the cracked plaster creating a familiar mosaic in the dim light seeping down the short hallway and into the doorless room from the single, dangling bulb in the kitchen.

Thoughts swirled in her mind. How could her mama still have so much empathy for others when the only emotion Anna felt was overwhelming gratitude that the jack-booted men hadn't come for her?

☭

Anna was up and dressed before their shared alarm clock clanged out its morning racket. She slurped down a small bowl of the watered-down *kasha* she'd heated up, even though she didn't have much of an appetite. She'd need some energy to make it through the work day. Wrapping a piece of black bread and a boiled potato in cloth, she nodded at her sister as she emerged from her room.

"You've been busy this morning," Nadya said.

"I couldn't go back to sleep after..." Anna gestured in the direction of the adjoining apartment. "So I just got up."

Nadya looked away and cleared her throat, the self-confidence she'd exhibited in the night all but gone. "Well, thank you for making the porridge."

"Of course." Anna put her lunch bundle in her bag and looked up when her mama shuffled into the kitchen. "Happy birthday, Mama." She kissed her cheeks and smiled.

"Thank you, dear."

"We'll have a nice dinner tonight to celebrate." Anna stepped toward the door even though it was early. She'd take her time walking to work today.

Mama grinned. "Is Nikolai coming?"

"Yes, Mama. But no flirting with my fiancé this time." Anna shook her finger at her mother, trying to look stern.

"Oh, but he's so handsome! I can't help myself." Mama's teasing smile faded as her eyes became wet with sentiment. "You two make such a handsome couple." She reached up and smoothed Anna's hair. "I'm so glad you inherited your father's gorgeous black hair and honey-colored eyes."

Nadya rolled her eyes, her mouth slightly turned up at the corners. "You do remind me so much of Papa."

"Where's Mikhail? Shouldn't he be up?" Mama asked, looking around.

"Anna wasn't the only one who couldn't sleep. He went to the office early. The Party Leaders will notice his extra efforts."

Anna doubted that. He spent more time at the office than anywhere else, often not returning home until long after they'd all gone to bed. He rarely took a day off, devoting all his time and energy to the Great Socialist Cause—as all good citizens should, according to him. Going above and beyond was expected, not rewarded.

"Well, I'm going to work. I'll see you tonight." Anna stepped into the hallway and shut the door. Glancing at the neighbors' apartment, she wondered how long the government would allow the man's family to stay there. She shook her head. They'd be lucky to be moved to a dormitory instead of being exiled—or worse, sent to a Gulag, a forced labor camp, where the husband and father who'd been taken in the dark of night would doubtless end up.

Anna's innate cheery disposition turned somber as she descended the three flights of stairs to the street. The atmosphere of constant fear dragged her down. *Anyone* could be an *Organ* of the Soviet Secret Police. She walked with intent, not meeting the eyes of the people around her in the streets, but staying alert, observing them peripherally. Any of them could be an Organ in disguise. The bicyclist avoiding the cracks in the road. The railway conductor. The bank teller, standing by the door to the bank, waiting to be let in.

She dodged a group of children, their white shirts and red scarves giving them away as Young Pioneers—any of them could be an Organ. An informer.

She often wondered if there'd been a time in Russia when people spoke at normal volumes. When they weren't afraid to have a conversation that wasn't whispered, eyes darting around to make sure no one was listening. Not in her twenty-one years of life, she was sure.

3

The whir of hundreds of sewing machines and the monotony of sewing the same pattern over and over wasn't helping Anna fight off the drowsiness that had taken hold of her after lunch break. She shook her head, trying to wake her mind up and keep her eyes open. If the supervisor saw her nodding off...well, any number of things could happen. Up to and including arrest for being a *wrecker*, which was considered counter-revolutionary sabotage.

Anna sat up straighter and tried to concentrate on creating a straight seam. When she'd first been assigned to work at the garment factory, she hadn't been exactly excited about it, but she was thankful she hadn't been assigned to somewhere much worse. Like the steelworks factory—she'd seen the scars that resulted from molten ore splashing the skin. Though the work was boring and repetitive, she was glad to do her part for the growth of the Soviet Union.

"Vera Ivanich!"

Anna jerked the garment she was sewing, causing the stitchwork to veer off the edge of the material. She stopped working the pedals with the distant thought that she'd need to unpick the thread, putting her behind on her work quota for the day. That muted thought was overpowered by the terror rushing through her chest as all the work stopped. A girl slowly stood from her machine, the blood draining from her face and a strangled cry hissing from her throat as she faced the factory supervisor and the group of NKVD officers behind him.

"Are you Vera?" One of the officers stepped up next to the supervisor.

"Y...yes," the girl stammered, wringing her hands.

Boots clomping on the cement floor, the officer moved to stand in front of her. "Empty your pockets."

"Why?" she cried, eyes darting around as if searching for help.

"Empty your pockets." The officer leaned in, his face only inches from hers.

With trembling hands, the girl reached under her apron and into the pocket of her dress. Before pulling her hand all the way out, she looked at the factory supervisor, eyes pleading. "Comrade Kirov, p... please. I didn't—"

The officer slapped her so hard she spun and stumbled into the sewing machine table behind her. "Show me what you've got."

The girl righted herself, tears now leaking from her eyes, down her face, to mingle with the blood trickling from her split lip. "I'm sorry!" she sobbed as she held out her hand, a small spool of thread resting in her palm.

"Quit your blubbering, girl!" an older woman scolded her from a few rows away. "You're a Russian! Act like one."

Wiping her eyes, the girl stood straighter, shoulders still slumped, but couldn't stop a terrified sob from escaping.

"Vera Ivanich," the officer said, "you are under arrest for violations of the law under Article fifty-eight, Section seven."

As the officers and factory supervisor marched the distraught girl out, Anna looked down at her marred garment and tried to slow her breathing. Why would that girl have stolen from The People? Was she a counterrevolutionary?

As if reading her thoughts, the woman assigned to the sewing machine next to Vera Ivanich said in a hushed voice, "She was just hungry. Her father was taken, and she's been giving her portions to her little brother. She was probably just going to trade it for some bread or potatoes."

The older woman who had scolded Vera for crying puffed out her chest and spat, "Are you saying that Comrade Stalin's Soviet government is not providing for its citizens?"

"No, no! Of course not. She must have—"

"Back to work, you shirkers!" the supervisor bellowed as he returned to the factory floor. "And this little interruption *will not* be used as an excuse to not reach the required output today. You'll stay until it's reached."

No longer worried about dozing off, Anna pulled the material out of her machine and set to picking out the errant threads, hoping she wouldn't be too late in getting home to celebrate her mother's birthday. As she worked, she wondered if the bossy old woman who'd yelled at Vera and her neighbor was an *informer* and if Vera's neighboring seamstress would be taken next.

☭

Anna managed to reach her quota only thirty minutes after the end-of-workday bell sounded. She dragged her feet to the factory exit, steering clear of the old woman she now suspected was an informer. She knew some of the girls whispered to each other as they sewed, and even became friends. But Anna always worried that she'd say something wrong, something that could be construed as agitation toward the Soviet power...or even just not show enough enthusiasm about the *ideas* expressed in the government run newspaper. Yes, it was best to keep to herself and save her conversations for her mother and Nikolai.

She only looked up once she stepped outside, and the weariness of the upsetting day lifted from her shoulders like a bird taking flight. There stood Nikolai, smiling as he leaned against a lamppost, a small bouquet in his hand and a bundle peeking out of the pocket of his peacoat. That smile was the best thing in Anna's world. Finding her own smile, she rushed to him and threw her arms around his neck, kissing his cheek.

"My Anna." Nikolai wrapped his free arm around her waist and pulled her close for a few seconds, whispering in her ear, "Those ruby-red lips of yours belong pressed up next to mine." He pulled back and looked at her. "That's not to say that I don't enjoy the warmth they bring to my skin no matter where they touch," he added, lifting his fingers to his cheek.

Anna blushed as she gazed into his dark-brown eyes in the waning sunlight. "We should get on our way." She unwound her arms from around his neck with a sigh.

"Yes, we should." He offered her his elbow as they made their way through the crowd of workers leaving the sewing factory. "We don't want to be late for your mama's birthday dinner."

The grip she had on his arm must have been tighter than normal, for he looked down at her with an uncharacteristic crease in his forehead. "Is everything all right? You seem tense, my love."

She loosened her hold on his bicep and looked around before answering in a quiet voice, "A girl was taken...arrested today right from the sewing room floor. She'd stolen a small spool of thread."

He nodded, pressing his arm, and her hand, closer to his body. "Did you know her well?"

Anna noted his use of the past tense. *Did* you. Not *do* you. Everyone knew the chances of that girl coming back were next to nothing. "No. Not at all, really." Her voice cracked just a little, so she clamped her mouth shut.

"But it was still hard for you to watch."

Leaning her head against his shoulder, Anna worked the muscles in her throat, trying to swallow down her sudden impulse to cry. Nikolai understood. She needn't give voice to her fears or misgivings about the hundreds—maybe thousands, she had no way to quantify it

—of citizens that had disappeared to the Gulags over the last year-and-a-half.

She raised her head as she remembered the scene from last night, the two arrests playing over each other in her mind. She whispered, "They came for our neighbor last night. The Black Mariah. The NKVD."

A chill rattled Nikolai's typically solid bearing, and he stopped, pulling Anna into a tight embrace. "I'd rather die than let myself be thrown into the back of one of those black beasts manufactured in the depths of hell," he whispered against her hair.

She shook her head. "Don't say that, Nikolai. I couldn't survive without you."

Clearing his throat, he released her and propped his lips up with a dashing smile that didn't quite touch his eyes. "Well, then, we'll just have to make sure we're very careful with our words and actions, won't we? So no one can question our undying support of the government and the Supreme Leader."

Of course, he was right. Wasn't he? That girl today *had* stolen property that belonged to the Soviet government.

And Anna had no way of knowing what kind of traitorous activities her neighbor might have been involved with.

And the teen boys who'd been arrested last week for distributing anti-Soviet propaganda—they were obviously working against the government.

And the saleswoman from the little mercantile over by Nikolai's dormitory—she'd used a newspaper to write down the number of items received in a shipment. She should have paid more attention to where the tip of her pencil rested. Defacing a picture of Comrade Stalin, even though it was just a small area of his forehead, was considered an act of terrorism. It didn't matter that there was no other paper available for her to write on.

And the children Mikhail had told them about as he defended the Decree of 1935 that stated children from the age of twelve on had full criminal responsibility...the kids who had been roughhousing and accidentally (well, Mikhail hadn't said *accidentally* when he told them about it) knocked a government poster off the wall. The two eldest were sentenced under Article 58. So were the parents of all the children, because, obviously, they must have told the children to do it.

Just be careful. The sick feeling in Anna's stomach didn't improve with that thought for some reason.

4

Mama's smile when Nikolai presented the small bouquet to her and kissed her on the cheek with a "Happy Birthday, beautiful!" helped to settle Anna's worried stomach, though a gnawing uneasiness remained in the background.

"Where did you get those flowers?" Mikhail asked with a frown.

Nikolai clapped the smaller man on the back and said, "Don't worry, Comrade. I paid for them."

Mikhail stiffened. "I wasn't suggesting otherwise."

"I bought them outside the railway station, in full view of two officers." He turned away from Mikhail, pulled a paper-wrapped package out of his pocket, and handed it to Nadya with a flourish. "A sausage for your pot, madame."

Her lips twitched as if considering a smile, but with a glance at her husband, a stern look returned to her face. "Thank you. It would have been nice to have it half an hour ago so we could eat on time."

Anna considered telling her about why she'd been delayed at work, but something held her back. Instead, she gestured to the couch and said, "Nikolai, have a seat while I help."

She pulled the old, cracked bowls down from the shelf and distributed them around the table.

"Get your fiancé and me a glass," Mikhail said. He worked to open a bottle of vodka he'd pulled from his overcoat. "One of my Party Comrades was able to get this for me." He winked at Nikolai, apparently no longer concerned about possible black-market flowers. "It's the new forty-percent stuff."

"You two take it easy with that," Nadya said as she dumped the sausage she'd just sliced into a boiling pot. "That's twice as strong as you're used to."

"We are Russian men, woman! We know how to drink!" Mikhail twisted the metal cap off and threw it on the table, where it bounced a couple of times before settling against a bowl. He filled each glass about a quarter of the way, then took one for himself and handed the other to Nikolai, who stood from the couch as soon as "vodka" was mentioned.

Holding up his glass, Mikhail said, "To the Supreme Leader, Comrade Stalin!"

They clinked the glasses together, then each downed their vodka in one gulp.

"Dinner is ready. Bring me the bowls, Anna," Nadya said.

"It smells delicious." Mama patted Nikolai on the arm before settling into her chair at the table. "Thank you for the sausage. It's always good to have meat in the soup."

He winked at her. "You're welcome, Mama Levitskaya. I'd do whatever possible to see that magnificent smile light up your face."

Mama blushed and slapped Nikolai's arm, her smile growing bigger.

Anna pulled out the wheat bread she'd bought the day before and sliced a piece for each of them, even Mikhail, and though Nadya had said he preferred the cheaper heavy black bread, he didn't hesitate to take it from her outstretched hand. With the added sausage and extra cabbage Nadya had added to the soup, it was the best meal they'd eaten in ages.

Mikhail mumbled between bites about "wasting food" and it being "excessive for a single meal" and "bourgeoise-like." His mumblings came less frequently as the bottle of vodka setting before him emptied into his and Nikolai's gullets.

After rare second helpings were doled out to the men, Anna and Nadya stood to clear the table. "Mama," Anna said, "you rest, we'll clean up."

Mama patted Anna's hand tenderly. "You spoil me, *solnyshko*."

Smiling at the nickname, *little sun*, Anna squeezed her mama's hand. "You deserve to be spoiled."

Anna dried the dishes the best she could with the threadbare dishtowel as Nadya washed and rinsed them.

At a loud snort of laughter from Nikolai, the sisters turned toward the men. Nadya scowled and whispered, "You'd better tell your fiancé to stop drinking before he gets too sloshed to walk home." She raised her nose into the air. "He is not spending the night here."

So bossy her sister had become since her marriage! "Oh, Nadya, let them have a little fun."

Nadya scowled, but whatever retort she'd prepared was interrupted by her husband's slurred words. "Ahh, Nik, we seem to have found the bottom of the bottle." He poured one last drink for each of them and held his glass aloft. "The first and the last toast should always be to the Supreme Leader. To Stalin!"

Their glasses clinked, and they downed the last of the vodka.

Anna gathered the glasses, setting them in the sink for her sister to wash.

She barely recognized Nikolai's garbled voice. She'd never seen him this intoxicated before, as he leaned across the table toward Mikhail. "Did you hear about the time Stalin was out swimming and he began to drown?"

Mikhail stiffened, and Anna's stomach clenched as she tried to signal to Nikolai to stop.

But either he didn't see her frantically shushing him with a finger to her lips, or he ignored her as he continued, "No worries, Comrade.

A peasant who was passing by jumped in and pulled him safely to shore. Stalin asked the peasant what he would like as a reward. Realizing whom he had saved, the peasant cried out, 'Nothing! Just please don't tell anyone I saved you!'" Nikolai laughed, slapping the table, oblivious to the icy tone that had descended on the room.

"That is not funny!" Spit flew from Mikhail's mouth as his face turned a dark shade of red. The vein on his temple bulged like a fat leach getting its fill of blood. "It's...it's treasonous!"

"No," Anna's throat closed, and she swallowed before choking out her next words in a whisper. "He didn't mean it." She looked to her sister for help, but the deep scowl of her forehead above her glowering eyes told Anna enough. Nadya would side with her husband.

Finally grasping his mistake, Nikolai sat up and replaced his drunken smile with a frown. "Mikhail, I...it was just a joke."

Mikhail shook his head. "Treason against the Supreme Leader is no joke."

"Mikhail," Mama's stern voice turned all heads toward her, "stop that nonsense about treason right this minute. He's obviously drunk and doesn't know what he's saying. Perhaps sharing a whole bottle of vodka wasn't the best idea." The way her eyes pinned Mikhail to his seat indicated exactly who Mama thought was to blame.

Anna shot a grateful look at her mother.

Meeting her eyes, Mama said, "Anna, why don't you walk Nikolai out? Thank you all for the wonderful dinner, but I'm afraid it's past my bedtime."

With a steadying grip on her fiancé's arm as he stumbled down the stairs, bile rose in Anna's throat. Mikhail was a Party Member, but he wasn't an informant, was he? He wouldn't denounce Nikolai... would he? She bit her lip as she remembered the anger etched across his face.

They stepped outside, the cool air helping to sober Nikolai up a little more. He turned to face Anna, gripping her arms at the elbows. "I'm sorry. I shouldn't have drunk so much."

Looking up into his glossy eyes, she held back tears. "You don't think Mikhail—"

"No." He placed a finger to her lips. "He'll see reason in the morning, after we've both had time to sober up."

Anna nodded, hoping he was right. "Okay, then. Are you able to make it home all right?"

"Yes, my love. I'll see you tomorrow night. Let's meet at the café at eight."

Anna had almost forgotten about their planned date. Nikolai had somehow procured tickets to a play. She nodded and leaned into him as he embraced her.

She watched him walk away into the darkness, swerving slightly across the sidewalk, before she went back inside and trudged up the three flights of stairs to the apartment.

Nadya and Mikhail, huddled together at the table, stopped talking as soon as Anna entered. She looked from them to Mama, whose face was pale, a worry line creasing her forehead as she pursed her lips into a tight seam.

Anna's anger pushed up against the fear boiling in her guts. She pulled out the chair across from her sister and brother-in-law and dropped into it. She swallowed down the anger; she needed to smooth things over, and anger wasn't going to help. "Listen, you know that was just the alcohol talking, right? I mean, it was just a joke. He didn't mean it."

"Drunkenness is no excuse," Mikhail said. "Alcohol only tends to loosen the tongue, freeing one to express their true thoughts."

Nadya nodded in agreement.

Anna clenched her fists under the table, her fingernails digging into the flesh of her palms. "Mikhail, please—"

"Please what, Anna?" he scoffed. "Please ignore the Directive issued in 1935?"

"Wh...what directive?"

He leaned forward, closing the distance between them across the table. "The Directive stating that the sharing of political jokes is as much a crime as leaking state secrets. The sign of a hidden enemy. Treason! Punishable by law under Article 58-10: Anti-Soviet agitation."

Anna couldn't swallow. Couldn't breathe. She looked at her sister with bulging, pleading eyes.

Nadya's face softened just a little. She took her husband's hand and spoke softly to him. "Nikolai was wrong to tell that joke. Could you, for my sister's sake, just talk to him about it privately, when you're both sober? Instead of turning him in? He made a mistake, Mikhail. I'm sure it's one he won't make again after you instruct him on the dangers of such propaganda. Not everyone understands that words can be used as weapons." She touched his chin. "You are such a magnificent teacher, I'm sure your influence will help him to change."

Mikhail glanced at Anna then Mama before returning his gaze to Nadya. "I'll consider it for you, my sweet." In a quieter voice, he added, "But I can't help but think that Anna would be better off with a loyal comrade for a husband."

Anna jerked her head up, and Mama gripped her arm under the table with a slight shake of her head. *Keep quiet* was the message.

"Yes, well," Nadya said. "Love is blind—especially young love. And I'm afraid if her heart were broken, she'd not be a very good wife for anyone."

"Well, yes, but—"

"No more talk of politics and love," Nadya said. "It's late, let's go to bed so you can sleep off that half bottle of forty-percent alcohol you downed." She pulled him to his feet and led him to their room without a backwards glance.

Mama released her grip on Anna's arm and whispered, "It's going to be fine. Mikhail will have forgotten all about it by morning."

Anna nodded, fear and exhaustion robbing her of her ability to speak. She trudged alongside her mother to their small room and undressed in the dark before lowering herself to her mattress. She tossed and turned as her thoughts raced.

Nadya won't let Mikhail denounce Nik.
But can she really stop him?
Party before family. I've heard him say that numerous times.
Mama's right, he won't even remember this in the morning.

5

The clanging of the alarm clock jerked Anna out of a restless sleep. She felt like she hadn't slept at all, but the drool she wiped from her face said otherwise. She dressed in the dark, her stomach falling as the events from the night before replayed in her mind.

She washed her face and pinned her hair up in a bun in the tiny bathroom. She'd been so grateful to be one of the few families in the building to have their own kitchen and bathroom—to not have to share those spaces with other families as they'd had to when living in a communal apartment. She'd thought at the time that the benefits of her sister marrying a Party Member outweighed the negatives. Now she'd give anything to be back in that abysmal, noisy, dirty place. To be rid of Mikhail and his religious zealotry toward the Party.

Stepping out into the kitchen, Anna shook her head as Nadya offered her a bowl of kasha. Her stomach was in even more of a turmoil than her mind.

"How...how is Mikhail this morning?" she asked.

Nadya glanced toward their room. "He has a bit of a headache, but he's up and getting ready for work."

Anna looped her purse strap over her shoulder, then twisted it in her hand. "Is he...has he..." She looked back at the room and whispered, "Has he said anything about...last night?"

The kasha bubbled, flipping a wet blob onto the stove. Nadya turned the burner off and removed the pot from it. "Not yet. But last night he agreed not to say anything. I think he'll stick to that."

Anna nodded. That was the best she could hope for. "Thank you. I'll see you after work."

She kept her head down as she walked to work, not wanting to see the government posters plastered everywhere, reminding her of the grave mistake the man she loved had made. She knew he wasn't an anti-Soviet agitator. He was a good citizen, a good student, who just wanted to do his part to help build a better Soviet Union. To help bring Comrade Stalin's plans to fruition. Surely Mikhail could see that?

Seated at her sewing machine, Anna checked the thread as she waited for the supervisors to hand out the day's allotment of material. The starting whistle had blown a few minutes ago, and from the corner of her eye Anna surveyed the two empty chairs—the one where Vera Ivanich had sat until her arrest yesterday, and the one at the sewing machine next to hers. A quick glance back at the old woman who had yelled at Vera and her neighbor yesterday told her all she needed to know. The woman nodded smugly at the empty chairs before bending to her work. She was an informer. She'd turned the neighboring seamstress in for uttering words of defense for Vera's predicament.

The dozens of women worked in subdued silence save for the whirring of the machines. Anna thought she may never utter another word inside this factory. It was safer that way.

She hurried home after work to clean up and change her clothes. Mama was there alone, hanging laundry on the clothesline strung across the kitchen.

"Where is Nadya?" Anna asked after stopping to give her mother a kiss on the cheek.

Mama shrugged, removing the clothespin from her mouth. "I'm not sure. She left hours ago to take Mikhail his lunch that he forgot."

Anna furrowed her brow. "I hope everything is okay."

"I'm sure she's fine. He often ropes her into helping out around the office when she visits him there. I believe it's his way of introducing her to the Party members so they might be inclined to vote her in next time she applies."

A squeezing pressure started deep in Anna's chest as she replayed Mikhail's reaction to Nikolai's drunken joke the night before.

"Don't you and that handsome fiancé of yours have a date tonight?" Mama asked.

Anna smiled and shook her head at her flirtatious mother. "Yes, Mama. I just came home to change."

She'd only been to the theater once before, when she was twelve and her class went to see a production put on by the older kids in the Komsomol. After washing up in the bathroom and deciding to wear her hair down for a change, she dressed in her best skirt and blouse, pulled her only good pair of stockings on, and secured them with elastic garters. She slipped her feet into the stylish chunky heels Mikhail had brought home for Nadya, thankful they hadn't fit her sister's big feet.

"How do I look?" She twirled for her mother.

"Beautiful." Mama pinched Anna's cheeks, her way of adding some color to her face without using makeup. "Take a sweater, though. It might still be summer officially, but fall is right around the corner. And it's still Russia out there."

Anna grabbed her sweater before leaving to meet Nikolai at the café.

"Did you choose this play because one of the heroes of the story is named Nikolai?" Anna teased as they left the theater. Although it had been violent and not at all a happy production, *The Days of the Turbins* had served to take her mind off of her worry that Mikhail would change his mind and denounce Nikolai.

"Heroism does seem to come with the name." Nikolai smiled, took her hand, and turned down the street toward his dormitory, stars twinkling overhead as it neared the midnight hour.

Anna laughed and tugged on his arm to bring him to a stop. "We're heading in the wrong direction, love. It's late, and I have to work in the morning." She frowned. "Unless you aren't planning on walking me home?"

He squeezed her hand and winked, a mischievous gleam in his eye. "Of course I'm walking you home. There's just something I want to give you, but I forgot to bring it with me. We'll just make a quick stop at the dorms so I can retrieve it before heading that way."

"Oh! What is it?" Anna asked, warmth flooding through her even though the night was cool. She was so lucky to have found such a caring man who did everything he could to spoil her.

"It's a surprise. You'll have to just wait and see."

On the short walk they talked about the play. "I heard it's one of Stalin's favorites," Nikolai said.

"I'm a little surprised, to be honest," Anna admitted. "What, with the White Army being portrayed in a somewhat positive light. I've always been taught they were a bunch of hairy demons or something."

"Perhaps it's now been long enough since the Civil War that we can see the opposition as human again," Nikolai pondered.

"Perhaps."

As they neared his building, Nikolai slowed and led her to the side of the structure instead of continuing to the entrance. In the darkness, Anna could just make out the slight tilt of his lips as he gazed down at her. "Have I told you that you look beautiful tonight, my love?" He pushed a strand of hair behind her ear, brushing her cheek with his thumb. "You should wear your hair down more often."

Before she could respond, he tilted her chin up and kissed her. It was by far their longest kiss, and Anna became lost in the increasing passion passing between them as Nikolai tangled his fingers in her hair, pressing her lips ever fiercer against his.

They broke apart only when a group of drunken young men stumbled down the sidewalk, laughing, as they passed by to enter the building.

With heavy breathing to match her own, Nikolai rested his forehead against hers, staring into her eyes. His voice came out in a husky whisper. "I can't wait to make you my wife, Anna Levitskaya. I love you more than a nightingale loves the rose. You are my soul."

Overwhelmed by his poetic words, by his intensity, Anna threw herself against his chest, hugging him so tight her arms shook. "I love you too, Nikolai."

With a sigh, he untangled himself from her arms and held her hands to his pounding heart. "Soon. Soon we shall be joined as one." He brought her hands to his lips and kissed them. "But it is getting late, and your mama will be worried if I don't get you home soon."

They walked to the entrance of the dorm. "Wait here. I'll be back before you can count to ten."

Anna tightened her sweater around her chest as he disappeared through the door, her lips still burning with the taste of his kiss. Her heart thumped from the fervor of it, from the depth of her love for him.

Headlights lit up the narrow street, blinding Anna for a moment as she stared into them. The vehicle stopped right in front of her—and her limbs grew weak as dread filled her soul.

A Black Mariah.

Stumbling deeper into the shadow of the building, Anna covered her mouth as acid rose to her throat. Four NKVD officers jumped from the cab of the police van, their jackboots hitting the ground like hammers to Anna's ears. They stormed inside the dormitory building and one of them shouted, "Nikolai Karakov! Come out of your room!"

Anna's blood turned to ice. *No!* She wanted to shout her protest out loud, to beg them to leave, to tell them Nikolai was innocent, that he didn't do anything wrong, but her body refused to obey her commands. She stood frozen to the sidewalk, trembling, tears spilling from her eyes.

"Nikolai Karakov! Last chance for you to come out voluntarily!"

A window on the other side of the stoop from where Anna stood burst open, and Nikolai pushed through the opening and dropped to the ground, looking toward her with a mixture of fear and anger in his eyes before running in the opposite direction.

One of the officers leaned out the window and yelled, "He's running! Get him!"

Three of the uniformed men shoved through the doorway, pulling their guns as they pursued Nikolai. The fourth officer, the one who'd yelled out the window, joined in the chase a moment later.

The icy fear that had held Anna in place since seeing the Black Mariah shattered as she rushed after the men. She swiped at the hair that had fallen over her eyes and clung to her wet cheeks, breaths hitching as she ran. Her mind clouded over, a single, driving force impelling her to reach Nikolai.

The smallest of the NKVD officers pulled ahead of the others and slammed into Nikolai, knocking him to the ground. The two men struggled for a moment, then Nikolai rolled away, the officer's pistol in his hand. He jumped to his feet, the gun pointed at the ground, and turned to run.

Repeated shots rang out, and Anna clamped her hands to her ears, screaming, "No! Nikolai!"

Several small crimson circles appeared on the back of Nikolai's white shirt, growing larger as he slumped to the ground beneath a streetlamp. A scream wrenched itself from deep inside Anna, ripping her soul into pieces. She pushed through the NKVD men surrounding her fallen love and collapsed onto him, her face and chest pressed against his blood-soaked back. "Nikolai," she sobbed. "No, no, no. Why? Why?"

Blood-tinged froth bubbled from his lips, his precious lips that had been pressed to hers only minutes ago. His eyes, wide and unseeing, stared into the pit of eternal darkness as one last agonal breath shuddered from his chest.

"No. Please. No." Anna sobbed as she clung to Nikolai's still body. A shiny metal tube fell from his lifeless hand and rolled to a stop a few inches away. *Lipstick,* Anna thought through the haze, *the surprise was lipstick.*

"Dammit!" one of the officers spat. "He was the last one we needed to fill our quota for tonight."

"We'll just drag his dead body in, yeah? That should count."

"No, it won't 'count', you idiot. They want live prisoners—dead ones can't serve the Motherland in the labor camps."

"Let's just take the girl, then. That will give us time to stop and get some vodka before transporting these criminals to the Lubyanka."

"Ha! You and your drink, Sergei. But that's a good idea, taking the girl. I'm sure she's guilty of something."

The four men laughed as two of them grabbed Anna's arms and yanked her away from Nikolai's still-warm body.

6

In shock, lips and hands numb from sobbing and gulping air, Anna remained flaccid in the officers' grip, forcing them to drag her back toward the Black Mariah. By the time her grief-addled mind realized where they were taking her, they were almost there. She staggered to get her feet beneath her then planted them and leaned back, trying to pull her arms from the hands of her captors. "What... what are you doing? I didn't do anything wrong. Where are you taking me?"

"Come on now, citizen." The man to her right jerked her forward. "If you've done nothing wrong, then there's nothing to worry about, is there?"

"Yeah," the officer walking behind her snickered, "it'll all get sorted out, I'm sure."

All four of them laughed at that.

They shoved her into the back of the Black Mariah and slammed the doors. As her eyes adjusted to the dark—only a small amount of light seeped in from the streetlamps through the narrow high windows and the slit of an opening into the cab of the van—Anna found at least a dozen men staring back at her.

"Well, what do we have here?" A burly man licked his lips and stood from a crowded bench along the side of the van, a tattoo darkening his bronze arm. "Come here, bitch, let's have a go."

Anna backed up against the doors, looking to the other men with pleading eyes. The few that returned her gaze leaned forward with anticipation, the same maleficence gleaming from their eyes as from the man now stalking toward her with a grin. The others, the men wearing suits or work clothes, looked at the floor.

Her hands shook as she held them out in defense. "Please. Don't—"

The man grabbed her left wrist, grinding the small bones in his large hand, and jerked her toward him. "Come on boys. Let's have some fun with this one."

"Help!" Anna screamed. "Leave me alone!"

But not a soul came to her aid as four or more of the others dressed similarly to the man painfully gripping her wrist, sprang from the benches.

Panic flooded her senses, the pungent odor of unwashed bodies, tobacco, and alcohol assaulted her nose as she drew in another breath to scream. The breath was knocked out of her as the men threw her to the hard metal floor of the Black Mariah. She landed a few kicks and scraped her nails across the burly man's face before the gang of men pinned her down, and the ringleader slapped her across the face.

"Let's see what you've got, whore." The man holding down one of her arms grabbed her blouse between her breasts.

"Don't rip it, idiot, we can trade it to the guards for something!" The burly man, now straddling her, slapped the other guy's hand away and hurriedly unbuttoned her blood-stained blouse, each brush of his clumsy fingers sent tendrils of disgust snaking across her skin.

Anna screamed and spit and begged until a man positioned at her head clamped his hand over her mouth. They didn't bother to remove her blouse or sweater, they just splayed them to the sides and pushed her bra up to her neck, exposing her breasts. The burly man stood and yanked her skirt and underwear down to her feet before dropping his pants.

Muffled screams pushed against the palm covering her mouth as tears fell from her terrified, bulging eyes. Pain shot through her at the first violent thrust, and her rapist grunted through rapid breaths, "Think we got a virgin here."

Anna wished she'd died on the sidewalk next to Nikolai. Wished she'd die right then as the men took turns with her, tearing her flesh, ripping her in half, she thought, as the stabbing, searing pain pulsed through her inside and out.

When they'd all had a turn, they released their grips, uncovered her mouth, and left her lying, bleeding, on the floor. Every muscle ached, and it felt like her arms and legs weighed a ton each when she tried to move.

The burly man jerked her to a sitting position by her shoulders. "Give us this shirt, now, girl."

She didn't even fight him as he pulled her sweater and blouse from her arms, she had no fight left in her. As soon as he released her, she flopped back to the floor and turned her head to the side, staring at the men's shoes as tears leaked from her eyes.

"Damn. The sweater's ripped, won't be able to barter with it." He threw it down on top of her. "What'd you do with her shoes, Oleg? I'm sure one of the guards will want them for a wife or mistress."

Anna laid there for several more minutes, no longer caring that her body was exposed. What did it matter now? She was dead inside. As the Black Mariah drove on, she slowly pulled her skirt and underwear on then pushed herself up to a sitting position and slid away from the men, clutching her sweater to her chest, until her back rested against the doors. A trail of blood painted the floor from the pool where she'd lain. The vomit that had been threatening ever since the NKVD had shouted Nikolai's name finally exploded up her throat and out of her mouth, spraying the wall next to her. She didn't bother to wipe the puke that had drizzled down her chin or the bloody snot trailing from her nose to meet it.

Her entire body trembled and twitched, making it difficult for her to pull her bra back into place and thread her arms through the sleeves of her ripped cardigan. She closed it over her chest, pulled her knees up—dried blood and bits of gravel staining the abrasions beneath the torn stockings—and wrapped her arms around her legs, rocking back and forth as a mewling sound she didn't recognize came from her throat.

This wasn't happening. It couldn't be real. Nikolai wasn't lying dead in the street.

But he was. She could still smell the metallic odor of his blood mixed with the stench of spent gun powder. The scene played over and over in her head, jumbled together with the violence she'd just suffered at the hands of the criminals sitting just inches away from her. In the Black Mariah.

One of the animals that had raped her pounded on the wall between the prisoner compartment and the cab. Anna whimpered at the sound and hugged her knees closer to her chest.

"What?" barked one of the officers.

"We have some goods you might wanna' look at," the animal said.

"Well, let's have a look, then."

The criminal shoved Anna's blouse and shoes through the narrow opening into the cab and said, "That oughta be worth some vodka, at least."

The officer grunted. "Maybe."

Vodka, Anna thought with disgust. *That's what started this whole nightmare.* She hoped whatever they brought back was poisoned—for the NKVD demons who had killed Nik and shoved her inside the van with a gang of heartless thieves, and for the criminals themselves who had held her down and—

The vehicle lurched to a stop. Part of her thought she should move away from the doors, but she didn't. Couldn't. Her muscles had turned to stone. She wished her brain would too.

The officers got out and were gone for only a few minutes before they returned and one of them handed a bottle of the cursed drink back to the thieves. The burly one with the tattoo took the first drink then passed it around to his gang while the other men—the quiet ones, the ones wearing suits or work clothes, the ones who had just sat there and watched what the pigs had done to her—looked on with longing, licking their lips as the bottle emptied.

Anna leaned her head on her knees, closing her eyes as the police van bumped along the poorly maintained roads of Moscow. She jerked back and opened her eyes, however, when terrible images of the past thirty minutes flashed in her exhausted mind. She shook her head, partly to clear it and partly to force herself awake. Then she stared at the floor, eyes blurred over, not seeing anything, as she filled her mind with multiplication tables to keep from thinking about anything else.

She'd only gotten halfway through the threes when the Black Mariah stopped again.

"You'd best move away from that door, bitch," the tattooed animal said. "It's about to be opened."

Anna glared at him with all the disgust and hatred raging inside her. She scooted forward a few inches just before the NKVD unlocked the doors and swung them open.

"Ahh, look," one of the officers said, "our girl wants to be first. She must be excited to be here."

Two of the officers grabbed her by the arms and drug her out of the van. Her stockinged feet slapped down on the cobblestone street and her knees buckled beneath her.

"Stand up, girl! We aren't going to carry you in!"

She stood, holding tight to her sweater to keep it closed over her chest, and through hitching sobs said, "They raped me. You threw me in with them, and they...they raped me."

The officer still holding to her arm yawned. "The government can't provide each of you with individual transportation. We don't have such facilities."

He let go of her and yelled into the van, "Okay, men, out with you!"

As the men jumped down from the prisoner van, the officers separated them—the rough-looking, *real* criminals to one side; and the dazed, quiet, pale men to the other. They shoved Anna into line with the latter group, then marched them all toward the oppressive building. Once inside, the criminals were taken through a door, and the two guards with Anna's group led them down a flight of stairs to the basement, into a darkened corridor, then into a small room where a tired-looking woman sat at a desk, a large ledger open in front of her.

"Girl, you first," the woman said, gesturing for Anna to step up to the desk.

Anna hesitated, and the guard shoved her forward.

"Name." The woman glanced at her with indifference before looking down at the ledger, pencil at the ready.

"I...there's been a...a mistake." Anna's voice was rough from crying and screaming.

The woman sighed. "Yes, I've heard that one before. Name."

"But they—"

"Name!"

All hope lost, she whispered, "Anna. Anna Levitskaya."

"Date of birth."

"Fifteen April, 1917."

The woman entered the date in the ledger next to her name, then gestured and said, "Through that door," dismissing her. "Next."

Anna stepped through the open doorway and a man barked, "Stand over there, face front."

She stood where he'd indicated, in front of a wall covered with dark paper. She adjusted her sweater, gripping it to keep it closed over her bra.

"Hands down! Face front." The man's voice was empty of any emotion.

Dropping her hands to her sides, Anna faced the man behind the camera. The flash left stars of light obstructing her vision as the empty voice said, "Profile."

She turned to the side, resisting the urge to reach up and hold her sweater closed. Immediately after the second flash, the man said, "Step over to the table," before turning to the prisoner who had come in behind her. "Stand over there, face front."

Before she could even process the items on the table, the uniformed man there grabbed Anna's right hand and pressed her fingers to an inkpad then to a card, followed by her thumb, then repeated the steps with her left hand. "Name."

"Anna Levitskaya." She longed for a glance, just something to show her she was still a human being. But she wasn't. Not to these people. She'd ceased to be a human the moment the NKVD had decided to arrest her in Nikolai's place. "Sir, please tell me what I've been arrested for," she pled, hoping the uniform meant the man had some authority.

He answered with an indifferent shrug and a jerk of his head indicating where she should go next. She stepped through the door into a corridor where another uniformed guard told her to sit on a bench. Though she lowered herself gingerly, the hard wooden slat sent a spark of pain through her tortured body. The squish of blood and...other fluids in her underwear made her retch, but there was nothing left in her stomach to expel.

Three of the male prisoners had joined her on the bench before a short, bespectacled guard stepped out from somewhere a few yards down the corridor. "Next."

The man standing guard in the corridor grabbed her arm and shoved her toward him. "Hurry it up, the warder's waiting."

A gush of fluid trailed down her thighs as she stumbled to right herself after being propelled off the bench. Clutching her sweater to her chest, Anna walked toward the warder, legs bowed apart to keep from feeling the slime rubbing against them.

The warder held a heavy door open and gestured for her to enter the stairwell beyond. The temperature in the stairwell was at least ten degrees colder than in the corridor. Anna hugged her sweater to her torso.

The door shut with a thud and the warder turned toward her. "Undress completely, put your clothes on the floor, then stand with your legs apart and your hands up."

Anna shook her head and backed away from him until her heels hit the stairs. "No, please—"

"Look, citizen, we usually do these searches with no less than five prisoners at a time, but I thought I'd spare you having to undress in front of the men out there. Any more defiance on your part, and I will change my mind about that." He scowled. "Either way, with or without your cooperation, the search will be done right now."

Though he'd said more to her than anyone else that night, his voice was still void of emotion, as if he were talking to an inanimate object instead of a fellow human.

Anna wished she could force herself to be like an inanimate object that felt no shame, fear, or disgust. But she couldn't turn her humanity off. Tears fell as her trembling hands removed the torn cardigan, the soiled skirt, the elastic garters and stockings one by one. She hesitated, pressure building in her throat as she forced her breaths around the sobs.

"Brassiere and underwear too, citizen. Hurry it up." The warder stood with his arms folded and eyes on her.

She turned her back to him and removed her bra, dropping it to the floor atop her other clothes. Biting her trembling lip, she slipped her bloody underwear off and kicked them to the side.

"Turn around, hands up."

Squeezing her eyes shut, she raised her arms and turned to face him. She heard him step toward her, and she held her breath, dreading whatever was coming next.

"Open your eyes." Without waiting for her to comply, he pried her right eyelid up then pulled down on the bottom lid to inspect it. His warm breath smacked her in the face as he repeated the act on her left eye.

"Open your mouth."

As he prodded inside her mouth, along her teeth, under her

tongue, stretching each cheek as he looked inside, Anna gagged, wondering how many other "searches" he'd done without washing his filthy hands. She could taste and smell the tooth decay, tobacco, bits of food, and other disgusting things his fingers had probed recently.

He tipped her head back, ignoring the choking noises in her throat as she fought against the unbearable urge to spit the nastiness out of her mouth while she stared at the ceiling. Pushing up on the tip of her nose, he used a small light to peer inside her nostrils before checking her ears.

Anna's arm muscles burned, but she didn't dare lower her arms until instructed to do so. The warder ran his hands down her sides, pushing his fingers into her armpits painfully, then lifted each breast, examining the underside and pinching her nipples.

"Let me see your hands, spread your fingers apart." When he was satisfied she didn't have anything hidden between her fingers, he searched through her hair. "Any hairpins in here?"

She shook her head, now shivering with both cold and disgust.

"Spread your legs, one foot here," he stomped his booted foot to the side of her bare one, "and the other over here." He stomped again.

She'd thought he saw her as an *object*, but as he slid his disgusting, dirty fingers deep inside her bruised and swollen body, then between every fold of skin between her legs, she knew—she was nothing more than an animal to him. To all of them.

She could no longer hold back and dissolved into hysterical sobs.

"Turn toward the stairs and bend over. Keep your legs straddled!" He raised his voice over her cries and hitching breaths. "Legs wider! Bend down more and stretch your buttocks out with your hands. Wider!" He put his hands on top of hers and roughly spread her buttocks to the point she thought her skin would tear. "Like this! Now, squat. Quickly!"

Anna squatted, her legs shaking.

"Again!"

The second time, she lost her footing and fell forward onto the stairs, catching herself just before face-planting.

"Okay. Almost done. Turn around and sit on that step. Spread your legs."

She covered her face, crying out once more as he shoved her knees farther apart and "searched" her with his fingers again.

"Stand up," he ordered, wiping his hands on a soiled towel hanging from his belt. He picked up her pile of clothes and handed her the underwear, sweater, and skirt, and stuffed her brassiere, stockings, and garters into a bag by the door. "I have to confiscate any items that may be used to harm or kill yourself."

"How..." Anna whispered, "with a garter?"

"Never you mind about that. You've taken too much of my time already." He shoved her toward the door and pulled it open. "Put your clothes on out there."

Anna tried to cover herself with her clothes as she whipped her head toward the bench full of male prisoners out in the corridor.

All but the guard looked away. He whistled and laughed. "You're going to make someone a nice little prison wife, girl."

7

Anna had to lean against the wall to get her underwear and skirt over her quaking legs. She put her cardigan on backwards, even with the large tear up the side seam, it covered her better that way. With much difficulty she tied the two sides together behind her.

She looked to the guard.

Still staring at her with a grin, he said, "Just wait right there. Someone will be along to take you over to the women's cells...or the box."

Never in her wildest imaginations had she ever thought that being locked in a cell with a bunch of other women would be a relief, yet the idea of it calmed her a little. But what had he meant by "the box"?

A large man in a jailer's uniform clomped down the corridor toward her, a scowl on his face. He grabbed Anna's arm. "Come with me."

As they walked along, Anna worked up the courage to ask, "Can I go to the restroom and...and clean up a little first?"

The guard snorted.

"Please...I—"

He jerked her arm and growled, "No."

Anna lost track of the number of corridors they turned down. The guard slowed his march only when they neared a closed door where inhuman screams permeated the walls. He nodded, eyes sparkling. "That one'll be confessing before long."

"What are they doing to him?" The question jumped to Anna's lips amongst the disorientation the animalistic screams invoked.

"Don't you worry, you'll find out soon enough."

Her eyes widened, and she stumbled as her legs grew weak. The guard jerked her arm, and she felt a stab of pain as something inside her shoulder popped in time with another scream from behind the door.

The scream ended with a defiant, "I won't...denounce...anyone," between panting breaths.

"We'll see about that!" An angry voice shouted. "You! Get another guard in here!"

The door swung open. Anna closed her eyes. She did not want to see what was going on in that room.

"Yuri, good timing," a hulking guard said. "Come give us a hand."

"What should I do with *her*?" The guard, Yuri, poked a thumb at her.

"Bring her in." He winked. "It'll be a good experience for her."

Yuri laughed and pushed her into the room in front of him.

A man lay face down on the hard floor, stripped from the waist down. A dark-haired man wearing an NKVD uniform threw a rubber truncheon on the desk. "Flip him over." The man, who was obviously in charge, breathed heavily, his forehead moist with sweat like he'd gotten quite a workout beating the prone man, whose lower back was red and swollen from the strikes.

"Stand right here and don't move a muscle," Yuri said to Anna, releasing her arm to assist in turning the male prisoner over onto his back.

Anna looked away from the skeletal man's nakedness.

"You two," the dark-haired man ordered, "spread his legs apart and sit on them. Make sure you hold his arms down."

Anna didn't want to be a witness to this. She closed her eyes, wanting to run, her heart pounding like she was already.

Boots stomped across the floor—and stopped near Anna. "Who is this?"

"A new prisoner," Yuri answered. "I was transporting her to the box when Aleksei asked for my assistance."

"Hmm. Very well, then. Woman! Open your eyes."

Anna stared into the face of the dark-haired man, fear prickling her spine.

"Keep them open. Watch. It will be a good lesson for you."

Expecting nothing but her strict obedience, the man turned from her and stepped between the prisoner's legs, placing the toe of his boot on the struggling man's testicles. As he steadily applied pressure, crushing the male organs between his boot and the hard floor, he asked, "Who else was involved with your Anti-Soviet, counter-revolutionary agitation? Give me ten names or say goodbye to your manhood." He leaned in, increasing the pressure of his boot, and shouted over the man's shriek, "Give me ten names, maggot!"

Holding her breath, Anna dug her fingernails into her cheeks, wincing with every rock forward of the torturer's boot, and she silently willed the man to stay strong, not to give in, not to inform on people. But no one, especially not Anna, would blame him if he did. And as his face turned red, eyes and veins bulging, throat working to release a scream wedged there—she opened her mouth to yell "tell them! Just tell them!"

"Okay! I'll do it!" the prisoner screeched, cutting off Anna's plea before its release.

The interrogator eased off just slightly. "You have fifteen seconds, then. Ten names, or I pop your bollocks like grapes."

As the prisoner forced the names through his constricted throat, the man pinning his testicles to the floor turned to look at Anna and barked, "Write these names down! There's a pen and paper on the desk."

She hesitated for half a second while her traumatized mind tried to decipher the meaning of the demon's words.

"Now! Do you want to be responsible for this man losing his balls, bitch?"

With a quick shake of her head, Anna hurried to the desk and, in barely decipherable handwriting, wrote down the names the tortured man spit out. Her hands shook, and she dropped the pen several times.

"How many is that?" the demon asked.

"T...twelve, sir," she stammered.

"Ahh! An overachiever, I see." He rocked forward one last time before removing the toe of his boot from the prisoner's genitals.

The guards released his arms and legs, and he rolled to his side and vomited.

"Anything else from me, comrade?" Yuri asked.

"No. You're free to go."

Yuri snapped his fingers at Anna and ordered, "Come on, let's go." He pulled her to him with a jerk as she neared.

After running on fear, pain, grief, and adrenaline for hours, Anna hit a wall of exhaustion. She could barely drag her feet fast enough to keep up with the guard. They turned down a hallway lined with short, narrow doors. The guard led her to the farthest one and said, "Take off your clothes and hand them to me. You can keep your underwear."

Her hazy mind wondered if these doors led to showers. She prayed they did. She turned her back to the guard and pulled her sweater off over her head, she didn't think she could get her fingers to work well enough to untie the knot at her back. She unbuttoned her skirt, pushed it down, and stepped out of it, covering her breasts with her folded arms.

The guard pulled the keys from his belt and unlocked the door, stuffed Anna inside, then slammed and locked the door behind her.

The darkness of a grave surrounded her in this new version of hell, and finding one last burst of energy, Anna screamed.

8

The door hit Anna's butt, and she tried to step forward, but there was a wall there and her folded arms pressed up against it. She jerked, trying to unfold them as they pressed into her chest. There wasn't room, she was stuck in that position. Panic raced through her veins and entangled her heart like a vise. She screamed. She would suffocate! What was this? Why? Why was she there?

She attempted again to untangle her arms, pushing her back against the door to make more room. The rough wood planks making up the wall tore at her skin, but it was no use. She was wedged in. She kicked back at the door with her bare foot, yelling, "Let me out! Please! Please..."

A vile odor unlike any she'd ever experienced assaulted her nose as she drew in a breath to continue pleading. The stench was overpowering—musty, organic, death-like. Her skin crawled. No. Something was crawling *on* her skin. A horde of something. All over her. Tiny insects dropped onto her from the ceiling, crawled onto her from the walls, the floor. She pressed her lips together and shut her eyelids tight; her nostrils flared with each repulsive, suffocating breath.

They bit her skin. Crawled into her ears and nose. She whipped her head around violently, trying to throw them off her face. *Bedbugs.* She'd been bitten before, at their old shared apartment. Anna thrashed against the confines of *the box*, stamping her feet to knock the insects off her legs. It was useless; she couldn't bend her knees properly, and the pitiful stomps she produced did nothing.

She could reach her face with one of her hands if she bent her head forward, curved her neck. So she swiped the blood-sucking fiends from her face as hysterical screams, muffled to the volume of a whimper by her sealed lips, tore up her throat.

Anna fought to rid herself of the hundreds—if not thousands—of crawling, biting, filthy insects for the next hour or more before she became too weak to so much as twitch a muscle. She leaned her forehead on the wood planks of the wall and let the vampiric bugs drink her blood.

Her hands had grown numb from the position they were stuck in. Her legs and back ached. If only she could sit down, just for a few minutes. How long would they keep her in there? How long had she been in there? In the complete darkness, she had no way to tell if it was night or day. How long had it been since she'd slept?

Bladder ready to burst, Anna held her urine, telling herself she was still human, that she wouldn't allow them to force her to wet herself. They couldn't plan on leaving her in there much longer... could they?

Oh, her legs! A sharp pain pierced her right calf as the muscle spasmed, and she gasped with the pain. She transferred her weight to her left foot and whimpered, unable to stretch the cramp away. A few minutes after it subsided, a new cramp struck her left calf, and the agony began all over again.

She could no longer hold her urine as her bladder, stretched to its limits, seized painfully, and she wept as this new humiliation streamed down her legs to puddle at her feet.

Had Nikolai known what went on in this place? What would happen to him if he was arrested? Anna remembered him saying that he'd rather die than be arrested. She now understood that sentiment, yet she still clung to her will to live.

Would Nikolai have gone quietly when they came for him had he known Anna would end up here in his place if he didn't? *Of course he would have*, Anna thought. *He loves...loved me. He would have done anything to protect me.* She swallowed, her throat dry. *But he didn't protect me. He ran and left me standing there alone.*

But no, she couldn't blame *him*. This was Mikhail's fault. That Communist Party bastard! That boot-licking Stalin worshiper!

Anna's thoughts flickered in and out of lucidity. If she could just sit down. Just sleep. Just talk to someone in charge. *Mama must be so worried.* She licked her dry lips. *How long have I been here? I need water. So thirsty. So tired.*

How long would they keep her inside this box? How long could they...before she died? *That's it*, she thought, *it isn't just a box, it's a coffin. A standing coffin full of demonic bedbugs.* After they were sure she was dead, when the odor of her rotting flesh could no longer be contained in this small space, they would just tip the box on its side and carry it out to the graveyard.

No. That couldn't be right. She thought about the man in the room. The man who'd come so close to losing his testicles. His screams. They'd wanted something from him. They wanted something from her. What did they want?

Anna smacked the back of her head on the door as another leg cramp hit. Her throat hitched as the prolonged cramp added itself to the pain and exhaustion covering every inch of her body, and the impulse to cry took over. But her eyes remained dry like her mouth and throat while her body spasmed, crying without the tears, adding to the pressure in her chest and the ache in her ribs.

The bedbugs continued to siphon her blood. Her skin itched and tingled and burned. And she needed water. She was so thirsty. So, so thirsty.

Anna had no idea how long she'd been in the box. The *standing coffin*, as she'd come to think of it. It had definitely been many hours, but could have been days. She fell in and out of lucidity, but never slept, was never able to give in to the much-desired oblivion of unconsciousness. The human body wasn't meant to stay on its feet for so long, to stay in one position for so long.

The door opened and Anna spilled out onto the hard floor of the corridor. She clamped her eyes shut, unable to lift her arms to protect them from the sudden harshness of the overhead lights.

"Get up, citizen."

Her arms tingled, like a million needles punctured them, as more blood was able to circulate. But she could still only move them in small, jerky motions. She tried to explain this to the guard, but nothing came out except a dry croak.

He nudged her with his boot. "Come on. The interrogator is waiting."

Rolling to her side, Anna was able to get one hand to work, and she pushed up to a sitting position then got her feet under her and squinting, found the wall to brace her hand against so she could stand.

"Put this on, you can't go in there looking like that." The guard shoved a plain gray, short-sleeved dress at her.

Anna had forgotten she was wearing only her underwear, and she turned her back to him, her sense of modesty having survived their attempts at turning her into an animal. The tortured muscles of her arms responded sluggishly as she pulled the dress on over her head. It hung on her thin frame like a half empty sack, but what did it matter?

"Follow me." The guard walked briskly down the corridor.

Bone-deep pain pounded her feet and legs with each step, and try as she might, she couldn't keep up with his pace. The guard looked back and scowled when he reached the end of the hallway.

"Either keep up, or I'll drag you there by your hair!" he threatened.

From what she'd experienced thus far in this place, she knew it wasn't just an idle threat. She scratched at her skin, at the hundreds of itching bedbug bites, and swiped at the bugs still crawling all over her as she forced herself to shuffle faster toward the guard. Maybe they'd let her sit down in the interrogation room. She wanted to sit down almost as much as she needed a drink of water.

Her eyes were dry and burning, and she shivered—chilled from losing blood to the voracious bedbugs—and again she wondered how long she'd been there, in the *coffin*. Her dry throat spasmed as she swallowed. Her tongue, swollen from thirst, prickled like she'd been licking a cactus.

Even though he'd threatened her to keep up, the guard seemed to have slowed his pace, the first act of kindness she'd experienced since watching her fiancé get gunned down.

They arrived at a different room than the one the male prisoner had been in. The man behind the desk—the interrogator—looked up as they entered. His cold eyes swept over Anna, still swatting tiny bugs off her skin—they'd started crawling out of her hair and onto her face and neck. A spike of fear hit her in the gut as the man narrowed his eyes into a glare and snapped at the guard, "Why are you bringing her in here with bugs crawling all over her? Do you think I want this office infested with the damned things?"

"Uh, no, comrade. S...sorry," the guard stammered. "I'll take care of it and bring her back."

"Be quick about it! I wish to be out of here in time to have breakfast with my wife for once!"

The guard nodded and turned about, shoving Anna back out the door as he grumbled, "Damn bug-infested whore," like it was her fault.

He jerked her around a corner then pulled his hand away and brushed his hands together to remove any bugs that might have jumped to him. He opened the stairwell door and said, "Upstairs! And be quick about it."

She tried. Her knees ached, and she was so weak she barely propelled herself up the first step. The guard pushed her from behind, and she fell, banging both shins into the edge of a stair. She stayed on all fours, hiking the dress up to her thighs so she could crawl up the dark, never-ending staircase. Anna didn't even question where he was taking her. She was so tired. She wanted to just lie down right there and sleep.

With panting breaths, she climbed her way to the top, the guard stomping heavily behind her.

He opened the door and ordered her to stand then led her outside to an enclosed courtyard. The only light came from the stars twinkling through the small portion of sky she could see above the building. So, it was night again. She'd been in that cursed box for at least twenty-four hours.

Clicking his flashlight on, the guard aimed it at a wall a few yards away. "Go stand over there."

Anna's brief glimpse of the wall showed dark splatters on the bricks. *Paint?* She wondered. *Why would they—*

The guard aimed the light at the wall again. "Right there, against the wall. Hurry it up!"

Even through her dry, inflamed eyes, she could now see the splatters weren't paint. It was blood. Fresh enough to drip from the bricks onto the paving stones at her feet. She whirled around to face the guard, expecting to see the flash of a gunshot ending the twenty-one years she'd spent on this earth. Instead of a gun, the guard aimed a large hose at her, and as he twisted the valve it was connected to, he said, "Take that dress off and set it to the side."

She turned her back and pulled the dress off over her head, then laid it on the ground.

"Underwear too!"

She closed her eyes, knowing there was no use in protesting, and peeled the stiff, filthy garment off her body, kicking it over onto the dress. The chill air raised prickly goosebumps on her skin, and she wrapped her arms around her torso.

With her back facing the guard, she had no warning as he unleashed a torrent of icy cold water on her. The force of the spray propelled her into the bloody wall, and she cried out as her hands touched the splatters of death. The water stung like the lash of a whip—a hundred whips. She pushed back against the onslaught, trying to get a little distance between her and the execution wall.

Anna's teeth chattered, knocking together with such force she thought they might all break.

"Turn around, arms up!" the guard shouted.

I'm just an animal, she thought, trying to ignore the shame that still lurked at being naked in front of a man. She turned, bracing herself for the blast of water to her sensitive breasts, and yet was wholly unprepared for the assault. She lost her breath as the pressurized water pounded her chest, and she reflexively put her hands out in front of her, trying to stop the spray with her palms.

"Arms *up!*"

She raised her arms again and turned her head to the side, gulping in little breaths of air. Her irritated throat burned as the cold air flowed through it, reminding her of her thirst, of her swollen tongue and cracked lips. Her fatigue-addled mind didn't even think before she turned her face back toward the water and dipped her head down to catch some in her mouth.

The guard lowered the spray before she could get more than a drop, aiming it at her pelvis. Again, her reflexes overrode her fear of disobeying the guard, and she dropped her hands to protect the tender area between her legs.

"Arms up! That's the last time I'm gonna tell you! Lower them again and I'll chain them to the wall!"

Whole body now shivering, Anna raised her hands, fists clenched against the pain and cold.

"And don't even think about trying to get a drink again." To emphasize his point, he blasted the stream at her face for a second— long enough to send what seemed like a gallon of water into her nose.

Her sinuses exploded in agony, and she inhaled sharply at the shock. Her freezing, weak body was racked with spasms as she coughed uncontrollably, natural reflexes taking over to expel the aspirated water from her lungs.

The guard barked out a laugh as he sprayed her legs.

The little amount of water that had managed to make it to her stomach came back up with the violent coughing, spewing out her mouth and nose. Panic engulfed her. Her throat spasmed. She couldn't breathe.

The water shut off, and the guard stepped closer to her. "Come on now, catch your breath. We need to finish up and get you back to your interrogation."

Anna's vision swam, and dizziness dropped her to her knees. The guard didn't yell at her, so she stayed there until she was able to breathe normally again.

"Alright. Let's finish up here. I still need to take the women's cells to the latrine." He lifted the hose, gripping the large nozzle. "Stay on your knees and bow your head."

He didn't open it all the way up this time, but the spray to her skull still felt like a sledgehammer to her already pounding head.

The deluge ended. Anna didn't move from her kneeling position as her long, dripping hair covered her face and nearly touched the ground. Her jaws ached as the chattering of her teeth grew more violent and her body quaked with the cold.

The guard's boots appeared on the ground in front of her, and he roughly searched through her hair. "Dammit. I'll never get all these bugs out of your hair." He pulled something from his belt. "Hold still."

He grabbed a thick lock of Anna's hair and sawed through it with a large knife, repeating the procedure until a pile of hair lay at her knees. It was too much. Losing her hair at the hands of this beast. It broke her. Of all the things she'd been through in the last—who knew? Twenty-four, forty-eight hours? Maybe more? It was the loss of her hair that finally broke her. She started to gather it up from the ground, her mind spinning with thoughts like, *maybe I can put it back. I'll ask for some glue. I can weave a wig out of it.*

The guard smacked it out of her trembling hands then turned the hose on her head once more. After another inspection, he was satisfied that he'd gotten rid of all the bugs from her now butchered, short hair.

"Stand up. We're almost done." He jerked her to her feet. "Go grab your clothes and hold them out to the side. Don't let any bugs get on you."

Like a convulsing, freezing zombie, Anna obeyed. The guard sprayed the dress and underwear on all sides before declaring them free of bedbugs and ordering her to put the cold, dripping-wet garments back on.

She had no idea how she made it back inside and down the stairs to the basement, but there she was, standing, trembling, her soaking wet dress dripping onto the floor, as she faced the interrogator's desk from several feet away. A guard sat on a couch behind her.

"You look like a drowned rat." The interrogator's voice dripped with cruelness. "Let's get started, shall we?"

9

"What is your name?" the interrogator asked.

"Anna Lev...Levitskaya," her weak voice whispered.

"Repeat your name." He stood and leaned forward over his desk, frowning. "*Louder.*"

Anna swallowed and tried again. "Anna Levitskaya." Her throat burned with the effort, but her hoarse voice came out only slightly louder.

"Again! Louder!" He slapped a ruler down on his desk with a loud *crack*.

Through chattering teeth and with a quivering voice, she half-yelled, "Anna Levitskaya."

"What was your job?"

"S...seamstress."

The interrogator poured water from a carafe into a glass on his desk then took a long drink. He set the glass down and narrowed his eyes at her. "Tell me about your anti-Soviet activities, Anna Levitskaya."

She ran her dry tongue across her cracked lips and stared at the water for a moment before his question broke through her addled mind. She shook her head. "There's been a mistake. I'm...I haven't done anything wrong. I didn't do anything. Please—"

He came around the desk so fast Anna hardly had time to blink before he was standing right in front of her. He slammed his fist into her solar plexus just as she took a breath, knocking the wind out of her and doubling her over. A choking sound was all that resulted as she tried to inhale.

The interrogator leaned down and said quietly, "We don't arrest people who are not guilty. And even if you aren't guilty, we can't release you—we wouldn't want people to think we are picking up innocent citizens, now would we?"

Black spots swam in front of her eyes, and Anna fleetingly thought she couldn't have heard him correctly. Her diaphragm finally relaxed, and she gasped in a breath.

"Stand up straight and answer my question!"

Anna straightened up, thinking that maybe she should just admit to something—anything—to end this. To get a drink. To sleep. Eat. But she *didn't* do anything wrong. If he'd just let her explain. She watched as the interrogator walked back over to his desk and picked up a rubber truncheon, slapping it against his hand as he turned to face her again.

She needed to say something. But what? Her thoughts moved in slow motion. She couldn't remember what he'd asked. She focused on the club's movement, it blurred in and out of focus. Anna blinked, her eyelids scraping against her eyes like sandpaper.

The man slammed the rubber truncheon down on the desk and she jumped at the loud *smack*. "Answer my question, Anna Levitskaya." His voice was low, menacing.

"Wh...what?" She needed to sleep. She closed her eyes and swayed on her feet. *Just a few minutes.*

Pain exploded in Anna's lower back, and her eyes flew open as she yelped. Waves of agonizing spasms shot down both legs, and she took an involuntary step forward, her knees ready to buckle.

The interrogator grabbed her upper arm and jerked her toward him. "Tell me about your anti-Soviet activities, whore!"

Panting as the stabbing pain subsided to a deep throbbing, the fog in Anna's head cleared a little. "Please, sir, I didn't—"

His grip on her arm tightened, his fingers digging into her flesh.

She groaned and shrank away from him, but he just gripped harder. A flood of words spilled from Anna's mouth. "They came for Nikolai, my...my fiancé! But he ran, and they killed him so they took me instead. Please," she whined, "I'm innocent!"

He released her arm with a shove that nearly toppled her. His jack boots clomped as he circled around her slowly, his intense gaze burning into her. He stopped in front of her and lifted her chin roughly with the tip of the club.

Anna flinched, the pain caused by the weapon still pounding in her back.

"We know all about Nikolai. I didn't ask about *him*, Anna. I asked about *you*." His hot breath, smelling of tobacco, brushed against her skin. He turned away from her.

Confusion pulsed through her head as she searched for something, anything, to tell him. To keep him from hurting her. "I don't know what you want me to say." It came out as a desperate plea.

The interrogator spun in a blur, lashing out with the truncheon and landing a powerful blow across her abdomen. A tortured wail escaped her lips as she crumpled to the floor in agony, folding her arms around her middle. She grunted with each quick breath, sure something had ruptured inside her.

The man kicked her square in the tailbone, the stabbing pain reverberating up her spine to her head. Through the haze of agony, she heard his words without really comprehending their meaning.

"Yakov! I'm going to go lay down for an hour or so. Get this wench back on her feet right now, and give her a kick if she closes her eyes for more than a second."

"Will do, comrade."

More clomping of boots, then the door opening and closing was followed by rough hands grabbing Anna by the hair—the earlier guard had apparently left it long enough to get a good grip—and pulling her to her feet.

Anna's intestines cramped, and a surge of nausea roiled inside her. She clamped one arm around her stomach and one hand to her mouth, standing, but still bent over.

"Stand up straight." The guard poked her in the arm with a beefy finger.

She tried, but the cramps intensified and her abdominal muscles tightened, not allowing her to move from her bent position. "Can't," she panted.

"I'll just have to help you then." He moved to position himself behind her.

Panic sliced through the fog of pain and Anna said, "No," and tried to straighten up again.

The guard ignored her attempt, placed a hand on each shoulder and his knee in her lower back, and wrenched her to a full standing position.

She screamed. It felt like a red-hot poker had been stabbed right through her. Squeezing her eyes shut, she concentrated on breathing and staying upright. Anna's clipped, shallow breaths weren't getting enough oxygen to her lungs, but she was unable to breathe deeper because of the pain.

Just as the cramping started to subside, the guard kicked her in the right shin with his heavy jack boot. "Eyes open," he commanded, voice calm, almost bored sounding.

Her eyes flew open, and a choked sob broke from her dry throat. She lifted her right foot off the floor to relieve the pressure as her bruised shin throbbed. Weakness and sleep deprivation had left her with no balance, and she tipped to the side, left leg wobbling, and had to put her foot back down to keep from falling over. A stabbing pain shot through her shin, but she suffered it quietly as it slowly dulled to an ache.

What was wrong with these people who could so readily inflict pain on another human being? Anna stared at the guard. He looked to be a little older than her, stout build, but only a few inches taller than her five-foot-three. He could have been a former classmate or a neighbor. Why did he not see her as a fellow human being? She was no different from his sister, his girlfriend, the woman selling flowers near the gates of the Kremlin. How, in his eyes—and all those she'd been in contact with since her "arrest"—had she morphed into something inhuman? How had she become someone worthy of torture? Someone undeserving of even the slightest of human dignities?

The guard stepped over to the desk and poured a glass of water from the carafe. He turned to face Anna and slowly sipped it.

Anna's throat hitched, spasming as she swallowed. Her dry, cracked lips parted, and the tip of her swollen tongue dragged across them as she watched the guard's Adam's apple move with each gulp. She was so thirsty. "Please..."

Tipping the glass toward her, the guard raised an eyebrow. "Oh, how rude of me. Are you thirsty?"

She nodded, not taking her eyes off the glass in his hand.

He stepped toward her and stretched his hand out, jerking it back with a laugh as soon as she reached for the water. "Did you really think I'd let you have a drink, you anti-Soviet bitch?"

No, she didn't *really* think he would. Her hand dropped back to her side. Her overwhelming thirst had taken over her senses for a moment.

The guard laughed again and leaned back against the desk, taking one more drink of the water before setting the glass down. He folded his arms across his chest and stared at Anna in silence for several minutes.

Her heavy eyelids scraped across her arid eyes, each blink lasting a little longer than the last until, giving in to the exhaustion, sleep took her away while she stood. A jack-booted kick to her left shin jolted her awake with a cry.

Without a word, the guard went back to leaning against the desk.

Anna had no idea how much time passed. Minutes seemed to last for hours as she swayed on aching feet, struggling to keep her eyes open. How long had she been awake? Her mind couldn't even begin to calculate it. Days. How long could she survive without sleep? Without food or water?

"Turn around." The guard straightened from his perch on the edge of the desk. "My legs are tired, I need to sit down." He grinned as his shoulder brushed against hers on his way to the couch at the back of the room.

She shuffled her feet around until she faced him.

He settled onto the couch with a sigh. "Ah. That's better." He crossed his legs and leaned back into the cushion, lacing his fingers behind his head. "This is a very comfortable couch. So soft, like a pillow." He yawned and looked at his watch.

Anna lost count of the number of kicks the guard landed on her bruised legs—he was very good at hitting the same spot each time. The kicks came with increased force each time her eyes stayed closed for too long, his annoyance growing every time he had to leave his comfortable seat.

Staring at the large picture of the Supreme Leader on the wall behind the couch, Anna's vision blurred. Her thoughts cloudy like her head was stuffed with cotton. She looked down at her hands, lifting them in front of her, turning them side to side as she gawked. Those weren't her hands. Her fingers. They stretched and ballooned, distorted in her vision. She looked back up at the picture, at the couch, at the guard. They weren't real. She wasn't real. She shook her head, and her vision blurred, the room became black and white.

Anna looked back at the guard, his face, void of color, a mask of twisted clay. Her lips tingled and her hands—*were* they *her* hands?— twisted into claws and she couldn't straighten them. Couldn't move her fingers.

The guard shot off the couch like a bullet and slapped her across the face, whipping her head to the side. "Stop breathing so fast, idiot! You're hyperventilating."

The sting of her cheek cleared her fuzzy mind, and the room came into focus again, the colors returning. This was real. She was real. But she still couldn't unclench her hands. Her chest moved up and down as she continued to huff air in and out of her lungs in rapid gulps.

Still standing close to her, the guard grabbed the hair on the back of her head and yanked, so she now looked at the ceiling. He growled in her ear, "Slow down your breathing. Now!"

He let go of her hair, and her head dropped forward. Anna concentrated on taking slow breaths, and gradually, her hands uncurled and the feeling returned to her lips. She looked at the guard. "What...?"

Shrugging, he said, "Sleep deprivation. Does weird things to a person." He looked at his watch. "It only gets worse, citizen. The interrogator will be back soon, you might want to just give him your confession when he returns." He slouched back to the couch.

He was right. She wasn't getting out of this. They didn't care if she was innocent. They'd already decided she was guilty. Not confessing would just prolong the torture, prolong the inevitable.

But what would she confess *to*? What did they *want* her to confess to? Her mind went round and round, too muddled by exhaustion to land on anything solid.

Anna's head jerked up when the door opened.

The interrogator marched in and sneered at her. "Let's get started, then, shall we?"

10

The interrogator was followed by another man, dressed similarly to him. The second man went to the desk and sat, pulled a sheet of paper and a pen out of a drawer, and prepared to write.

"Anna Levitskaya," the interrogator circled around her, "tell me about your anti-Soviet activities."

He stopped right in front of her, pulled a rubber truncheon out of his belt, and slapped it against his hand.

Anna swallowed. "I..." Her mind spun. What should she say? What should she confess to? She knew very little about Soviet laws; it wasn't something they learned in school. "I umm..."

The interrogator grabbed her face, digging his fingers into her cheeks. "Confess, dammit! We know you're guilty!"

"I'm trying." Breath hitched in her throat, terror squeezed her chest. "I can't think. I...I'll say whatever you want. Just tell me what you want."

"Just talk! You know what about!"

The thought of Nikolai popped into her head. He'd done something that Mikhail didn't like. What was it? "I..." Anna strained to remember. It seemed like so long ago. "I told a joke...or laughed at a joke."

"What kind of joke?"

"It was...it was about the Supreme Leader."

"So you admit you are a sworn enemy of Soviet power." He leaned in close to her face. "What else?"

Anna closed her eyes, shaking her head. What else. What else. She thought about Nadya. What things had her sister gotten mad at her for saying?

"Tell me!" The interrogator stepped to the side of her and swung the truncheon, connecting to Anna's lower back, the exact same place as before, with a dull *thwack*.

Her agonized scream hurt her own ears as pain flared down both legs and all the way up to her head. "Please..." she sobbed. "Please... I'll tell you." Pain and nausea surged through her entire body.

"Go on then! Tell us!"

Nadya... Mikhail... The informer at the sewing plant. Anna's thoughts jumbled together and came tumbling out of her mouth before the horrible man could strike her again. "I ridiculed the Five-Year Plan. I...I questioned my neighbor's arrest. Complained about bread prices. Showed pity for a co-worker who stole from the government." Her voice rode higher, more hysterical, with each "confession."

The interrogator nodded and spoke with fake pleasantness. "See? That wasn't so hard, was it?" He took Anna by the arm. "Let's just go over here to the desk so you can sign your depositions."

Flinching at his touch, Anna forced her stiff limbs into motion, spasms racking her lower back and legs with each step. She knew she was innocent, but also knew it was no use fighting it—they'd marked her as guilty, and not giving in just meant more torture, eventually ending in death. Her thoughts touched on the man whose torture she'd witnessed her first night there, and she was thankful that at least she hadn't betrayed anyone else. She couldn't do that.

At the desk, the man sitting there slid the paper he'd been writing on toward her. "Read and sign each deposition."

The words swam in her vision. She glanced at the half-full carafe with longing and tried to blink the sensation of burning sand out of her eyes. Anna read and signed the five depositions against her and the declaration that she was a sworn enemy of Soviet power. She barely recognized her own shaky signature. *Maybe they'll let me eat and drink now. And sleep.*

She dropped the pen onto the desk and looked again at the water.

The man at the desk grabbed the paper and placed it in a folder. He pulled a new piece of paper from the drawer and wrote: *Deposition No. 6* at the top.

Anna's head swiveled to look at the interrogator standing at her side, her sunken eyes wide with confusion and fear.

The twisted grin on his face only served to spike her terror. "Stand up straight, now, citizen. No leaning on the desk." He pulled her a step back.

The urge to defecate hit her with a flurry of cramps. "I need to use the restroom," she said with a desperate plea.

He laughed. "Oh, no, Anna. We aren't finished here. You'll have to wait."

"I can't! I'll mess myself!" She tightened her buttocks together, humiliation coloring her face.

"Yakov," the interrogator snapped at the guard, "lay down some plastic here in case she makes a mess."

Anna's stomach rumbled loudly with the next roiling cramp. "Please—"

"No! If you cooperate, we'll have you in a cell with a latrine bucket in no time."

Yakov spread a large square of plastic onto the floor and the interrogator shoved her to stand in the center of it.

Her legs and buttocks shook with the effort of holding the liquid stool in.

"Name the others in your group, your co-conspirators." The interrogator moved to stand next to the desk.

Anna shook her head. It was one thing to confess to crimes she didn't commit, but she refused to falsely accuse anyone else. "There are no others. I...I acted alone." She bent one of her knees slightly and held her breath, fighting against her own body. She turned to Yakov, the guard, then to the man at the desk, pleading, "This has to be illegal. You can't torture people like this!"

The three men laughed, and the interrogator said, "Oh, little bitch. Of course it's legal! The Supreme Leader himself confirmed the Central Committee's decision to allow the use of 'physical pressure' on prisoners who take advantage of our *humane* interrogation methods in order to shamelessly refuse to give away conspirators. We must prevent you from impeding the exposure of those conspirators that are still free."

"Humane?" Anna couldn't believe the demon had dared utter the word! "What, about any of this, is *humane?*"

"Well, you wouldn't know that, would you? Seeing as you were uncooperative from the very beginning." He dragged her back over to the desk, Yakov followed with the plastic, arranging it beneath her. The interrogator forced her right hand, palm down, onto the desk. "The vise, Yakov."

The man sitting at the desk opened a deep drawer and withdrew a device, handing it to the guard. Yakov positioned a circular piece of metal on top of her hand and hooked the vice under the edge of the desk, then he tightened it, pinning her hand to the surface. The interrogator forced her other hand into the same position, and Yakov repeated the process with a second vise.

"Viktor, would you like to do the honors?" the interrogator asked the man sitting across from her.

Viktor nodded eagerly and pulled a small case the size of a wallet from his pocket.

The interrogator held up a hand and looked down into Anna's eyes as she was forced to bend slightly over the desk. "Last chance.

Give us the names of your co-conspirators, and I'll have Yakov take you to a nice cell with a latrine bucket and a bunk."

Oh, how she longed to give in. To blurt out the names of everyone she knew. But she couldn't. She'd already written herself off, there was no escape for her. But she wouldn't do this to someone else.

"Come on now. There have to be others. Your sister. Your mother. Friends or co-workers. Friends of your dead fiancé. His professors."

She gritted her teeth, resigned to suffer through whatever came next—especially after his mention of her mother. "I will not name anyone. There are no co-conspirators."

The interrogator nodded to the man behind the desk, and he opened his little case, extracting a thin, wooden needle.

A scream she didn't know she had in her tore through her ravaged throat as he rammed the needle under the fingernail of her right pointer finger. She lost the battle with her bowels, but she barely registered the warm liquid running down her legs, splatting onto the plastic beneath her.

Anna's screams persisted until she had no voice left, yet her lungs continued to force bursts of air through her damaged vocal cords, producing hoarse, almost silent, warbling noises like a dying bird. As the devil before her proceeded to each of the fingers of her right hand, ramming the needle in then pulling it out slowly, a curtain of red fell over her vision. She pulled against the vises in vain, her skin bruising and tearing beneath the metal clamps. The spasms in her lower back intensified with the effort and the partially hunched position she was forced into.

Blind and delirious from the torment, Anna continued to pull against the restraints and scream silently for several seconds after the man paused in his torture. She fell to her knees, gasping for air, hands still flattened against the desk by the vises.

"Are you ready to give up your accomplices, Anna Levitskaya?" the interrogator asked.

Fury gave her strength. She *would not* denounce anyone. She turned her head and focused on the man through the red haze. "No." Her voice was like gravel, her throat raw and inflamed.

He sighed and crossed his arms over his chest. "Stand up!"

Anna's foot slipped on the watery stool beneath her, and she hit her head on the desk.

"Release her hands."

The guard, careful to avoid the mess on the floor, removed the vises then stepped back.

"Now," the interrogator said. "Stand. Up."

Pressure and burning pain pulsed in her fingertips with every rapid beat of her heart. Anna somehow clawed her way to her feet using the desk as leverage, and stood, head down, looking at the floor.

The interrogator drummed his fingers on the desk. After a moment of silence, he said, "We'll continue her questioning tonight, as it's time for breakfast. We want her to think about us until then, though, so Yakov, let's give her a *drink*."

Anna glanced at the carafe, but what little hope his words brought were crushed by the evil glint in his eye.

Yakov nodded and left the room, returning after a few minutes with a clear bag, water sloshing inside it as he tipped it from side to side. A clamped tube close to an inch wide came from the bottom of the bag.

"Back on your knees, girl," the interrogator commanded.

Anna dropped to her knees, wondering vaguely why he'd made her stand up a few minutes ago if he was just going to make her kneel again. But she knew why. It was all about cruelty.

Taking the bag from Yakov, the interrogator explained, "This is what we refer to as a salt-water douche." He looked at the guard. "Hold her steady."

His words were still scrambling around in her head, trying to find purchase, when the guard stepped behind her, straddling the mess, clamped one hand down on her shoulder, and grabbed a fistful of her hair with the other. He yanked her head back, her neck hyperextended, and her eyes staring at the ceiling.

The interrogator shoved the tube to the back of her throat and said, "If you don't want to drown, I suggest you swallow."

Yakov took his hand from Anna's shoulder and clamped it around her bottom jaw, forcing her mouth to close around the tube. Her eyes spun wildly as she tried to comprehend what was happening.

The interrogator raised the bag above his head and opened the clamp. Salt water gushed into her mouth. She sputtered and coughed, her throat constricting at the onslaught. The briny water spurted out of her nose and the corners of her mouth, with much of it, though, being forced down her throat. She fought against the guard's grip to no avail. She couldn't breathe. She may as well have been immersed in the Dead Sea.

Through her panic, she heard the interrogator say, "Swallow, bitch."

Her throat rebelled against her attempts, but she was able to gulp down a few swallows. He yanked the tube from her mouth and the guard released her. She fell forward onto her hands, coughing so hard she thought her burning throat would rupture. Her nose and eyes burned like she'd been snorting embers. The salt water stung where it touched her skin as it seeped into the miniscule bug bites covering her body.

"Take her to a punishment cell and send someone in to clean up this mess."

The guard didn't wait for her to stop hacking. He grabbed her under the arms and pulled her to the door, dropping her to the floor while he opened it and yelled into the corridor, "Yuri! Give me a hand here."

They each grabbed one of her arms and dragged her down the hallway as she continued to cough up salty water.

"Where we taking her?" Yuri asked.

"Punishment cell, if there's one available."

"There is. I just took a guy out of number three and dropped him for questioning. He won't be needing it anytime soon."

As the coughing started to settle down, Anna became aware of thirst beyond any she'd ever experienced. The bitter taste of salt coated her dry mouth and lips, her swollen tongue pressed against the roof of her mouth like the teeth of a hacksaw. She lay slack in the grip of the guards, allowing them to drag her along. Weakness permeated every cell of her body.

They turned down a short hallway, the dull roar of fans or machinery muffling the clomp of the guards' jack boots. Another guard met them at a door with a stenciled "3" on it and unlocked and opened it, raising his voice over the noise, "She's gonna have a crappy day."

An insane urge to laugh filled Anna at his words. Crappier than she'd already had? What more could they do to her?

11

The door slammed behind her. The guards had hefted Anna to her feet and shoved her inside the confined space. She slumped against the wall, legs too weak to fully bear her weight. This cell wasn't as tight as *the box*. There was room to turn a full circle, but not enough room to sit. And instead of pitch-black darkness, a harsh overhead light bore down on her, reflecting off the white walls of the cell into her inflamed eyes.

Despair overcame her, and she wished for nothing more than death. Her life was over anyway—it had ended as soon as the bullets entered Nikolai's body. She craved the peace death would bring her. The freedom from pain. And knowing—hoping—she might soon meet the Lord, her resolve not to denounce another soul to these monsters was cemented in her heart.

Anna closed her eyes, glad, at least, there was no guard standing by to kick her awake. Her chin dropped to her chest as she dozed off at last.

Pounding at the level of her head jolted her awake almost immediately.

"Wake up, citizen! No sleeping!" A guard yelled through a small peephole in the door.

The hum of machinery from somewhere down the hall was drowned out as a noisy fan kicked on nearby. Icy air blew through a low vent in the wall at her feet.

It took no time at all for prickling numbness to grow in her toes and fingers. Anna held her hands up and looked at them. The tips of her fingers were as white as the walls. She wrapped her arms around herself, trapping her damaged fingers in her armpits. The freezing air blew up her dress, swirling around her bare, stool-splashed legs.

Anna let out an anguished moan as her teeth chattered, feeling like a jackhammer to her pounding head. Her body was racked by violent shivers, pain shooting through her fatigued muscles with the uncontrollable contractions. She raised and lowered her feet, marching in place as much as she could in the confined space. She'd never been so cold in her life. It was indescribable. She couldn't feel her fingers or toes, the tip of her nose, her lips.

Even with the agony of freezing to death, the intense thirst plaguing her was worse. If she had to choose between a warm fire or a glass of water, she'd grab that water and gulp it down so fast...

Another pounding on the door. Anna squinted up at the peephole where an ugly brown eye peered in at her.

"How's it going in there? Cool enough?" His laughter followed him down the hall.

His knuckles rapped on the door of the cell next to hers, but she couldn't make out the words he yelled to the prisoner inside.

Closing her eyes, Anna prayed for God to take her. The bright light glaring down on her penetrated her swollen, burning eyelids. How long could she survive at this temperature? She opened her eyes, and the world became distorted. The perception of floating outside her body slowly materialized, and she became angry that the disembodied version of herself could still feel every pain and every chill of her bones.

The fan in the wall shuddered and slowed to a stop. The sudden quiet crept in like an eerie presence.

Still trembling from the cold, Anna was surprised to feel grateful the icy air had ceased to blow. Maybe she *wasn't* ready to die. She pulled one of her hands from the shelter of her armpit and stared at it as it shook, blurring as her eyes or her brain, or both, had trouble keeping up with the motion.

She jumped as the guard pounded on the door again. Was he going to keep doing that all night? Or was it day?

"You awake?" he yelled.

She rolled her exhausted eyes to look at the peephole, only able to raise her eyelids halfway.

"Bet you're glad the cold air stopped, huh?" Another laugh as he walked away.

Moving in slow motion, Anna folded her fingers into a fist, raising her thumb to the ceiling—a way of telling him to "shove it."

The quiet only lasted about thirty seconds, then the fan rattled to life again. Anna shook her head. No. Her body hadn't even had the chance to stop shivering. Her teeth were still chattering. It took her several minutes to realize the air coming from the vent wasn't cold. That it was, in fact, warm. Anna lifted the hem of her dress, letting the warm air blow against her legs.

She dropped her dress and leaned her head back against the wall, closing her eyes as the warmth engulfed her. She slipped into a standing sleep but was soon roused by a new discomfort.

Heat. Stifling heat. Like standing inches away from a roaring fire. Anna panted like a dog. The cracks in her dry lips turned to fissures in this new hell. She was too dehydrated to sweat.

The guard pounded on the door, repeating his rounds. "Your skin is looking awfully red, everything okay in there?" He didn't wait for an answer before moving on.

Anna lifted her dress to expose her torso and chest, using her left hand to hold it there, trying to decrease the heat. The fingers of her right hand pulsed with pain where the needle had been thrust under her fingernails. Her already weakened muscles lost all strength, and she dropped the dress, her arm flopping down to her side, as she slumped against the wall. The hot air blowing from the vent singed the backs of her legs, the acrid odor of burning flesh filling the cell.

The walls shimmered, rolling like waves, as Anna struggled to make her weakened muscles move, turning to face the back wall so the heat now blew on her bruised shins. Her pulse raced, and she fought to stay erect, fearing that if she fell she'd be wedged against the walls—the vent—and unable to move.

Her head ached, and the dizziness and nausea increased. The hot air stung her nostrils as she breathed quick huffs in and out, so she switched to breathing through her mouth until her raw throat and dry tongue couldn't take it anymore. Alternating agonies.

The guard pounded on the door again but didn't say anything this time.

Moaning, Anna blinked as fuzzy images floated in her vision. Sneering faces—guards, interrogators, NKVD, her rapists, Stalin—all baring their teeth like ravenous wolves. Her legs, the heat had to be melting the skin off them. She rolled her head forward to look down, a distant spike of alarm ringing somewhere in her mind, muffled, as gray-colored flames licked at her feet. She closed her eyes for several seconds, and the muted flames were gone when she opened them.

"You're hallucinating, Anna," Nadya's stern voice echoed in her head. "Get it together. Turn around again."

Anna obeyed the disembodied voice, shuffling her feet until she again faced the door.

"Mmm, something smells delicious."

"Mama!" Anna whispered, hearing her sweet mother's voice.

"What's for dinner, Nadya?"

Anna swiveled her head, looking for the source of the voices.

"It's Anna, Mama," Nadya said, "they're roasting her alive."

The fan slowed to a stop; the voices of Anna's sister and mother floated away in the silence.

Hallucinations, Anna thought, eyes closed against the dizziness.

A fist pounded against the door. "Warm enough for you?" The guard chuckled and moved to the next cell.

Maybe she'd tell the interrogator the guard was an enemy of the people...

The fan kicked on again, blowing freezing air through the vent.

☭

Anna spilled out into the corridor when the guard opened the door, having just endured another round of scorching heat. She had no idea how long she'd been in there or how many rounds of the alternating extreme temperatures they'd put her through.

Two guards rolled her over and one of them shook her by the shoulders. "Wake up, woman! Open your eyes!"

Her inflamed lids scratched across her eyeballs as she forced them halfway open. One of the guards, at least, looked relieved—or was she hallucinating again? They grabbed her under the arms and dragged her to the interrogation room.

In front of the desk, they lifted her to her feet and ordered, "Stand up!"

She swayed and stumbled to the side a couple of steps before finding her balance. The room spun around her, and she tipped to her right. One of the guards grabbed her arm, preventing her from falling.

"Get her a stick to prop herself up with," the interrogator said.

While one guard steadied her, the other hurried out of the room.

The interrogator smiled at her and asked, "Did you get some sleep today, citizen?"

"Huh," Anna lifted her chin. Her throat muscles worked as she tried to speak and finally managed a garbled "Not allowed."

"They didn't let you sleep?" He shrugged. "Well, after all, this isn't supposed to be a vacation resort, Miss Levitskaya. The guard was awake too."

The guard holding her up snorted.

"Of course, he's probably snuggled up next to his mistress about now." The interrogator leaned toward her. "After eating a hearty dinner, I'm sure."

The second guard returned and handed Anna a walking stick. "Use that to steady yourself, woman. Dmitri doesn't want to keep standing there with your stink getting all over him."

Anna's weak grip on the stick was enough that she could stand without assistance.

The interrogator walked to the side of the desk and sat at a small table Anna hadn't noticed before. There were two chairs at the table. And atop it sat what, with her fuzzy vision, Anna thought was a pot of borscht, a couple of pork chops, a chunk of bread, and a pile of fried potatoes. As starved as her body was, she only had eyes for the carafe of water placed directly in the middle of the table.

The interrogator said, "I hope you don't mind if I eat while we talk, Anna. I slept a little later today and didn't have time for dinner at home." He poured water into a tall glass and drank it slowly, gazing into Anna's eyes as he did so.

"Please..." Anna stared at the glass. She'd never wanted—no, *needed*—anything so much in her life.

"You know, Dmitri," the interrogator nodded to the guard, "a human being cannot live more than a few days without water. Their organs shut down, their brain swells, they can have seizures." He shook his head. "Not a pleasant way to go, my friend."

"No, comrade, not at all," Dmitri agreed.

The interrogator took a spoonful of borscht, slurping it before swallowing. He turned his attention to Anna. "Miss Levitskaya, how many days have passed since you last had a drink? I mean, besides the salt-water douche this morning. That actually makes the 'dying from thirst' process happen faster."

Oh, how she loathed this man. She continued to stare at the carafe, swaying. Dizzy and weak.

"Answer the question, Anna. How many days?"

She peeled her tongue from the roof of her mouth, painful ulcers shooting sparks through the dry tissues. "I..." her voice came out as a croak, "I don't know."

"Yes, well, a little confusion is understandable under the circumstances." He tore a piece of bread from the small loaf and dipped it in the borscht, then continued as he chewed. "If my calculations are correct—and assuming you had something to drink the evening of your arrest—you have gone more than forty-eight hours without water. And factoring in the salt water we were forced, by your noncooperation, to give you last night...I'd say you are nearing the end."

The thought of death didn't scare her, not after what she'd been through the last forty-eight hours—if only the thirst wasn't so all-consuming. So painful. So tormenting to body and soul. She could focus on nothing else. The pain and exhaustion thrumming through her every cell were weak in comparison to her need for water.

"But, good news!" The interrogator continued to eat noisily as he spoke. "I won't let that happen. I'm enjoying our time together, Miss Levitskaya, and I wouldn't want it to be cut short."

Anna dry swallowed, her throat going through the motions even though there was not so much as a drop of saliva there, as the interrogator lifted a second glass and filled it halfway with water from the carafe. He gestured to the guard and said, "Dmitri, give this to our guest."

She dropped the stick and grabbed the glass out of the guard's hand before he could pull it away. The glass clinked against her teeth as her hands shook. Much of the water slid out the corners of her mouth and down her neck, but the bit she was able to swallow soothed her tongue and throat. But it was but a drop in the bucket of what she needed. She held the empty glass out. "Please. May I have more?"

"No." The interrogator stood, walked over to her, and took the glass. "Now it's your turn to give me something, bitch."

12

A man's scream penetrated the wall from an adjoining room. The interrogator glanced in that direction then back at Anna. "Let's not try to outdo whatever *persuasion* is going on next door."

Anna put her hands behind her back, the memory of the needle sliding beneath her fingernails bullying its way to the front of her mind. "I...I already signed a confession."

He tilted his head to the side and frowned. "Yes, well, that deposition seems to have been misplaced. We'll need to start over."

Despair filled her chest. She couldn't remember a single thing she'd "confessed" to. What game was he playing?

He rapped his knuckles on the desk thoughtfully then put a finger to his chin. "I have an idea. We got off to a rough start, Anna. Let me make it up to you." He turned to Dmitri. "Let her sit on the couch—but *no* sleeping! I'll be right back."

It had been over two days since Anna had sat. Her knees forgot how to bend, and the joints grated against each other as she lowered herself onto the soft surface, falling into the cushion when she lost her strength about a foot from it. If she could have produced tears, she would have cried at the sheer relief of taking the weight off her feet. She leaned her head back and closed her eyes.

Dmitri slugged her in the thigh. She flung herself forward, sure he'd stabbed a large knife through her leg from the sharp cramp that wouldn't subside.

"No sleeping," he said.

Nausea bubbled in her stomach as the muscle continued to spasm. She swallowed and breathed fast. She couldn't throw up the measly amount of water she'd just drunk. She needed every drop.

The cramping dulled to an ache by the time the interrogator returned. He carried a metal bowl in his hand. The man who'd shoved the needle under her nails trailed behind him, and Anna retched, nearly losing her battle to keep the liquid down. What kind of new hell did the two men have in mind for her this time?

He held the bowl out to her. Anna shook her head, thinking about the salt-water he'd forced down her throat... When had it been? That morning?

Placing a hand over his heart, the interrogator frowned. "I am offended that you do not trust me, Anna. Eat. I know you must be starving." It wasn't a suggestion.

He shoved the bowl closer, and Anna flinched before taking it from him. She had trouble getting the thin gruel from the bowl to her mouth, her trembling hand shook most of it out of the spoon before it reached her lips.

The interrogator paced in front of the desk where the man he brought back with him sat writing on a sheet of paper. After several minutes, he returned to Anna and snatched the bowl from her, sloshing the gruel onto her lap. "That's enough." He walked to the table and poured a small amount of water in the glass she'd drunk from earlier, then handed it to her.

Throat working a little better now, Anna was able to drink it all before he took it from her. Her eyes wandered to the carafe. The small amounts the interrogator had given her weren't enough to even begin to slake her thirst. Her mouth and throat returned to being just as dry as soon as the water slid down her esophagus.

"How's it coming, Ivan?" the interrogator asked as he glanced over his shoulder at his comrade.

The man waved a dismissive hand and grunted. "Few more minutes."

With a sigh, the interrogator went back and stood next to the table, eating fried potatoes with his fingers.

Anna's eyelids drooped. Her head nodded forward. She jerked it up and opened her eyes as wide as she could. She couldn't let herself fall asleep. But it was no use, she couldn't withstand the pull of slumber after being awake for over seventy-two hours. She awoke with a gasp as the guard, Dmitri, slammed his fist into her thigh again. Her muscle seized, and she cried out, rocking forward as she tried to rub the cramp out with her left hand. She moaned, the pain worsening as she tried to straighten out her leg.

Shaking his head, the interrogator said, "You will not be allowed to sleep, Anna Levitskaya, until you are truthful in your testimony."

Truth? she thought through the haze. *That is the last thing you want.*

"I am finished, comrade," Ivan said, laying the pen neatly on the desk. He stapled two pages together.

Anna didn't even see the interrogator move from the table before he was standing in front of her. He yanked her to her feet, and she crumpled to the floor, her spasming leg unable to hold her weight.

"Get her to her feet, Dmitri, and bring her over to the desk." The interrogator nudged her with his boot before walking away.

The guard hefted her up. The muscle cramp subsided into a powerful ache, and she was able to stay erect. Dmitri shoved her toward the desk. She stumbled then limped over to stand in front of it.

Ivan slid the papers he'd been writing on across to the interrogator.

He tapped it with a finger and said, "Now, Anna Levitskaya, here is what you have testified to this evening in the presence of two witnesses. Sign here."

She knew it would do no good to protest that she hadn't *testified* to anything, she'd barely even spoken "this evening." Anna's vision blurred as she tried to read what the man had written. She picked up the pages, bringing them closer to her face, and read:

1. *Anna Levitskaya, in collaboration with fiancé, Nikolai Karakov (now deceased), admits to Collusion to Commit Treason to the Motherland through various contacts, leading to Suspicion of Espionage as follows: A. Levitskaya and N. Karakov had contact with C. Vyshinsky, an acquaintance of A. Novikov who had a dress made by the same seamstress as L. Turner – wife of a foreign diplomat.*

She had no idea who any of those people were, except Nikolai.

1. *A. Levitskaya admits to Undermining of State Industry by means of wrecking with Counter-Revolutionary purposes as follows: subversion of property from Garment Factory #76; tampering with equipment, such as sewing machines, to slow production; and shirking her duties as a seamstress by refusing to fulfill quotas.*

None of this was true. She was a good worker and never "subverted" so much as a piece of thread!

1. *A. Levitskaya admits to the spreading of Anti-Soviet and Counter-Revolutionary Propaganda and Agitation through the telling of political jokes about the Supreme Commander and criticism of the Soviet Union.*

It had been Nikolai that told a joke—while drunk. Not her. But, she remembered vaguely, she had confessed to doing this last night, just to get the torture to stop.

> 1. *A. Levitskaya admits to Failure to Renounce N. Karakov for his Anti-Revolutionary activities.*

Anna knew she was innocent of all these things she'd supposedly "confessed" to, but she had no fight left in her. It didn't matter. They'd just keep torturing her until she signed—again. She struggled to flip to the next page, the skin of her fingers too dry to gain purchase on the paper. The interrogator reached over and turned it for her, and she continued to read.

> 1. *A. Levitskaya testifies that the following citizens have committed or intend to commit acts consistent with Anti-Soviet, Counter-Revolutionary, or other crimes against the Motherland:* Olga Levitskaya—

Blind rage overpowered Anna's fear, pain, thirst, and exhaustion at seeing her mama's name written in the small block letters by the demon seated at the desk. With a defiant cry, she tore the papers in half, crumpled them in her fist, and dropped them on the desk. She turned to the interrogator. "I will *not* denounce anyone." Her chest heaved with anger. How dare they invoke her mother's name! *These monsters of hell had better—*

The red-faced interrogator back-handed her, sending her sprawling to the ground. "Strip her and hold her down!" he yelled.

The guard pulled the dress over her head then ripped the soiled underwear off her. The man sitting at the desk moved to sit on her upper back, smashing her chest into the hard floor, and the guard held her legs down. A trickle of blood dangled from her lip until, in slow motion, it fell, staining the floor beneath her face.

A rubber strap brandished by the interrogator came within her limited line of vision for a split second. The first strike of the strap landed on her lower spine, in the same spot that was already bruised and swollen from the truncheon strikes the night before. Intense pain exploded, like boiling water had been poured over the sensitive skin there. An inhuman howl erupted from Anna's throat, continuing as the interrogator struck the same site repeatedly before moving down to beat the soles of her feet.

Anna screamed and sobbed, suffocating from the weight on her back and the prolonged screams that seemed to come from another person, another dimension.

The beating stopped, but Anna continued to weep as bolts of pain shot out from her spine, and her feet burned such that there couldn't possibly have been any skin left on them. Her screams died down to moans and gasping breaths.

The interrogator leaned over near her head and blew a puff of cigarette smoke into her face. His forehead dripped with sweat. "You can let go of her now, comrades."

Ivan pushed down on her head to stand and Dmitri let go of her legs.

Her only movement was the rise and fall of her chest as she breathed, and the involuntary twitches of her muscles.

The interrogator grabbed Anna's left hand, flipped it over, and extinguished his cigarette on her palm, wrenching another scream from her tortured body.

"Take her back to a punishment cell."

"There aren't any available," the guard replied.

Their voices sounded distant, like mere echoes from the far side of an empty cavern.

"Then put her on a stool!" the interrogator yelled.

Darkness closed in on Anna, and she succumbed to it, closing her eyes.

13

With a sharp inhale, Anna's eyes flew open to see the guard holding something close to her nose. She jerked her head back, away from the abrasive odor burning her nostrils. Her respirations picked up, quick and shallow, groaning with each exhale as consciousness returned—bringing the world of pain with it.

"Come on now, on your feet." The guard straddled her and lifted her under the arms.

She screamed, her surroundings fading out for a moment as agony flared in her back. She was still in the interrogator's office. She must not have been out long since she still smelled the burned flesh of her palm from his cigarette and the remnants of smoke.

The guard hefted her to her feet, and she cried out again as the bruised and swollen soles took on her weight.

"We don't have far to go. I'm not gonna carry you," he said. He removed his support and bent to pick up her dress. He leered at her bare chest for several seconds, grinning.

No, she thought. *No, not again.* Her thoughts flashed to the back of the Black Mariah, the men, the gang rape.

The guard shook his head and draped the dress over her shoulder, gesturing to the torn underwear laying nearby. "Those are ruined. You'll have to go without."

She swayed, dizziness wafting over her.

"Let's go. Follow me." The guard spun and headed toward the door.

Each step was a new lesson in agony as she shuffled her feet slowly. She somehow made it to the corridor where the guard waited several yards away, next to a stool. Jaw clenched against the torment, she hobbled to where he stood.

He gestured to the wooden stool, positioned a couple of feet out into the corridor, away from the wall. "Sit. Do not move either your ass from the stool or the stool from this spot. Do not sleep. Sit up straight, do not attempt to lean against the wall."

The stool was tall enough that she didn't have to lower herself much to reach the seat. Her feet just touched the floor—they might not have touched at all had they not been swollen from the internal bleeding the rubber-strap-wielding interrogator had caused. Muscle spasms tore through her lower back, and she closed her eyes, grunting through the pain.

When she opened them, the guard, Dmitri, stood staring at her heaving chest again. She tried to lift an arm up to cover herself, but it just dropped back to her side, too weak to carry out the simple command.

Dmitri stepped forward and fondled her breasts, nodding to the dress draped over her shoulder as he backed away. "You might want to put that on. Not all the guards have as much self-control as me."

His jack boots echoed on the cement floor as he walked away, whistling. He stopped and looked over his shoulder at her. "And don't even try to disobey any of the rules. A guard will be around to check on you every couple of minutes."

Dropping her head, Anna balanced on the stool, in too much agony to appreciate that she was sitting down. And it didn't take long for her to realize the stool was just another form of torment. The hard surface pressed against her tailbone with a deep ache. With nothing to lean back against, keeping herself erect caused more back spasms, and she had to put pressure on her bruised feet to keep herself from sliding off.

She became aware of a rank odor as she sat there, and she searched her surroundings for the source before realizing it was her. Dried stool still clung to parts of her legs, and she vaguely recalled urinating herself at some point too. Maybe more than once. Unwashed skin and hair and festering bug bites added to the aroma. She smelled like a dead animal on the side of the road.

Footsteps came toward her, and she looked down at her nude body, remembering Dmitri's warning about other guards not having self-control. It felt as if she were fighting against a riptide as she moved her arm, heavy with fatigue, to grab the dress. The rough material rubbed against the fresh burn on her palm as she closed her hand around it. She flinched, and the dress slipped to the floor.

No!

Anna glanced up at the approaching guard, panic and shame adding to the strain on her rapidly beating heart. She looked down at the dress. Dmitri had told her not to move from the stool. What would happen if she did—just long enough to grab the garment? *Bad things*, she thought. *Bad things would happen.* But...worse than what a horny guard would do upon seeing her naked?

Blinking to clear the fuzziness from her vision, she looked toward the guard and covered her breasts with one arm and her crotch with her other hand. A strangled sob caught in her chest as the man neared.

Anna blinked again. No. Not a man. A woman. A female guard.

She stopped in front of Anna and frowned. "Looks like they worked you over good."

"Please," Anna whispered, "I dropped..." She nodded to the dress.

The guard picked it up, grumbling, "Damn male guards. They have no sense of propriety. Let me help you with this." With a gentleness Anna couldn't believe existed in this hellhole, the woman slipped the dress over Anna's head and helped guide her hands through the arm holes before tugging the back of the garment down over the seat of the stool and stretching the front almost to Anna's knees. "I can't let you stand to pull it down properly, but at least your woman parts are covered now."

"Thank you," Anna said with more gratitude than she'd ever felt in her life.

"Yup." With a stern look, the guard admonished, "There are three guards, including me, patrolling this corridor tonight. One of us will be by every few minutes. Don't let any of us catch you sleeping, slouching, standing, or moving this stool from this exact spot."

Anna straightened her back, trying to hold in a groan as muscles contracted and knotted up.

The guard continued on down the hallway, disappearing as she turned the corner at the end.

Hours passed. Anna chanced closing her eyes between the guards' rounds, not to sleep—the intense pain coursing through her body made sure that didn't happen—but to help focus all her depleted energy on staying erect and to force herself to take slow, deep breaths to help stave off the muscle spasms in her back and to cope with the pain.

Her legs had gone numb early on, yet she could still feel her pulse hammering in her feet like a red-hot poker. She was afraid to look at them. Last time she'd dared to peek, they'd grown to twice their normal size. The red, blue, and purple bruising had started seeping up around the sides of her feet, the blood pushed against gravity by the pressure. She wondered how far her skin could stretch before ripping apart.

Once again, hallucinations tormented her. Anna didn't know what was real and what wasn't. The urge to sleep ultimately overpowered all else, and she slunk to the floor. Agonizing pain shocked her awake when one of the male guards kicked the damaged sole of one of her feet.

"Get your lazy ass back on that stool, bitch! What do you think this is? A hotel?"

Weeping, Anna used the stool to pull herself to her knees, but she couldn't put any weight on either foot—the pain too severe for her body to allow it. Between sobs, she said, "I...can't."

"Lazy piece of shit," he mumbled. He wrapped his arms around her waist and lifted her, dropping her onto the stool from about a foot above it.

She yelled as the jolt sent a lightning bolt of pain up her spine. Darkness invaded her vision from all sides, and she fought to remain conscious. She tipped to the side. The guard caught her then waved something in front of her nose. Smelling salts. She inhaled sharply on reflex and jerked her head away.

The guard watched her for a few more seconds, then said, "No more sleeping. I'm going to increase the patrol of this hallway, so don't even think about disobeying."

A change in guards alerted her to the fact that the day shift was over. They'd be taking her to the interrogator's office soon. What was she going to do? What would they do to her if she refused to sign again? Maybe they would just execute her. A big part of her wished for that. To be at peace.

"No, my Anna," Mama's voice said. "Do not let them take your life. You are strong, *solnyshko*."

"Mama," Anna sobbed. "What should I do?"

"You know what is the right thing. I love you." Mama's voice faded, floating away.

And, looking down at her savaged body, she knew what she had to do. She could not subject another human being to this hell. Especially not her mama.

14

No longer able to keep her back straight, Anna slouched over, hanging her head. She didn't even attempt to straighten up when she heard the clomping of jack boots coming her way on the cement floor of the corridor.

Two guards, she thought distantly as they positioned themselves on either side of her.

They each looped an arm under her armpits and hefted her off the stool without a word. Someone whimpered like a lost puppy as they dragged her down the corridor, her feet dragging behind her.

It took a while for her to realize it was her—the whimpering was coming from her. She closed her eyes. Maybe she could sleep while they escorted her to the torture chamber. They couldn't see her eyes from their positions. She had to get some sleep. Even for just a few seconds.

She must have dozed off, because she had no recollection of arriving at the interrogation office. She was in the hallway near the stool, then she was being dumped on the floor of the office in front of the desk.

"Stand up, bitch!" the voice she'd come to despise more than Satan himself ordered.

It was all she could do to push herself to her knees.

After watching her struggle for several minutes, the interrogator said, "It seems that you'd rather kneel at my feet today, citizen. Fine then, but there will be no sitting back on your heels and you will keep your back upright!"

When had she started trembling? Her whole body shook. She stared at the interrogator's boots blindly, fighting to stay erect.

"Now, Anna Levitskaya, I'd like to be done with you. I have other enemies of the state I need to question. So let's make this quick, shall we?"

She remained silent, concentrating on keeping her position through the twitching muscles, exhaustion, and dizziness.

"Comrade Gorbatov," he pointed to the man behind the desk, "has graciously recreated the deposition you so childishly tore up last night. We'll just need your signature, and then we can get you situated in a common cell with others of your ilk."

Anna looked up at him for the first time since entering the room. Her resolve had only strengthened since hearing her mama's voice out in the hallway. "I will not denounce anyone." The shakiness of her voice was borne of fatigue and pain, not fear. Losing her mind bit by bit to sleeplessness had caused her to forget her fear—at least for the moment.

The interrogator crouched down in front of her, puffing smoke in her face. "So...there's *nothing* we can do to convince you to name your co-conspirators?" He held his burning cigarette close to her cheek.

"Nothing." And though the heat from the cigarette singed her skin, Anna didn't shy away. "Because there *are* no co-conspirators."

He sighed and stood. Leaning over the desk, he and his comrade whispered to each other. She caught a word here and there, "worthless," "labor camp," "need for workers."

Ivan Gorbatov wrote again, the pen scraping across the paper the only sound in the room. An occasional scream or begging wail could be heard from the rooms on either side, but Anna's torture chamber remained silent.

Wavering on her knees, the time passed with ethereal slowness. Even her pain dulled as sleep deprivation induced a sensation of disembodiment.

She twitched when the interrogator shoved a paper in front of her. "Sign."

Anna watched with detached curiosity as her hand—which didn't feel as if it were a part of her—raised to take the paper from him. It took a moment for her to figure out how to get her fingers to close around it. She held it close to her face, the words swimming in her fevered vision. The four depositions from—was it yesterday?—were written there. She flipped it over. Blank. No denunciations or accusations against anyone else. She nodded. "Okay."

The interrogator took the paper from her and laid it on the desk. "Get over here so you can sign."

She scooted her knees across the hard floor until she reached the desk. He handed her the pen, and with a light grip to not exacerbate the pain in her fingers, she took it and signed her name on the line he indicated. The shaky scribbling only looked vaguely like Anna's signature, but it was the best she could do.

Ivan whisked the paper away, placing it in a folder with a pile of others.

"Take her to a women's common cell," the interrogator said to the guards. "And bring me the next one."

The two guards grabbed her under her arms and dragged her backwards, her bruised and swollen heels bouncing across the floor. She cried out with the intense pain, but they continued to tow her along without even a glance down at her.

By the time they reached their destination, she was sure she'd never walk again. They dropped her in front of the gray metal door to the cell as one of the guards pulled out a ring of keys and unlocked the padlock. They pulled the door open and shoved her inside, slamming it behind her.

Anna landed on someone's legs and was pushed away with a curse. She scrunched up, bringing her legs to her chest to make herself as small as possible in the overcrowded cell. Bright lights lit up the space even though it was still night, Anna assumed, since the prisoners were all sleeping or trying to sleep. She couldn't shrink herself enough not to sit on someone's feet or other body part. There was no window. In the sweltering heat created by so many bodies pressed together, many of the women had stripped down to underwear and bra, their clothing folded beneath their bodies. Anna didn't have that luxury—as she had neither underwear nor bra.

An older woman sat up from a bunk she shared with another, laying head to foot on the narrow surface. "Hey," she whispered. "I'm the *starosta* in this cell. There's a small spot for you over by the *parasha*, the bucket. Make your way over there. And disturb as few as you can. We'll talk in the morning." She laid back down, folding her hands over her abdomen.

Anna looked to where the woman had pointed. The cell wasn't large, the distance to the open space on the floor next to the latrine bucket was only about eight feet away. But there were women sitting or lying, some even standing, across every inch of that eight feet. And Anna couldn't stand or walk.

She rolled to her knees, almost kneeling on a sleeping woman's hand. She inched forward, bumping into a thin redhead.

The redhead cursed and raised up on her elbows. "What are you doing?" she whispered. "You'll never make it over there like that. You need to stand up!"

"I...I can't." Anna lowered her head.

"Well, why not? Don't you have fee—" The redhead sat up, going silent as she stared at Anna's tortured feet. "Oh. Your feet..." She shook her head and looked into Anna's eyes. "You've already been interrogated, then."

Anna nodded. "Hasn't everyone in here?"

"No, they don't—"

"Hush, Natalia!" the *starosta* whispered. "You can talk in the morning!"

The food hatch in the door lifted and an angry "Shh!" hissed through the opening before it slammed shut with a bang.

In a much quieter whisper, Natalia replied, "Well, she isn't going to make it to the bucket, Ev. We'll make room for her here." She nudged the woman next to her. "Make some space."

The woman grumbled but complied.

"There," Natalia whispered, "if we both lay on our sides, I think you'll fit."

Heat wafted off the nearly nude bodies that flanked Anna. Between that, the uncomfortable position, the pain, thirst, and hunger, she didn't think there was any way she'd be able to sleep. But being forced to stay awake for days on end had made sleep her body's number one priority. She was out in a few minutes.

Pounding on the door was followed by the rattling of keys and the guard pulling the door open. "Six o'clock! Wake up!"

Women all around Anna sat up, but she remained still, eyes closed even though she'd heard the guard. *Just a few more seconds,* she thought.

Someone nudged her from behind and whispered almost silently, "Get up."

The urgency in that whisper made Anna's heart leap, and her eyes snapped open. She struggled to push herself up from the side-lying position she'd been in for whatever had been left of the night after her time with the interrogator—a couple of hours maybe? Every muscle ached, and her lower back screamed with agony when she moved. She clamped her teeth together to keep from crying out, and with a gentle push from behind her, she was able to sit up.

The guard peered around the cell then nodded, seemingly

satisfied that no one remained sleeping. "No trip to the toilets this morning, ladies," he said. "We're short-staffed. You'll have to all use the latrine bucket. You have fifteen minutes!"

There were a few groans, but no one complained out loud.

The older woman who had introduced herself in the middle of the night as the *starosta*, stood and said, "Line up. Let's get a move on or we'll never get through all of us."

Anna crawled toward where her cellmates lined up. She was last in line.

"Move your line over to the side, ladies, I need to be able to *watch* you." The guard grinned. "I have to make sure you aren't breaking any rules."

Anna had already been worried about relieving herself in front of the other women, but the thought of doing it in front of the leering guard... "Excuse me," she said, tapping the woman in front of her.

"No talking!" the guard yelled.

She just wanted to know how often they were typically taken to the toilets. As dehydrated as she was, she could probably go some time before the need to urinate became unbearable.

Her stomach growled and a sharp cramp lit up her bowels. *No!* She'd only eaten such a small amount of the watery gruel the interrogator had given her—how could she need to pass stool already? She knew it was because of the havoc her body had been through over the last several days. How could she expect any of her organs to work as they should?

The line of prisoners grew more anxious as it moved forward. Women grumbled under their breath if anyone took more than half a minute.

"Five minutes," the guard said.

There were still at least ten women in front of Anna. Her stomach clenched again. As she watched the others, she realized she'd have to stand, there was no seat on the latrine bucket, the women just stood, straddling it, to complete their business.

Anna reached the nearly full bucket as the guard yelled, "Thirty seconds!"

Another cramp twisted her intestines. Anna clamped her mouth on a yelp of pain as she shoved herself to her battered feet to straddle the bucket. She lifted the back of her dress, but left the front to cover her.

"Twenty seconds!"

Had her intestines not cramped again at that moment, Anna doubted she would have been able to make them perform on-demand, but a small amount of watery diarrhea trickled into the bucket beneath her, and the *starosta* handed her a small piece of frayed material to wipe herself with. She nodded her thanks, wiped, then dropped the material onto the pile next to her.

"Time's up!" the guard shouted. "Now, Evgenya, whose turn is it to empty the latrine?"

The *starosta*, Evgenya, pointed at two of the women, who moved to pick up the fetid bucket. "Can I assign someone to take the rags to the toilet to wash them?" she asked the guard.

"No. It will have to wait until tomorrow."

Evgenya put her hands on her hips and huffed out a breath, but she kept her thoughts to herself.

"What?" The guard shrugged. "It isn't like anything's going to improve the odor in here, anyway." He followed the latrine bearers out into the hall and shut the cell door.

Anna continued to stand near where the bucket had been, feet burning with the weight of her body pressing them into the floor. She hadn't inspected the cell when she'd been dumped there in the night, and she took a moment to look around.

There was a small table with a little pile of books atop it. The only seating, besides the bunks or the floor, were two stools that had been pushed under the table. The bunks were nothing more than raised wooden planks all along the edges of the cell—no mattresses, or even blankets. Not that they needed blankets in the sweltering heat caused by so many bodies being pressed together in the small space.

Evgenya made her way to Anna's side. "Let's sit. Your feet must be causing you so much pain," she whispered, looking side-eyed at the peephole in the door. She took Anna's arm and slowly helped her over to the nearest bunk.

They sat, Anna with a groan that made it through her clenched teeth.

"What's your name?"

"Anna."

"So, Anna," Evgenya began, "as I said a few hours ago, I am this cell's *starosta*, the elder prisoner who's sort of in charge. We whisper because we aren't 'allowed' to talk—they don't want us to compare stories, I guess. Always keep an eye on the Judas hole, there," she gestured to the peephole, "and clam up if you see a guard looking in."

Anna nodded.

"I'll give you a quick rundown before the guard returns. Bedtime is eleven, wake-up is six—sometimes earlier. That is the only time we're allowed to sleep, no sleeping during the day, no laying down. They never turn the lights out, so you'll have to get used to that. We can't cover our faces or arms, so when it gets cold in here, your arms have to stay uncovered, on top of the blanket—if you're lucky enough to get one of those."

Anna had a hard time concentrating. Her mind was still fuzzy and kept wandering as she watched the other women whispering or standing alone.

"They take us to the toilet first thing in the morning, at least half the time, and again at night before bedtime, if we're lucky. That only happens about a quarter of the time. They let us have the slop bucket at night if we don't get to use the facilities."

Looking down at her filthy, itchy, skin, Anna asked, "When do we get to shower?"

"Hah!" the woman said a little louder than a whisper. Her eyes moved to the peephole before landing back on Anna. "We're supposed to get a shower every ten days...but it's been at least three weeks. The guards are lazy, and they just keep shoving more of us into this place."

The guard's eye appeared in the peephole, and the whispers stopped. He opened the door and ushered the two prisoners back inside, without the latrine bucket. "Breakfast. Line up."

Natalia's red hair bobbed toward Anna through the crowd. "I'll get yours," she whispered when she lined up.

Gratefulness flooded Anna's chest. If she'd had any tears to shed, they would have started falling. *Thank you*, she mouthed. It had been so long since she'd had a glimpse of humanity. A smile. She had to remind herself she'd been there less than a week—it had only *felt* like forever.

Natalia cradled a bowl against her stomach with her arm and held two cups by the handles in that hand. In her other hand she held two small pieces of bread. She kicked one of the stools out from under the table and scooted it over to where Anna sat on the bunk. "Take one of these." She nodded to the cups.

Anna examined what appeared to be water in the lukewarm cup while Natalia situated herself on the stool at Anna's knees.

"Warm water," the redhead whispered. "Sometimes we get lucky and they put a little tea or coffee in it. Not today, though." She set the bowl on her lap and handed Anna a piece of bread and two sugar cubes she'd had in her fist.

The warm water slid down Anna's dry throat, coating it. She closed her eyes and let herself enjoy the sensation.

"We have to share the gruel. Not enough bowls."

"Quiet over there!" the guard yelled.

Anna dropped the sugar cubes into her water, following Natalia's lead, then nibbled on the bread, trying to pace herself to make it seem like a bigger portion. Same with the water—she wanted to guzzle it all down at once, but took small sips instead, her goal was to make it last until she was done eating. She and Natalia took turns sipping the watered-down gruel from the bowl.

"All right!" The guard straightened from where he'd been leaning on the doorpost, watching them. "Finish up. Stack your dishes on the cart."

Anna drank the last of the sugar-water in her cup, and Natalia took it from her and made her way over to the cart. After the guard closed the door behind him, Evgenya returned to her spot on the bunk, next to Anna, and Natalia again sat on the stool, pulling it in so close, their knees touched.

"So," Evgenya whispered, "where were we?"

Anna shrugged, she had no idea. Her memory was all messed up.

"Doesn't matter," the older woman said. "So, that was breakfast. They're supposed to take us out to the yard for a twenty-minute walk, but that hasn't happened for at least a week. Other than that, it's just a whole lot of the same thing. Whispering to each other while we watch the Judas hole. You can read, but we only get a couple of books at a time, so we have to take turns."

Anna glanced over at the table, the books she'd seen there earlier were gone.

"They'll bring us lunch and dinner. Take us to the toilet after dinner, if we're lucky. There are some sinks in there, so you can wash your clothes—but only in the mornings, and only if everyone hurries."

Natalia leaned forward, eyes wide. "And they come and get us, one or two at a time."

Alarm spiked in Anna's chest. "What for?"

"At night...for interrogation. During the day," she glanced toward the peephole, "to see the prosecutor, for sentencing."

"Do the prisoners come back, after sentencing?" Anna asked.

"Not always."

She was afraid to ask what that meant.

"What...what did they do to you?" Natalia's eyes moved quickly from the top of Anna's head, down to her feet.

"Have you been interrogated?" Anna asked.

Her red hair fell across her face as she shook her head.

"How many of you haven't been?"

Evgenya answered, "About half."

"And you?"

"Yes. Months ago." She frowned. "But I fared much better than you, young one. I knew resistance was futile. Holding out wasn't worth losing my health."

"Or your teeth," a toothless woman standing nearby whispered with a lisp. "You can't get new teeth."

"Yeah," another woman agreed. "I've heard that they'll convict you whether you confess or not."

Anna felt the truth of that statement deep inside her soul.

"So..." Natalia looked at the door again. "Why did you resist?"

Staring down at her feet, Anna whispered, "Because I knew my life was over no matter what. And I wasn't about to condemn another innocent person to this fate. Especially not my mama."

The redhead's eyes flashed with both fear and anger. "They wanted you to denounce your mama?"

Anna nodded.

The room went silent. At first, Anna thought it was because everyone was listening in on their conversation, but with a glance at the door, she realized the guard was peeking in, watching them.

After he moved on, Natalia whispered again, "What did they do to you?"

15

A group of her cellmates closed around her to listen, their curiosity outweighing the negative effects of their combined body temperature. A blonde-haired woman, who, unlike most of the others, looked to be well fed, tried to nudge her way into the crowd but was denied—often with nasty looks from the others.

Their obvious disdain for this woman confused Anna. They'd all been, if not friendly, at least civil to her. She looked at Natalia with a confused frown.

"She's an informer," Natalia whispered. "There's always at least one in every cell."

Evgenya nodded. "Don't say a word to her—or to anyone else when she's within earshot."

Anna swallowed and looked to make sure the woman wasn't close enough to hear her whispers. Then she told them everything she could remember about the moment she'd been shoved into the bug-infested box until her placement in the cell with them. She didn't tell them what happened in the Black Mariah. That horror was hers to bear alone.

When she was finished, the cell remained silent for a full minute.

One of the women who looked even younger than Anna, whispered, "You must really love your mama."

Anna's throat grew thick, and an ache formed deep in her chest. She wanted to go home. She missed her mama. She missed Nikolai. She longed for the days when she and Nadya laughed together.

The crowd around her dispersed as much as possible in the tight quarters. Everyone seemed to be lost in their own thoughts. Anna wiped a tear from her eye—the first her body had been able to produce in a couple of days. She pressed a hand against her aching heart.

"Let's see what we can do about those feet," Evgenya said. "Ladies, Anna needs some foot coverings. Bring me the extra material or towels you have stashed."

Anna was surprised that there was little hesitation. Once one woman came forth with a strip of cloth, others started passing more down.

"Very good," Evgenya said. "That should be enough. Thank you."

"Yes," Anna's voice caught. "Thank you so much."

The *starosta* knelt at her feet with a grunt and wrapped the donated strips of material around them in a crisscross pattern, first one, then the other. "There. Hopefully that will help with the pain when you walk."

Anna tried, but she couldn't fight the urge to hug the older woman. Evgenya allowed it for only a few seconds before pushing her away with a blush.

Keys rattled outside the cell. The silence inside intensified, as if they were all holding their breath.

The door opened, and a different guard said loudly, "A. L." as he looked around. "If your initials are A.L., step forward."

Anna's gaze met Natalia's. Her widening eyes did not give Anna any comfort. She stood and limped toward the guard.

Without another word, he led her out of the cell and down the corridor. The makeshift foot dressings helped a little, but Anna ground her teeth against the pain as she shuffled behind him, trying to keep up. When he opened the door to a stairwell and gestured for her to go up, she had to choke back a sob.

By the time they reached their destination, an office on the second floor, Anna was ready to fall to her knees and crawl.

The guard knocked on the door and a bored voice said, "Come in."

Anna limped across the parquet floor, eyeing the chair positioned in front of the desk.

The well-nourished blond man looked up at her impersonally and said, "Sit."

She sat on the edge of the chair, trying to balance just right so not too much pressure was on her feet or her lower back.

"State your name," the man said as the guard left the room, shutting the door behind him.

"Anna Levitskaya."

In a calm, disinterested voice, he said, "I'm Lieutenant Colonel Kotov, one of the prosecutors here. I'll be conducting your questioning by the prosecutor."

More questioning? Anna rubbed her hands on her dress nervously.

Opening a file with her name on it, Lieutenant Colonel Kotov yawned as he examined the contents. He spent fifteen minutes acquainting himself with it while Anna watched, wondering why he hadn't looked at it prior to her arrival.

Finally, he raised his eyes, staring at the wall instead of looking at Anna, and asked with a lazy drawl, "What would you like to add to your testimony?"

Confused, she took a moment to answer. "What...what would I like to add? Do I...am I required to add something?"

The Lieutenant Colonel sighed, his slumped shoulders collapsing further inward. "Not required, Miss Levitskaya. It's just something I have to ask before signing off on it."

Remembering how the interrogator had tried to add

denouncements to her "testimony," Anna bit down her fear and asked, "May I...umm...take a look at it?" She nodded at the file.

He crinkled his tired brows. "Sure. Why not? It isn't like I have forty more of these to get through today." He pushed the file toward her. "Make it quick." He leaned his head back and closed his eyes.

Anna opened it and quickly scanned through the typed pages. The last page contained the charges against her—all of them listed under Article 58, Counterrevolutionary Activity. She expected this, though she knew almost nothing about Soviet laws. But this term had been mentioned multiple times during her interrogation.

The prosecutor shifted in his seat and cleared his throat. Anna glanced at him, and he gestured for her to hurry. She quickly read through the individual charges.

58-6: Espionage

58-7: Undermining of State Industry

58-10: Anti-Soviet and Counterrevolutionary Propaganda and Agitation

58-12: Non-reporting of a Counterrevolutionary Activity

Aggravating Factor, 58-11: Organizational or support actions related to the preparation or execution of the above crimes.

Anna read the last line again then looked up at the prosecutor. "I don't understand this last charge." She pointed to it.

Kotov leaned forward with a sigh, glancing at the paper. "It means you committed the crimes as part of an organization."

"But I didn't...I...I wasn't part of any organization."

He pulled the file to him and leafed through it for another five minutes. "You conspired with one Nikolai Karakov to commit these crimes," he said, as though that answered everything.

"Nikolai?" It hurt to say his name, and her voice cracked. "But, he is...was, he *was* my fiancé. How is that considered an organization?"

Kotov spread out his hands. "What is there to say? One person is a person, and two persons are...people."

Anna opened her mouth, incredulous at his reasoning, and thought, *But...one person and a corpse? Is that an organization?*

He flipped to the last page and signed it, stamping it with the date before closing the file and pushing a button on his desk.

The guard came in and led Anna back to the crowded cell. From her position near the door, wedged, standing between several other women, she looked for a place to sit, but every bunk was packed with three or four women sitting squished together. The two stools were occupied. She couldn't even see a spot on the floor big enough to sit.

Anna sucked in a breath as someone stepped on her foot. She pulled it back, clamping her mouth on a cry.

"Anna," a loud whisper came from the back of the cell.

She looked in the direction of the whisper and saw a wisp of red hair in the crowd. Murmuring "excuse me" as she went, Anna shuffled and nudged her way through the tight-packed bodies until she reached Natalia.

Evgenya stood near her and gestured to the corner of a bunk. "Sit, Anna."

Lowering herself to the small section of plankboard, she apologized to the woman next to her as she tried to make more room for Anna.

"I'm so glad you're back," Natalia whispered. "Where did they take you?"

Anna shook her head. "He called it 'questioning by the prosecutor.' He didn't ask many questions, though."

With a nod, Evgenya said, "It's part of Soviet law, *required procedure*." She barked a derisive laugh. "It is one of the few requirements they cling to while they violate our legal rights in every other way."

The woman sitting next to Anna snorted. "We have no legal rights."

"No. No we don't." Evgenya glared at the cell door and waved her arms in an all-encompassing circle. "This entire building, and the thousands of others like it, is based on violations of legal rights. There is no freedom in the Motherland anymore." She looked around sharply, as if remembering there was a stool pigeon in the cell with them, relaxing slightly as she spotted the informer across the room.

A hush fell on the prisoners as the guard's eye appeared in the peephole. He opened the door, scowling as he nudged a woman sitting against the wall with his foot. "Wake up! No sleeping!"

He pulled a cart up to the door and said, "Line up for lunch."

Again, Natalia gestured for Anna to stay seated as she got in line near the front. She was able to get a bowl for each of them this time, and two cups of warm water.

The scant amount of cabbage floating in the broth looked and smelled rotten, but Anna ate it anyway, knowing it was the best she was going to get.

The rest of the day passed in sweltering heat and minimal movement in the packed cell as Anna tried to stay awake. She didn't feel like talking, but she listened as Natalia chattered on in nervous whispers, jumping anytime the guard looked in. She'd been there for two weeks. She knew her turn with an interrogator was overdue.

Dinner consisted of the same soup they'd been given for lunch, after which two female guards opened the cell door and one of them shouted, "Prepare for the toilet!"

Natalia helped Anna to stand, and the women all silently lined up in pairs. Once in the bathroom they were given ten minutes to eliminate and wash their hands.

"No washing clothing!" one of the guards yelled as a prisoner removed her shirt and shoved it under the running faucet. "Save that for the morning trip!"

Anna never thought she'd be ecstatic to be able to sit on a filthy toilet to relieve herself. The small amount of urine she voided into the bowl was dark yellow, almost brown. She didn't have time to coax her bowels into emptying before the next in line started cussing at her to hurry. But even better than the toilet was the few seconds she spent at the sink. She washed her hands, splashed water on her face, and did what she could to clean the dried stool and blood from her thighs before the guard yelled at her for taking too much time.

She and Natalia walked silently back to the cell side by side, Natalia stepping slowly to match Anna's shuffling gait. When the door clanged shut and the guards' footsteps could be heard walking away, Evgenya found Anna and whispered, "Tonight you can sleep on the floor over by where the latrine bucket goes. That's where the new prisoners go, no exceptions. You'll be able to move to a better place as you attain some seniority."

Anna nodded. Anything was better than being shoved back inside one of the *boxes*.

"Best make your way there now so no one can encroach on your space."

Wondering if the guards would bring the slop bucket back in, Anna made her way over to the corner. She vaguely recalled Evgenya saying something about the bucket only being brought in if they weren't taken to the toilets. Having a little more space and not having the odor of the bucket right next to her brought some consolation to her worry about not having a place to go to the bathroom if she needed to.

She sat with her knees drawn up to her chest, arms wrapped around them, and did everything she could to stay awake. By the time a guard yelled "bedtime" through the peephole, her eyes were inflamed and dry from the effort to keep them open. She curled up on the floor, but was soon forced to straighten out and lay on her side as the women all tried to find a place to lay down. The brightness of the lights boring into her closed eyelids and the heat wafting off the partially nude bodies surrounding her made it difficult for her to find sleep, exhausted as she was.

At some point she drifted off, only to be awakened by a guard opening the door and saying loudly, "N.V. If your initials are N.V. get your ass up and come with me."

Natalia stood slowly, a shaky hand pressed to her mouth as a low cry escaped around it. She looked back at her cellmates as if one of them could help her, and she locked eyes with Anna for a brief second before the guard yanked her out by the arm.

16

Eyes squeezed tight, Anna trembled as she prayed for her new friend. Wondered if she'd ever see her again. Relived her own recent torture. Her mind wouldn't stop showing her alternating images of Natalia screaming as the interrogator tormented her, and Anna, herself, reliving the agony of the nights spent in his office.

The sweltering heat and sweaty bodies pressed against her made the healing bug bites sting and itch. The sensation of bugs crawling on her skin and in her hair made her want to scream, but she held it in as she scratched at the areas on her body she could reach with her left hand. Stabbing pain penetrated the fingers of her right hand anytime she instinctively used them to scratch, forgetting for a moment about the wooden needle that had been so skillfully and leisurely thrust under each fingernail.

"Hold still!" whispered the woman plastered against her back as Anna's elbow bumped her for the umpteenth time.

Anna clenched her jaw, grinding her teeth against the incessant itchiness. She opened her eyes, the bright lights tricking her mind, making it hard—among all the other distractions like pain, worry, heat, and irritated skin—to sleep. Anna jerked her head back with a stifled squeal as a plump, white louse wiggled its way deeper into her neighbor's thick, black hair.

"What is wrong with you?" the woman behind her asked, clearly annoyed.

"Lice. She has—" Anna clamped her mouth against the twisting nausea spiraling up her throat.

"Yeah? So what? We all have 'em, princess. Even you, in your butchered hair." The woman sighed. "Just go to sleep. And if you can't sleep, at least hold still."

Crawling sensations covered Anna's scalp. Whether real or imagined, she had no clue. She'd never wanted a warm shower more in her life. She closed her eyes and forced her thoughts to Nikolai, to their last kiss. She imagined what their simple wedding ceremony would have been like. What their children would have looked like. And she drifted to sleep with thoughts of his lips on her mind.

The cell door opening jolted Anna awake. A muffled sob sounded as the guard pushed someone into the room and slammed the door. Anna squinted, her eyes adjusting to the light after being asleep, and she raised up on her elbow. Natalia was curled up in a ball up against the wall, the tremors of silent tears rippling through her body.

"Natalia," Anna whispered. "Are you all right?"

Her straggly red hair fell over her shoulders as the young girl shook her head, face pressed to her knees.

"Shh!" someone in the middle of the crowded cell said. "Talk in the morning."

Anna wished she could reach her new friend, but wall-to-wall bodies prevented it.

The remaining hours passed agonizingly as Anna tried to get back to sleep, an occasional snuffle or stifled sob reaching her from across the cell.

Pounding on the door. "Six o'clock! Wake up!" the guard yelled as he pushed the door open. "Prepare for the toilet! Hurry it up!"

Every muscle in Anna's body screamed as she pushed herself to her agonized feet. They lined up in pairs, and as she glanced at the woman next to her, she realized it was the stoolie. She searched for Natalia's red hair, just remembering as the fog of sleep faded that her friend had been interrogated in the night.

Anna spotted her up near the front of the line, of course, because she'd been right by the door.

The stool pigeon looked Anna up and down and smiled. "It looks like you got quite the workover." She raised her chin to the front of the cell as the line began moving. "Your friend up there doesn't seem to be worse for wear. She must have spilled her guts."

Anna looked straight ahead, clamping her mouth on the crude retort that popped into her head. She shuffled forward on her tortured feet.

The woman leaned closer to Anna and whispered, "You must have told them everything, what with all the persuasion they obviously used on you. I'm sure you didn't end up holding anything back." She shook her head. "You poor dear."

The stool pigeon continued to talk as the prisoners trudged down the corridor to the bathroom. If Anna could have, she would have walked faster—or run—to increase the distance between them. Evgenya was a few people ahead of them in line, and she whipped her head around and glared at the woman. "Shh!"

Anna realized that the guards hadn't shushed her as they normally would have, solidifying in her mind that the woman truly was an informer, working for the Organ.

When they reached the bathroom, the guards stood just inside the door. "You have ten minutes. Get on with it," one of them said. The two men leered as the women relieved themselves and washed up at the sinks.

Anna's bladder was ready to let loose as the back of the line reached the three toilets. She lowered herself gingerly to the seat of one, muscle spasms raking across her lower back, and was able to mostly keep covered with the dress as she relieved herself.

Most of the other women had stripped down to their underwear and hurriedly washed their clothes in the sink, splashing themselves with the cold water in the pitiful semblance of a bath.

Anna glanced at the guards as she approached a sink. She wanted so desperately to wash the filthy dress and her filthy skin. But she didn't even have underwear to partially cover her body.

What does it matter? she thought. *I'm nothing but an animal to them.*

"But *you* know you're not an animal, my Anna." Her mama's voice chided from deep within her mind.

"Three minutes!" a guard shouted.

Anna glanced once more at the men. One of them stared right at her with a leering grin. *Maybe tomorrow we'll get female guards.* Anna sighed and splashed the cold water on her face and arms, then lifted the hem of the dress a little further up her thighs than was decent, and scrubbed her legs as best she could.

"You really should wash that dress, bitch," the leering guard said. "It's disgusting."

She pulled the hem down, covering her legs, and, looking at the ground, stuttered, "I...I'll do it tomorrow. No time now."

Back in the cell, Anna made her way over to the corner where Natalia stood, slumped against the wall and staring into space. Anna examined her before speaking. She had a swollen, split lip, and both eyes were rimmed with darkening circles, the bridge of her nose swollen.

"Natalia?" Anna whispered. "What happened?" She knew better than to ask if she was okay.

The young woman shook her head and looked down, avoiding Anna's eyes. In a weak whisper, she said, "I'm not brave like you." A sob rocked her petite body, and she covered her face with her hands. "I gave them everything...everything they wanted. Names of people I barely know. Names of people I know well. Family—" Her voice cut off with a choking sound.

Anna pulled her into a hug and whispered, "Oh, Natalia. I'm not brave—my fear for my mama is just stronger than my fear for myself."

Face buried in Anna's shoulder, the red-haired girl said, "But I couldn't do it. I couldn't handle the pain. I'm nothing but a weak, foolish girl."

Anna grabbed her shoulders and pushed her back so she could look at her face. "Look at me, Natalia," she commanded. When the girl's red-rimmed eyes met hers, she said, "No one—least of all, me—can judge you for doing what you had to do. They don't care about truth, and it's no use trying to stay truthful because the result will be the same. They will convict whoever they want and enjoy their barbaric *persuasion* techniques along the way."

Natalia shook her head. "I've never been punched before. Never really felt pain beyond cramps and skinned knees. How did you endure it, Anna?"

"I don't know." She hugged her friend to her chest again. "I'm just stupidly stubborn, especially when it comes to the truth."

Keys jangled out in the hallway, and the cell went silent. "Line up for breakfast!" the guard yelled as soon as he pushed the door open.

The day continued much the same. No twenty-minute walk outside as Evgenya had told her was supposed to happen. As much as Anna would love to get some fresh air, she was glad. Her feet were in no shape to go for a forced stroll.

Shortly after their evening meal of cabbage soup, three sugar cubes, and a cup of warm water, a tall, severe looking female guard opened the cell door and shouted, "A.L. Prisoner, A.L."

When Anna stood from her perch on a bunk, a spike of fear stabbing her heart, the guard jerked her head toward the hallway. "Come with me."

Now what?

Anna followed the guard down the cold corridor and up two

flights of stairs, back to the same office where she'd undergone the "questioning by the prosecutor."

"Wait here." The guard shut the door behind her.

Alone in the office, Anna stood in the middle of the room and looked around. She hadn't noticed the sculpted bronze clock atop the marble mantel before. Now the fireplace blazed with a hearty fire. It must be getting cold outside.

Anna jumped as the door opened and quick steps with the distinctive sound of jack boots approached her from behind.

"Miss Levitskaya."

The voice of her interrogator, her torturer, turned her blood to ice.

"Sit. This won't take long."

Anna shuffled over to the chair in front of the desk and lowered herself into it. Her heart galloped in her chest as she wondered what this sadistic man would do to her this time. She'd hoped to never lay eyes on him again unless it was to watch him twitching as an executioner's bullets pierced his body.

A frown creased the interrogator's brow as he sat across from her. "No need to look so scared. Your questioning is behind you, and, after all, I was only doing my job. Nothing more, nothing less." He pushed a file toward her. "You're here tonight for a 206 procedure, which is, in accordance with the provisions of the Code of Criminal Procedure, your—the defendant—review of the case before your final signature."

He started writing on a piece of paper dismissively, no doubt whatsoever that she would sign it.

With a shaky hand, Anna opened the cover of the file. The first thing to greet her tired eyes, right on the inside of the cover in printed text, was an astonishing statement. It seemed that during the interrogation she'd had the right to make written complaints against anything "improper" that had occurred. And the interrogator was obliged to staple the complaints into her record.

She read it again to make sure she understood. It clearly said she'd had this right *during* the interrogation. Not after. Not at the very end of the process.

Anna turned more pages, reading the signed affidavits of the two interrogators—nothing matching up to what she'd experienced at their hands. She studied the charges closely, wanting to ensure they hadn't slipped something else in. Then she turned back to the statement clipped to the front cover of the file, and a surge of anger emboldened her. "I won't sign. You conducted the interrogation improperly."

He looked up, compressing his lips in a snarl. "All right then, let's begin all over again, shall we?" He reached for the file.

Anna held tight to it. The bronze clock sitting on the mantel quietly chimed.

All over again? Anna's stomach flipped painfully. *I'd rather die.*

She turned to the last page and signed on the line labeled "Defendant."

The interrogator returned to his writing and, when finished, pulled the file to him and added it to the papers there. Anna caught a glimpse of the words at the top: Conclusion of Indictment.

He rifled through some papers in a wire basket until he found the one he wanted, then he shoved it at Anna. "Read, then sign."

The title of the document, typed in all caps, read: NONDISCLOSURE AGREEMENT. Anna read the short statement. *I, the undersigned, under pain of criminal penalty, swear never to tell anyone about the methods used in conducting my interrogation.*

Part of her wanted to laugh at the ridiculousness of it all. After all, who would she tell that could do anything about it? Anna signed the document and dropped the pen on top of it, too exhausted to hold it in her grip any longer.

17

The days wore on as more and more women were shoved into the small cell. So many, that several of them could only stand, even at night, and others squeezed themselves into the small spaces beneath the bunks to sleep. Anna's feet slowly healed, but they would never be the same. She'd moved up in seniority and now shared a bunk with two other women—Natalia and an older woman named Alexandra. They laid head to foot, on their sides, in order to fit.

About once a week they'd come and get anywhere from one to ten of the prisoners for sentencing. The women would be gone for hours before some were returned, not knowing where the others had been taken.

Anna figured she'd been there for three or four weeks. She often wondered if her mama knew what had happened to her. To Nikolai. She watched with envy and sadness each time a prisoner received a package from someone on the outside. Packages were given to Ev, the *starosta*, to distribute to them.

Scrunched up against the wall as she sat on a bunk with four other women, Anna's eyes glazed over as she stared at the pages of a tattered book of poetry from the prison library. The door opened, but she didn't look up.

Several seconds passed before the door closed again.

"Anna," Ev said as she made her way through the forest of sweaty bodies, "you got a package." The older woman smiled at Anna's shocked expression.

It was a large bundle compared to what usually came from the outside. The brown paper it had been wrapped in was tattered and sloppily thrown back around the bundle, barely keeping the items enclosed with a piece of twine wrapped about it. All the prisoners' packages were searched before being allowed into the prison.

Anna ran her fingers over the wrinkled paper where her mama's hand had written her name. Tears leaked from her eyes onto the ink.

"Aren't you going to open it, Anna?" Natalia whispered.

She nodded, slowly moving to untie the twine. She put the letter aside, to read after the others had lost interest in seeing what she got. Anna's vision became blurred as the tears increased. Mama had sent her a work skirt, a plain white blouse, and shoes with knee-high stockings. Laying between the skirt and blouse was a smaller package wrapped separately. As she peeled the paper back, the smell of boiled potatoes wafted out. Anna's mouth watered. In her lap, atop her clothes, laid a half-dozen small, peeled, boiled potatoes—a hole pierced through each from the guards' inspection—and a small piece of black bread.

Eyes blurred with tears, Anna could only stare for a moment at the food—more food than she'd seen since watching her torturer eat in front of her—food prepared with tender care by her loving mama's own hands. She looked up at the four or five faces staring down at her. Natalia licked her lips but remained silent. No one expected her to share, at least not without having something to trade, she'd learned that early on when other prisoners had received packages. But Anna couldn't eat all of it herself, and saving it for later was out of the question. If the guards didn't take it from her, one or more of the prisoners was sure to give in to their hunger and steal it away.

With a determined nod, and knowing she didn't have enough for the dozens of women packed into the cell, Anna handed a potato to each of the women she'd grown closest to: Evgenya, Natalia, and Alexandra.

"You don't have to share with us," Ev said, even as she took the food from Anna's outstretched hand.

"I know. But I want to." Anna bit into one of the remaining potatoes and closed her eyes as she chewed. The plain, starchy vegetable tasted better than anything she could remember. She wanted to savor it, take her time, but her starving body had different ideas. She swallowed and shoved the rest of the potato in her mouth, chewing only enough to send it down her gullet. She finished off the remaining two, but gathered her willpower and rewrapped the chunk of bread, saving it to have with the watered-down broth she'd get for supper. Weeks of starvation-level rations had shrunk her stomach, anyway. For the first time since her arrival to this hell hole, she felt full.

"Anna," Natalia licked the palm of her hand to get every bit of the potato Anna had shared with her, "thank you so much. I promise I'll share with you if I ever get a package of my own."

"You're welcome. But I don't expect anything in return, and you shouldn't make promises you may not be able to keep." Anna didn't mean it as an insult or reprimand, and the gentle way she said it demonstrated that. She knew what being deprived of food could do to a person, and she didn't want Natalia to beat herself up over it if her hunger won out over her promise.

"I will share, Anna. I swear it!"

Anna grasped Natalia's hand and half-smiled. "I know you will, Nat. Thank you."

The small crowd surrounding her went back to whatever they'd been doing before the package arrived. Anna glanced at the peephole in the door and didn't see a guard peering in. She stood in the constrained space, set the unwrapped package of clothes on the bunk, and lifted the skirt from the crinkled paper. A feeling of joy like opening a present on her birthday before her father died flooded her as a bra and underwear fell from the skirt's folds. She'd forgotten what it was like to be fully clothed. She slipped the underwear on under the dress and with another look at the peephole, turned her back to the door and peeled the ragged dress off over her head. The bra gaped around her shrunken breasts, but the added layer of protection from the guards' leering eyes and roving hands was priceless. She tucked the worn blouse into the waist of the skirt, wishing she was allowed a belt, as the weight loss affected the way it fit as well.

The filthy rags wrapped around her feet fell away with only a small nudge, and Anna sighed with gratefulness as she pulled the stockings onto her feet then slipped them into the well-worn shoes.

She tucked the wrapped bread into a pocket and folded the tattered dress into a square. She could use it as a pillow as long as it didn't get stolen. Anna reached for the letter, hands shaking a little as her heart broke with homesickness. Oh, how she missed her mama!

Unfolding the short note, she thought about how writing paper was hard to come by, and she wondered where her mama had found even this small piece. She read:

My Dear Anna,

My heart is breaking for you. For Nikolai. Blame for the delay in getting this to you lies squarely with your sister's husband (I refuse to say his name). He kept the truth from me for weeks while I searched for you, asking everyone where you were. I love you, my Anna. Please, please stay alive. Please return to me when you can. Wish I could trade places with you. I will send more packages as able. Couldn't send sweater, you were wearing your only one—hope you still have it.

Love, Mama

The last couple of sentences were squished at the bottom of the small paper. A tear fell on the note, smearing the ink. She patted it dry with a corner of the old dress, folded the note, and placed it in her pocket with the bread.

Of course her mama wished she could trade places with her. Anna shuddered at the thought. They would have to kill her before she'd allow that to happen! She jumped as someone tapped her arm.

"You'll need to give the paper to me, Anna." Ev nodded to the paper the bundle had been wrapped in. "The guards'll be back for it."

They weren't allowed to have paper—they might try to communicate with the other prisoners or slip a note to someone on the outside. Anna folded it and handed it to the older woman. She'd hold on to the note for as long as she could—just seeing her mama's slanted handwriting comforted her. Knowing she was still free. Still alive.

☭

The small chunk of bread lasted through two meals—that was all Anna could gather the willpower for. She'd broken it in half and dipped it in the broth that night, savoring the extra bites, then finished it off with breakfast the next day.

Now, a few days later, she wished she'd drawn it out a little longer as she sipped at the gruel that seemed to be getting thinner by the day.

Sometime between breakfast and lunch, Anna and two other women were summoned from their cell. They joined a small group from another cell and were marched up the stairs to the first floor and into the baths. As wonderful as it sounded to be able to take a real bath after weeks of just splashing cold water on herself at the bathroom sink, Anna was worried about leaving her newly acquired clothing with the guards. Not that she had a choice.

After disrobing and leaving their clothes on benches outside the bathhouse, the women were forced to walk past several male guards who looked them up and down and commented on the condition of their bodies. Anna covered her breasts with one arm and her lower body with the other.

"Hands by your sides, bitch." The guard jabbed his club into her side.

Face hot with embarrassment and anger, Anna lowered her arms and continued her shameful march into the bathhouse.

They were each given a sliver of black soap that smelled of ash and lye. Anna was surprised to find that the water in the shared baths was warm. She worried, though, as she enjoyed the feel of clean skin and hair, what this was all about. Were they giving the prisoners one last impression of what it was like to be human before executing them?

No. Other women had been returned to the cell after being brought there. After sentencing. It clicked then. They were being taken to their sentencing hearings. Anna's stomach churned, acid creeping up her throat. Maybe she'd get a light sentence. There were even rumors of one woman prisoner being granted amnesty! Anna wouldn't let herself hope for that, but a light sentence...that was possible. Wasn't it? Six months, a year maybe. Then she'd be back with her mama. Back at the factory.

"Out of the water! Dry off and get dressed." The guard's gravelly voice roused Anna from her daydream.

She was relieved to see that her clothes and shoes hadn't been touched. Once the women prisoners were all dressed, the guards marched them outside through a courtyard, where the chill stung her freshly washed skin, and the trees were bare, the last of their fall leaves crunching underfoot. Even as Anna shivered from the light breeze touching her wet hair, she breathed in deeply, enjoying the fresh air.

They entered an area of the enormous building Anna had never seen before and were led down a short corridor to what she could only describe as a box. It reminded Anna of a train car, only a little more spacious. Benches lined the walls, and for once, there was room for all to sit. Though most of them didn't. Anna paced with some of the others, too nervous to be still. The sun peered through the one small, high window in the box—at least until a cloud blocked its light.

Nothing happened for at least two hours, and by that time, Anna's feet had tired, and she sat on a bench next to a woman from another cell.

"Do you really think we're here for sentencing?" the woman asked.

Anna nodded. "I don't know what else it would be, what with the bath and all."

"I'm scared." She looked down at her hands and her voice quivered. "I heard one girl got *twenty-five* years."

Anna whipped her head up to look at the woman. "That...that can't be right. It must be a rumor. Unless she did something horrible."

"She was a fifty-eight, just like the rest of us."

"Just pray the man doling out the sentences had a pleasant night with his mistress," a gray-haired woman who'd been listening in said. "If he's in a good mood, maybe he'll go light on us."

"That's ridiculous," another prisoner scoffed. "The punishment is based on the crime. The Party would allow it to be no other way."

Anna narrowed her eyes at the woman. A Party member. Like Mikhail.

The gray-haired woman huffed and rolled her eyes. "Oh, shut it, Lena. If 'the Party' is so great, then why are you here? Aren't you a perfect little Communist?"

Lena the Communist glared at the older woman. "I deserve to be here just as the rest of you do. Our great Soviet leaders do not make mistakes. I will serve out whatever sentence they hand down, proud to know that justice is being done."

"Oh, save it for your comrades," the gray-haired woman spat. "We've all heard enough of your prattle."

The door crashed open and one of the prisoners was summoned. Not one that Anna had seen before, probably from the other cell. Anna jumped to her feet again, anxiety pumping through her blood anew. Less than ten minutes later, the door flew open again as the woman was readmitted and another one called to go out.

Several of the prisoners rushed to the woman, who stumbled across the floor. "Well?" the gray-haired one asked.

In a choked voice, the woman blurted, "Five years!" She crumbled to a bench and sobbed into her hands.

Again, the door crashed open and the previous prisoner was shoved through. Before anyone could ask what sentence she'd gotten, the guard called for Anna. She swallowed and moved forward on shaky legs, thinking, *Five years isn't so bad. I can endure for that long.*

☭

A bored looking, black-haired NKVD officer sat at a table on the right side of the room, a stack of papers about half the size of normal typewriter paper, an inkwell, and a simple lamp the only things on its surface. "Sit," he said, gesturing to a stool across the table from him.

Anna sat, wringing her hands in her lap.

"What's your name?"

"Anna Levitskaya." Her voice came out barely above a whisper.

The officer leafed through the pile of papers until he found the one with her name on it. "Anna Levitskaya, for the offenses of…" He read off the crimes she had been charged with and ended with, "Ten years in corrective labor camps."

The air left her lungs. *Ten years?* She must have heard wrong.

While Anna tried to wrap her head around this, the officer flipped the paper over and wrote on the back of it with a fountain pen. He finished up and pushed the paper toward her.

Anna blinked down at it and the schoolchild's seven-kopeck pen with a flattened point that now lay there in front of her. Her mind and body had gone numb.

"Sign here." The officer pointed to a spot below his writing.

She pulled it closer and read: *I certify that the text of this decree has been read to me on October 29, 1938.*

"I...I'd like to read it myself." Her voice came to her as if someone else had spoken the words. Someone far away.

The officer sighed. "Do you really think I would deceive you?"

When she didn't answer, he rolled his hand at her impatiently. "Well, go ahead. Read it."

Anna flipped it over and fixed her eyes on the typewritten words:

EXTRACT

From a decree of the OSO of the NKVD of the U.S.S.R.
of October 29, 1938, No. 43.

....

Case heard:

Accusation of Anna Levitskaya,

Born in the year 1917 in Moscow,

Russia, U.S.S.R.

Decreed:

To designate for Anna Levitskaya for espionage, undermining of state industry, anti-Soviet and counter-revolutionary propaganda and agitation, non-reporting of counter-revolutionary activity, and for an attempt to create an anti-Soviet organization, 10 (ten) years in corrective labor camps.

Copy verified. Secretary Makarov

She looked up at him. Was she really just supposed to sign it and leave in silence? She felt as though she should say *something*.

But the officer had already nodded to the guard at the door to take her away and get the next prisoner.

She frowned. "But, ten years? Why?" Her words sounded false even to her own ears. She knew why. Because the government did whatever they wanted. She wasn't even a human to them.

The officer grabbed the paper from her, flipped it over to where he'd written the statement, and pointed. "Sign. Right there."

Anna signed. What else was she going to do?

After another hour in the boxy room with the others who were there for sentencing, Anna was taken back to the crowded cell. She avoided Ev and Natalia's eyes as she pushed her way to a corner, sat on the hard floor, and curled up, unable to even cry.

Ten years. She'd be thirty-one—if she even survived. Mama would be sixty.

PART II

Winter 1938-1939

18

I n the early morning hours, pounding on the cell door woke Anna
with a start. A guard flung the door open and shouted names, one
of which was Anna's. She got to her feet and hurriedly put her skirt
and blouse on. It was still too hot in the packed cell to wear them
while trying to sleep, so most of the women slept in their underwear,
lying on their clothes like they were a thin mattress of sorts. She was
slipping her stockinged foot into her shoe when the guard yelled,
"Out of the cell! Follow me!"

The group of women followed the guard, surrounded by more
guards than Anna had ever seen in one place as they stepped into the
corridor. They stopped at multiple other cells, on a couple of
different floors, the same routine being played out at each. More than
half of the prisoners joining their ranks were men, many of them
looking even more bedraggled than the women.

They were led up to the ground floor and outside, at the back of
the Lubyanka where deliveries were made. Three heavy-goods trucks
were lined up on the pavement, painted black except for the word
"BREAD" printed on the side of each.

Confused and shivering in the cold November air, Anna thought, *Are they going to make us unload the trucks?*

They split the prisoners into three groups, opened the large back doors of the trucks, and herded the groups into them. Puffs of white steam poured from their mouths and noses with each breath, dissipating into the freezing air.

"All the way to the back! Squeeze in!"

Anna moved forward, somewhere in the middle of the pack. She recoiled when she reached the truck, the person behind her bumping into her back. It was pitch black inside, no windows or openings of any kind. Would they even be able to breathe in there?

"Move it!" one of the guards standing beside the door gave her a shove.

She climbed in. The long benches that ran along each side of the cargo truck were full, male and female prisoners squished together as tight as possible. Anna looked back at the guards, wondering what to do as more prisoners were prodded into climbing in.

"Go to the back and sit down. Spread your legs so the next idiot can sit between them. Keep moving!"

Anna's heart raced, and she glanced at the prisoner directly behind her, her panic receding just a little when she saw it was a woman. She stumbled to the back of the truck, holding her hands out in front of her as the dim light from the guards' flashlights near the doors gave way to impenetrable darkness. Her hand hit the wall at the back, and she turned around, bumping into the woman behind her as she felt her way into the abyss. Neither of them spoke as Anna lowered to the floor and rested her back against the wall, spreading her legs so the next in line could sit between them, pinning her skirt to the floor.

"Where you takin' us?" a male prisoner blurted as he climbed aboard.

"Get in there, sit down, and shut up. You'll find out soon enough."

Even in the tight quarters, Anna shivered. She was sure it was below freezing outside and not much warmer inside the truck. The guards shoved the last half-dozen prisoners into the box even though there was no room and it seemed impossible they would fit. A couple of them remained standing as the guards forced the doors shut.

The woman in front of her pressed back even more into Anna. She couldn't breathe. Suffocating. The darkness surrounding her brought flashes of memories. Bad memories. The Black Mariah. The rape. The standing coffin full of bed bugs.

Her breaths started coming rapidly, shallow, teeth chattering, lips numb. Her arms didn't want to move. She tried to bend her legs a little as the truck started up and lurched forward, but the way the woman in front of her was sitting on her skirt severely restricted her movement.

"Slow down your breathing, girl, before you pass out," the woman said.

"Can't breathe," Anna huffed.

"Just slow it down. You'll be all right."

"Why do you care?" a raspy male voice sounded in the darkness. "Let her pass out an' smother to death. More air for the rest of us."

Ignoring the man, the woman in Anna's lap continued to whisper encouragement to her until her breathing returned to as close to normal as it could while packed into the truck like sardines.

Anna's knees ached and her calves cramped as they bumped along the road. She wished she'd thought to hike her skirt up before sitting, so her legs wouldn't have been pinned to the floor.

Someone toward the back, someone on one of the benches from the sound of it, asked the question Anna had been wondering since they started packing them into the trucks. "Where do you think they're taking us?"

"Where do you think, dumbass? To the Gulags. The labor camps."

"Or outside the city to execute us." The man who spoke these words sounded lifeless, flat, all emotion removed from his being.

"Nah," came another voice. "They need us to work. They won't kill us."

A woman laughed, harsh, like a cackle. "Oh, we're dead already. Doesn't matter if they shoot us outside of town or take us to the Gulags to work till we die. We're dead already."

That silenced them. No one spoke again until the truck came to a halt. Anna figured they'd been traveling for over an hour.

The doors opened. Wafting in with the icy air came the sound of a train whistle. They were at a train station.

Anna was one of the last to disembark, pins and needles shooting through her legs and feet. A gust of wind carried small flakes of snow straight through her thin blouse as she climbed from the truck. It was still dark, but there was a promise of light glowing on the horizon.

"Over there, get on your knees! Keep the lines straight!" The guard pointed to a flat expanse of gravel. They'd pulled up behind the main building, where train cars waited on the rails.

Anna and the few stragglers joined the large group and dropped to their knees at the end of one of the lines. Guards carrying rifles stood behind and to the side of the group. A dozen others patrolled the perimeter, large dogs on leashes walking with them, occasionally growling or barking.

Two guards walked along the columns of prisoners, counting them. Soon, Anna's knees ached as the gravel dug into them. She studied the train cars she could see from her position. They looked like regular train cars except for the several strands of barbed wire wrapped around them, wooden platforms on the outside where guards stood, and small windows protected by thick iron bars.

Then they counted again. And again. The light snow intensified, sticking to the ground. Anna shivered and put her hands under her armpits, envious of the guards and the few prisoners who had warm coats. If she could only stand and stomp her feet or something, maybe she'd be able to feel her toes again. A few minutes later, someone else had that same thought, and acted on it.

An older man, two rows in front of Anna, stumbled to his feet and turned toward the nearest guard. "I need—"

Several shots rang out, and the man slumped to the ground, half his face missing. Warm blood and brain matter splattered the kneeling prisoners surrounding him, including Anna, who choked back a scream.

Guards shouted.

"Stay on your knees!"

"Don't move!"

Two guards grabbed the dead man under his arms and dragged his body away.

Shocked at what she'd just witnessed, combined with the freezing cold, her shivering intensified until Anna's whole body convulsed. She was afraid to lift her hand to wipe the gore from her face. Afraid the trigger-happy guards would shoot her then drag her body away unceremoniously.

Please, please stay alive. That's what her mama had written to her. And that's what she planned to do.

Another thirty minutes passed as the guards counted the prisoners again. Then recounted them.

Anna trembled, teeth chattering, feet and hands numb from the cold, leg and back muscles strained and hurting from the kneeling position. But she'd endured worse.

Finally, row by row, the prisoners were commanded to stand and, flanked by armed guards, were loaded onto the train cars. The *Stolypin* cars, as Anna had heard them called, specially outfitted to carry prisoners.

When at last Anna's row was called upon to stand, Anna lurched to her feet, only able to shuffle slowly toward the car. She chanced one swipe at her face to remove the blood and bits of brain and skull, but it had dried—or frozen—to her skin and hair, so her effort was useless.

A bit of relief broke through her traumatized state as she climbed into the car and saw that they were separating the men from the women.

The *Stolypin* car looked like an ordinary passenger train car, divided into compartments. Anna passed by two men's compartments before being shoved into one containing only women prisoners. The compartment was dark, but not pitch black like the truck had been, as the early morning light peeked through the barred windows across the corridor.

Anna took in her crowded surroundings. On each of the upper baggage shelves, two women huddled, half-sitting in uncomfortable hunches. She counted five women—hard-looking women, thieves or prostitutes—lying on the middle bunks that were joined together into one continuous bunk except for where it was cut out beside the door. On each of the lower bunks, five women sat crammed together. That left only the floor for Anna and the other three women the guards had pushed in after her.

A guard shoved the last prisoner out of the way with his boot as he slid the iron-framed door made of crisscrossing bars shut. Anna and the other three women wriggled their way to the floor, sitting wedged, cross-legged, between the legs of those on the bottom bunks.

Before the train even started moving, torment from the *blatnye*—the criminals, the non-political prisoners—began. One of the women laying comfortably on the middle bunk, leaned over the side and spat in Anna's hair.

"Hey, bitch, what happened to your hair? Looks like it got caught in a fan," the spitter said.

Anna touched her hair. It had grown out some since the guard had cut it off with his knife. She clamped her mouth shut on the retort that sprang to mind. The woman was much bigger than her and appeared to be well-fed. Plus she was a criminal, she could probably rip Anna to shreds.

"You too good to talk to me, *frayer?*"

Frayer? Anna hadn't heard that word before, didn't know what it meant.

"Leave her alone, Marietta," said an older woman, lying flat in the bunk next to her, knees bent and arms beneath her head. "You'll have plenty of opportunities to harass the politicals once we reach the Gulags."

The spitter, Marietta, flopped to her back and examined her fingernails. "It's gonna be a boring ride if I can't play with my food."

Anna and several others whipped their heads to look at her.

Marietta laughed. The other four criminals on the middle bunk joined her. "Ahh, don't worry, we ain't cannibals. At least not yet."

Anna wiggled around until she could bend her knees then laid her head on them, exhausted and wondering how long this ride would be and where they were going. The train hadn't even started moving yet.

She really wished they wouldn't mix the political prisoners with the criminal element—but it was better than being in with the men.

Being closely packed in the train car didn't even have the benefit of keeping her warm like it did in the cell at the Lubyanka. She'd stopped trembling like she had been outside, but she was still miserably cold. The women on the middle bunks all had warm coats, gloves, boots—even scarves. They'd probably stolen them from other prisoners.

Two guards patrolled up and down the corridor, their shadows casting a deeper pall over the caged prisoners each time they passed between the barred windows and the barred train compartment. A weight pressed into Anna's chest at the sight of the rifles slung across their backs. The guards at the Lubyanka hadn't carried rifles, hadn't shot and killed someone right in front of dozens of prisoners.

As horrible as the conditions had been at the prison, Anna knew her life was about to take a turn for the worse.

She hugged her knees to her chest and watched the snow fall through the slit of a window she could just see across the corridor.

19

Hours later, the train finally moved. These guards didn't seem to care if the prisoners spoke to each other, as long as things didn't get loud. Anna guessed it no longer mattered if they passed information to one another at this point—since the bogus "trials" were done and they were all headed to the labor camps.

There wasn't much conversation between the Fifty-eights—the political prisoners, the "enemies of the people"—they were mostly despondent. Anna was still trying to wrap her head around the *tenner* she'd been sentenced. Ten years—for what? Even if the things she'd "confessed" to had been real...how had the Soviet Union come to the point of a *joke*, of *words*, being a crime worthy of ten years of hard labor? Why was that a crime at all?

Her mind went round and round all day, trying to make sense of it all. But, she finally decided, evil doesn't need to make sense.

"Hey, citizen chief!" yelled one of the criminals from the middle bunk.

The guard stopped mid-stride and glared in at her. The compartment was dark, the waning day no longer providing much light through the windows and the lights in the corridor not having been turned on yet. "What do you want?"

"You gonna feed us today? I'm starving."

"Not today, nothing was issued for you for today."

Some cursing and grumbling came from the prisoners in Anna's compartment and the ones to either side of it, at least.

"Well, how about some water? I'm parched." That request came from Marietta.

The guard sighed and shook his head. "If we give you water, then you'll have to pee." And with that terse explanation, he pivoted and resumed his patrol of the car's corridor.

"Well, no shit, chief! Does that mean you aren't gonna give us water this whole trip?" Marietta spat after him.

Anna didn't think one of the politicals, the counter-revolutionaries, would get away with talking to the guards like that. Yet this common criminal, this *real* criminal, didn't even get a mild reprimand. She doubted the women on the middle bunk had gone through the same "interrogation" process she and the other Fifty-eights had, either.

She vaguely remembered Nikolai talking about how criminals—real criminals, like thieves and murderers—were considered by the Soviet leaders, especially Comrade Stalin, to be *one of our own people* as opposed to traitors of the Motherland. They could be *reformed*, whereas a counter-revolutionary was an enemy of the people, and there was no reforming them. Nik had said something about it being "progressive doctrine." Anna didn't know what that meant, and thinking about her dead fiancé made her heart ache. And the thought of thieves and murderers having more rights and better treatment than her—a law-abiding citizen—made her head spin with confusion. It just didn't make sense.

"Move it, *frayer*," Marietta said as she reached down from her bunk and slapped Anna's head. "I'm coming down."

Anna had nowhere to move to, but Marietta had already swung one leg off the bunk and into Anna's face, so she struggled to her feet and pressed herself against the group of women sitting on the bottom bunk across from her.

The criminal dropped to the floor with a thump of her thick boots. A gold cross dangled from a chain around her neck. She nudged the woman Anna had been sitting beside with her boot. "I know some of you have food stashed. Dig it out and hand it over."

And, to Anna's astonishment, several of the women did just that! Without so much as an utterance of resistance. Her astonishment faded, though, as she thought about what she would have done it she'd had any food. Probably the same thing, handed it over.

"Come on," Marietta chided, "there's got to be more than this. Don't make me strip search you."

And the guard strolled past without so much as a glance their way.

A couple more women coughed up parcels of food from their pockets or hidden pouches created in the hems of their skirts.

Marietta handed it up to her fellow *blatnoi*. They waited for her to climb back up then divided the food amongst themselves. Anna and the others watched, silent, as they ate every last crumb of black bread, every potato, and even a portion of sausage.

Anna's stomach growled. She hoped that sausage had been poisoned. Before returning to her wedged-in seat on the floor, she looked up at the middle bunk and asked, "What does *frayer* mean?"

The group of thieves laughed, and the older woman spoke while chewing noisily. "It means non-thief. It's an underworld word, dearie. Non-thief, nonhuman. Same."

Anna shook her head and squeezed her way back to her seat on the floor. The dim light coming through the windows disappeared as night fell. The only light in the compartment came from the lamps in the corridor. Some of the women on the bunks were able to twist and turn until they laid head to foot, with one curled up lengthwise at the end.

Anna nudged the woman next to her. "Maybe if we lay down on our sides, we'll all fit and be able to get some sleep."

The woman nodded.

Anna wriggled her way to a side-lying position. With effort, she could fit under the bottom bunk. If one of the prisoners did the same on the other side, they'd all have a place to lay.

"Thank you," one of the women whispered as she lowered herself to the floor.

Anna nodded and closed her eyes.

Anna awoke, stiff and sore, while it was still dark in the compartment. She tried to swallow the panic that rose inside her when she realized she was trapped under the bunk. Her heart pounded ever harder and ever faster, her breaths coming like the wings of a hummingbird in flight. Unable to control the panic, she pushed against the woman who lay blocking her in. "Move. Please. Can't breathe." Memories of the bedbug box and the hot and cold torture box bombarded her until she felt like she was back there, arms pinned to her chest.

The woman mumbled something but didn't attempt to change position.

Pushing harder against her back, Anna's voice rose in pitch and volume. "Move! I can't breathe!"

The woman pushed herself up to a sitting position and scooted down as far as she could. Anna twisted her torso and banged her head on the bottom of the bunk. Her head swam until she realized she'd been holding her breath and took a few deep breaths. She wriggled her torso out from under the bunk and stopped to regain her composure from the claustrophobic panic she'd awakened to.

She scraped her shin on a metal bar supporting the bunk, jostling the other two women stuck riding on the floor with her, before emerging from the dark crevasse. She curled into a sitting ball and thought, *I won't be sleeping under there again.*

Even though it was still night and the other prisoners in the compartment were sleeping, Anna couldn't get back to sleep. She swallowed, her throat dry with thirst. It had been over twenty-four hours since she'd had a drink of water. And even with that, she needed to pee. Her thoughts went to the dire thirst she'd experienced during her interrogation period. The days she'd gone without food or water, the salt-water being forced down her throat, the crusted sandpaper her mouth, throat, and lips had become. She really hoped they weren't planning on forcing that torture upon her again.

When morning light glowed through the window, the guards changed shifts. As two of them stood just outside of Anna's field of vision, the off-going guard said, "You'll need to give them water. Then they'll need to go to the bathroom, of course."

"So, let me get this straight. First shift has to water them, take them to the pisser, and feed them supper. Remind me again what second and third shifts do?" Irritation was apparent in his voice.

"Seniority has its benefits, comrade. Good night." The stomping of his boots joined others as the night shift guards headed to their compartment.

The new guards grumbled amongst themselves before one of them sent two of the others to fetch water.

"Wake up you lazy *zeks*! If you've got mugs, get them out," he shouted from the corridor.

"But they took all of our belongings at the prison!" a male prisoner from another compartment complained.

"Guess you'll just have to share, then. Better get it figured out what order you're drinking, we aren't going to stand here all day."

The five middle-bunk criminals in the women's compartment all had their own mugs, and they pulled them out of coat pockets or bags they'd been allowed to bring with them.

The woman whose legs Anna now leaned against said, "The healthy drink first from the shared mugs. Those with TB or other illnesses go next, and if you have syphilis—go last!"

Such an order would make sense—if each compartment got their own supply of water and mugs. But as it turned out, the women's compartment was third to get the pails of water rolled to them on a noisy cart. The thieves pushed to the front and stuck their mugs through the bars on the door. The guards dipped the mugs in the water and handed them back before dipping the two communal mugs into a pail and handing them to two of the political prisoners through the iron bars.

One advantage to being stuck on the floor was that Anna was one of the first, after the *blatnye,* to get a drink. It took a moment for her throat to start working.

"Hurry it up," one of the guards said, "we don't have all day!"

Anna hurried, even as she wondered what else the guards had to do, stuck on the train just like the prisoners. She handed the mug back to the guard and squeezed back past the next in line even though she wanted more—she knew better than to ask for a second cup. They were all like well-trained dogs at this point.

Even before the last compartment in their car had been watered, some from the first compartments called out, asking, "When can we go to the bathroom?"

"Later. Maybe after we all take our breaks." The guard didn't even try to hide the annoyance in his voice.

"Maybe they should line the cells with straw and we can just piss like animals," a man from the next compartment over mumbled.

"They already treat us like animals," another replied. "Don't give them any new ideas."

"Don't think we haven't thought of it," a guard growled. "The Supreme Leader doesn't want you messing up the Soviet's train cars."

The next couple of hours were miserable as Anna's bladder filled up until she thought it would burst. From one meager cup of water. Well, not exactly, she'd had to pee before then, just not as bad.

The guards finally started making their way from one compartment to the next, allowing one prisoner at a time to walk down the corridor to the toilet. It was an agonizingly slow process, and Anna thought she might soil herself if she had to wait much longer. When the guard tasked with letting the prisoners in and out finally made his way to their compartment, the thieves climbed down from their perches on the middle bunk and shoved their way to the front. Anna lost her balance and landed on the lap of a woman sitting on the lower bunk. She ended up staying there, as there was nowhere else for her to go with the five *blatnye* crowding the narrow aisle between bunks.

Anna stood when the last of the thieves was let out for her turn. A few other prisoners lined up behind her. When the thief returned, the guard opened the door just enough for her to slip back inside the compartment then motioned for Anna to go out. She glanced down the corridor in the opposite direction to see a guard standing at the end, so no one would try to escape that way, she thought.

"Come on! Get a move on!" shouted the guard stationed next to the toilet door.

Anna hurried to the tiny bathroom. Once inside, she turned to shut the door.

"Leave it open," the guard said.

She should have been used to them watching her in all stages of undress and performing all sorts of bodily functions...but she wasn't. Her face burned, even in the cold bathroom. She hiked her skirt up enough to pull her underwear down while keeping herself covered as much as possible. Her bottom had just touched the filthy toilet seat when the guard said, "Come on! Come on now! That's plenty, that's enough for you!"

Anna didn't bother to respond to him. He could strike her if he wanted, but she was going to empty her bladder. As she squeezed the last drop out, the guard moved to the door and reached for her. She stood in a rush, pulling up her underwear as he returned to his stance near the door. Anna turned toward the small sink but stopped short at the guard's harsh voice.

"Don't touch that, move along!"

She guessed washing her hands was too much to ask. Hurrying back to the women's compartment, Anna glanced inside at the men next to it. They were even more crowded than the women—standing so smooshed up against each other that she swore a couple of the men's feet weren't even touching the floor, they just hung suspended between the bodies of those taller than them.

With one last glance out the window at the snow-covered trees rolling by, Anna slipped through the iron-barred door the guard held open for her. Before the next woman in line could even make it to the toilet, the guard there said loudly, "Hurry it up! Number one only."

The first-shift guards must have figured they'd done enough work for the day, what with giving the prisoners water *and* allowing them to go to the toilet—a process that took over two hours by Anna's estimate—because they didn't distribute any food. Marietta caught one of the politicals sneaking a bite of something hidden in her bra and swung her foot down to kick her square in the mouth, knocking a couple of teeth out.

The woman whimpered, holding her hand to her bloodied mouth, as Marietta jumped down and reached inside the woman's bra to retrieve the dry crust of bread hiding there. "Anyone else holding out on us better produce what they have now, or I'll knock *all* your teeth out."

Several more women dug in their hiding spots and handed various food items to her. Anna wondered if it would have been as easy for the thieves to take what they wanted from the women on the outside. She doubted it. They hadn't been beaten down on the outside. They'd still been human then.

Second-shift replaced the day-guards in the afternoon, and they grumbled as they pushed a cart down the corridor, handing out half a salted herring and a small chunk of bread to each prisoner. Anna ate the herring and saved the bread for later—but not much later, she didn't want the thieves to end up with it. Less than an hour passed before she regretted eating the salty fish, as thirst once again tore at her throat.

"Do you think they'll give us any water before lights-out?" she asked the woman pressed up beside her on the floor.

The woman only shrugged.

One of the prisoners seated on the bunk behind them said, "Nope. Then they'd have to take us to the bathroom again. Shoulda' saved the herring for later, for when they're headed towards us with the water again."

"Yeah," Anna said, "that would have been a good thing to tell me an hour ago."

"Live and learn."

Anna noticed a couple of the thieves looking around at the other prisoners a short time later, eyes focusing in on pockets and other places food might be kept. She pulled her bread out and ate it before it could be taken from her.

"Guard!" yelled one of the men in another compartment. "Guard! Please! I...I need to use the toilet."

"No. You've already done that today, citizen. You'll have to hold it till tomorrow." The guard strolled on down the corridor.

"But...please! I...I can't hold it. It's...it's *number two*." He loudly whispered the last two words as if that would keep others from hearing him.

There was no answer from the guards.

The next sound Anna heard from that compartment was a loud groan followed by what could only have been an explosion of stool hitting the floor—and cursing from the other prisoners locked in there with the poor man.

The lowest ranking guard hurried to the door of the compartment. "Dammit, man! Pick that up in your hands. Now!"

Anna almost retched at the thought, glad she couldn't see the action.

"Now, come on." The guard opened the door then closed it behind the man holding his own loose stool in his hands. "Take it down there and dump it in the toilet, nothing else! No shitting or pissing, no washing up!" he yelled after the prisoner.

Anna caught a glimpse of the man as he returned to the compartment. The redness of his cheeks stood out in contrast to the sickly pale skin of the rest of his face. His downcast eyes said all there was to say. Animals. That's what they were to these soldiers. These guards. And everyone else they'd come across outside the bars of their cells since being arrested.

20

———

For over three weeks they rode that train. Some days the guards strolled by in the late afternoon and said, "We aren't going to be feeding you today; nothing was issued for you." Sometimes that happened several days in a row. The thirst was worse than the hunger —the salted herring and lazy guards making it worse. At one point, after almost three days without receiving water, the train stopped at a deserted station. The guards let the prisoners out in groups, telling them to find a place to squat because there wouldn't be another opportunity to go to the bathroom until the next day. Anna and several others, desperate for a drink, broke off blackened icicles from the train cars, letting the dirty ice melt in their mouths before finding a spot to pee and empty their bowels if they could.

Three weeks of sitting and sleeping on the floor. Too infrequent trips to the filthy bathroom. Salted herring and stale bread. A cup of water a day, if they were lucky. Guards tromping up and down the corridor twenty-four hours a day. Guards pounding on the outside of the train car—the undercarriage, the walls, the roof—at every stop to make sure no one had sawed through trying to escape. Anna had to roll her eyes at that one—what would any of them use to saw through metal? They didn't even have utensils!

When, finally, they disembarked at the train's final destination, Vladivostok on the Pacific Coast, Anna saw for the first time just how many prisoners had been on the train. She looked down the snow-packed expanse where the prisoners had been commanded to stand in lines in the freezing cold, and she gaped at the hundreds—if not into the thousands—of men and women. And, she knew, many had died on the trip there. Two from her own compartment.

Anna hugged herself, tucking her hands under her armpits to keep the biting wind from freezing them solid. The little hairs in her nose froze the instant she stepped from the train car onto the icy ground. A trickle of snot had frozen at her nostril like a tiny icicle.

She stomped her feet to keep her circulation going and wondered where they were taking them now. They'd unloaded the prisoners a good distance from the station, but Anna could still see the building, and others deeper into the city, through the winter haze. Guards walked up and down the rows of prisoners, counting them.

When they were satisfied that every *zek* was accounted for, the guards issued the command to march. Surrounded by soldiers with rifles and vicious looking dogs, Anna and her fellow prisoners trekked through the snow for the next hour. Prisoners who stumbled and fell were met with the swinging butt of a rifle, the kick of a jack-booted foot, or the teeth of a dog—sometimes all three. Anna stared at the ground in front of her, stepping as carefully as she could at the fast pace the guards had set.

The wind bit at her face until she could no longer feel it. Her feet and hands were numb as well, and she looked with envy at the prisoners who had coats, warm boots, and gloves. She could tell in which season each one of the politicals had been arrested by the type of clothes they wore. Many were in lighter summer clothes like her. She mourned the loss of her sweater, even knowing it would do little to stave off the bitter cold.

The columns of prisoners were brought to a halt when they reached an encampment surrounded by barbed wire, a tower with armed soldiers overlooking the area. Anna looked up, teeth chattering, and read *"Vtoraya Rechka"* burned into the wooden frame above the gate.

Once through the gate, they were forced to stand in formation while the guards counted them again. Anna and most of the others not wrapped up in winter clothing stomped their feet and alternately slapped their arms and rubbed their hands together as their exhaled breaths were carried away on the wind like frozen specters.

What little amount of the sun's rays that filtered through the gray sky dipped below the horizon, plunging them into the dark, starless night. And as the sun sank, so did the temperature. Anna just knew she would freeze to death before they finished counting. And she couldn't bring herself to care, as her thoughts turned sluggish and her knees knocked together with tremors.

"All right! Women, line up and follow Dasha to your barracks. Men, we'll call you line by line. Don't move until you're told to or you'll be shot." The guard added this so matter-of-factly that, in another life and time, Anna might have thought he was joking.

Anna got in line to trudge after Dasha, hoping the barracks were at least warm, but not expecting it. "Fifty-eights in here, all others wait where you are." As the female guard opened the door and ushered them inside the barracks, the first thing that struck Anna was the odor. It smelled like sickness. Vomit and stool. And just...the smell of sickness. She covered her mouth and nose as she entered the crowded building.

In the light of the single, dangling lightbulb, Anna surveyed her surroundings. Thin, ashen-faced women lay three or four to a bunk and on the floor beneath and near the lower bunks. The bunks were three rows high, with only enough room between the top one and the ceiling for a person to lay flat. A woman leaned over the side and vomited into a pail before rolling back with a moan.

"Un-diseased on this side," a woman said, waving the newcomers over. "Not that any of us'll stay that way for long."

Anna tore her gaze away from the moaning, fevered-looking women and moved as far away from them as she could in the overcrowded barracks. Which wasn't far. "What's wrong with them?"

The woman scratched at her scalp beneath a scarf. "Mostly dysentery from drinking unboiled water in this pit of a camp. Some typhus, which ya' get from the bugs."

"Shouldn't they be in a hospital or something?" one of the newcomers asked.

The woman barked out a mirthless laugh. "There's no medicine here anyway—at least not for the likes of us—so no sense sending anyone to the hospital."

Anna glanced over at the sick prisoners. "Is there any water, *boiled* water in here? We haven't had any for a couple of days."

The apparent welcoming committee chairman shook her head but pushed her way over to a wood-burning stove toward the back of the long building. She grabbed a dented pail hanging above the stove's surface. "Here." She handed it to Anna. "There's a spout in the middle of the camp. Better hurry, it's closing in on lights-out."

"So...I can...we can just leave the barracks? Are you sure I won't get shot?"

"You can leave the barracks until lights-out, then they lock us in. And they *will* shoot you if they find you out then."

The pail rattled in Anna's shaking hands as she held it close to her chest, the bit of heat it had picked up from the stove as it hung above gave her a small degree of warmth. "Will you...or someone... come with me?"

"Not me. My dogs are tired." She pointed to a woman that looked younger than Anna. "Maria, go with her. And find something to burn in the stove, the fire's about out."

Anna did not want to go back into the penetrating cold, but her thirst drove her out the door. Hunger too, as she had a couple pieces of the salted herring hidden away in her pocket, waiting until she had access to water before eating it. They'd also not been given any bread the last few days of the train ride, and thus, most of the prisoners hadn't eaten anything, knowing better than to eat the salty fish without having anything to drink.

Anna and Maria followed a worn trail through the snow, Maria searching their surroundings in the dark for something to burn, which seemed futile since the grounds were clear of anything burnable.

"Maria?" Anna asked. "Is this the labor camp?" She'd been wondering since they'd disembarked. The guards ignored all inquiries from the prisoners, and the women around her had argued about it—some saying it was and others insisting it was but a transit prison, a holding place before they were sent to the real labor camps.

The shy girl shook her head and said quietly, "No. They're just holding us here until we can be shipped off to one of the Kolyma camps."

"Oh." Anna didn't know if that was a good thing or a bad thing. Maybe it didn't matter either way, because there were really no more "good things" to come in her life, at least not for the next ten years. "How do we get there? Isn't this the end of the line for the trains?"

"Boats. That's why there are so many of us here. There aren't enough ships to keep up with the influx of prisoners." Maria stopped in front of a bronze spigot attached to a pipe rising from the ground. "Here's the water."

Try as they might, the women couldn't get the frozen handle to turn. A guard watched them from twenty yards away, eyes smirking above the scarf wrapped around his lower face and neck.

"Ugh," Maria huffed. "Forget this. There might be some fresh snow behind one of the buildings." She tromped off in the direction of a half-finished brick building, rickety scaffolding and ladders clinging to its side. A wheelbarrow laid tipped over at the base of a ramp made of thin sheets of wood that looked as if a stiff breeze would tear it apart.

Anna followed, glancing back at the guard, who had turned his disinterested attention elsewhere.

Maria climbed over a pile of bricks and exclaimed in a whisper, "Aha. Snow *and* wood."

After stumbling over the brick pile, Anna scooped up a pailful of the dingy snow then packed it tight with her already freezing hands before piling more on top and repeating the process until the bucket was full to the brim. "Are you sure this snow is okay to ingest? It looks dirty."

"Yeah. It's no dirtier than the water that comes out of that frozen pipe we just came from. Besides, we're going to boil it first, remember?" Maria picked up scraps of wood she'd brushed the snow off of and handed a few pieces to Anna. "Untuck your shirt and hide that in the waist of your skirt."

Anna sat the bucket down, able to stuff several strips of wood between her torso and waistband, thanks to the weight she'd lost since being arrested. Maria hid more beneath her worn coat.

They headed back to the barracks, and Anna held the pail tight against her abdomen. "What if they catch us with the wood?" she whispered.

Maria shrugged. "Depends on the guard and what kind of mood he or she is in. They'd probably just make us put it back, but might send us to the punishment cells."

Anna shuddered above and beyond the trembling from the cold. That didn't sound like something she wanted to experience. Luck was on their side, though, as they hurried past the lone guard out in the middle of the compound, he was preoccupied, smoking a cigarette with one arm wrapped around a warmly dressed woman. The woman pressed her body into him, and he dipped his head to blow smoke directly into her open mouth.

"I guess that's one way to share a cigarette," Maria mumbled.

Anna, confused, asked, "Is she...Did he bring his girlfriend here?"

Maria stifled a laugh. "No. She's one of the *blatnye*. It's not uncommon for them—and for us, when we can—to trade sex for favors."

Shaking her head, Anna thought, *Never. I'll starve or freeze to death before I do that.*

The girl looked at Anna's clothes and shivering body then dipped her head and said quietly, "That's how I got this coat. And mittens, but they got stolen."

Anna wasn't about to judge her. This godforsaken place could turn a nun into a prostitute. But after the Black Mariah... Anna tightened her grip on the pail full of snow. No. A nun, maybe, but not Anna. Not if her life depended on it.

They reached the barracks just as Dasha and two other guards headed toward it. "Best get inside, you two. Ten minutes to lights-out."

Anna and Maria made their way through the crowded barracks to the stove. Anna set the pail on its surface before she joined Maria in unloading the bits of wood onto the floor below it.

A loud groan came from the sick side of the room, and the woman who it came from stood from a bottom bunk, steadying herself on the support post before lurching toward the latrine bucket. She barely got her underwear down in time, squatting as a torrent of diarrhea splashed into the nearly full bucket. The new odor mingled with all the others, and Anna pressed her nose into her shoulder to stifle the smell.

"Lights-out!" Dasha yelled into the barracks as the wind whipped through the open door. "I'm locking you in." She shut the door, and a padlock clicked then banged against it. The electricity was cut to the lone lightbulb, and they were plunged into darkness except for the glow from the embers at the bottom of the now open stove.

After one of the women stoked the fire with the wood they'd brought back, Anna stood watch over the pail of snow as it melted, then boiled. Pain spread through her fingers and toes as her proximity to the stove warmed and thawed them, but she had other concerns. She was so thirsty, as were the others who'd been with her on the train. They gathered around her as she used a cloth someone had handed her to lift the pail off the stove and place it onto a small table a few steps away, a blackened ring on the top showing her where it had obviously been set many times before.

"Umm," Anna looked around the darkened room. "Does anyone have a cup we can use?"

The woman who'd directed them to the "un-diseased" side of the barracks spoke up. "You can use mine for tonight, but tomorrow, you'd best be finding your own." She handed a thin metal mug to Anna. "My name's Sonya. What's yours?"

"Anna." She dipped the cup into the still bubbling water then set it on the table to cool as her throat spasmed at the thought of a drink. She bent down to blow on it, and after it cooled enough not to scorch her throat, she drank it down in greedy gulps, pausing only to spit out bits of wood or dirt, before dipping the cup in the pail again. To protests from some of the others, she held it and blew on its contents as before. "I didn't see any of you volunteering to go get water or to come with me, so I think I deserve to drink two cups before passing it along to any of you."

"She's right, leave her be," said a prisoner she didn't know well but recognized from her cell in the Lubyanka.

After drinking another cupful of water, Anna handed the mug to her then backed away, a little closer to the stove, and ate one of the herring halves she'd stowed in her pocket while on the train.

"All the bunks are taken." Sonya's no-nonsense way of getting to the point reminded Anna of Evgenya, and a pang of sadness hit her in the gut at the surety she'd never see the Lubyanka *starosta* again. Sonya continued, "You'll have to find a place on the floor or under one of the bunks to sleep."

Anna wasn't about to crawl under a bunk again.

Maria touched her shoulder and said quietly, "There's a spot on my bunk, if you want. Anya died last night. You'll just have to help me move her body under the bunk."

Anna's eyes widened. "You mean...her body's still in here? On your bunk?"

The girl nodded. "There are too many of us for them to take roll every night, so when someone dies, we stuff them under a bunk until they start stinking. That way, we can still get their food rations."

As Anna grasped the legs of the small, dead woman and helped move her lifeless body, she thought, *Maybe we really are animals.*

21

The single dangling lightbulb flickered on, and the rattling of keys outside the barracks' door brought Anna fully awake where she was curled up next to Maria on the narrow bunk. The fuel in the stove had long since run out, and Anna shivered, her breath floating in white puffs above her as she resisted the order to get up for just a moment longer.

"Get up you lazy wenches!" The guard burst through the door. "Those with work assignments line up for chow. The rest of you will have to wait."

"Wait for what?" one of the new arrivals asked as Anna forced herself to a sitting position.

The guard ignored her question, but one of the women, wrapping a scarf around her head and neck as she joined the queue, said, "They only feed those who work, and there are more prisoners than work here."

Alarm spiked through Anna's chest as she turned to Maria. "Is that true?"

"Mostly." She rose to join the line of workers. "You might be able to get some gruel after we eat."

Panic caused Anna's voice to come out high-pitched, almost like a whine. "But how do we get work?"

Maria shrugged as the line moved toward the door. "Beg."

As the last of the "workers" shuffled through the door, Anna looked around at those left behind with her. Her stomach twisted with equal parts hunger and anger. None of this made sense. They'd all been sentenced to the *labor camps* because, supposedly, the Soviet needed more workers to accomplish its second "Five-year Plan." And, as she'd heard her vile brother-in-law say on more than one occasion, "forced labor is the only way to reform and re-educate the anti-Soviet scum." Yet, here she was, maybe not at a labor camp yet, but at a waystation on her way to one, forced there by lies and a government that cared only about Stalin and his sycophants and their unattainable Communist utopia!

Anna made her way to the door where some of the prisoners who'd been there more than a day were heading. "Where are you all going? Can we just leave the barracks?"

A woman pulled her tattered scarf down to uncover her mouth. "Yes, we can leave whenever it's unlocked. Most of us are going to line up at the kitchen behind the workers. There won't be any bread left for us, but there's sometimes some gruel left."

Anna rubbed her hands up and down her arms as the frigid air outside met the freezing air inside the barracks. "Then what?"

"Then you try to find some job to volunteer for—or a guard or trusty to screw. That might even get you some warm clothes." She pushed the scarf back up to cover her nose and mouth and turned her back to Anna.

The wind had blown most of the snow to drift against the buildings and perimeter fence. The icy air pierced the thin fabric of her blouse, and Anna wondered if she'd ever be completely warm again as she stepped outside, following the others to the kitchen. Waiting in the long line behind hundreds of men and women prisoners, she gazed with envy at those wearing warm coats, boots, mittens, and scarves. Even those who wore lighter coats that looked to be prison issued made her jealous. She was far from the only prisoner whose clothing was ill-fitted for the winter weather. It was easy to discern those who had been arrested in spring or summer months by the lack of warm clothing they wore.

Anna stomped her feet and rubbed her hands together, tucking her chin into the collar of her blouse. It was an hour before she reached the doorway, and the warmth radiating from the back where the stoves were almost made her cry for joy. Crudely constructed tables and benches crowded the large room. Prisoners sat at the tables and stood along the walls as they slurped up the gruel, some of them also drinking from whatever random container they'd found that would hold water. There was little conversation in the room full of people.

Limping, a balding man with gray stubble on his face carried a tray of empty bowls to the serving window. The gruff man behind the window took the tray from him and dished up the next serving of gruel into one of the dirty bowls.

Anna took the half-full bowl he proffered her, urging her hands to stop shaking so as not to spill any of the precious, watery gruel. She looked down at it and turned to walk away when an idea struck and she turned back. "Umm...excuse me."

The server scowled in her direction with a grunt.

"Would you have need of a dishwasher...or, or anything else I could help with?"

He spat out a harsh laugh. "Only thing I need help with back here is a bitch to suck my—"

Anna spun and hurried away, her cheeks burning as more than one person's laughter followed her. She gulped down the thin gruel as the guards stationed at the door shouted, "Kitchen closed! Everyone out!"

Reluctant to leave the warm building, Anna set her empty bowl on the limping man's tray and, avoiding the serving window, made her way slowly outside. The thirst that never seemed satisfied snaked its way to the front of her mind, just behind the bitter cold. As the prisoners disbursed around her, she surveyed her surroundings, trying to get her bearings. Trying to prioritize her needs as her earlier anger dissipated, replaced by uncertainty and fear.

A group of thin, sickly men stood around the water spigot she and Maria had tried to use the night before. She needed water, and she needed to find work that would allow her to receive more rations—some bread, at least. She continued her list as she stood watching the men pass around the stump of a cigarette. Warm clothes. A cup. Anna's mind spun, and it was getting her nowhere as her teeth chattered and her face went numb.

She drew in an icy breath and turned, walking toward the partially constructed building she and Maria had collected snow and wood from last night. The work site was starting to buzz, mostly men dressed in ratty, quilted jackets. Some wore warm boots and others felt boots wrapped in whatever material they could find to help keep out the cold and wet. Anna stood back and watched, hoping to find a need—other than sexual favors—she could provide.

Two men alternately filled their wheelbarrows with cement or brick mortar from where it was being mixed in an area central to several buildings under construction. They trudged back to their worksite, pushing the heavy load across the frozen ground and up the sketchy ramp to the first level of the scaffolding. Once there, they parked the wheelbarrow, then filled two buckets with the cement before carrying them up to the highest level where the bricklayers worked and dumping their contents on the scaffolding between them.

Anna had an idea. When the man returned, she swallowed down her fear, stepped up the ramp to where he stood, and cleared her throat. "Excuse me."

He turned a weary gaze on her.

"Could I, maybe, help out here?"

He sighed. "Doing what?"

"Well." she looked from the two empty buckets in his hands to two more on the ground below. "Maybe while you're carrying two buckets up to the bricklayers, I could fill those other two, then you could leave the newly emptied ones here for me to fill while you take those up." She shrugged and rubbed her arms. "It would be more efficient."

A cynical laugh escaped the man's throat. "No one here cares about being efficient."

Anna scrambled for another reason for him to let her help. "Okay...but, it would be less work for you if you didn't have to fill the buckets before carrying them up there."

He sighed again. "What are you hoping to get from this?"

"Food." She looked down, her voice shaking along with her chattering teeth. "Maybe a coat...and a cup."

"Might as well be asking for the moon, Miss."

She bit her lip and nodded, turned to make her way back down the ramp.

"Wait. Let me talk to the boss." He pointed to the side of the ramp. "Wait down there."

The man returned with a red-faced, shorter man who asked, "What's your name?"

"Anna."

"Well, Anna, I'm Ivan." He glanced at her arms. "Thomas here told me about your idea, and it isn't a bad one, but what makes you think you can keep up with the two wheelbarrowers? You look awfully frail."

A glimmer of hope sparked. "I'm stronger than I look." She regarded him with pleading eyes, seeing a glimpse of kindness in his face. "We could give it a try, and if...if I can't keep up I'll go. I'll find something else. Please."

Ivan nodded. "Fair enough. Get started, and I'll round up a jacket. Getting you a cup shouldn't be too hard, and I'll let the kitchen know to give you a worker's ration today—*if* you can give a full day's work."

"Thank you!" Anna grabbed the two empty buckets at the bottom of the ramp, carried them to the wheelbarrow, and set them on the uneven boards. The shovel was heavier than she thought it would be, and she struggled to fill the first bucket while Thomas watched.

"Here." He pulled a trowel from a loop on his pants and handed it to her. "This might be easier for you. But I need it back at the end of the day."

Anna nodded and took it from him.

While she filled the second bucket, he asked. "Why are you doing this? I mean, I get that you need to eat and all, but most of the women just cozy up to one of the trustees and get assigned easy jobs. Jobs that are inside like cooking, cleaning, laundry, medical."

Her guts boiled as she answered in a hoarse whisper, "I will never 'cozy up' to one of those horrible *blatnye* thieves. I'd rather die."

"Admirable thought, but we'll see how long your conviction lasts." His voice held a tinge of sadness rather than the cruelty Anna expected from those words.

Thomas's wheelbarrow partner pushed his way to the bottom of the ramp and looked up at them.

"Come," Thomas said, "let me introduce you two."

Anna followed him, still holding the trowel.

"Maxim, this is Anna," he introduced. "She's going to help us out by filling the buckets up for us."

Maxim glanced up, grunted, and set his wheelbarrow down, waiting, Anna assumed, for Thomas to get finished with his load so they could trade spots.

"Max is a man of few words," Thomas said as he trudged back up the ramp. "But he's an alright fellow."

By the time they broke for lunch, Anna's arms were as wobbly as earthworms, but she couldn't let the men see that. She followed behind them into the mess hall where Thomas waited for her to catch up before saying quietly, "We all sit together, and Ivan goes to get our food. He's a great foreman. He looks after us as much as he can, being a Fifty-eight himself."

Anna breathed a sigh as she lowered herself to the bench beside Thomas. It was the first time she'd sat since leaving her bunk that morning. More workers filtered in, filling up the tables around them.

Ivan carried a tray over to them, one bowl of watery soup and a small chunk of black bread for each of the men—and Anna—in his crew. He stopped beside Anna, set the tray on the table, and set a worn quilted jacket over her shoulders. "It's way too big for you, but it's the best I could do. You'll find a tin cup in the righthand pocket." He moved to sit across from her. "You did good work this morning. Think you can keep it up till quitting time?"

She put her arms through the sleeves, warmth from more than just the jacket flooding through her. These men—these Fifty-eights, anti-Soviet agitators, so-called "fascists"—had shown her more kindness in one morning than she'd seen in months. She nodded. She wasn't sure her arm muscles agreed, but she would use every ounce of strength in her body to keep working—and to not let this kind man down. "Thank you so much." She blinked back tears and hung her head to hide them while she worked on rolling up the sleeves of the jacket.

"Better hurry and eat, we only have ten more minutes." Ivan broke his bread in half, put one half in his coat pocket, and took a bite out of the remaining piece.

As badly as she wanted to shove the whole piece in her mouth—it was the first bread she'd had since leaving the prison in Moscow weeks ago—she copied the foreman and put a piece in her pocket for later. Or maybe she could trade it for something. Gloves or a scarf.

They worked until it was too dark to see, the lights on the perimeter fence giving out only a dim glow to the prison grounds. As Anna trudged from the mess hall after a sparse dinner of cold cabbage soup and a small chunk of bread, the muscles in her arms ached, and it was an effort to hold the collar of her jacket closed against the cold.

A thin, sickly figure stumbled toward a group of prisoners

gathered around a barrel fire, smoking and telling jokes. The figure, a man, Anna thought, approached the group, and with a gravelly, weak voice offered, "I will recite my ill-fated poem about our Supreme Leader for just a half-day's ration."

"Go away, Osip. Off with you!" The man shooed him away then turned to the others. "The great poet, Osip Mandelstam, is nothing but a blithering idiot now."

The others around the barrel laughed and kicked snow toward the shuffling man.

Osip Mandelstam, Anna had heard of that name. There had been talk of him at the Lubyanka, whispered tales of the poem that had gotten him arrested. No one could recite it—it was said that the poem had never been written down, only spoken to close friends. *Ha!* Close friends indeed! At least one of them had turned the poet in. With burning hatred, Anna thought of Mikhail. She was sure her brother-in-law had been the one to turn Nikolai in.

The poet caught his toe on a rock and stumbled to the ground a few steps away from her. Anna hurried over and helped him up, astonished at how thin his arm was beneath her weakened grip.

"Thank you, dear." He looked at her with watery, red eyes. The man wasn't well.

"You're welcome." She let go of his arm and moved to step around him, wanting nothing more than to visit the latrine before going to the crowded barracks and collapsing on her shared bunk.

The man reached a trembling hand toward her. "Would you like to hear my poem, young lady? For just a crust of bread, perhaps?"

Anna felt the weight of the small chunk of bread in the pocket of her jacket as if it were a heavy stone. She *had* eaten more today than she had in weeks, maybe months. She could spare a little for this poor man, couldn't she? Shouldn't she?

The men and women at the barrel watched to see what she would do. She looked up at the poet and sighed. "I'd love to hear your poem, Mr. Mandelstam, but let's go somewhere more private."

She held out her arm for him to hold to as they walked a short distance away from the jeering prisoners. Osip headed toward the perimeter fence, where a large stone was wedged into the ground beneath a buzzing light. He lowered himself to the stone with a grunt. Under the light Anna realized that he wasn't as old as she'd thought. The way he stooped over, his skin hanging from his bones, she'd thought him an old man. But as she watched his quickened breaths puff white steam from his lips, she determined him to be much younger, perhaps in his late forties.

His eyes glazed over, and he mumbled incoherently under his breath for a moment before be blinked a few times and looked up at Anna. He lifted a fist to his mouth and coughed into it, then said, "The poem then. For some bread?"

Anna nodded.

Osip Mandelstam recited with near perfect clarity:

> *"We live, not feeling the land beneath us*
> *We speak, and ten steps away no one hears us,*
> *But where there's even a whispered conversation*
> *The Kremlin's mountaineer, murderer, and peasant-*
> > *slayer will be mentioned.*
> *His fat fingers, like grubs are greasy*
> *His cockroach moustache sneers*
> *His boot rims shine..."*
> *The poet coughed into his fist again.*
> *"And all around him, a gaggle of spineless leaders,*
> *Half-humans, serve as his toys.*
> *One whinnies, one purrs, one whines,*
> *Only he shouts and points,*
> *Throwing decrees like horseshoes*
>
> *"Hitting a groin, a head, an eye—*
> *Every death sentence tastes sweet*
> *For the broad-chested Ossete."*

Anna stood solemnly as his words hung in the air between them. In decades past, a poem like this would have elicited chuckles, maybe even been published in the newspaper alongside a political cartoon. But now? Now it wasn't poetry, but a suicide. Though it didn't really matter who heard them here, already imprisoned, Anna couldn't quell the instinct to glance around like a frightened rabbit to see who might have heard. In a lowered voice, almost a whisper, she asked, "Mr. Mandelstam, why? Why did you not keep this to yourself when you were a free man?"

"Free? When was I free?"

She thought he'd retreated back into his confused state of mind until she looked in his eyes—they were as clear as they'd probably ever been. Anna waited for him to elucidate.

"Censorship isn't freedom, my dear. Being unable to voice an opinion that differs from that of the reigning government party without fear of execution or prison—which, it turns out, are one and the same more often than not—is not freedom. Having to whisper, even when you think what you're saying is toeing the party line...but just in case you use the wrong word or a newly outdated phrase—*just in case*—you whisper, in the dead of night, lying next to your wife in bed. The walls have ears, and this is not freedom."

Anna nodded. The poet was right. The Soviet people were not free.

Osip, seemingly encouraged by her nod, continued in that sickly, raspy voice of his, "You see, dear, I detest imitation and censorship, and I've never pretended to be loyal to the Stalinist regime, the Bolshevik's—though it would have drastically improved my and Nadezhda's lives." He took Anna's hand in his and narrowed his gaze as his eyes bore into hers. "Compromising my beliefs in such a way is simply out of the question. I don't possess the constitution for it." He sighed and dropped her hand, a chill taking him by force as his eyes glossed over again.

Anna dug in her pocket and placed the small piece of bread in his hands.

"Thank you, dear." He looked up at the sky and his eyes widened as if he'd had no idea it was night. "My, it's getting late. I should get home. Nadezhda will be worried."

This poor man! Anna thought. *Look where his convictions got him.* She looked around at the wretched camp, her gaze following the fence to the watchtower where the silhouette of a rifle-wielding guard could be seen. She nearly choked on the bitter laugh that stuck in her throat. *Look where my* lack *of conviction got me. At least Osip Mandelstam will go to his grave with the knowledge that he stood for something, that he didn't cave to the thought police like I did—like most of the Soviets have.*

The poet stood and looked down at the rock he'd been sitting on. "My first book was called 'The Stone,' and the stone will be my last book."

Anna watched as he wandered off into the dark, stumbling in a meandering course toward the row of barracks.

22

Time was funny. How, when sitting in an overcrowded prison cell in the midst of a large city, with nothing to do but wait day in and day out, weeks could feel like years, but when working from dawn to dusk in the subzero, Siberian temperatures, the weeks rushed by. Anna moved slowly through the teeming camp, absently looking for the poet amongst the crowd while her mind wandered. It was too dark to see far. She hadn't seen Osip for a couple of weeks, and she wanted to give him the crust of bread she had saved in her pocket. His mental health had been gradually deteriorating, reaching the point that he only occasionally recognized Anna as a friend as exhaustion and paranoia took over his mind. She worried that he'd died and been carted off with all the other bodies, but she held out hope that he was just lost in the huge influx of prisoners.

Not seeing him, Anna hurried to her barracks, hoping someone had found something to burn in the stove so she could warm her icy hands. With one last glance around before stepping through the door, Anna knew she should be grateful. She had a work assignment which afforded her a full worker's ration of food, and even though the small amount was never enough to satiate her constant hunger, it was more than many others got. She had a place in the barracks to sleep. It wasn't warm by any means; just that morning she'd awakened to find her hair frozen to the wooden planks of the bunk she still shared with Maria. But it was shelter from the arctic elements outside.

They just kept dumping more and more prisoners into the transit camp, and the ships that were to carry them to their assigned Kolyma labor camps were few and slow as they made their way through the icy waters. Thousands of prisoners were forced to reside out in the cold or in half-built barracks where snow fell through unfinished roofs and the wind slipped through the poorly and hastily built walls as if they were made of muslin. Some had been given tents, but there just wasn't enough shelter for the influx of men and women. Between the frigid temperatures, lack of food, and illness, at least a hundred corpses were hauled out of the compound every morning.

Anna made her way through the packed barracks, disappointed to see that the stove sat cold and empty, though with all the bodies packed inside, it was warmer than she thought possible. She sat on her bunk and surveyed the crowd. Maria must still be at the laundry building—or entertaining her *trusty* overlord and his *blatnye* friends. The things he made her do weren't worth an easy job doing the camp workers' laundry, not to Anna, at least. And often not to Maria either —when she'd come in with bruises to her face, walking with a limp. Those were the nights she curled into Anna's back and shuddered as she cried herself to sleep.

Sounds and odors of sickness came from the other side of the barracks. Moans and coughs, vomiting and splashes of diarrhea into the latrine bucket—and sometimes the floor. Anna scratched at her head, her hair had grown quite a bit since the butchering it took in the Lubyanka. All the prisoners were infested with lice and bedbugs —and as a result, a typhus epidemic had struck the camp. That was part of the reason for the overcrowding—the camp had been quarantined, and no prisoner transports had been allowed to leave it for almost four months. Yet the transports from Moscow to the transit prison continued without taking this into account, shoving more and more prisoners into the camp with nowhere to house them and not enough to feed them.

Ivan had told his work crew that they were to get the day off tomorrow—a first since Anna had arrived at the camp. She'd heard rumors that the prisoners were supposed to get a day off every ten days—but that certainly hadn't happened.

Anna curled up on the bunk, barely registering when Maria shook her and asked her to scoot over sometime after lights-out. The trusties had a deal with the guards, when the women they were *involved* with came back to the barracks after lights-out, the guards unlocked the door and let them in without question.

Before first light in the morning, the door to the barracks was opened and six guards shouted, "Everyone up! On your feet!"

Anna stood and helped Maria up, scooting out of the way as much as possible so the two women lying on the floor beneath their bunk could crawl out.

"Anyone with a cough, fever, diarrhea, or vomiting line up at the door!" One of the guards yelled. He turned and pointed to three of the other guards. "Go make sure we get them all."

The three pulled their scarves over their mouths and noses and pushed their way into the barracks, pulling sick women off bunks and nudging with a toe of their boot those still lying on the cold, filthy cement floor.

"What do we do with the dead ones, chief?"

"Leave 'em. We'll send some *zeks* in later to gather them."

The six guards spread out around the forming line and ushered the sick prisoners out the door, some of them, too weak to stand, were forced to crawl out into the snowy compound.

"Where are you taking us?" one of the women asked.

"Quarantine barracks."

Anna hurriedly wrapped her shoes and lower legs in strips of felt she'd gathered from the torn piece of an old prisoner coat she'd come across. She was thankful to have the shoes her mother had sent to her, but wished she had warm boots. She immediately felt guilty for her wish, knowing there were many prisoners without footwear at all. Any scrap of rubber, fragment of an old tire, or pieces of torn-up padded jackets were strapped to the bottom of their feet with discarded wire or electrical cords. She looked down at her worn shoes —she'd be there before long.

Following the slow-moving line of sick prisoners at a distance, Anna thought about Osip. Maybe that's where he'd been the last couple of weeks. Maybe they'd quarantined him. He'd grown more emaciated and frail over the last few weeks, his cough worsening, and his body wracked with fever. Anna hoped to get a glimpse inside whichever barracks was being used to house the quarantined prisoners. They'd been told that typhus wasn't something you could catch from someone else who was infected, it came solely from the bites of bugs that carried the disease...but it wasn't the only illness going around camp.

The line of quarantined women wound through the prisoners sleeping or mulling about the camp grounds—many of those still on the frozen ground having taken their last breath sometime during the night.

She pulled her hands inside the long sleeves of her jacket and ducked her chin into the collar to fend off the worst of the cold. She waited several yards off as the guards shoved the sick women through the door to join the men already inside.

"No one is to leave this building!" the chief guard shouted as the last woman, crawling on all fours, collapsed just inside the door. "I'm leaving it unlocked so the orderlies can get in and out—any quarantined person caught trying to leave will be shot immediately!"

One guard stationed himself twenty yards away, leaning against a poorly constructed cabin-like building that housed some of the trusties—all criminals, *blatnye,* who somehow were held in high esteem by the prison and camp directors. Unlike the Fifty-eights—the politicals, the *zeks,* the "enemies of the people"—whom they treated worse than animals. The guard slung his rifle across his back and dug out his pouch of tobacco, rolling a cigarette while his comrades dispersed, off to take care of other duties.

With a wary eye on the remaining guard, Anna moved to stand several feet away from the doorway of the quarantine barracks to where she could peer inside. The odor that wafted out of the building nearly knocked her to her knees. She shielded her nose and mouth with her sleeve-covered hands and swallowed down a retch.

Two stories of bunks lined the walls. Anna watched in horror as a man lying on a top bunk moaned and clutched his stomach before watery stool spurted through his already soiled pants, pouring onto the people curled up on the bunk below him.

Anna tore her eyes from the sickening sight and searched the faces in the dim light. She thought she recognized a huddled form, curled up and shivering on the floor near a row of bunks. She couldn't be sure it was Osip, but the wisp of filthy brown hair swept over his bald crown looked familiar.

Heavy footsteps crunched behind her, and Anna turned. The guard, still smoking his cigarette, stepped toward her. "What are you doing?"

Her heart sped up, and she stammered, "Just...just looking for a friend."

"Well, if your friend is in there, you'd better say goodbye. I don't suppose many of them will be coming out alive." His tone was matter-of-fact, and somehow that made his words all the more chilling.

Anna swallowed her fear and said, "The...uh...your chief said something about orderlies. Does that mean they will be getting treatment? Medication?"

He shrugged. "There is no medication. The orderlies will just be bringing them water and carrying the dead out."

Anna glanced back inside the dismal barracks.

"Now move along."

Almost every day for the next week Anna walked past the quarantine barracks hoping to catch a glimpse of Osip, maybe even talk to him through the open door. Several times she was there as they were hauling dead bodies out and tossing them onto carts pulled by *zeks* who looked very much like they might be next.

It was dark, and Anna's arms ached from filling what seemed like a thousand buckets, but she'd promised herself she'd give it one more try tonight, and if she wasn't able to talk to the poet this time, she'd give up.

She trudged to the quarantine barracks, but she couldn't get near the open door. A couple of guards and three or four trusties stood around it. One of the guards demanded, "Everyone on your feet and strip down. The orderlies will gather your clothes."

"Why?" one of the quarantined asked.

"We're going to treat them with chemicals in a special chamber to get rid of the bugs, shithead. Now strip down!"

The orderlies gathered the clothing as the men and women disrobed and stood naked, shivering in the below zero temperature.

"Aren't you going to give them blankets or robes or something so they don't freeze?" Anna blurted as the orderlies and all but one guard walked away.

"Mind your own business, bitch," the remaining guard said. "They'll be fine, the decontamination process doesn't take long."

Anna frowned and looked inside the barracks again. There! She spotted Osip near the door and stepped forward.

"Hey!" The guard held out his arm to stop her. "Get back!"

The emaciated poet, Osip Mandelstam, looked up and met her gaze just before he collapsed to the cement floor.

"Osip!" She tried again to go to him, but the guard shoved her to the ground and pointed his rifle at her.

"One more attempt to enter that barracks and I'll shoot you."

"Help him. Please," she pleaded.

The guard looked from her to the prostrate man and cursed. He pointed at two prisoners huddled in a group outside, trying to keep from freezing. "You and you. Take this man to the camp hospital..." He looked at the crumpled form on the floor. "Or dump him with the other dead bodies."

"No," Anna gasped, though she'd known he was on his last leg, her heart still hurt for the brave poet.

The two prisoners dragged him out the door, away from the mass of naked, sick people, then lifted him, one holding him under his arms and the other by his legs.

Anna stepped up beside him and looked down at him. "Osip."

The man's blue lips moved slightly, and he moaned without opening his eyes.

"He's still alive." She looked at the two prisoners who carried him. "Please, take him to the camp hospital."

The one at Osip's head nodded with a grunt, and they trudged off in the dark toward the small brick building that served as the camp hospital.

"Now you," the guard tipped the barrel of his rifle toward her, "get back to your barracks, or wherever you turn in for the night. It's almost lights-out."

Wanting desperately to go with Osip, to make sure the prisoners truly carried him to the hospital, but not wanting to push her luck any further with the guard, Anna's shoulders drooped as she made her way to her barracks.

The next afternoon in the mess hall, word spread that Osip Mandelstam had died in the camp hospital that morning. His body was on its way to be dumped in a mass grave with all the others who had succumbed throughout the night.

Anna only nodded at the news, unable to feel anything. Maybe he was the lucky one.

23

Several times a week the prisoners were made to stand in lines of five abreast—sometimes for hours on end—either in the morning or evening for headcount. This time was different, though. The Camp Commander followed on the heels of the guards as they stopped before each prisoner and demanded, "First name! Surname! Crime! Sentence!"

As each prisoner answered in quick succession, the Camp Commander checked the papers on his clipboard then either moved on to the next one or ordered that prisoner to go line up at the gate.

The guard stepped up to Anna and shouted his questions in her face. "First name, surname, crime, and sentence!"

"Anna Levitskaya, Article Fifty-eight, ten years."

The Camp Commander shuffled his papers then made a mark on one of them. "Over there." He nodded toward the ever-enlarging group by the gate.

Anna swallowed the lump that flared in her throat—she thought it might have been her heart as it had leapt so when she'd been told to move—and walked over to the separated group on shaky legs. She briefly met eyes with one of the other women and recognized her own fear mirrored there before they both looked away. Whispered reports had been passed through the camp for months that Moscow had ordered the number of prisoners to be "reduced." Which meant executing many of them and dumping them in mass graves. They'd all heard the gunfire shortly after large groups of prisoners had been marched off for "transport."

Anna waited with the others as hundreds more joined them in the numbing cold. She glanced up occasionally at the soldiers surrounding them, rifles at the ready, vicious dogs straining at their leashes. She'd thought many times since the night of her arrest that she'd be better off dead—like Nikolai—than a victim of this cruel system. But Anna wasn't ready to die. Her mama had begged her to stay alive, and she so desperately wanted to see her mama again. Wanted to feel the warmth of their little apartment as they shared their meager meals—meals that now seemed like feasts. She even missed Nadya, but not her sister's Party-loving husband.

They stood in the cold for hours while the guards continued their roll call. By the time they finished and sent those who hadn't been separated back to work or barracks, Anna figured there were at least fifteen-hundred standing in rows by the entrance gate.

The Camp Commander marched toward them, still holding his clipboard full of papers, stopped in front of the large group, and announced, "Say goodbye to Vtoraya Rechka, citizens. You will now walk in single file to the docks. Any malingering or straying from the line will result in immediate execution."

Anna searched the faces of those near her to see if she recognized anyone, hoping if this was a transport to a Gulag one of her friends would be going, but if it was a trip to a mass grave site, she hoped none of them were included. She saw no sign of Ivan, Thomas, Maria, or even the quiet Maxim.

Keeping her head down, eyes on the ground, Anna followed behind the person trudging before her. When they reached the docks they were separated by gender, then herded up the gangplank of the cargo steamer like cattle.

She'd never been on a boat before; it might as well have been a spaceship blasting off to another planet. She stared up at the letters "DS" painted on the smokestack—the letters stood for *Dalstroi,* the construction and mining organization that had recently been placed under the NKVD. The last things Anna noticed before being forced below deck into the hold were machine-gun nests placed on the deck of the ship. At the bottom of the ladder soldiers shoved her into one of several sections that had been blocked off from one another with iron grates. She and the other women crammed in the cage hurried to secure a spot on one of the crude wooden bunks that lined the hold. Anna plopped down on one of the lower bunks, knowing her chance of keeping an upper bunk if there were any criminals amongst them was slim.

As the soldiers thrust more and more women into the space, Anna's chest tightened. When it seemed that not one more body could be squeezed inside, they shoved five more in. Worse than the Stolypin car had been, they were truly packed inside like sardines. She worried that she wouldn't be able to stand up for the duration of the trip, and those who were standing, smashed up against one another, wouldn't be able to sit. They'd gone from enduring the frigid air for hours outside, to wilting in the heat of so many bodies pressed together in the windowless hold. Anna struggled to get her quilted jacket off among the crush of women, holding tightly to it once she succeeded. She would need it where they were going, she was sure.

Iron grills separated the men's compartments from the women, and there were at least three times the number of men as women. And, as she'd predicted, the criminals, the *blatnye,* took to the top bunks, already harassing the politicals below them.

Anna's legs grew numb before the ship even began to move. She tried to shift her position, but the prisoners were packed in so tightly it was impossible. The air seemed thick and void of oxygen as her lungs worked to breathe. Rethinking her earlier comparison to being herded like cattle, she decided that wasn't true—they wouldn't treat cattle like this, they were too important to the welfare of the Soviet Union.

The hatch leading from the deck to the hold slammed shut with the finality of a coffin lid. Anna breathed faster, almost panting, as the closing of the hatch seemed to have sucked all the air out of the cargo space turned prison. The sound of the engines rose, and the ship vibrated all around them as it embarked on its journey. The Sea of Okhotsk rose and fell as the ship rode the winter waves, breaking through ice as it propelled forward. Anna's stomach lurched with the movement, nausea rolling inside her. The first vomit hit the floor shortly after and created a chain-reaction as more women—and men in the other compartments—heaved what little contents were in their stomachs out onto the floor.

Anna bent over so her forehead rested on her knees and closed her eyes, trying to breathe through the nausea. A stream of partially digested gruel and bread splashed onto her head from above, and Anna lost the fight with her stomach. Her vomit hit the floor at her feet, splashing the legs of the standing prisoners, and soon her stomach muscles ached from repeated dry-heaving.

With no idea how long they'd been in this new hell, Anna guessed it had been several hours as the ship continued its incessant rocking back and forth. At some point, several of the women who were forced to stand, slumped, held up only by the close-packed bodies of the others. Finally, one woman pleaded, "Please, I need to sit. Can we try sitting against each other?" Her voice wavered.

"If we sit between each other's legs, we might be able to fit," one of the few who hadn't thrown up suggested.

Oh, how far we've fallen, Anna thought, *that not a single person has voiced concern about sitting in the vomit splattered all over the floor.*

After much shuffling and some cursing, they were all sitting, either pressed together on the bunks or straddling each other on the floor. The woman leaning against Anna's legs moaned, "Why don't they at least open the hatch? Get some air down here?"

Anna had mostly ignored the grumbling and cursing coming through the grates from the men's compartments, but she perked up when a deep voice answered through the grating. "They won't open it for at least three days."

His proclamation was met with multiple questions and responses:

"Why not?"

"How do you know?"

"We'll run out of air!"

"How will we get food and water?"

The man's voice broke through, quieting the murmurs. "I used to work on one of these steamers, before I got arrested and thrown in with the rest of you. They won't open the hatch except on the rare occasions when they throw down some food or lower down a bucket of water, until after we are well past the coast of Japan." Bitterness coated his next words. "They wouldn't want any Japanese fishermen or the like to see what the Great Russia does to its own citizens. As far as they're concerned, these are just cargo ships transporting goods and supplies. They must keep the true contents of their 'cargo' boats a secret."

Sleep was impossible with the constant seasickness roiling in Anna's stomach, the dreaded thirst, the moaning, and the torturous confines of the packed cell. There wasn't enough room for anyone but the criminals in the top bunks to lay down. Standing for more than a moment brought unbearable dizziness. Her legs and feet were numb from all the bodies pressed up against them. And the heat brought back the horrible memory of the hot box she'd been placed in at the Lubyanka.

On what she guessed was the second day at sea, the hatch opened and from the darkness above, bits and pieces of salted herring were thrown down into the hold. As much as they could, the prisoners who were still in good enough health scrambled for the food, lunging over each other, pushing, elbowing, just to reach a head or other dried piece of fish not fit for pigs.

Anna snatched half a herring as it fell and hurriedly stuffed it in her skirt pocket. She'd learned her lesson on the train—she wouldn't eat the salty fish until water was available. Still seasick, it wasn't all that hard to resist the urge to eat it immediately, anyway.

Later—could have been the same day, could have been the next, she had no real way of knowing—a bucket of water was lowered down on a rope, first within reach of the men's compartments. The bucket had only one cup hooked to it, and even though about half of the men had their own cups, the process to get everyone a drink was lengthy. Cups had to be passed from the back to the front, dipped in the bucket, then passed back to the owner or whoever was next in line for the community cup. And, of course, the criminal element lounging on the upper bunks got to go first.

Anna's compartment got the fourth or fifth bucket, and she handed her cup forward, glad she kept it in the pocket of her coat. She worried about passing it forward, worried she'd never get it back, but her thirst won out, and she trusted her fellow prisoners with the precious cup, thankful that the criminals in her compartment stayed on their upper bunks and had their own cups.

After Anna drank a cupful of the gritty water, she let the women around her use her cup, keeping a close eye on where it was at all times. She breathed a great sigh when it was safely tucked away in her coat pocket again. She folded her coat in a way that would keep the cup from falling out, and hugged it close to her sweaty body.

Even though the cup of water wasn't nearly enough to slake her thirst, she needed to eat. Anna dug the small piece of salted herring out of her skirt pocket and bit into it, longing for the watered-down soup and small chunk of bread she'd be having if she was back at camp eating lunch with the bricking crew.

Things in the hold quieted down after the last bucket was withdrawn and the hatch slammed shut and stayed that way.

The same deep voice of the former barge-worker who had spoken up the first day broke the relative silence. "They gave us water, that must mean we're close to being past the Japanese coast. They'll have to let us use the toilet soon."

"I ain't about to wait for that."

Anna watched in disgust as a criminal on the upper bunk of the men's compartment closest to her, showered the politicals below him with urine. Other *blatnye* joined their brother-in-crime, laughing as some of the men tried to cover their heads and others just let it rain down on them, giving in to the inhuman treatment they'd suffered since the day of their arrests.

Anna cringed away from the disgusting display, glancing up in fear that the female criminals would join in the harassment on their side. They hadn't yet, but probably only because it was a little more difficult for women to pee from a bunk.

At least twelve more hours passed, and Anna's bladder was about to burst. The water and herring had stayed down even through the nausea the ship's motion caused, and she was thankful for that. But she needed to pee.

The hatch opened, and a shaft of light beamed down into the dank, malodorous hold. Anna squinted at the shadow of a soldier standing on deck, yelling down at the prisoners. "Toilet! Female's first. Line up at the ladder when I unlock your cage!"

The thieves on the top bunks jumped down, not caring where or on whom their booted feet landed, and shoved their way to the front. The soldier unlocked the gate and stepped aside as the *blatnye* made for the ladder. Anna stood when there was room to do so, her legs wobbling like all the muscles had been removed. Pins and needles pricked at her feet and calves, and as the line moved slowly out the gate, she half-shuffled and half-stumbled her way forward until her legs woke up. She put her coat on as the frigid sea air wafted through the open hatch.

It was an hour before Anna made it out of the hold, up the ladder to the deck. And another hour before she came within sight of the "toilet." As the barge moved up and down beneath her unsteady feet, she blanched, a pang of fear piercing her chest. The "bathrooms" were mere crudely constructed box-like contraptions made of boards, attached to the side of the ship. The prisoners were forced to climb over the ship's railing and into the box. Anna watched in horror as an older woman balked at climbing from the safety of the deck, over the railing, as the vessel rolled to and fro. The guard prodded her with a club, and either that or her necessity to relieve herself caused her to overcome her reluctance and climb over the rail. The woman lost her grip as she slung her second leg over, and only avoided an icy, watery death because the women in line behind her grabbed her and steadied her while she stepped into the box.

Anna's turn came after waiting in line for almost three hours. She paused to look down at the roiling sea before steeling herself and, with a vise-like grip on the railing, climbed over into the box.

It had to have been at least eight hours before the toileting process was completed with all the prisoners. Darkness bathed the open hatch where the last of the men still waited to climb the ladder onto the deck. When they were all locked back in their compartments, the soldiers threw more salted herring down into the hold. Anna was only able to snatch a small, bite-sized portion this time, and again, she saved it for later.

She was lucky to claim a spot back on one of the lower bunks after the trip to the toilet, as uncomfortable as it was. The tarred floor slathered with vomit and who knew what else seemed far worse. She was even able to sleep a little, leaning against the woman behind her. Awakening sometime in what she assumed was still the night, she nudged the woman leaning heavily against her lower legs, trying to get her to change positions and take some of the pressure off. The woman slumped sideways, all the weight of her torso falling stiffly into the woman next to her on the floor. Her neighbor grunted and pushed on her. Anna and the second woman looked at her and then at each other, realizing at the same time that she was dead.

But death didn't mean what it used to. Instead of being sad or horrifying, it was just an everyday occurrence. Something to be expected until it was your turn.

The next time the hatch opened, sunlight dulled by cloud-cover penetrating the darkness of the hold, someone from the men's cage beside theirs called out, "We have dead in here."

"Here too," said the woman on the floor near Anna.

"We'll get to them later...unless you don't want water today?" The soldier lowered the water bucket down without waiting for an answer.

24

———

Anna awoke with a start to a woman's scream, followed by several others. In the dim light provided by a single kerosine lamp in the hold, she could barely make out several of the male prisoners lined up at the open gate to the women's cage. By their style of clothing and gruff demeanor, she knew they were *blatnye.* Criminals. How had they gotten the gate open?

"Time for a Kolyma tram, bitches."

Terror froze Anna to her spot as the man at the head of the line bulled his way in and grabbed the first woman he came to. He threw her skirt over her head and ripped her underwear from her twisting body. Other men pushed through the door, latching onto the first victims they came to as the others waited for a turn. They brutally raped them as the women kicked and clawed at their attackers, the men punching them and holding them down.

Anna came to her senses through the screams and grunts. She glanced at the waiting line of men, standing with their pants down, obviously ready for their turn. Using every ounce of her panic-fueled strength, Anna pushed with her feet until she'd scooted between the women behind her on the bunk, back into the darkened corner. She curled her knees up to her chest, making herself as small as possible, and hid behind her coat and the other women, trembling and sobbing, the neck of her coat shoved in her mouth to muffle the sounds.

"Stop the fun!" a man yelled.

Through a small slit between women, Anna watched, unable to tear her eyes away from the horror. The men who were abusing the women on the tarred floor gave one or two last thrusts before reluctantly heaving themselves off of them and going to the back of the line. The men next in line fell on their victims, savagely ramming their cocks inside them.

"Stop the fun!" the tram "conductor" yelled again after a few minutes.

As the next group fell on the women, one of the men growled, "This one's dead." He dragged her by the legs, throwing her body over the threshold before grabbing another woman and ripping her clothes off amid terrified screams.

The women on the top bunks cheered the men on, laughing and shouting jeers at the victims. The women on the floor and in the lower bunks pushed back against one another, trying to stay out of the rapists' reach—but there was nowhere to go. Bodies pressed against Anna until she thought she would suffocate—which was a better way to die than being part of the carnage stacking up on the threshold. Body after body was added to the pile of dead women. And those who were confirmed not to be dead, but just unconscious, were slapped to bring them back around.

Hundreds of men, political prisoners, hung from the bed boards in their cages, watching. Not a single one of them tried to stop the rapists.

The women who Anna hid behind were pulled down one-by-one as the "Kolyma tram" continued. She looked around, frantic to find some way to end her life before the animals reached her.

The hatch opened. Guards on the upper deck blasted the hold with freezing sea water, dispersing the frenzied crowd of rutting males, leaving a pile of dead women in their wake.

The guards forced the men back into their cage and locked them in. The dead women were dragged away, up the ladders, and thrown overboard without so much as their names being asked, much less written down. A few of the more severely injured women were taken away by the guards.

"Dante's hell has nothing on this place," a woman beside Anna spat in an angry whisper.

When the guards once again sealed the hatch, shutting them in the darkened hold, the criminals came alive again on the other side of the grate. Some of the bulkier men, obviously not having had enough pleasure for one night, turned to searching the bunks in their own compartment, hunting, apparently, for young men.

Anna cringed with each wail of pain from the unfortunate adolescents who were added to the list of casualties, afterwards lying still on their stomachs, bleeding and sobbing on the floor.

They'd been at sea for at least two weeks, and Anna prayed it wouldn't be much longer till they made it to their destination, as she knew she wouldn't be sleeping until then.

A loud clang followed by a weak shaft of light from overhead woke Anna from her half-slumber. They hadn't been given any food or water for at least two days, ever since the rapists had somehow breached the women's cell. She blinked, trying to elicit some moisture for her dry, stinging eyes.

"Get up! Form a line!" Several guards made their way down the ladder into the hold. They banged on the iron bars with their truncheons. "Come on, now, your new home awaits!"

Amid the myriad groans around her, Anna's raspy voice joined in as she untangled her weak, sleeping limbs and forced herself upright for the first time in days. Her determination to stand in the slow-moving line increased as she watched those who were too weak to do so get beaten by the impatient guards. Some of them found the strength to comply, but those who couldn't... The guard in charge told the others, "Just leave them. We'll deal with them when we get back."

Anna cringed, her stomach dropping. She knew exactly how the guards would "deal with them," just like they'd deal with a lame mule.

Muscles shaking with fatigue, Anna climbed the ladder and was roughly lifted onto the deck of the ship by a guard stationed on each side of the hatch. Her eyes stung, and she pulled her jacket closer about her as the coldest wind she'd ever experienced whipped across the deck. The prisoners were herded onto a transport truck—more like a cattle truck with open sides. They stood, crushed together, trembling in the cold.

Anna was somewhere near the middle of the pack, encompassed about by people taller than her, so their surroundings remained a mystery to her as they bounced along a rutted, pothole-filled road. She looked up as the truck jolted to a stop, a dim light lit up the gray clouds where the winter sun tried, and failed, to penetrate the darkness.

The back of the cattle truck rattled open, and the prisoners jumped down, forced to stumble along between two rows of guards and their barking, snarling dogs. As she trudged through the camp gate, Anna glanced up where hung a large piece of plywood with a banner draped over it that read: *Labor in the USSR is a Matter of Honesty, Glory, Valor, and Heroism!* And another that said: *With Just Work I Will Pay My Debt to the Fatherland.*

Anna snorted at the absurdity. There was no honesty or valor left in the Soviet Union. Only pain and torture. Lies. Forced silence. Hunger. And there was certainly nothing "just" about any of this.

A sharp jab to her side brought Anna out of her dark thoughts.

"Move it!" the guard said. "Through the gate, women to the right, men to the left!"

They lined up, standing on the frozen ground, the trampled snow like ice. Anna's worn shoes were no match for the cold, and her toes soon ached from it. She stomped her feet and kept her hands in the pockets of her quilted jacket, her right hand resting on her precious cup.

When all the prisoners had been unloaded, the counting started. Several NKVD officials walked along their ranks calling out, *"Odin, dva, tri..."* writing down each number on their clipboards.

After three rounds of counting, one of the officials marched up to the head guard from the ship. "These numbers are not adding up, citizen chief. Explain."

"You've added the numbers we reported who died en route?"

"Of course I did!"

The guard flinched as the NKVD official stepped closer, nose to nose with him. "Yes, of course you did, sir. The privates must have miscounted as they threw the dead overboard. I assure you, the live prisoners are all here."

Just as Anna thought, those left on the ship were considered dead —and would be as soon as the guards returned.

The official scribbled something on his clipboard then shoved it toward the guard. "Sign here. I won't take responsibility for your ineptness."

For a brief moment, the guard looked as if he would refuse, then with a sharp nod, he took the clipboard and signed.

The men and women were led into a poorly constructed building, the men disappeared through a doorway on one side as the women were instructed to go through one on the other side.

"Undress and hand your clothes over for treatment," a male trusty barked out at them.

Anna hesitated as she looked around. All the trusties lining the room were male, and they watched with lascivious smirks as the women prisoners removed their clothing. A word of protest caught in Anna's throat as the faces of the convict trusties melded into the faces of those who had raped her in the Black Mariah and those who had participated in the "Kolyma tram" on the transport ship.

Other women cried out in protest, "No!"

The few soldiers among the trusties quieted their wailing with a threatening gesture of the truncheon.

Anna undressed, her face blushing even in the freezing cold room as she handed her clothes and shoes over to the waiting hands of a leering trusty.

"We...we'll get them back, won't we?" a woman about her same age asked in a whisper.

"Yeah," the trusty grinned, "sure you will."

Anna looked longingly at the jacket Ivan had given her, knowing she'd likely not see it again—or if she did, it would be on the back of one of the *blatnye*. Her guts wrenched sharply when she remembered her cup hidden in the pocket. She didn't have long to mourn the loss of her only worldly possessions. Covering her breasts with an arm and her crotch with her other hand, she was forced down a hallway. Trembling with fear and cold, she followed the other women as they walked one at a time through a gauntlet of male soldiers and trusties. Lewd comments and an occasional fondling touch followed her down the hallway. Anna's arm was torn away from her breasts a number of times.

Their words landed like blows as she shuffled slowly down the unheated corridor.

"This one's still got some perkiness to her tits."

"Those ruby lips will feel fine wrapped around my cock."

"What's your name, bitch? I wanna' put my claim on you. I can show you what a real man feels like between your legs."

"She's a shy one. Bet she'll scream like a banshee when—"

Anna clamped her hands over her ears. She'd rather let them gawk at her breasts than hear their horrible words.

Trembling from fear and cold, exhaustion and hunger, Anna stepped through the doorway into a room lined with trusties holding razors. A soldier shoved her to one of the waiting "barbers" who leered as he demanded, "Raise your arms above your head."

Anna swallowed, closing her eyes while she did as commanded. She flinched as the icy razor touched her armpit, and the barber said, "Best hold still, woman. I wouldn't want to cut such fine flesh."

Biting her lip, Anna held as still as her shivering muscles would allow while the man shaved the hair from her armpits. When he moved down to remove her pubic hair, she choked out a cry, the tears she'd been holding back finally breaking free.

"Spread your legs. Can't have any body hair hiding the lice."

Bile rose up into Anna's throat as the barber's warm breath wafted over her thighs while he crouched before her to finish the job.

With a slap on her butt from the now standing barber, her eyes jolted open, and she lowered her arms.

"Over there now, to the baths." He gestured to an open doorway where other freshly shaved women were headed.

Anna didn't dare to hope that the water was warm...but maybe it wouldn't be near freezing. She entered the room, which wasn't really a "bath" but just a line of faucets, water swirling into drains in the floor. A plump woman handed her a sliver of black soap and instructed, "Lather up good, the guards are watching, and if they don't think you've been thorough, they'll lather you up themselves."

With a quick glance at the male guards on the far side of the room, Anna trudged through the ice-cold water accumulating on the floor and stopped in front of an available faucet. Her hands trembled as she stuck them beneath the running water. She struggled to grip the soap sliver with her numb fingers but was able to make enough of a lather to wash the grime from her body.

"Hair too." A guard stepped over to her and shoved her head under the faucet.

Anna gasped, then hurried to use what was left of the soap to lather up her hair, teeth chattering. She gulped some of the water as she bent to rinse the weak lather from her hair, knowing she might regret it later, as the water hadn't been boiled. The guard must have been satisfied with her efforts because he stomped back to his post.

A soldier shoved her out into another hallway, where she stood shivering with a few other prisoners, water dripping from their hair and naked bodies. When she reached the front of the line, the male trusty—big and burly, reminding her again of the horror in the Black Mariah—commanded gruffly, "Spread your legs."

Her muscles were slow to react. The man "helped" her along by shoving his knee between her legs and muscling one to the side a couple of feet, gripping her upper arm painfully to keep her from slipping to the floor. He dipped his bare fingers in a tub of tar ointment, then smeared the medicine between her legs.

Ushered into another room, Anna was handed a pile of clothes—not the ones she'd been wearing upon arrival, as she'd feared—and told to get dressed. The issued clothing was ill-fitting with rips and tears: the padded stockings too large, the short padded jacket missing several buttons and not nearly as warm as the one they'd taken from her, and the rubber-soled boots at least two sizes too big, with cracks through the soles and sides. At least the skirt she got was thick wool, though worn through in several places and too big for her shrunken waist. The underwear, bra, and long-sleeved tunic were in no better shape.

She dressed as quickly as her numb fingers would allow, looking longingly at the thick mittens sticking out of the pockets of some of the soldiers.

"Okay, *zeks*, line up and follow me!" The soldier pulled his fur-lined hat down over his ears, wrapped his wool scarf around his lower face, and put his mittens on before leading them out into the wind-blasted snow.

Anna ducked her head, trying to keep the biting cold from tearing at the skin of her face. Icicles formed in her wet hair before she'd even taken two steps. Night had fallen, and so had the temperature.

Sorry, Mama, she thought. *I don't think I'm going to survive this place.*

25

The weary prisoners trudged through the snow to a long, rectangular wooden building. The soldier opened the door to complaints from inside of letting the cold in.

"Get in there," he said, shoving the first in line through the doorway.

Anna's eyes adjusted to the dim light of a kerosene lamp hanging from a peg near the door. The barracks was crowded, of course, just like the one at the transport prison and her cell in the Lubyanka. She searched the rows and rows of poorly made bunk beds, all full of women leaning against the unplastered walls, the cracks stopped up with what appeared to be mud.

She pushed her way over the frozen mud floor to a small, crude table stationed near the metal stove. A hardened looking woman a few years Anna's senior—perhaps more, perhaps less—scowled as Anna was pushed from behind and bumped into her.

"Watch it, sister." On the other side of her frown, the woman was pretty, her dark eyes rimmed with thick eyelashes. Belying the gruffness of her voice, the woman made room for Anna to warm her hands at the stove.

Anna nodded her thanks and bit down on her chattering teeth, taking note of the nearly empty bucket of water sitting on the table. She'd been trying so hard to hold it together, but the reminder that her cup, along with the jacket Ivan had given her, was no longer in her possession, broke the weakly constructed dam keeping her emotions in check. Head bowed, she wiped the falling tears on her slumped shoulders.

The woman beside her sighed. "Get it together, sister. You're here now and there's nothing to be done about it." She turned to face Anna. "I'm Zoya. What's your name?"

After swallowing the lump in her throat, Anna whispered, "Anna."

"Listen, things don't have to be so hard here, Anna. You're young, pretty, still holding on to most of your womanly shape. All you need to do to make life easy here is hook up with one of the trusties." Zoya looked her up and down. "Hell, you might even be able to hook one of the camp chiefs and get assigned to the medical section or the bookkeeping office."

Anna's eyes widened, and she shook her head.

"What do you mean, 'no'? I do it. Most of us do it, those of us who still can, anyway. It's the only way to get food and to keep away from general labor." Zoya narrowed her eyes. "Or do you think you're too good to screw around? To whore yourself out like the rest of us?"

"No. No, that isn't it." Anna looked away from her, screwing her eyes shut on the intruding thoughts of gang rapes.

"I hate to break it to you, but your only chance at survival is to give in."

Anna shook her head. "I'd rather die."

Zoya grunted. "Well, then, that's exactly what's going to happen, stupid girl." She shook her head. "We'll see how fast you change your tune when they send you out to do hard labor."

Looking down at the worn rubber boots on her feet, Anna remained silent. She'd been through the worst of it—hadn't she? Been tortured in every way imaginable. She would never give in. Could never. Her traumatized mind wouldn't allow it, no matter the consequences of refusing to do whatever it took to survive. Survival was no longer at the top of her list of priorities.

"Lights-out in ten!" a guard yelled as he pounded on the door.

Anna searched the crowded barracks for a free bunk. Everything was filthy to go along with the oppressive odor that hung in the air. Some of the bunks were walled-off with hanging rags, and as Anna turned her attention to one of them, she heard sounds like rutting pigs to go along with the rhythmic swishing of the make-shift curtains. She slapped a hand to her mouth and turned to face Zoya with wide eyes.

Zoya shrugged. "They've got to finish up and get back to the men's barracks before lights-out. At least they're trying for a little privacy. Some don't even care to try." She nodded toward a man and woman going at it in one of the bunks a few feet away—the woman's skirt flipped up to her chin and the bare-assed man standing beside the bunk, thrusting with his pants down around his ankles.

A disgusted whimper fled from her throat as Anna spun away from the sight.

"You really are a prude, aren't you, Anna?" Zoya tilted her head, her eyebrows forming a V that deepened as she looked into her eyes. "No. That isn't it, is it?"

Anna tore her gaze away from the woman and looked down at her boots again. She couldn't tell her what happened in the Black Mariah. To speak it out loud would be to relive it. And she couldn't do that. Anna squeezed her eyes shut and shook her head.

"Well, never mind, then." Zoya nudged her with her shoulder. "Let's find you a place to sleep."

Exhaustion slammed into Anna with the force of a charging rhino, and she trudged along behind Zoya to the back of the barracks. All the bunks were overflowing with women. Zoya pointed to a lower bunk where two women lay head to feet. "This is my bunk. You can sleep underneath for tonight."

A stabbing jolt inside her chest reminded her of the last time she'd slept under a bunk like this. But one last look around before a guard took the kerosene lamp, and her fatigue won out. She curled up under the wooden planks of Zoya and friends' bunk, and shivered until she fell into a fitful sleep.

☭

The sound of her own voice woke Anna from the nightmare. The word "no" still rang in her ears as her heart raced out of control and tears froze to her cheeks. Her chest rose and fell rapidly with her panting breaths as lingering images from the nightmare flashed in her mind. Nikolai, twitching on the sidewalk as his blood pooled beneath him. Anna, sobbing, draped over his chest. The NKVD officers and the criminals from the back of the Black Mariah tearing at her clothes as she mourned and screamed.

"Hey, sister," Zoya whispered as she hung her head over the side of the bunk. "Slow down your breathing. You're okay. It was just a dream."

Anna wished it had just been a dream. Wished that this was all just a horrible, long dream and she would wake up in her family's apartment, go to work at the sewing factory, and meet up with Nikolai after work. But this was reality. The true dream was her life before, when she'd thought she could stay safe by being careful. That was the fantasy. No one was safe in the Soviet Union.

Biting down on the collar of her coat to stifle a sob, Anna concentrated on taking slow, deep breaths until her heartrate returned to normal. She stared out into the darkness from under the bunk, listening to snoring, breathing, and occasional whispers of her fellow prisoners until a loud siren signaled it was morning.

"Get up!" The tiny amount of warmth that had remained from the ashes in the stove was whisked away by the frigid wind blowing through the now open door. "Those who have a work assignment, make your way to the mess hall. Those without an assignment, line up in front of your bunks!"

Anna crawled out from under the bunk before the other women could block her in.

Zoya stood beside her and squeezed her arm. "Just think about what I said last night. It's a small price to pay to stay out of the forest." She wrapped a wool scarf around her head and face, buttoned up her coat, and put on a pair of mittens before heading out the door.

Standing among the new arrivals and at least a dozen women who looked too sick or old to work, Anna stomped her feet and slapped her arms to get her circulation going.

When the last of the women with jobs filed out, the guard stepped back outside, saying, "They're all yours. New batch came in last night."

A group of trusties—criminals—sauntered in and slowly, deliberately strolled down the center of the barracks, ogling the women standing in front of the bunks. Inspecting them like cattle. Anna shrank back into the corner before they reached her, cowering there as she clutched her coat tight around her chest.

A couple of the trusties stopped to talk to women before reaching her, but when she glanced up from gazing at the floor, three of the men approached, staring at her with vile grins on their faces. She started shaking her head before they even reached her.

"This one's a pretty one," one of the men grabbed her face and lifted her chin. "What's yer name, doll?"

Anna clamped her mouth tight and fought the tears prickling in her eyes.

"Yeah," the shorter of the three men said, "I'd take her."

"You two clear out. This one's mine." The big man pushed the other two away and sat on the bunk next to where Anna stood. "Have a seat, darlin'." He didn't wait for her to comply as he pulled her down beside him. "What's your name?"

"Anna," she whispered as she searched for a guard—not that she expected them to help her.

"I'm Isaak." The criminal laid his hand on her knee and squeezed.

Staring at the sleeve of his new padded jacket, she forced herself to sit there, biting her lip as every instinct told her to get up and run.

"I have my own cabin. Why don't you come visit me? We'll have some privacy there." He leaned in close to her ear, his rancid breath warming her cheek. "I have a hotplate and a frying pan. We can fry us up some potatoes and have a good time. I'll make sure you get assigned to an easy job."

Anna's throat froze on the words she wanted to say. *No! Never!*

"Come on, now." He patted her thigh. "I can get you into the kitchen or the bookkeeping office. Or maybe you'd prefer the sewing shop or laundry? I can get you in there too. What do you say? Let's go." He stood and held his hand out to her.

She found her voice then. "No. I won't. I...I *can't*." She tried to think of an excuse to give him, but could only come up with, "I'm engaged."

His deep-throated laughter filled the long building, and others looked over at them. "So what! I'm married. None of that matters. The rules are different here in the Gulags, bitch."

Anna shook her head, fear rising in her chest, making it hard to breathe.

"Now come on. I'm not gonna offer again."

"No. No, please. I can't."

The slap caught her off guard, though it shouldn't have. Brutality had been her reality for months now. She held a hand to her stinging cheek and looked up at him defiantly.

"Do you think you're too good for me, bitch?" He grabbed the front of her coat and lifted her to her feet. "Do you?"

Shaking her head again, she pushed against his broad chest, trying to move him away from her. *He's going to rape me. He's just going to take what he wants. They all do. I'm just an animal to them.*

"Please," she pushed harder, "please just leave me alone. There are others who are more than willing. Please leave me alone."

He let go of her coat with a shove that toppled her back into the bunk. "I'll assign you to general labor. You won't last a month out there."

"I don't care." Anna's voice was a whisper.

With a growl, Isaak said, "Don't come crawling back to me when you're a last-legger. When your breasts are hanging down like little dried-out sacks and your ass is nothing but sagging, wrinkled skin."

Anna looked at his feet. His fur-lined boots.

"Last chance."

She shook her head, still looking down.

"Fine!" he roared. "You're going out with the logging crew. Right now! Stand up, bitch!"

As she pushed herself up to stand, Isaak grabbed her roughly by the arm and jerked her toward him. He growled in her ear. "You'll come crawling to me tonight, begging me to take what's under that skirt. Logging's just a dry execution. You won't last a month."

He drug her past the other trusties and women, out into the bitter cold, where he shouted to a warmly dressed female prisoner exiting a cabin. "Svetlana!"

The woman strolled over, adjusting her scarf around her face so only her eyes showed.

"Take this *zek* to the logging camp." Isaak didn't wait for a reply as he turned and stomped back to the women's barracks.

Svetlana scowled, her eyebrows crouching down below the scarf for a few seconds as she glared at Anna. "Like I have nothing better to do with my time." She took a few steps toward the front of the camp then turned to her. "Well, come on! I'm only going to take you to the head of the trail. You can find your way from there on your own."

Before they'd even reached the front gate, the snow had found its way through the cracks in Anna's boots. Her feet slid around inside them like a child's wearing her father's shoes. Her toes were numb, and she pulled her hands up into the sleeves of the short, padded jacket they'd issued her, folding her arms about her chest to stave off the frigid air.

The guard at the gate nodded them through after Svetlana explained Isaak's directive, adjusting his rifle over his shoulder as he went back to the fire barrel, laughing with his comrade.

Anna figured they'd gone about a half mile outside of camp when the woman stopped at a trail where the snow had been tramped down, leading into the thick trees of the forest. Pointing to it, she said, "Follow that. You'll run into them in about three miles."

"Wait," Anna said, "what do I do when I get there? What do I say?"

Svetlana was already several paces away, heading back toward the camp. "Ask for the brigadier. He'll set you straight."

Setting out on the trail, Anna noted that the snow to either side of it was at least two feet tall, well over the tops of her boots. She wondered how long it would take for frostbite to turn her toes to deadened lumps of stone. Or her nose. She'd seen a picture once of a man who'd lost his nose to frostbite while trying to climb some mountain. She tucked her chin and covered her nose as best she could with the collar of her jacket, tilting her head toward the ground to take the brunt of the wind to the crown of her head. Her mind became as numb as her fingers and toes as she trudged along without coherent thought.

Anna had no idea how long she'd been walking before spotting the first of the workers sawing at the trunk of a tall tree. She approached them, but it took her several tries at speaking to get her voice to work loud enough for them to notice her. Finally, as one of the men turned and spotted her, she was able to ask, "Where is the brigadier?"

With a nod of his head, he said, "You'll find him over by the fire."

She followed the sounds of men and women working through the trees, muffled by the thick layer of snow, until she saw the smoke of a fire wending its way to the sky above through the branches of trees, like a stream picking its way along a rocky bed.

Several men stood near the fire, but only one of them was dressed like a worker—the others were guards, guns slung over their shoulders.

"Where'd you come from," one of the guards said as she made her way to them.

"C...camp. I was...I was told to find the brigadier for an assignment."

"Well," the man looked her up and down, "you found me. Come with me."

Anna followed him into the woods, the snow topping her boots, her frozen skirt making the trudge even more difficult. They stopped amid a group of thin, haggard looking women cutting the branches off the fallen trees with axes.

The brigadier pointed to a couple of axes laying in the tramped down snow next to a tree. "Grab one of those and get to work. Work norms are the same for women as for men. You'll get fed according to how much you get done."

Only one of the women looked up as Anna lifted the heavy axe, her frozen, bare hands struggling to hold the thick wooden handle. She watched for a moment as the women pounded away at the branches, barely managing to make a dent in them.

The woman who had looked up as she approached, voice muffled by her icy scarf, said with scorn, "What are you doing here? A looker like you just has to spread her legs to stay safe from the general work detail."

Anna shook her head and took a whack at a branch of the fallen tree, the dull axe hitting it with a thud.

The woman growled, "Idiot, you'd best lose any bourgeoise thoughts of virtue—and fast—it's only a matter of weeks before you lose those looks out here, then no guard or trusty will want you, and you'll be worked to death right beside us ugly ones."

There was no more talk from any of the women. Steam from Anna's panting breaths drifted up into the trees as she lifted the heavy axe, whacking over and over at the same thick branch. By the time the brigadier called for the supper break, she couldn't lift her arms or feel her fingers.

She followed the other women over to the fire and waited in line to receive her rations, only to be told by the guard when she reached the front, "No rations for you, you came late."

Standing off from the others, Anna held her hands tightly under her armpits and stomped her feet—but it was no use. She'd never be warm again.

26

———————

The trek back to camp in the dark seemed to be twice as far as the trek in. Anna's muscles were weak not only from the hard labor, but also from lack of food. She stumbled along toward the back of the pack of prisoners—freezing, starving. A skeletal man tripped and fell beside her. He struggled to get to his feet, too weak to accomplish the task.

One of the guards unleashed his dog. "Get him!"

The man cried out, "No! Please. I can—" He broke off with a shriek as the dog's teeth sank into his leg. His shrieks merged with the dog's bestial growls to form an off-key symphony of nightmares as the animal made its way to his throat.

Anna froze, unable to take her eyes off the grizzly scene.

Another guard slammed the butt of his rifle into her ribs. "Keep moving or you're next."

She somehow found the strength to walk faster as the prisoner's screams faded and finally ended with the report of a gunshot that knocked the snow from the surrounding trees. Anna made her way to the middle of the pack and somehow compelled her weak muscles to keep pace.

Upon reaching camp, they were forced to line up for headcount as the guards called out the assigned numbers that were sewn to their coats. Thankfully, the numbers added up, and they were finally released to line up again in front of the mess hall for dinner. Anna's work group had been the last to return to camp, and she'd been afraid they'd missed dinner.

The men and women lined up with some shoving and cursing, and Anna joined the queue toward the back, relieved she'd made it back in time. As she got closer, she watched as the guard ladled watery soup into the waiting bowls, cups, and other containers belonging to the prisoners in front of her. Her heart sank. She didn't have anything to hold the soup. Or water.

The trusty looked at her with a bored expression as she stepped up to his cart. "No bowl, no soup." He handed her a small chunk of bread and nodded to another steaming pot. "Get a drink of warm water with the community cup, but be quick about it."

Anna swallowed the water as quickly as her dry throat would allow, savoring the warmth of the gritty liquid as it slid into her stomach.

Trudging back to the barracks, Anna knew her feet and hands were festering with blisters she was unable to feel. Inside, the barracks was dark compared to the compound, which was illuminated with flood lights. The single kerosene lamp hung by the door. She found her way to the back near Zoya's bunk and lowered herself to the frozen-mud floor, resting her head and arms on her bent knees for a few moments. She couldn't remember the last time she'd had anything to eat. It had been days, she was sure.

She lifted her head and crouched on the floor to eat her bread.

A shadow blocked the scant light from the lamp, and Anna looked up to see Zoya standing over her.

"You ready to lose your useless honor and join us sinners in the land of sex-for-security?" Zoya asked.

Anna blanched, nearly choking on the dry bread. Her exhausted mind rushed to remind her of her tearing flesh, the blood, the pain, the stench of the disgusting animals in the back of the Black Mariah. She shook her head and dropped the remaining portion of bread to her lap, no longer hungry.

Zoya shrugged. "Suit yourself. You'll be dead within a month."

Meeting her gaze with fierce resolve, Anna whispered, "There are worse things than death."

With a snort, Zoya replied, "You're already dead, then," and walked away.

Anna stared after her until losing her in the crowd. She looked down at the bread in her lap. Though her appetite had vanished, she knew she couldn't afford to waste any food. She slipped the small portion into her jacket pocket, saving it for later.

Heavy, booted footsteps came toward her then stopped right in front of her, the toes of the boots nearly touching hers. Her chest constricted, cutting off her breath as she looked up into the sneering face of Isaak.

"Last chance, Anna Levitskaya. I have a pair of nice, warm mittens, sausage and potatoes to fill your stomach, and this"—he thrust his pelvis toward her—"if you come back to my cabin with me right now."

Hunger churned in her stomach at the mention of the food—it'd been so long since she'd tasted potatoes, and sausage...she hadn't had that since Mama's birthday. She held back a sudden sob at the thought of her mother. The hunger pangs evolved to a wave of nausea as he shoved the bulge in his pants toward her face. Slapping a hand to her mouth, Anna closed her eyes, shaking her head.

Isaak grabbed her by the hair, pulling her to her feet. Spittle flew from his mouth as he shouted, "You think you're too good for me?" He jerked her face close to his. "I don't need your permission, bitch. I'll just take you right here, on this filthy floor like you deserve, like the traitor to the Motherland you are."

He pushed her to the floor. Anna scrambled to back away from him, but he stomped on her leg as she tried to crawl away. He grinned, seeming to find joy in her terror, as he unbuttoned his pants.

Shaking her head, tears and snot tracing lines in the dirt on her face, all she could do was wheeze, "No. No. No," over and over.

Anna had no idea where she came from, but when she looked up again, Zoya stepped up to Isaak and caressed his arm. "Why ya wasting your time on her? Let's go back to your cabin and I'll show you and the boys a new trick I learned."

Isaak scowled at her. "Back off. I'm gonna teach this bitch a lesson." He bent over and pulled at Anna's skirt as she kicked and cried.

Zoya shrugged and stepped away. "Your loss. Lev almost lost his mind when I tried it on him. Gave me an extra bread ration when I was done. But if you want to waste your energy on her..."

Isaak straightened up and licked his lips. "What's your trick?"

Leaning in, Zoya whispered in his ear as his eyes grew wide. He licked his lips again and grinned like a wolf about to devour its prey. He kicked Anna and growled, "This little fascist will have to wait." He hurriedly buttoned his pants before grabbing Zoya's arm and pulling her out of the barracks.

Anna pushed her skirt down and hugged her knees to her chest. Many of the other prisoners stared at her, talking in hushed tones.

"That is not at all like Zoya."

"What's she playing at?"

"Now you're gonna owe her."

Every muscle in Anna's body trembled with cold and nausea. How was she going to keep Isaak away from her? And not just him, but all the other men who knew they could just take whatever they wanted? She didn't understand why the criminals, the *blatnye*, were treated so much better than the politicals—most of whom, she'd come to realize, were innocent—and were given free rein in the prison camps. Anna rocked back and forth. Death was the only way to avoid him—his death or hers. Could she take another life? Even one so vile as Isaak's? No. She didn't think she could. Could she take her own life? Again, she thought not, at least not overtly.

Anna's thoughts were interrupted when a guard stomped into the barracks and pointed to her and two other women. "You three— firewood duty. Bring it to the guard quarters."

Muscles protesting, Anna pushed herself to her feet and slogged back out into the freezing night to find fuel for the guards' fire while the one in the women's barracks remained cold. She followed the other two prisoners, unsure of where to "find" firewood in the snow- covered camp.

"Go look over where they're building a new barracks. You can grab any broken boards but leave the good ones." The woman pointed in the direction she wanted Anna to go, then headed off in the opposite direction.

It took at least an hour for Anna to find an armful of wood and another twenty minutes for her to find the guards' quarters where she dropped it from her shaky arms next to the door. She followed two guards back to the women's barracks and stepped inside just in time for an extra headcount.

"Find a spot to plant yourself, then stand still!" one of the guards yelled.

Anna searched the crowded barracks until she spotted Zoya, then she walked toward her, nodding when Zoya's eyes met hers with a scowl and a return nod. Anna stood near the cold stove, shivering, while the guards counted.

"Lights out!" one yelled when they were satisfied with the numbers. The barracks plunged into darkness as the guards took the only lamp and shut the door, locking it from the outside.

Anna curled up on the floor next to Zoya's bunk, the cold keeping her awake only for a short time as utter exhaustion won out.

A loud siren woke Anna from her dreamless sleep. She stood and followed Zoya and the others as they pushed through the deep snow that had fallen overnight to line up at the mess hall. Upon reaching the front of the line, Anna looked longingly at the watery gruel as the trusty ladled it into Zoya's bowl.

"No bowl, no gruel," the trusty repeated to Anna.

Her spirits dropped even further as she realized there was no bread being handed out this morning, either. She hurriedly drank some of the warm salted water using the community cup, then moved to stand near Zoya, digging the small chunk of bread from last night out of her pocket.

Zoya leaned over to her and whispered, "Find yourself a tin can or something today. You can't keep missing meals."

Anna nodded, wondering why the woman cared.

In the relative warmth of the mess hall, the cold relented just enough for the body and hair lice to wriggle around and bite at her skin. Anna scratched at her scalp with torn and broken fingernails. Blisters and raw sores stung at her feet and the palms of her hands.

Another siren sounded, alerting the prisoners to roll-call and inspection. Anna found the brigade she'd been assigned to yesterday and lined up with them in front of the gate as the guards stood with their guns on either side of each group. A guard and a work-assigner walked among the columns, the work-assigner holding a finely planed signboard on which he wrote the number of workers in each brigade and the number of brigades.

Anna's brigade was checked off first and sent out on the three-mile trek through the new layer of deep snow, five prisoners abreast as the front row blazed a trail, the guards yelling orders from behind the group. They traded places whenever the guards determined those in front were slowing down. When it was Anna's row's turn to battle with the two to three feet drifts, the snow fell over the tops of her boots beneath her skirt that froze around her legs, making the chore even harder to accomplish. After only a few minutes, she was ready to lay down and let the guard-dogs end her life. The memory of the man's screams from the night before was all that kept her pushing forward.

By the time the guards called for a change, Anna had fallen behind, almost to the front of the second row. The only thing that likely saved her from getting the butt of a gun to her back or head—or worse—was that the guards were bringing up the rear and couldn't see that she was shirking.

Her mind grew numb as the trek seemed to take twice as long as the day before. She couldn't help but think of the mittens Isaak had offered her as she shoved her hands deeper into the pits of her arms. Then her weakening mind turned to the "kept" women who'd flounced off to their easy, light-duty jobs that morning—laundry, clerks, assistants, cleaners, hospital workers. They didn't even have to leave camp. They worked in warm buildings, were fed better and given tobacco. They were protected... Was Anna fighting a losing battle? Should she just give in now, before she lost her fingers to frostbite—or her life to starvation? She'd almost been raped again last night. The criminals and guards would just take what they wanted anyway—and she'd get nothing for it.

Anna slogged along, her feet sliding in the too-big boots that did nothing to keep her feet warm or dry. A flashback of the Black Mariah caused her to stumble. No, she refused to freely give herself to those animals. She'd had the courage to resist denouncing anyone while being tortured and interrogated, she could resist this. Ducking her head against the biting wind, her thoughts turned to Nikolai. Her heart wrenched in her chest as she recalled his insistence that they wait until they were married before giving themselves to each other. And now he was dead, and she was in this frozen hell, and he would never be her first—and only—now. She thought of how proud her mama would have been to know she and Nikolai were waiting. They didn't attend church like Mama and Papa had before the revolution— that was a good way to get on the wrong side of the NKVD for sure— but Mama had taught her daughters about God's love.

When they reached the work area deep in the forest, the guards tied ropes to the trees around them to show where the boundaries were. If a prisoner stepped one-half of a foot outside of those boundaries, they'd be shot instantly.

Anna took up an axe and copied the others as they tamped down the snow around whichever tree they were assigned to work on. She knew they'd never even come close to making the "work norms" that had been set for them, it was impossible even under the best of conditions. The snow slowed down the work even more—and the prisoners would pay for that with decreased rations that were already too little to survive on.

By the time the guards called for the supper break, Anna didn't think she'd be able to lift her hands to her mouth. The brigadier handed her a small piece of salty herring, and she moved off by herself. Oh, how she wished to sit down for this thirty-minute break. But everything was covered in snow—and she didn't know if she'd be able to get up again anyway. She stared out at the icy river as she chewed the frozen piece of fish.

A man stepped up next to her, causing her to flinch before she recognized him as a fellow *zek*—one of the so-called "socially hostile" prisoners—and more likely than not, he wasn't a threat to her. She scoffed inwardly at the absurdness of it all. How the criminal element —the "socially friendly"—prisoners were treated well, never sent out on work details, basically ran the prison camps. And they had much shorter sentences. The world she lived in just didn't make any sense.

She and the man stood in silence for a few minutes. He held his handmade cigarette out to her, offering her a drag. She gratefully took the scant tobacco rolled in a piece of newspaper and closed her eyes as she breathed in the smoke before handing it back to him and finally looking into his face. She figured him to be an older man by the wrinkles apparent next to his eyes.

"My name is Pyotr." His voice was softer than she thought she'd ever hear out there.

"I'm Anna."

"Is this your first Gulag?"

Anna nodded.

He took another drag on the cigarette. "I've been moved around a few times in the four years I've been in the Kolyma." He tamped out the remaining bit of his smoke and put the butt in his pocket then wrapped his scarf around the bottom of his face, covering the gray stubble. "I'm a priest. That's my crime."

"Break over! Back to work, you sloggers!" the brigadier yelled.

27

Anna could only concentrate on putting one foot in front of the other on the trek back to camp. She wondered fleetingly how far below zero it was. She had no reference point for this icy hell. Her hands, feet, and face were numb, and her muscles were ready to give out. The wind blew the snow against her cracked lips and froze the snot around her nostrils.

Again, their brigade was the last to enter camp, but they made it just before the mess hall shut down for the night. Anna's dinner consisted of a small chunk of bread and a cup of warm water as she still didn't have anything to use for the soup. She ate half the bread and shoved the rest in her jacket pocket just as the siren signaled for the prisoners to line up for headcount.

She'd barely made it to the barracks when a guard sent her back out into the frigid cold to collect firewood again. Remembering what Zoya had told her that morning, she searched not only for firewood, but for some sort of container in which she could get gruel and soup. She wandered toward the mess hall, slowly making her way to the back as she picked up small twigs and fallen branches. Next to the large metal barrel they used to burn trash in, something silver glinted just beneath the snow. Anna bent to inspect it, and she'd never been so happy in her life to see a tin can. Further inspection showed it to be intact, and she slipped it inside her jacket pocket with relief. She'd have gruel come morning!

☭

The morning siren sounded, and Anna checked for the tin can in her pocket, breathing easier upon feeling it there. After lights-out, she'd eaten the bread she'd saved from dinner last night, knowing—hoping—she'd have a little more to eat come morning.

She headed to the mess hall with the others, almost smiling with cracked lips as she held her can out to receive the ladleful of watered-down barley from the kitchen worker. She put the bread in her pocket and almost wept as the warmth of the gruel settled in her empty stomach.

After headcount the trek to the worksite began. The added calories, small though they were, and the lack of snowfall overnight made the journey easier. Pyotr nodded to her, and she nodded back, as they weren't allowed to talk to each other while marching. Anna glanced at the guards, guns, and dogs walking on either side of the brigade of prisoners.

As the guards stretched the rope around the area they were to work in that day, the brigadier gruffly gave out the assignments. He pointed at Anna and the woman behind her. "You two will cut down trees." He handed an axe to Anna and a two-person saw to the other woman.

Anna looked to her partner, hoping she knew how to cut down a tree, because Anna sure didn't. But that was too much to hope for, as the woman stared at the cumbersome saw for a moment before looking up at Anna with a worried shrug.

They made their way to a tree within the roped-off limits, Anna watching others as they got to work with axes and saws. She and the woman stopped at a smaller tree that was still so big around Anna feared it would take them a week to fell it. She looked at her new partner and cleared her throat before saying quietly, "I think we need to use the axe first, to make a starting point for the saw."

The woman nodded and set the saw on the ground, out of the way. "I'm Eva. We can take turns with the axe if you want to start."

Nodding, she replied, "I'm Anna," before struggling to lift the heavy axe to take her first swing. Her grip on the wooden handle faltered as the axe head hit the frozen tree, and showers of chips flew in her and Eva's faces. After four strikes, Anna's strength was depleted, but she took one more swing, glancing the dull metal off the trunk of the tree.

Eva's turn yielded about the same, as Anna stood watching with her icy hands clamped tight under her armpits, stomping her feet to keep from freezing to death. It might have made a difference if either of them could hit the same mark more than once in a row, but after each of them had taken several turns, it just looked like a woodpecker had been pecking away at the bark in various places. The two men working near them had downed two trees and were close to finishing off their third by the time the brigadier called for the first break, a ten-minute smoke break.

Anna moved to the edge of the roped-off area so she could stare down at the icy river, her arms trembling from the cold and muscle fatigue.

Pyotr again came to stand next to her, holding his lit cigarette out to her. "This is my second time being sentenced to a camp."

Anna raised her eyebrows as she took a drag on the cigarette then handed it back to him.

"I see it as a big game of solitaire, my life these last two decades. Prison, exile, camp, prison, exile, camp." He drew smoke into his lungs then let it out through pursed lips.

"They...they can do that? Send you back?" Anna knew the question was a naïve one as soon as it left her lips. Of course they could send you back. They could do whatever they wanted.

"Indeed they can." He stared off at the river. "This time when they 'summoned' me to the Lubyanka, the thieves stole my priest's hat. The government official there proposed that I become a member of the Synod." A bitter laugh sounded in his throat. "The official said 'I thought you might allow yourself some respite from prison.' But, I refused."

Anna shook her head. "Why?"

"Ahh," a grim smile spread across his cracked lips, "because it is not a pure synod—not a pure church. They only want those who will have one ear turned to heaven and the other to the Lubyanka."

Quietly, Anna asked, "How did this happen? What happened to truth and honor?"

"We are all to blame. The citizens of this once great country."

"But it's the government that's doing this. How is it our fault?"

"Because people just allowed the lies to proliferate, accepted lies as truth even though they—we—knew they were lies. We've become a country full of people who are afraid to speak out. Afraid to speak the truth." His fists curled up into balls as he whispered angrily, "That's where totalitarianism starts—citizens giving up their right to free speech."

"Back to work!" shouted the brigadier.

Anna nodded her understanding to the priest as he put out the burning end of the stub of cigarette and placed it carefully in his jacket pocket.

Wind whipped the crystal-like fallen snow about her as she returned to the tree.

Eva stood looking up at it. "I think we should forget about the axe. Let's just try to saw through this thing."

"Okay."

They each grabbed a handle of the two-person saw—Anna glancing with jealousy at Eva's worn gloves—and placed the teeth on the rough bark of the tree. Anna stumbled as Eva pulled the saw toward herself, not quite expecting her to start. Then they got the hang of it, jerkily...for a couple of minutes. The saw got stuck, and this time Eva stumbled at the unexpected halt to its movement.

Time and time again the saw stuck, and the women struggled to get it moving again. They'd hardly made a dent in the tree when the brigadier called for the supper break.

Anna lined up to receive her ration, and when she and Eva reached the guard handing it out, the brigadier scowled. "Only partial rations for these two shirkers."

The guard broke a small piece of bread in half and handed one chunk to each of them, no herring. Anna took her measly ration over to where Pyotr stood in their earlier spot. She was strangely drawn to the man. Unlike the fear she felt around others of his gender, she trusted him, and that surprised her. Maybe it was his age. Or that he was a religious man. Most likely, it was a combination of those things plus that he treated her like a human—looked at her without leering, talked to her even if she didn't respond.

The two ate their scant meal in silence—Pyotr with twice as much as her, but still not enough to live off of for long. When he finished, he took his gloves off while he rolled a cigarette with his shaking hands.

Offering it to her after lighting it at the guards' fire, he took up his story where he'd left off as if several hours hadn't passed. "So, I refused the offer to join the Synod, refused to denounce my religion, and they arrested me. Again. 58-10—Counterrevolutionary Propaganda!" He shook his head. "Another tenner. Barely survived the last one..."

"That's horrible." Anna gave the cigarette back to him.

"The most horrible part is that they sentenced several nuns for private notes they'd written each other at the same time as my sentencing. The Soviet government is very afraid of *words* it seems."

"What do you mean?"

"To quote Article Fifty-eight, Section Ten: 'propaganda or agitation, containing an appeal for the overthrow, subverting, or weakening of the Soviet power...and equally the dissemination or preparation or possession of literary material of similar content.'"

"What does all that mean, though?"

"It means any idea that goes against that of the Soviet government, anything that doesn't coincide with or rise to the level of intensity of the ideas expressed in the state-run newspaper on any particular day, equals ten years hard labor. After all—anything which *does not strengthen* must *weaken* the great Motherland. We must all *fit in, coincide* with their beliefs or else be guilty of *subversion*." He took a long drag on the cigarette then looked out toward the river as he whispered, "Woe unto them that call evil good, and good evil; that put darkness for light, and light for darkness; that put bitter for sweet, and sweet for bitter."

"Isaiah 5:20," Anna said softly.

Pyotr looked at her with surprise.

She shrugged. "My mama quoted that one quite a bit. But the question I have is this: when can we expect the 'woe' for the evil ones?" She sighed.

"All in the Lord's time, my dear."

2 8

The tree and the saw continued to mock Anna and Eva until neither of them could lift their arms. Snow had fallen from the branches as they struggled, finding its way into the collar of Anna's coat and further inducing hypothermia. As the saw slammed to a stop for what must have been the hundredth time, nearly toppling Anna to the frozen ground, she was ready to give up. The look of defeat on Eva's face proved she felt the same.

A shrill whistle from one of the guards signaled the end of the work shift. The prisoners piled the tools up against a tree then covered them with a tarp.

The march back to camp grew worse as dark clouds rolled in and the wind picked up. Anna's arm strength was as far below zero as the temperature, and she couldn't even lift her hands to the protection of her armpits. Instead, they dangled at her sides. She couldn't feel her fingers anyway, and her sluggish thoughts rested on the idea that she no longer cared if she lost all of her digits to frostbite.

A woman a few paces in front of her fell to the snow-packed ground and didn't even try to get up. She folded her arms and closed her eyes. Anna bent to help her as a guard closed in, and the woman opened her eyes, staring into the darkening sky, and her mouth tilted into the tiniest of smiles as she said, "I'm going home." Her head fell to the side, eyes still open and mouth slack.

Anna stepped back as the guard reached the woman. He nudged her with his boot then dragged her body to the side of the tramped down snow and looked up at the chief guard with questioning eyes.

"Leave her, we'll gather the body tomorrow."

Anna gave the woman one last look then glanced up at the gathering storm clouds and rejoined the march before the guards set the dogs after her.

Anna's work brigadier motioned her and Eva to the back of the line when they reached the mess hall. She looked at her sawing partner who just scowled back at her. As they approached the server, Anna clumsily pulled the treasured tin can from her jacket and held it toward him.

"These two didn't even fulfill fifteen percent of their norm, and I don't intend to throw away precious food on traitors who can't fulfill their norms." He looked from one to the other of them, then back at the server. "Give them only fifteen percent of a ration."

The man shoved a scant piece of bread at each of them and waved off Anna's can when she held it out toward the pot of soup. "No soup for shirkers."

Anna's shoulders dropped, and she lowered her pounding head. She dipped some warm water into her can, took a bite of the bread and put the rest in her pocket, then headed back out into the cold toward the barracks. She didn't want to watch other prisoners slurping the watery soup or eating their larger rations of the black bread.

Before reaching the barracks, the siren sounded and, like a trained animal, Anna trudged to the front of the compound for headcount. Weakness drenched her like a crashing wave. Her muscles quivered as she stood there, slapping her hands against her legs to keep from freezing. Her stomach knotted as if it were eating itself from the inside.

The dark clouds that had been amassing since Anna's workgroup started their trek back to camp opened up, depositing crystallized snow on the camp. The wind whipped the falling crystals, mixing it with the dirty snow covering the ground and structures. By the time the guards were satisfied with the headcount—subtracting those who had succumbed to death at or on their way to or from the work details—Anna's hair was frozen, her face, hands, and feet completely numb.

Back at the barracks Anna fought for a spot by the stove and gently rubbed her hands over the heated cast iron, grateful that a fire was burning inside it. As the feeling returned to her fingers, pain replaced the numbness, and she bit her lip to keep from groaning.

Zoya came to stand by her side, holding out an old pair of mittens to Anna, who looked at them with glazed eyes. Was she teasing her? Wanting her to grab for them just to yank them back away?

"Take them." Zoya's gruff voice broke through the fog in Anna's cold-deadened brain. Zoya pushed them toward her.

Anna took the mittens from her and looked up into her eyes, holding back tears. "Are...are you sure?"

Zoya shrugged. "They're yours. I got a new pair from one of the trusties I shack up with."

"Why are you so nice to her?" said a young Polish woman whose name Anna had yet to learn. She scowled at both Anna and Zoya. "She's too good to spread her legs to help herself—let her freeze."

"Mind your own business, Basha." Zoya waved her away.

Leaning closer to Zoya, Anna asked in a whisper, "Why *are* you so nice to me?"

Zoya shrugged. "Maybe you remind me of someone."

A bunk near Zoya's had an open spot that night—it had belonged to the woman who had died on the trail back from the forest that day. For the first time since arriving, Anna slept on a hard, wooden bunk, shared with two other women, instead of curled up on the frozen floor.

Among the usual sounds of sexual activity that Anna would never get used to hearing, she focused in on the conversations happening around her as she tried to get comfortable on the wooden rack.

"Are they really giving us a day off tomorrow?"

"That's what my foreman said. I can't remember the last time that happened. It's been months."

"Yeah, at least three months. And they're *supposed* to give us two days off per month."

That statement brought about a round of embittered laughter.

Anna, stomach churning from hunger, drifted off to sleep before the guard came to take their lamp and lock them in for the night. Hopes of a day off from the grinding work of the logging camp floated in her head.

☭

A nudge from behind woke Anna in the dim light of early morning straining through the small barred window high up on the back wall of the barracks.

"Move it. I need to pee."

Anna's weak muscles reacted slowly, resulting in a huffy sigh and a shove from her bunkmate. Her head swirled from lack of food as she forced herself to stand—all she wanted to do was lay on her bunk all day.

Swaying on her feet, eyes closed, Anna waited for her bunkmate to return from using the pail before laying back down. She curled her hands inside the mittens, glad for at least that added layer of warmth even as she wished for a blanket.

Unused to having a day off, most of the women were up and mulling about before any guard or trusty arrived to rouse them. Anna lay curled up on the bunk after her two bunkmates vacated the space.

Zoya sauntered over. "Scoot," she said.

Anna scooted back on the bunk but remained laying down.

Sitting on the edge of the wooden slats, Zoya asked, "What are your plans for the day—in the unlikely event that they actually allow us a day off?"

Fatigue enveloped her, increasing at the thought of leaving the uncomfortable bunk. She shrugged, wincing at the pain it caused in her neck and shoulders. "This." Forcing the single word out caused her to have a coughing fit.

Zoya waited for her to stop coughing, then turned to better face her. "You can't just lay here. The guards and trusties will see that as an invitation to help themselves to your lady parts. You can come with me to do laundry and clean yourself up if you want."

Normally, the chance to wash herself and her clothes was something she'd jump at, but the decreased rations and heavy labor had sucked every ounce of energy from her body. The only thing that compelled her into pushing herself up off the bunk, was the thought of Isaak or one of the others forcing himself upon her. She nodded, and Zoya moved out of her way. Dizziness once again attacked as she stood, and her friend, for she now thought of Zoya as such, reached out a hand to steady her.

"They should be coming to let us out for breakfast soon." Zoya drew her eyebrows together in concern. "What kind of rations have you been getting?"

Anna shook her head. "Not many. I can't even come close to making the norms out in the forest."

Zoya scowled, but kept whatever she was thinking to herself.

Anna knew what she was thinking—that if she didn't give in and shack up with one of the guards or trusties soon, she was a goner—and part of her agreed with Zoya's apparent assessment that she was crazy not to. But the bigger part, the louder part, the insisting, terrified part, screamed "no" at the very thought. She couldn't do it.

Keys rattled at the door to the barracks, and after a moment it swung open. Isaak and a few others marched in, and Anna shrunk beside Zoya.

"Camp Chief has decided to give you worthless *zeks* a day off." His eyes roved around the dim room. "But that doesn't mean you can just ignore what needs to be done around here."

His eyes landed on Anna, and he stalked over to her. "You, Anna Levitskaya, take that bucket out," he pointed to the slop bucket, brimming with human waste, "empty it, clean it, and bring it back here. Then you can go chop down the piss pyramids and haul them off."

"You mean after breakfast, right, Isaak?" Zoya asked as she rubbed up against him.

With a grunt, he glared at Anna, but nodded.

Anna released her held breath as the men departed, then checked her pocket for the tin can and followed Zoya and the others to the mess hall.

Waiting in line, Anna cleared her throat and asked Zoya, "What is a 'piss pyramid'?"

Zoya barked a disgusted laugh. "Haven't you noticed the poles outside the men's barracks? The ones with the white rag tied to the top?"

"I..." Anna frowned, trying to remember if she'd seen these poles, "I don't think I have noticed."

"I'm not surprised, leaving before daylight and coming back after dark makes it hard to see anything in camp." She rolled her eyes. "When it gets this cold, no one wants to make the long trek to the outhouses, so the men in particular, just whip it out and piss wherever they find most convenient—which most often ended up being the well-beaten paths we all use. The snow would have little yellow spots all over where we were walking. And come late spring— well, you can imagine the stench once the snow starts melting."

Anna grimaced and nodded.

"So, the geniuses that run this place decided to fix it by putting up these poles outside the barracks and announcing another decree.

Anyone caught peeing anywhere outside other than the outhouses or on the poles, is sentenced to ten nights in the punishment cell." Zoya looked at her and, reading the confusion still spread across her face, rolled her eyes. "That's why the piss pyramids form. And a couple of times a month someone is tasked with chopping them and carting the frozen pieces out of the camp zone."

"Oh." Anna's arm muscles cramped up at the word "chopping." But chopping frozen urine had to be easier than chopping frozen trees.

With no brigadier around to tell the server any different, and maybe in part because she was with Zoya, Anna got a full women's ration for breakfast. The thin gruel slid down her throat and warmed her belly. She couldn't make herself save any of the chunk of bread she was given this time, instead eating the whole thing as she sat with Zoya.

Zoya went off to the laundry, leaving Anna to traipse back to the barracks alone. The bucket was full to the brim and smelled like someone's insides were rotting. She didn't want to soil her new mittens, so she tucked them under the piece of twine she had tied around her skeletal waist to keep her skirt up. The bucket was far too heavy for her to carry, so she dragged it across the frozen mud floor of the barracks as the nasty contents sloshed over the side.

Nobody had told her where she was to dump the vile contents, so she dragged it all the way to the outer compound where the outhouses were, straining to lift it enough to dump it in the hole. The odor wafting up at her from the bucket and then the disturbed contents of the outhouse pit made her retch, and she struggled to hold on to the meager breakfast sitting in her stomach.

It took the rest of the day for her to find all the urine pyramids, chop them down, and dispose of them on the outskirts of camp. It shouldn't have taken that long, but her sore, weak, cramping muscles made the work difficult.

Anna trudged back to the barracks after a dinner consisting of a small chunk of black bread, warm salted water, and fish stew in which she was lucky to get a couple of pieces of slimy cabbage but no fish. She stopped to watch as several transport trucks rolled up to the gates with hundreds of prisoners stuffed into them. Shaking her head, she continued on to the women's barracks and sat on her bunk before the new prisoners were shoved inside the crowded structure.

The other women had the same thoughts as her as they all crowded in and staked claim on their bunks by sitting on them. Zoya sat next to Anna, a hardness in her eyes as she said, "One of your bunkmates, Helene, was killed while trying to escape today. I'll take her spot on your bunk."

Anna nodded then looked down at her mittened hands. The emotion that welled up inside her wasn't grief for the dead woman, but for the strong impression she got that Zoya was switching bunks in order to better protect her. And she still had no idea why. Perhaps Anna reminded her of a younger sister or friend? She didn't know, because any attempt she'd made to get Zoya to talk about her life before her arrest was met with cursing and something like "It doesn't matter. Life before may as well not have existed."

So, she sat quietly next to this rough woman who had reluctantly shown her so much kindness, and she leaned her head on Zoya's shoulder to show her gratitude without speaking, almost surprised when Zoya didn't shrug her off. Knowing it would be awhile before the new prisoners were finished with the arrival procedures, Anna closed her eyes, hoping to get some rest before the chaos of crowding more people inside the barracks ensued.

A female trusty entered and disrupted the moment of calm. "Mail!" she announced.

Anna hadn't received a package or letter since just before leaving the Lubyanka. She remained motionless except for the movement of her chest as she breathed in the fusty air of the barracks and half listened to the names being called.

"Anna Levitskaya!"

It took a moment and a bump of the shoulder from Zoya before she realized her name had been called. Then, as she forced her battered, undernourished body to stand, jumbled thoughts started dumping into her brain. *Was it a package from Mama? A letter maybe? A pardon?! Something from her sister? A friend?*

The trusty handed her an official-looking envelope with a smirk.

Anna stared at it for several moments until the trusty gave her a shove. "Get out of the way."

The envelope wasn't heavy or large enough to contain any food or clothing items as she'd hoped. Her name and prisoner number were typed on the front. Though she'd heard of people being pardoned and sent home, and the thought had briefly crossed her mind when she'd heard her name called, she didn't dare hope for it, and tamped the idea down with force.

She sat next to Zoya and removed her mittens, setting them in her lap. With shaky hands, she opened the already unsealed envelope and unfolded the official document inside.

This is to inform prisoner Anna Levitskaya (Article 58; Ten-year sentence) of her sister, Nadya Levitskaya Riazanov's declaration — enclosed herein.

Anna set the document aside and proceeded to read a copy of the declaration, written in her sister's handwriting:

I, Nadya Levitskya Riazanov, am convinced that Anna Levitskaya is an enemy of the people and I hereby renounce her and request that my relationship to her be regarded as non-existent.

Her sister's neat signature followed.

Anna dropped her hands to her lap, crumpling the papers into a ball. Dry-eyed and flush with anger and hurt, she pushed her way to the stove, opened it, and threw the papers into the flames, slamming the cast iron door before returning to sit on the bunk.

Zoya handed her the mittens she'd dropped and patted her hand. "Those on the outside sometimes have to do what they have to do to *stay* on the outside."

Anna squeezed Zoya's hand and sat in brooding silence as the new prisoners were shoved into the already overcrowded room.

29

Zoya curled around Anna like a protective hen when the lights went out. Though she was utterly drained and wanted nothing more than to sleep, her thoughts wouldn't let her. She remembered Nadya being her best friend when they were growing up—always the protective, if somewhat bossy, big sister. Things changed when Mikhail entered the picture. But how could Nadya denounce her? Didn't she know what Anna had been through in order to protect her and Mama? All the torture because she refused to denounce them? A tear slid down her cheek onto the wooden planks beneath her face.

At some point in the night, Anna drifted to sleep only to be awakened by her own whimpering as she relived the Black Mariah in her dreams. She lay shivering, her back pressed against Zoya's, as the vision faded.

The pounding on the door and rattle of keys in the lock came before daylight. All but the new prisoners shuffled out into the blasted cold. As they lined up at the mess hall, one of the men cursed the cold. "It must be thirty below out here! Do they really expect us to work in these temperatures?"

His companion snorted, a puff of white air escaping through the tightly wound scarf around his face. "Rule is no work outside if temps drop to less than *sixty* degrees below zero. We have a ways to go for that!"

Another man chimed in, "They'll still make us work, though. It's like a free day for the work norms—the chiefs write it off so the records show none of us went out to work, but they send us anyway and add whatever they squeeze out of us to the other days to raise the output percentage."

"Yep. Then the medical section writes off those who freeze to death as something else."

"And they shoot anyone having trouble making it back to camp."

Anna looked at Zoya with furrowed brows, teeth chattering.

Zoya nodded. "It's all true, sister."

They stepped inside the mess hall, which was only slightly warmer than outside there by the open door.

"S...sixty below?" Anna said, looking down at her worn padded jacket and boots.

"Yeah," Zoya scowled, "you aren't going to survive long out there —it isn't even close to getting as cold as it will yet. You really need to—"

Anna shook her head. "No. I won't do it." She knew what Zoya was going to say, and she didn't want to hear it. Didn't want the nightmare to return to her mind.

"You're so stubborn," Zoya mumbled under her breath.

The two women stood off to the side after receiving their rations, Anna holding the heated tin can of gruel in her hands to warm them. Zoya looked her up and down. "You're skin and bones, sister. Something's gotta give if you're going to survive this winter."

Anna sipped from the can to keep from answering. She knew that. But at the moment, she didn't care. She glanced at the open doorway where the wind picked up the snow from the ground and carried it off to pile up against the buildings. She'd care as soon as she stepped outside again, though.

"Alright, shirkers! Time for headcount!" a guard shouted.

Zoya reached a hand out and pulled Anna back when they neared the door. "Here," she unwrapped her scarf from around her head and face, "at least take this, stupid girl." She shoved it in Anna's hands before she could refuse—not that she would have. Zoya was off to the laundry—inside and warm—after head count, she'd be fine without it.

"Thank you." Anna donned the scarf, already thankful for the added protection from the wind and cold.

Over the next week Anna and Eva didn't even come close to making the norms that were set for them. Their productivity diminished each day as their food rations were cut and their weakness increased. They stumbled into camp each night, skin and bones, numb to their cores.

Zoya stuck close by Anna whenever she could, keeping the trusties and guards at bay. She kept her thoughts to herself, but Anna could see it in the way she looked at her sometimes that she still didn't understand why Anna refused to do what was necessary to save herself.

Sometime in the middle of the week—Anna had lost track of the days, what did it matter anyway? There were no "weekends" there—a female prisoner was somehow able to escape. It was thought she caught a ride—hidden, of course—back to Magadan on a transport truck. No one knew where she'd gone from there.

As they stood in the cold for head count that night, her absence was discovered and the guards were whipped into a fury.

One of the female brigadiers standing near Anna yelled, "Oh, I hope they catch her, the bitch! I hope they take scissors and cut off all her hair in front of the line-up!"

Anna, cold and weak and hungry, unable to form a coherent thought, said, "At least she can have a good time out in freedom for all of us."

A guard heard her.

And before releasing everyone back to their barracks, he called her forward and commanded her to stand at attention, back straight and hands down at her sides, in front of the gatehouse.

Anna's head hung as the wind tugged at her skirt and Zoya's scarf still wrapped about her head. Her feet were already numb from working in the snow and standing while the guards counted them—but this was a new kind of cold as she stood motionless in the dark of night, the only light nearby that of a bright lantern hanging above her. The temperature seemed to be dropping several degrees per minute.

The guards ordered the other prisoners back to the barracks, and soon, Anna was alone except for the two guards positioned in front of a fire barrel near the gatehouse. She gazed at the fire with deep longing, too far away from it to feel even a modicum of its heat. She shifted from one foot to the other.

The guard who had stood her there pointed his club at her and shouted, "Stand at attention, whore, or else it will be even worse for you!"

Anna forced her body to stand straight, but she couldn't will the tears away. Each drop that left her eyes froze instantly until tiny icicles clung to her eyelashes and the skin of her face.

She shivered uncontrollably, teeth chattering. Her back ached from being forced to stand strictly erect for so long. It had been two or three hours. Lights-out had been called at least an hour ago. "Please, citizen chief!" Anna begged through chattering teeth. "I didn't mean it. I won't do it again. Please, let me go to the barracks."

"You'll go when I say you can go, traitor!" the guard barked at her.

Closing her eyes, she thought, *Maybe I can just fall asleep and float away. Leave this horrible place.*

She barely felt the hard slap to her face, eyes flying open only because her head jerked back from the blow.

"Open your eyes, whore!"

Prying her lids apart with great effort, she only succeeded in keeping them open for a couple of seconds. Her body swayed and her head drooped.

"Stand at attention!" the guard screamed into her face.

She swayed again. "Please…"

The second guard called to the first from his position by the fire, "She's about done-for, Boris. Better get her back to the barracks or we'll have more paperwork to do when she dies on our watch."

An angry grunt came from deep in Boris's throat. "Fine. You take her."

The guard left the warmth of the fire with a curse and grabbed Anna's arm, yanking her toward the row of barracks. She stumbled, falling to her knees on the packed snow. With another yank she was back on her feet, but her knees didn't want to bend. A bone-deep ache set in, and with each jarring step, more pain was added.

The barracks seemed like it was miles away, but finally, the guard unlocked the door and shoved her inside the dark building. She stumbled her way through sleeping bodies to the bunk she shared with Zoya and Eva. The stove was out, so there was no sense in wasting energy to get to it to warm herself. She dropped onto the bunk and lay head to foot next to Zoya.

"Dammit, Anna, you're like an icicle!," she said in a gruff whisper. She tugged on the thin blanket covering her torso and slipped a portion of it over Anna. "Get some sleep, dumb girl."

When the morning siren blared through the compound Anna's eyes scraped open and she attempted to push herself up from the bunk. Something was preventing her from raising her head, and at first she thought maybe Zoya was lying on her hair.

"Your hair's frozen to the bunk." Zoya sighed. "Let me help you." She pried at Anna's hair with her fingers until the cement-like ice broke off—with some of her hair still attached to it—and she was able to sit up.

Anna kept her head bowed through breakfast, headcount, and the march to the worksite. The ordeal of last night had broken her. She'd never been so cold, not even in the Lubyanka torture chamber. Her bones ached, and she had no feeling in most of her toes. She was afraid to remove her boots, knowing she'd find frostbitten flesh there.

The two women, Anna and Eva, hadn't improved much at their job, but they'd at least acquired a sort of rhythm to their work. They still hadn't even come close to reaching their assigned norm.

There was an unusual stillness in the air when they returned to work after supper break, and Anna looked up into the sky, but all seemed fine—the winter sun even peeked through the branches of the tall trees.

They'd almost sawed all the way through the tree they'd been working on for two days, both a little worried about which direction it would fall, when the wind started up with a terrifying howl. It whipped wildly through the trees, forcing everyone down to the ground.

"*Buran!*"

Wind muffled the shouted word from the men working only a few feet from her. A sudden winter storm, unpredictable and severe. She'd heard of them, but never seen one. The snow swirled up into the air, and everything disappeared in the white fog. The barking of the guard dogs came to her as if her ears were stuffed with cotton.

The high-pitched whistle of the guards pierced the wave of sound coming from the wind. Arms spread wide, Anna and Eva slipped and stumbled their way toward it, supporting each other as best they could.

When they reached the guards, one of them held out a rope that others of the crew already held to. "Grab this and *don't* let go."

Bent over, fighting against the strong wind, the crew made their way to the road following the guard dogs as they continued to bark and howl. Anna barely hung on to the rope with her mittened hands. Thunder clapped above their heads, and the sky burst open, pelting them with a violent stream of ice and snow. The wind—Anna could hardly breathe, it blew in her face with such force.

The work crew followed the dogs, hoping they were headed back to the prison camp. Anna couldn't see anything past Eva's back in front of her. She clung to the rope for her life. With all the familiar landmarks gone, it was like trying to find their way on an alien planet. After what seemed like hours of blundering along, Anna's foot came down on something soft—another prisoner who had let go of the rope.

Anna shouted, "Stop!" But the wind stole away her voice. No one heard her, and no one stopped. She leaned down, working to keep her balance as she shuffled along, and gripped the person's arm, pulling it toward the rope. "Hold on!"

But it was no use. The arm fell to the ground as soon as Anna released it, and the brigade was sure to move on without her if she let go of the rope to help the unfortunate soul.

3 0

Five people from Anna's brigade were found to be missing when they finally returned to camp through the horrific storm. The *buran*. The guard performing the head count—inside the mess hall instead of out in the storm—shrugged his shoulders and said, "We'll find them in the spring, after the snow melts."

Anna searched the frosted faces of those around her, silently praying to find Pyotr in the crowd. A relieved puff of air broke free from her throat where her fear had been holding it hostage. Pyotr's eyes demonstrated the same sentiment, as he nodded to her from a few rows away.

Never had she seen a storm such as this. It was a hell made of tiny daggers of ice, slicing away at any exposed skin. As she stood trembling, even in the relative warmth of the mess hall, Anna thought she might prefer the hell crafted of consuming fire.

The prisoners were allowed to stay in the mess hall until the storm died down, and by that time, the dinner siren had sounded. For the first time since arriving at the Kolyma camp, Anna was in the first group to be served. She took a drink of the warm salted water then held her tin can out to be filled with soup, carrying that and her small chunk of black bread over to sit next to Pyotr. She pulled down the scarf covering her mouth and nose and raised the soup to her face, surprised to see not only the usual scant amount of spoiled cabbage and a piece of potato, but a herring head. She hadn't seen "real" meat in her soup since arriving. Must have been one of the advantages to being first in line—which she'd probably never have the opportunity to do again.

Anna sipped some broth from her can and took a small bite of the bread. Pyotr ripped into his bread with malice, causing Anna to pause her chewing and look at him.

"They've started piling the bodies along the side of the barracks... ground's too frozen to bury them." He dropped his head and whispered, "So many lives taken. And for what?" He turned to her, hurt and anger flashing in his eyes. "For what?" His voice rose enough to earn a look from the nearest guard.

Anna looked away from his blazing eyes and shook her head. She'd asked herself the same question, over and over.

"How did humankind fall so far, so fast? As if killing off its citizens in scores wasn't enough for them, the Soviet powers have twisted everything. Made good evil and evil good."

They'd talked about this before, out in the forest. But Anna stayed silent, letting Pyotr vent his frustration.

"The real criminals are given posts of power in the camps, lording over those of us that are here for our *thoughts*, for our *beliefs*, for *nothing at all*. They don't go out into the sixty-below weather. They don't waste away from eating rotten food in such small portions it wouldn't keep a rat alive! They get the top bunks in the barracks—or their own cabins! Allowed to rape the women and beat the men and steal any belongings one of us might have been able to hold onto from the outside."

Anna placed her hand on his arm as his thin shoulders heaved with emotion.

"And they aren't the ones whose dead bodies are dragged out of the barracks every morning, to be piled alongside the poorly constructed buildings we're forced to live out the rest of our short, miserable lives in."

"Like garbage," Anna said.

Pyotr nodded.

They finished their dinner in silence, Anna's thoughts forced from where she'd locked them the last few weeks. The morning ritual of the guard shouting through the door, "Are there any stiffs?"

And the answer was always "yes." Then they offered a bread ration to anyone who would drag the corpses outside and throw them on the ever-increasing pile of frozen bodies. It was always the criminal element, those who needed the extra rations the least, who volunteered.

Anna stood near the stove, thankful that someone had stoked the fire within and added a real chunk of a log they'd been able to sneak in somehow. One of the problems with getting warm, though, was that it woke up the lice. She scratched frantically at the most urgent itches. She unbuttoned her padded jacket and pulled out the neck of her shirt, peering at her flesh in the dim light. Several white, bloated lice wriggled in her loose bra—and she could feel the sickening movement of dozens of others all over her body. She snatched the disgusting bugs away from her skin and crushed them between her fingers, the splash of ichor in her face no longer causing her to gag, or even react at all. Her nails were covered with the stuff. She wiped her fingers on her skirt, scratched some more, then buttoned her jacket back up. It was too cold to undress or to stay unbuttoned for too long.

Thinking about the last time she'd undressed, when she'd first arrived there, she grimaced as she remembered the handfuls of lice and other bugs that had fallen off her bare body, sure there were loads more of them now.

The itchiness went beyond the bug bites. Anna had developed a rash around her neck area that looked like a collar. It was dry and scaly. She may have had more areas, but she wasn't about to undress in this cold to look. The cough she'd developed over the last few days was also getting worse, and she didn't want to expose herself to even more cold.

"Lights out!"

Anna slipped her mittens on and plopped down on the bunk after waiting for Zoya and Eva to lay down. Darkness closed over them as the guard took their lantern and locked them in for the night. She awoke sometime later with chills coursing up and down her body. Her stomach clenched as cramps rolled across it. She made it to the bucket just in time, thankful it was dark enough that no one would know who was making the dreadful sounds as watery stool shot into it.

Upon laying back down, Zoya stirred beside her. "Are you okay? You're burning up."

Answering with a groan, Anna curled up as another cramp twisted her guts. She fell to the crowded floor halfway to the bucket and crawled the rest of the way. Her legs trembled as she squatted over the rim, wondering how a body could make so much watery stool out of the meager amount of food she was allowed to eat.

Instead of making the trek back to her bunk, Anna curled up on the floor next to the foul-smelling bucket, where Zoya found her after the morning siren sounded.

31

Anna's mind was fuzzy, confused one minute and lucid the next as the guard shouted through the open door, "Any stiffs?"

Zoya charged up to him. "Forget about those who are already dead. You need to help Anna before she joins them!"

Did he laugh at her? Anna wasn't sure as she drifted away.

Two male *zeks* had Anna's arms draped around their scrawny necks, her boots dragging across the packed snow. Zoya's voice came to her from behind. "They're taking you to medical, Anna. You're going to be fine."

She'd never been inside the medical building in camp. She'd scoured its outside edges for firewood, but that was as close as she'd gotten. Squinting at the brightness of the lamps, Anna groaned as the men dropped her onto a bed. A real bed. The sheets were dingy and worn, but there *were* sheets on the thin mattress.

"You men can go now. Better get to the mess hall before headcount." A gentle male voice wafted over Anna. The man in a lab coat sat on a stool next to the bed and looked down at her. "You're the lucky first patient today, but there's sure to be many more. Always are." He shook a thermometer then held it toward her. "Open up."

Her teeth chattered as she held the thermometer between them, trying to keep it under her tongue. Everything ached. She groaned and clenched her arms around her stomach as a deep pain took up residence there.

"I'm Dr. Kopelev. Let's see that thermometer before you break it in half." He pulled it out of her mouth and held it up, twisting it in front of his eyes until he found the line of mercury. "Oh my. You really are sick—though I could tell that just by looking at you." He stood and called to a nurse, "Tamara, get her coat and boots off, we need to cool her down."

"How high is her fever?"

"Inching toward 105. She'll be getting on the transport to Magadan later today."

Anna grabbed his hand before he could step away. "What's wrong with me? Am I dying?"

As the nurse worked to pull her jacket off, the doctor leaned over her and examined the rash around her collar, pulling her shirt down a little to better view it. "My educated guess is that you have pellagra, an upper respiratory infection, and an intestinal virus. And, no, you aren't going to die. Not on my watch, anyway."

Anna dropped in and out of consciousness as the nurse wiped her face and neck with a wet cloth, mumbling soothing words Anna couldn't put together into sentences that made sense. She awoke a while later, but the nurse had moved on to other tasks as more and more prisoners filled up the large room, adding to those who'd already been there when Anna had arrived.

She shivered on the bed, covered in a light sheet, not because the building was cold—it wasn't—but because of the fever.

The nurse awakened her mid-day, making her sit up in bed and handing her a cup of warm broth. And sometime that afternoon an orderly or trusty or something, pulled her up to a sitting position on the side of the bed and told her to put her jacket and boots back on.

Were they sending her back out to general labor? To the forest? There was no way she'd even make it out there.

The man shoved her jacket into her chest with an agitated scowl. "Hurry it up, the transport truck will be here any minute."

"Transport?" Where were they transporting her? Another camp?

"To the prison hospital in Magadan. The doctor already told you this!" He dropped her coat in her lap and stomped off.

Soon Anna found herself being crowded into a cattle car with other sick and dying prisoners. They were packed in so tight they had to remain standing. Even after her knees buckled from weakness, the close-packed bodies around her kept her from falling to the floor. She remembered little of the hellish journey, just pain, stench, and freezing cold. She had no idea how long it lasted—could have been an hour or days.

She awoke briefly when the cattle car lurched to a stop and the soldiers opened the back to let them out. Those who could, jumped or climbed down, the rest of them, including Anna, were dragged to the edge by the soldiers then allowed to drop to the muddy ground.

She tried to push herself up, her hand landing in an icy puddle, but a coughing fit took all the air from her lungs, and her vision faded to black.

☭

She awoke in a bright, clean hospital ward, lying on a cot covered with clean white sheets. For a moment, she thought she must have died and gone to heaven. Clean sheets. It had been so long since she'd seen sheets at all, much less clean ones. Now she'd found herself resting on them twice in one day...or had it been more than one day?

And she, herself, was clean. Tears sprang to her eyes as she peered under the top sheet at her ravaged but scrubbed skin. Not a bug in sight. She touched a spot of rash on her arm, miraculously not itching, and her fingers came away with some sort of strong-smelling ointment.

She wore a threadbare tunic, and flushed with alarm as her thoughts finally caught up with her surroundings: who had stripped her, washed her, and redressed her?

Pulling the sheet up to her neck, she looked around. There were both men and women prisoners in the beds stretching down the rows as far as she could see. And men and women orderlies and nurses busily moving from patient to patient. Closing her eyes, she searched her memories, landing on a broken remnant of one. A patient older woman, gently removing her clothes, *tsking* at the state of her filth and skeletal body. She breathed in relief.

A small man with a gray mustache strode over to the side of her bed and looked down at her with a slight smile. "Anna Levitskaya?"

She nodded, pulling the sheet all the way to her chin.

"I'm Dr. Lazarevna. I'm glad to see that you're finally awake. Your fever broke a few hours ago." He helped her to sit up then placed a stethoscope in his ears and pressed the other end to her back. "Breathe in and out."

The deep inhale triggered a coughing spell that made black dots swim in her vision. The gentle doctor patted her back until the irritation in her throat faded. He attempted to listen again, this time with success. He straightened up and said, "Luckily, the infection hasn't reached your lungs, it's all in the upper respiratory tract. Do you feel like eating?"

Anna's hand absently went to her stomach, where hunger had been a constant companion for months. She nodded, wondering what kind of ration she'd get for not fulfilling any work norms at all.

"Very good, then. I'll have an orderly bring you something to eat."

Now Anna stared down at a tray bearing six pieces of bread. Six! Three pieces of black bread and—unbelievably—three pieces of white bread! She hadn't had white bread since... She shook her head to keep the memory from forming.

Still, her eyes filled with tears at the sight of the bread *and* turnips and carrots lying next to it! The vegetables weren't even spoiled! The orderly had told her that these were the anti-pellagra rations.

Slowly, with the care and the food given at the hospital, the diarrhea dried up, the cough subsided, and the rash disappeared. And then she was forced to leave paradise and return to hell, asking herself why they'd bothered to save her when it seemed like, in the end, they only wanted her tortured death. Logic was long dead in the Soviet Union.

32

Anna returned to camp early in the morning. They'd celebrated New Year's Day the night before at the hospital by giving each of the prisoner patients just enough *makhorka*, the cheapest form of tobacco, to roll a single cigarette, which she'd savored. The new year meant nothing to her, though—1939 would be no different from the last four months of 1938. And no different from the next nine-and-a-half years, were she to survive that long, which she doubted.

She'd put on a small amount of weight during her two weeks of being well-fed in the hospital. Enough that her breasts weren't sagging like deflated balloons. Which was not something she was exactly happy about—the sooner her body turned into a shriveled shell the better, as far as she was concerned. Maybe it would keep the disgusting trusties and guards away from her.

Returning to the barracks shortly after the work crews had gone out for the day, Anna stood by the barely heated stove, warming her hands. She was freezing, of course, thanks to the ride back to camp in the back of a cattle truck. At least, thankfully, the hospital had returned her clothing items—including the worn jacket and mittens—cleaned and de-loused. The guard at the gate had told her and the others who had returned with her that he would check them in, and to go to their barracks and await assignments.

Anna looked up as the door opened, her knees nearly buckling when Isaak walked in and shut the door behind him. She backed away, putting the stove between her and him.

"Relax, Anna Levitskaya. I'm just here to check up on you." He stepped around the stove and took hold of her arm. "And to give you one more chance."

She shook her head, and Isaak increased the pressure on her arm.

"Now, hear me out before you refuse again." He looked her up and down and licked his lips. "You aren't going to be desirable much longer—hell, you almost aren't at this point. You might as well give in and save yourself. I mean, the next time you get sick...you might not make it to the hospital in time. You'd best become my whore and get an easy job assignment, because you won't survive much longer doing general labor."

"No. I told you I don't care about that." Her voice cracked with fear. "I can't. I can't do what you're asking."

"Oh, I'm not asking. I'm done asking." His face contorted with anger and his grip on her arm became painful as he pulled her closer to him, his spittle flying in her face. "Too bad your little whore friend isn't here to save you this time."

Though she knew her screams were futile, she couldn't stop the terrified sounds from ripping her throat on their way out. The criminal trusty threw her to the floor. She pushed back with her feet, trying to scramble out of his grip, scratching at his face with her free hand, jagged nails tearing at his skin.

His fist came down on her jaw so hard everything went black for several seconds, her body limp. When she semi-recovered from the blow, he already had her skirt pulled up and her underwear down around her ankles, one hand pressing on her chest while the other worked to unfasten his pants.

No one was going to step in and save her—she knew that, she'd been here before. She continued to struggle, her feet scrambling on the frozen-mud floor. Isaak took her by the shoulders and slammed her head and upper back into the ground. He pried her legs apart with his knees and forced himself inside her as she sobbed. The tearing pain flooded her mind with images of the Black Mariah. Her flinches and cries seemed to fuel him on, and she shut her eyes tight to keep from seeing the malevolent grin on his face.

When he was done, she pushed her skirt down and curled up into a ball while he stood over her, buttoning his pants and refastening his belt.

"Get up!" He yanked her by the arm, and she stumbled to her feet. "That was fun, but it doesn't count to get you out of general labor unless you participate willingly. Unless you come crawling to me. Begging."

Something broke inside Anna, filling her with rage. She spat in his face, a glob of saliva dripped down his cheek. His slap knocked her to the ground, where bloody drool dripped from her split lip and her left ear rung.

"Get up and get your worthless *zek* ass out to the logging camp!"

Isaak yelled for a young criminal prisoner, couldn't have been more than fifteen years old, to "escort" her there. He'd been taught well by his criminal family, as Anna endured his foul mouth, shoves, and kicks all the way to the edge of the area where the loggers were working. She hardly felt his abuse. Her mind had shut down, her vision glossed over, and her hearing muffled as she stumbled her way over the tramped down trail.

The boy marched her right up to the brigadier. "Brought ya' another low-life *zek*." He pushed Anna toward him.

The brigadier glanced at her and scowled. "Did you do this to her?"

"Nah. That was Isaak."

"Not surprised," he grumbled. "Go on then, get out of my work site."

The boy peeked at the fire around which a couple of guards stood then back at the brigadier, obviously wanting to warm himself before heading down the trail again. The criminals weren't as brave when not surrounded by their gang. He cowed a little at the brigadier's frown and started back toward camp at a healthy clip.

"Your partner's been assigned to chop off branches while you were gone. Go find her, and you two get back to sawing down trees."

Anna tripped more than walked as she tried to find Eva with her half-glazed eyes. Even in the freezing cold, she felt the pain and disgust between her legs. She stopped and dropped to the snowy ground, unable to focus on the task at hand. She put a mittened hand to her face, wondering in a blurry moment why it hurt, then tried to remember what she was supposed to be doing.

"Anna, you're back," Eva's voice traveled through the haze of her mind. "What are you doing just sitting there? You're going to get in trouble."

It took several breaths before she could make herself answer. "I'm... I don't know. I'm supposed to find you...and saw down trees."

Eva came closer and frowned. "What happened to you?"

Anna shook her head.

"Come on. The guards are looking over here. Let's go find a saw."

Anna was able to put more effort into pushing and pulling the saw, having been well fed over the last two weeks, and the repetitive physical labor helped to numb her mind.

At the whistle for first break, Anna dropped her end of the saw and stood frozen in place. Pyotr found her there after a few minutes, throwing worried glances her way as tears froze to her cheeks. She hadn't even wrapped her scarf around her face, it still hung about her shoulders where it had fallen during Isaak's attack.

Pyotr didn't ask what had happened or try to get her to talk, he just handed her his lit cigarette and hummed a hymn he often sang. It was like that for supper break, too, when she shoved the chunk of bread and dried herring into her pocket, too sick to her stomach to eat. She wanted to tell him that his quiet support was more appreciated than she could ever express. But her throat closed off every time she thought of speaking. Oh how she wished she was back at the hospital where they'd treated her like a human!

Back at camp, Anna forced herself to wait in line for dinner rations, the exhaustion returned as if she'd never spent any time recuperating in the hospital in Magadan. She looked only at her shuffling feet, not wanting to see or be seen by anyone. She left the mess hall, taking her rations with her back to the barracks. It was more crowded than it had been when she left. More prisoners must have been transported there. Anna wondered if it would ever end. They already didn't have enough room or enough food for the droves of prisoners they'd shipped there. But she knew they didn't care. The government officials sitting inside their warm homes, gulping down vodka, and eating like kings—they didn't care.

She made her way through the crowd and dropped to the floor in the darkest corner, forcing herself to eat even though her stomach clenched at the thought.

Someone, standing over her, cleared their throat.

Anna looked up into Zoya's eyes. Her friend frowned down at her before plopping herself down next to her. "What in the hell happened to you? I thought you went to the hospital to get better, not get beat up."

Anna looked down and mumbled, "It didn't happen there."

"On the way back then?" She lifted Anna's chin to look at her. "Anna, tell me what happened."

She couldn't. Anna couldn't speak the words. She shook her head as the tears started falling again, oozing out of her swollen eye.

"It happened here. When you got back." Zoya waited for a nod from Anna before continuing, "Was it Isaak?"

Anna looked away, flinching at the name of her assailant.

"I'll kill that son of a bitch," Zoya whispered fiercely.

Anna rested her head on Zoya's shoulder, and they stayed like that until lights-out called them to their shared bunk.

33

Anna hurried through the subzero compound, careful not to slosh out the rapidly cooling soup in her tin can. She was lucky to get any soup at all as her brigadier was quick to reduce her rations again after another unprofitable day in the logging camp.

Zoya sat on their bunk as she entered the barracks. Anna sat down next to her, taking a sip of the watery soup.

"Isaak won't bother you ever again."

A mouthful of broth entered Anna's lungs as she inhaled sharply. Zoya didn't really kill him, did she? When the coughing spell ended, she looked up at her friend.

Zoya just gave a tough nod then looked away. "But, sister, there will be others, and you need to toughen up or just give in. I won't always be here to protect you."

Anna sat in silence, looking down at her remaining broth.

"Look, it isn't a matter of morality or moral degradation—it's a matter of survival." Zoya sighed and looked around the barracks. "There *is* no morality in the prison camps."

Eyes blank, Anna replied in a whisper, "I have nothing to survive for. Nikolai is dead. My sister dis...disclaimed me." She downed the rest of her soup and shoved the can in her jacket pocket.

"That's just stupid, Anna. There's always—"

"Lights-out!" the guard yelled as he pulled the lantern outside with him, plunging them into darkness.

Zoya stretched out on the bunk behind Anna.

Anna whispered fiercely, "I will keep my morality even if—no! Especially if—it means dying in this God-forsaken place." She laid down with her back to Zoya and curled into a ball. She couldn't sleep as Zoya's words turned round and round in her head all night.

Standing in line at headcount, Anna looked up at the clear sky, thankful there were no clouds to pour down snow on them, but shivering in the extra cold the cloudless sky brought to the Kolyma. The men seemed more restless than usual, whispering in their ranks and looking around nervously.

"Everyone shut up!" the camp director shouted.

Anna straightened up. The camp director never came out to morning headcount.

"One of the trusty's had his throat slit last night."

Dead silence from the *zeks*. Shouts and curses from the criminals. Isaak's name tossed around.

"Shut it!" the camp director yelled. The guards pointed their rifles in the direction of the prisoners. When the crowd settled down, the director continued, "If any of you know anything about this murder, you'd best step forward now. There *will* be camp-wide consequences if this isn't solved in a timely manner."

Anna forced herself not to look at Zoya while wondering why, with all the death and murder in this camp, this was such a big deal.

As if reading her thoughts, the director said, "We will not allow for one of our citizens, the socially friendly prisoners whose worth is far above any of you anti-Soviet pieces of garbage, to be slaughtered in such a way without repercussions!"

The women, at least those around Anna, bowed their heads, not looking at anyone.

"Off with all of you! Off to your assignments. But there'd better be an answer to who killed Isaak by the evening siren."

Anna's thoughts were a jumbled mess all day as she worked alongside Eva. Neither of them mentioned Isaak. Anna's relief that Isaak was gone was invaded by her guilt for being glad he was dead. Guilt that Zoya had committed murder for her, had given herself to him and others to keep Anna safe.

Isaak's murder must not have been as important as the camp director had stated that morning, as another influx of prisoners kept him from fulfilling his threats. Things went on as normal for dinner and then headcount, except for the growling and whispered threats issued by Isaak's gang.

Anna sat on her shared bunk, still thinking about what Zoya had done for her. Her work detail always came back into camp so late that most of the socializing that took place in the women's barracks was over with. A calm quiet took over as women sewed with hidden needles and thread, wrote letters on stolen scraps of paper that would likely never find the recipients, or left to shack up with their "camp husbands."

But tonight was different. The old woman in the bunk above Anna's, a last-legger unable to work and nearing death, began talking —almost desperate to tell her story—as she peeked her head over the side of her bunk and stared at Anna with rheumy eyes. "This is my second stint, you know."

"I...I didn't know that," Anna said, wondering what purpose there was in sending an elderly woman to a labor camp. Why not just execute her? The result would be the same. Bitterness swept through her, tightening her chest, her stomach roiling.

"Oh, yes." Her eyes got a far-off look. "But there are worse things."

Anna thought, *what could possibly be worse? Even death was preferrable to this place.*

"I did eight years in one of these 're-education' camps. Survived its horrors only by focusing on one thing—to return to my children. They'd been so young when their father and I were taken, only four and six years old."

"So they were taken to an orphanage," Anna guessed.

"Yes, like so many others." The woman's tale was interrupted by a coughing fit that racked her emaciated body, turning her cracked lips blue. After catching her breath, she continued, "After my release, I spent weeks trying to get to them and days scouring the orphanages in Moscow to find them."

The women who were close enough to hear her, stopped what they were doing and listened, looking up at her quietly.

"They'd grown so much—but I still recognized them immediately. I held my arms open in anticipation of the embrace I'd been dreaming of for eight long years. But they just stood frowning at me from afar." She wiped at a tear trailing through the grime on her wrinkled face. "I moved toward them, but my son, the older of the two, stepped back, pushing his sister along with him. He said, 'We won't go with you, woman. You are an enemy of the people. An anti-Soviet scum. You are not our mother.'

"I tried to reason with them, but the workers shuffled them off and told me to leave and never come back."

The only sounds in the overcrowded room were the grunts and other disgusting noises coming from the curtained off bunks.

The old woman sighed. "I don't blame my children. They'd been brainwashed, taught that their father and I were 'enemies of the people' who did not deserve their love. I found out later that they had been specifically instructed to refuse to leave if I came to get them."

"But you're their mother!" someone in the crowd said.

The old woman shook her head sadly. "No. Not anymore. Our children—all of them—belong to the Soviet Union now. There is no such thing as a family anymore."

"What did you do?" another woman asked.

"What could I do? I went into exile for three years as the court demanded. I never found out what happened to my husband, and when I finally returned to my home, to the town I grew up in, I was once again arrested and sent back here—this time without a trial."

"They...they can do that?" asked a young newcomer, still rosy-cheeked from so recently being on the outside.

Harsh laughter was her reply, followed by a rough-voiced, "They can do whatever they want."

"But...no trial? What did they charge you with?"

"Article fifty-eight something or another. What does it matter? I did nothing wrong, yet here I am, dying in this cesspit." After another bout of coughing, the woman rolled over and mumbled, "I'm tired. So very tired."

The next morning when the guard called, "Any stiffs in there?" the woman's bunk mate pushed her dead body off the bunk to land on the prisoners below who were too slow to move out of the way.

34

A commotion at the river below interrupted Anna's conversation with Pyotr during their first smoke break. They peered over the edge, careful not to step foot outside the roped-off boundaries lest they be shot.

The men below had been rolling logs off a flat car—using two other logs as a ramp—and onto the platform in preparation to float them down the river once the ice broke up. Like pulling a block from the bottom of a tower a child had built, twenty or more logs were loosened and came plummeting down the ramp.

"Out of the way!" several of the men yelled.

But one man was too slow, and was buried beneath the mountain of heavy logs.

Anna put a mittened hand to her scarf-covered mouth and looked away for a moment. When she looked back, the other men were pushing the logs off the pile he lay under, and when they came to his crushed and lifeless body, two guards shoved it out of the way on the platform.

"Get back to work!" one of them shouted. "You can carry his body back to camp when night falls."

Pyotr bowed his head then made the sign of the cross. "Like an animal, his carcass will be added to the pile back at camp. Spring thaw is going to bring much work and a great stench from the rotting bodies of our fellow detainees."

Anna slogged her way back to the tree she and Eva were working on for the second day. Their meager strength was spent already, as they endured more and more reduced rations for not even coming close to making the impossibly set work norms.

At supper break, after receiving a pittance of bread and no herring, she noticed a woman, her name was Galya, who seemed to, only recently, always get a full ration—and she was assigned to the same work of cutting down trees, but *by herself* with a one-handed saw. It was impossible to think that she could meet the work norms.

Instead of going to her usual spot to eat with Pyotr, Anna pulled Eva over and nodded toward Galya. "How does she do it?"

"I don't know." Eva stared after her. "Let's find out." She gripped Anna's arm and marched toward the woman, Anna in tow.

They stopped right in front of her, close enough to whisper without anyone else hearing what they said. Eva didn't mince words. "How are you reaching the norms?"

Galya swallowed the bite of herring she'd been chewing. "I'm just doing my work."

Anna narrowed her eyes, and Eva shook her head and said, "Not possible." Her voice softened on her next words. "Come on, Gal. We're dying. Right before your eyes. Please...tell us how you do it."

She glanced around furtively before stepping even closer and whispering, "I'm sure you've noticed that this forest is full of piles of timber cut by previous work gangs. No one ever bothered to count how many there are."

Anna frowned. "But anyone can see that they're not freshly cut..."

With another scan of their surroundings, Galya said, "The only reason you can see that is because the cross sections are darker. If you saw off a small section at each end, it looks like it's just been cut. Then you stack them up in another place—and there's your norm."

Eva and Anna looked at each other, their eyes crinkling as they half-smiled.

Anna had wondered why it was so essential that they all work themselves to death in order to meet the work norms when there were actual piles of felled trees just rotting away in the forest. But she knew why, it wasn't about reaching norms or helping build a new Soviet Union—it was about inflicting as much pain as possible on the *zeks* until they eventually died, then replacing them with more like a never-ending cycle of Dante's Inferno.

The two women reached their norms that day—all in the half day after supper break. Moving the felled trees to a different location to make their own pile was back-breaking, but full rations for dinner that night made up for it. At first, they watched nervously for the guards or brigadier to notice what they were doing, but soon realized they were paying no attention to the work of the prisoners, it was too cold for that. Instead, they stood around a fire, talking and laughing, only occasionally glancing around to make sure no one was trying to escape. They only checked on progress at the end of the thirteen-hour day.

Anna's lighter mood crashed as they lined up for the trek back to camp, watching as four men struggled to carry the dead prisoner who'd been crushed beneath a mountain of logs. As they marched along, she wondered why the guards hadn't just told them to leave him in the snow as they had so many others. But she should have long ago stopped trying to understand the workings of their minds—the human mind cannot comprehend that of a monster.

Either the days were becoming ever so slightly warmer—if you can call a temperature change of fifty below to forty below warmer—or the bit of health Anna had regained from receiving full rations just made it feel that way. The trick Galya had told them about had paid off. There was no shortage of felled trees—as there was never a shortage of prisoners to keep cutting them down.

She sat near the stove on a rare day off, sewing her prisoner number back onto her jacket after having it re-inked. This was only the second day off they'd been given in the months since she'd been in the Kolyma. Her fingers and toes had been damaged by frostbite, but she'd been able to keep from losing too much weight on full rations, and she was beginning to believe she might make it through the winter.

Putting her jacket on, she moved back to sit on her bunk so someone else could have her spot near the stove. Placing her mittens back on her hands, she stared up at the posters on the walls of the barracks. All propaganda. She stared at the picture of Marx for a moment before turning her gaze to that of Stalin. She narrowed her eyes at the Supreme Leader. Her will to survive had grown; she refused to sit idly by and let the system win. To let Stalin win.

She'd been so naïve before her arrest, always telling herself that the people who'd been taken away in the middle of the night must have done *something* to deserve it. Reassuring herself that as long as she followed the Party rules she'd be fine. *Hmf,* she snorted, garnering looks from women nearby. There were no real rules—only quotas. Only feeding the cannibalistic machine in the name of another "Five-year plan."

Ooh, how her eyes were opened on that horrible night in August. How a drunken joke heard by the wrong ears could cost you your life. How being in the wrong place at the wrong time could change you from a human to a Fifty-eight—a subhuman, treated worse than the horses used to pull the sledges full of the corpses of the Fifty-eights.

In her willful ignorance—some of which was forced upon her by the Soviet school system and Soviet citizens' fear of words, some because of her own belief that the less she knew the safer she'd be— she'd had no idea about the extent of the disaster created in the early '30s with the creation of the collective farms—the *kolkhoz*. Ration cards and long ration lines in Moscow were inconvenient, and her stomach never felt all the way full, but they weren't starving to death in the city. Pyotr had told her about the hundreds of thousands of *kulak* families that had been removed from their farms and relocated to labor camps or elsewhere. And the millions who had suffered death—not only by execution, but by starvation. How, many people resorted to cannibalism—even eating their own children—just to stay alive. Her mind could not have conceived such things before her arrest. But now...she'd witnessed first-hand the barbarism of the Soviet government, the zero regard for individuals, for families, for property, for God—the Communist way of thinking.

Yes, she'd learned so much in this place. The only thing the Soviet children were taught in the schools was how wonderful the Socialist/Communist systems were. What genius underlay Marx's fanatical ideas. So many children brainwashed—and so many parents afraid to teach them the truth.

Lies.

All lies.

She tightened her hands into fists inside her mittens to keep from leaping at the pictures of Stalin and Marx and ripping them from the walls.

Anna would survive, if for no other reason than to spite those bastards.

PART III

Spring-Summer 1940

35

The unseasonably warm March day coaxed Anna to stay outside after dinner. According to the thermometer outside the mess hall, it was almost forty degrees. She looked down at her scarred and calloused hands, amazed she had made it through another winter.

She smiled slightly as Pyotr made his way over to her, Zoya, and Eva, thankful that her three friends had made it through the harsh winter too. Zoya continued to be her protector. She never came right out and said it, but Anna thought she reminded Zoya of the little sister she talked about sometimes. Thankfully, the men had mostly left Anna alone since Isaak had been killed over a year ago.

Raucous laughter came from the group of criminal trusties standing around a fire across the central compound from them. There was no such laughter from Anna's group—or most of the Fifty-eights for that matter.

The trusties still caused her heart to race with fear, and it made Anna increasingly sick to her stomach to see or hear the guards or trusties having sex with women in the barracks, so she'd started leaving the building whenever she could while they performed the disgusting act. The *zek*—Fifty-eights—men didn't screw out in the open like that. Those who weren't too exhausted from months or years of heavy labor and little food, and were lucky enough to find a willing participant, at least tried to be discreet about it. Anna had become less timid around the male political prisoners, almost able to trust them.

Pyotr had become her closest friend, even closer than Zoya, as they'd spent many hours together out in the forests during breaks. The four friends sat on stones near the border fence, boots slopped in mud from the thawing of the ground. Their conversation had turned from lighthearted to serious after Eva, looking out at the first stars to appear in the dimming sky, sighed and asked, "How do men become so evil? I don't mean just a single man or a few men—my mind can conceive of that—but half of the men and women in Russia? What makes them hate us so?"

"Ahh, a question I've pondered for twenty years or more." Pyotr scratched at the stubble on his head, having just been sheared again a few days earlier.

"And," Zoya asked, "what answers have you come up with?"

"Well, one must first understand that it's human nature to seek justification for his actions. In order to do evil, a human being must be convinced that what he's doing is good, or at least that it is a well thought out act conforming with natural law."

"But what could possibly justify the cruelty, starvation, death—everything that's been suffered by their hands—of *millions* of people?" Anna shook her head. "I can't even fathom it."

"Ahh," Pyotr held up a finger, "let's use Shakespeare's villains as an example of Eva's comment about a single man committing evil: his villains' imagination and spiritual strength stopped short at a dozen or less corpses. Why?"

The women glanced at each other, then back at him with shrugs or shakes of their heads.

"Because they lacked *ideology*." Pyotr looked at each of them in turn before continuing. "Ideology is what gives evildoing its much sought after justification and steadfast determination. It's the social theory that helps make a person's acts seem good instead of bad in his own and others' eyes, so that he won't be admonished and scourged, but, just the opposite, he'll be inundated with praise and honors!"

"Ideology..." Anna tried to wrap her head around what he meant. "Like Marx's ideas about Communism and taking down the class structure."

Pyotr nodded, smiling slightly. "Yes, Anna. I see you've been listening to my ramblings out in the forest. It's good to know our friendship is based on more than just *makhorka*."

"You've taught me a lot."

"I think I understand what you're saying," Zoya said. "They believe that Communism is the greater good, so that excuses everything they do in its name. But...it's just sheer insanity to think that so many people believe this and defend it! Even those who were and are victims of Stalin's purge the last few years. Party members who go to their deaths shouting praises for the Supreme Leader who sent them there!"

"Oh, but if they admitted they were wrong at that juncture, how would they excuse their actions prior to that? It's become a competition among them about who can praise their failed ideals the loudest—right up to the end." Pyotr looked up as the perimeter lights flickered on, bathing them in light. "There is a precise line that Shakespearean evildoers would not cross. But the evildoer with ideology does cross it—with clear and dry eyes, leaving humanity behind, without, perhaps, the possibility of return."

The small group stood in silence, pondering his words.

After a moment, Pyotr said, "Might you pray with me, my friends, before the siren sounds?" It was something he asked every time they gathered together in the evenings. Eva and Zoya usually refused his offer, neither of them putting much stock in there being a loving God, but tonight, they both nodded along with Anna.

Pyotr smiled gently and held out his hands. He prayed as the four of them grasped hands in the cooling air. A beautiful, brief prayer of thanksgiving and blessings of safety for the women.

Anna turned to go to the barracks, but was stopped by Pyotr's hand on her arm. He rarely touched her, instinctively knowing her fear of men, so it startled her a little. When she looked up at him, a shadow hiding most of his face, the sadness in his eyes made her heart hurt.

"What's wrong?" she asked.

A morose smile touched his lips. "Nothing. I just want you to know that I love you like the daughter I never had. Thank you for being my friend."

"Thank you for befriending me." Anna leaned in and hugged him, something she'd never done before. His demeanor worried her, but before she could question him about it, the lights-out siren sounded. "See you tomorrow."

He answered with a nod as they went their separate ways.

Worry ate away at Anna's gut on the march back to camp the next evening. Pyotr hadn't been with the brigade that day, she'd searched for him at each break, but was afraid to ask anyone about him. Eva suggested that maybe he'd gotten sick, stating he had looked rather pale last night.

She took her dinner to the barracks with her, hoping to find Zoya there, hoping she'd know where Pyotr was. Fear stabbed through her chest at the looks of sympathy some of the other women gave her as she stepped inside. "What's going on?" she asked.

An older woman, Veta, put her hands on Anna's shoulders. "Zoya. She was—"

"Where is she?" Anna's eyes darted around the barracks.

"She's gone. Transferred hours ago, along with many others."

"No! Where to? Where did they take her?" She choked on the words, trying to hold back tears.

"No one knows, Anna. They don't even tell the ones they're transferring where they're going. I mean, does a zookeeper tell the animals where they're going if they move them to another zoo?"

Anna sat on her bunk. Her and Zoya's bunk. Maybe that's where Pyotr had gone. It cheered her up only slightly to think her friends might be together. She swallowed the soup, having a difficult time getting it past the lump in her throat. What would she do without Zoya? Would she become a target again? She hadn't looked into a mirror in a long time, but hoped the last year-and-a-half had done its work on making her undesirable.

Two men clomped into the barracks, looking around. Fear prickled her senses, fear she wouldn't have felt had Zoya been by her side. She swallowed hard, pulled her scarf over her face, and hurried outside. She searched for Pyotr, going to all the places they usually met up.

Wrapping her scarf tighter around her nose to stave off the stench of decaying bodies, she approached Pyotr's barracks. Several unlucky souls were outside, tossing the thawed bodies that had been collecting there all winter onto a sledge. One of the men stopped to catch his breath, wiping his forehead with the sleeve of his jacket as he noticed Anna. "You looking for the priest?"

Anna nodded.

The man averted his eyes and the other men stopped to listen to the exchange. "He...uh...he isn't here. They—"

Another prisoner, emaciated to the point that he looked to belong on the sledge with the other dead men, interrupted. "They transferred him."

Their shifting eyes and uncomfortable stances told Anna they were lying. The way he'd acted last night...expressed his love for her.

He'd been executed.

And he'd somehow known it was coming.

Anna whirled around and ran, finding refuge behind the kitchen. Back to the wall, she slid to the ground and sobbed.

36

The brief respite the warmer spring weather brought with it crashed with a late winter storm. Anna stood in her row during headcount the next morning, stomping her feet and slapping her arms with her hands, trying to get her circulation moving. The wet snow disregarded her boots as if they were sandals. She'd found some used tire tread to bolster the soles and wrapped twine around it, but the snow found the cracks and holes and seeped inside.

She'd made it back to her barracks just before lights-out, and she'd cried until her shattered mind and body gave in to sleep.

Zoya was gone.

Pyotr was dead.

Eva was still there, thank goodness, but they weren't close like she'd been with Zoya and Pyotr. Their relationship was based on working together to cut trees in order to survive. Eva couldn't get over the fact that Anna wouldn't cave in to the trusties in order to live easier in the camp, because Eva would have, had the offer ever presented itself.

The only other person in the world Anna cared about was her

mama—and the chances of ever seeing her again were slim. She didn't even know if Mama was still alive.

All these thoughts kept circling around and around in her head as they stood amidst the falling snow for what seemed like hours. Finally, Anna's brigade was ordered to move out, but their brigadier wasn't the one giving the orders. A new guy stood in his place. A trusty by the looks of his clothes and the meanness in his eyes.

"Move it, you dirty bastards! Let's go!" he shouted, letting them all pass him so he could take up the rear with a couple of the guards.

Once they reached the work site, the new brigadier stood before them. "I'm Brigadier Anatoly. The last guy is gone, don't ask any questions. There will be no more smoke breaks. You will get ten minutes to get your supper and eat it. Anyone caught shirking will be punished. If you don't make norms in the regular thirteen-hour day, you will stay until norms are met." He looked down at his clipboard, wet papers fluttering in the wind. "Assignments are as follows..." He read off the same assignments they'd had all winter, only changing up to accommodate for those who weren't there—like Pyotr.

Anna and Eva took their saw and axe and moved into the forest to find an old pile of chopped-down trees as they'd been doing over the past year, carefully keeping an eye out for the new brigadier. They needn't have worried, he spent the entire cold day at the fire, watching only those within his sight.

At the end of the day, he screwed up his face into a frown when Anna and Eva showed him to their pile of "freshly" cut trees. He counted them and marked them off for meeting the required norms, but kept looking from them to the pile with suspicion.

Anna looked at her work partner and raised her eyebrows. They were going to have to be really careful with this brigadier around.

The next day, the two women moved farther into the forest, careful to stay within the roped-off boundaries of where they were allowed to go. They looked around nervously as they sawed the ends off of the fallen trees.

Anna strained as they dragged one of the trees to a different location to start their pile for the day. They moved it far enough away from where they'd originally found it to be safe, eyes still roving their surroundings for the brigadier or guards.

Returning to get the next tree, Anna gasped and tears instantly sprang to her eyes—there stood Anatoly, the new brigadier, holding one of the sawed-off ends up with a vicious grin on his face.

"Well now, *zek* bitches. I knew you were cheating somehow. There's no way a couple stupid, skinny, women could make norms so easily."

They didn't dare look at each other or him, both stared only at the ground.

"From now on, you two will need to stay where I can keep an eye on you." He stepped over and slapped Anna's butt. "Especially you."

She flinched, panic settling in her stomach like it had just returned home from a long trip.

"Let's get going, then. You two have a long day of catching up ahead of you. You'll work through the supper break, shirkers don't get rations anyways." He started walking through the trees, following the path he'd made in the snow, then stopped and turned back to them. "Oh, and, if you happen to make it back to camp tonight, you'll go straight to the penalty cells."

Night fell long before the brigade was allowed to tramp back to camp. Anna and Eva weren't alone in not making the impossibly set norms. Even working the extra hours, they didn't come close, but the new brigadier decided to call it a night when he realized he'd have to stay out there with them. He smugly escorted Anna and Eva to the punishment cells, telling the guard there, "Seven days for these two, but let them out to work in the morning—I'll bring them back to you every night." He shoved them both inside one of a long line of small cells made of soggy logs—and no roofs. Looking in at them before slamming the door, he said, "If you don't make norms tomorrow, you'll be in here without your clothes for the remainder of your time."

The two women sat on the muddy ground, knees drawn up to their chests because it was too small for them to stretch their legs out, shivering as the temperature fell.

The guard returned a while later. "Here's your penalty rations, citizens." He didn't bother to unlock and open the door, he just tossed the two small chunks of bread over the top of the enclosure.

One piece landed on Eva's head and bounced into her arms. The other piece, Anna's, landed somewhere in the mud near her feet. Only the dim echo of a light reached them from the perimeter lighting of the compound, and Anna had to feel around on the ground to find it. She lifted it near her face and tried to rub some of the dirt off of it before eating it.

"This must be less than ten ounces," Eva complained.

Anna took a bite of her bread, dirt grinding in her teeth as she chewed. "There's no way we can make the norms. What are we going to do, Eva?"

Eva was silent for a moment, then whispered, "We're going to die."

Leaning her head back against the sodden logs, Anna closed her eyes and tried to ignore the hunger eating away at her insides and the ice forming on the wall behind her. She willed the bone deep exhaustion to win out, hoping to be able to sleep through the torturous night.

She awoke long before the siren calling the prisoners to breakfast sounded the next morning, shivering next to Eva. Anna was so hungry, all she could think about was food. Those in the punishment cells weren't allowed to go to the mess hall with the other prisoners. Instead, a guard, different from last night's, unlocked the door and allowed each of them to take a cupful of salted warm water.

"What about food?" Eva asked.

"You'll only be fed once a day while you're in here." His face betrayed a touch of pity for the women. "Seven ounces of bread for dinner, and a portion of gruel or soup every third day."

The women looked at each other, Anna wondering how they were going to work without eating.

"I was instructed to take you to headcount. You'll be going out to your work detail today then back here when you return." He held the door open. "On your feet. Let's go."

"What I wouldn't give for a potato," Eva growled as they lined up for headcount.

Of course the women didn't make the impossible norms, though they had become more adept at sawing and were able to down one and a half trees under the watchful eyes of their new brigadier. Anatoly was true to his word; as soon as they reached the awful punishment cell, he ordered them to strip down to their underwear. Anna looked at the guard, a different one than had been there that morning, and asked, "Do we have to, citizen chief?" The brigadier was, after all, only another prisoner, not NKVD.

He scowled. "Do it now or I'll do it for you!" The guard took a step toward her.

Anatoly slapped her. "Don't ever question my authority again, bitch."

With numb fingers and heavy arms, Anna had a hard time unfastening the buttons of her jacket. She glanced at Eva, who seemed to be having the same difficulty.

"Come on, now! I don't have all night!"

Anna shivered. It certainly wasn't the coldest she'd ever been, or probably the hungriest, but more than just her muscles were weakening—her emotional state was breaking. She handed over her clothing items one at a time, putting an arm across her chest to cover the areas of worn cloth on her bra.

Holding their clothes in his arms, Anatoly grinned and nodded. "That's better. I'll drop 'em by in the morning so you can get dressed before heading out to work."

Anna's neck and shoulders were stiff and cramping from shivering all night. Muscle spasms shot through them when she lifted her arms to get dressed in the early morning. All she could think about was that, tonight, she'd at least get some gruel or soup with her measly portion of black bread.

Seven days of hard labor without enough to eat to keep a mouse alive; Anna thought about food almost every second of the day. It's all she and Eva talked about, when they'd still had the energy to talk, torturing themselves with memories of meals they'd eaten back at home. Their clothes had been taken from them each night, and even though the temperatures were warming, it was still well below freezing at night after the stars came out.

She'd been back in the barracks and back to receiving three meals a day, at reduced rations of course, not being able to meet norms, for a few days. April had come sometime during the last week, but the passing of one month into another meant nothing to her as almost eight more years of this torture loomed ahead. Miraculously, Anatoly had returned all of her clothes, even her tin can. Sitting on her bunk after dinner on her third night back, weakened down to her marrow, Anna lifted her weary head as the sound of trucks rolled into the compound. A new transport of prisoners had arrived. She looked around at the overcrowded barracks, wondering how the newcomers were going to fit.

"Anna," a younger, healthier girl named Irena who'd taken to Anna, said, "let's go watch them unload."

Anna shook her head.

"Come on! All you've done since you got back is mope around

and sleep. It'll do you good to do something besides work and sleep." Irena pulled on Anna's hand.

Sighing, Anna relented and slowly got to her feet.

They watched from a distance as the men and women were unloaded from the backs of the trucks like cattle. Some of the men wore military uniforms, including long, dark trench coats. Most of them walked with bowed heads and slumping shoulders, but one man stood out. Anna followed him with her gaze as he marched with his head up, back stiff, looking straight ahead. There was something different about that one.

He only broke his stride to help a woman who had fallen get back to her feet.

Part of her wanted to listen to the headcount, find out what the man's name was when they made the prisoners shout out their names, crimes, and sentences. But exhaustion won out, and she returned to her bunk to lie down.

37

The tall soldier Anna had noticed the day before was assigned to Anna's brigade. She caught herself more than once watching his long strides as they marched to the forest. There was something different about him. Or was it just that he seemed unbroken? She looked away from him. He'd be broken soon, just like the rest of them.

Anatoly, the brigadier, split Anna and Eva up and sent Anna to chop branches off felled trees with a dull axe, always keeping her where he could see her.

Only a few hours into the work day, Anna could barely raise her arms and was making little progress on the tree she'd been working on for the better part of an hour. She struggled to lift the heavy axe again, but lost her grip and watched it fall to the muddy ground. Standing as if in a stupor, Anna swayed as she stared at the axe. *I'll just rest my arms for a few minutes, then try to pick it up.*

Pain shot up her spine and down both legs as Anatoly bashed her with his club just below the small of her back. She dropped to her knees in the mud of the thawing ground. She looked up at him, tears forming in her eyes, as he raised the club to take another swing at her.

The soldier-prisoner, the one with the long strides and the

straight back, appeared from nowhere and plucked the club from the brigadier's hands, flung it past the rope marking the allowed boundaries, and walked back to the tree he'd been working on, picking up the single-person saw to continue.

Anatoly spun around and stared at the man, mouth open, for several seconds before spluttering, "You stinkin' traitor!" He turned to the guard nearest him. "Did you see that? Aren't you going to do something?"

The guard shrugged. "It's your brigade, citizen. I'm just here to keep them from escaping."

The red-faced brigadier looked back at the soldier-prisoner with a touch of fear and a whole lot of anger in his eyes. "Well, asshole, you can do your own work and then finish hers"—he jerked his head toward Anna, still on her knees—"even if it means we all have to stay out here all night!"

Anna reached for the handle of the axe and used it to get to her feet, back muscles spasming. She snuck a glance at the soldier as he sawed through his tree. There was definitely something different about him.

She worked through her pain and fatigued muscles, trying to get as much of her work done as possible so the soldier didn't have to. Still, she didn't even come close to the norms. After finishing his work, he came over without a word and started chopping off the branches on the other side of the tree Anna was working on.

The whole brigade continued working well after darkness set in and returned to camp late, after the kitchen had closed for the night. Anna watched as Anatoly escorted the soldier to the punishment cells and shoved him toward the guard with a curt, "Two weeks! And take his clothes!"

Sitting on her bunk just before lights-out, Anna rubbed her tired arms and thought about food. Eva plopped down beside her and, after a few minutes of silence, said with a weary voice, "The work will kill us, but we are only able to survive by working."

Unlike with Anna and Eva, the brigadier commanded that the soldier stay the whole two weeks inside the punishment cell instead of being let out for work each day. It had been a few days since he'd stood up for her then worked alongside her in silence. She was still only getting a small percentage of her rations, since it was impossible for her to meet the norms set by some sadistic bureaucrat far from the forests of the Kolyma. She wondered, as she ate the small portion of moldy black bread given to her for supper break, if the soldier was getting any food at all.

It was during these solitary breaks that Anna missed Pyotr most of all. Instead of eating with a group of other prisoners as Eva often did, she preferred to find a solitary place where she could have imagined conversations with the priest, telling him things she'd never had the guts to tell him when he'd been there. This day, she thought about Zoya and imagined meeting up with her after... When they were both free and had somehow survived. It was easier to think about surviving in the still cold but warming Spring.

The guard's whistle brought her out of her fanciful thoughts, and she went back to her tree and hefted the heavy axe.

Most of the prisoners, probably all that weren't bedridden or in punishment cells, milled about outside as night fell. The sun had shone down on them all day, further thawing the ground into dregs of mud, but also warming the weary prisoners. They were reluctant to spend this time before lights-out inside the dreary barracks, Anna included.

Hands on the small of her back, Anna arched, stretching out her tight muscles, as the last rays of the sun disappeared behind the horizon.

"I bet there's still some nice tits under that jacket," slurred a trusty she'd seen often inside the women's barracks. "Come back to my cabin with me so I can take a look."

Anna shook her head, frantically wondering when these animals would leave her alone. Her body was wrecked—all loose skin and sagging breasts—her face had to look at least a decade older than she was after two winters working out in the frostbiting, freezing cold of the Kolyma.

"Come on now." He stepped closer. "I've had my eye on you for a while. I can get you some light work, I have an in with the laundry." He reached for her arm.

Anna ran as fast as her worn-out legs and adrenaline would allow, losing him in the crowd of people. She ran until her breaths came in painful gasps, lungs burning and side splitting, not stopping until she feared she would faint. She slumped down behind a pile of wood near one of the punishment pits—used when the other cells were full or just whenever a guard or trusty wanted to inflict even more misery on a *zek*.

As her breathing gradually returned to normal and her heart rate slowed, she heard a voice coming from the nearest pit. A beautiful voice singing an old hymn from the time before the revolution. She closed her eyes and listened, the voice soothing her fear and making her forget about her pain. She couldn't be sure it was him, but imagined the lovely sound coming from the soldier.

The siren sounded, signaling lights-out in ten minutes, and Anna reluctantly got to her feet and joined the group of people headed toward the barracks. She looked around like a scared rabbit, hoping to stay hidden from the trusty who had propositioned her. She really missed Zoya.

Anna returned to the woodpile every evening she could during the next week and a half. She knew he must be miserable down in the muddy pit, likely with nothing but his underwear on. She wished she could give him some food, knowing from experience that he had to be starving. But she couldn't give up any of her meager portion—even if she could figure out a way to get it to him. He sang or hummed every evening, his voice growing a little weaker each day, yet still beautiful. Even through a cold bout of rain, rivulets running into the pit turning the damp soil into thick mud, he hummed, though the sound was muffled, like he hid his head beneath his arms.

When at last, two weeks after the club incident, the soldier returned to the morning line-up, Anna risked a glance at him. He was pale and gaunt, his uniform hanging looser than before, but he still had a sparkle in his eyes. He caught her looking at him and smiled. Before she looked away, her mouth curled into a half-smile without her permission. A long-hidden sensation crept from behind the thick wall she'd built and fluttered in her stomach for the briefest of moments before the logging work brigade was driven out of camp and down the soggy road. She kept her eyes focused on the ground in front of her for the entire hour-long trek.

When they broke for their ten-minute supper break halfway through the workday, Anna went to her usual spot overlooking the river, now overflowing its banks with the spring thaw. She hummed one of the tunes she'd heard the soldier singing while in the pit, her voice a terrible substitute for his.

Boots slurping through the mud alerted her to someone approaching, and she turned with a start to find the soldier standing a few yards to the side of her. Anna took a step back, fear from old wounds making itself known—yet somehow, her instincts insisted this man was safe. Not at all like those who had hurt her.

"It's okay. I won't come any closer." His soft voiced soothed some of her fear. "My name is Georgi."

"I'm Anna," she whispered.

"What are you here for?"

Many prisoners asked this of each other, even though the answer was almost always the same. Anna replied as she usually did, bitterly saying, "I'm an enemy of the people, of course. What about you?" A part of her urged her not to talk to this stranger, but a bigger part really missed the supper break talks with Pyotr. And...this man had stood up to Anatoly for her, and suffered the consequences of that action.

"Officially?" He shrugged and frowned. "They say I was 'active in traitorous activities while in captivity'."

"Captivity?"

"Yes. I am...was...a soldier fighting in the Winter War against Finland that just ended last month. I was unfortunate enough to be captured by the Finns and held as a POW. As soon as the war was over, they released all of us back to the USSR, and we were immediately taken under heavy guard to special camps, interrogated by a huge team of people, and..." He looked out over the river, silent for a long moment. "Some were sentenced to death, others were released, and most of us were sentenced to the Gulags."

Anna raised her eyebrow as his gaze returned to hers.

"I'm in for twenty-five."

"Twenty-five! That's awful! That seems like an especially terrible thing to do to a soldier just fighting for his country." Anna hadn't even known they were at war. She may have heard some mumblings about it, but she tended to block all the chatter out these days. She rarely even spoke with Eva anymore. So, why had she opened up to this soldier? Georgi?

A guard blew his whistle, and the brigadier shouted, "Back to work, you shirkers!"

Anna and Georgi fell into a sort of routine over the next few days, him finding her during supper break, sitting with her and talking. Mostly it was him talking, as Anna was content to just listen, not wanting to share too much with him. He sometimes found her when trekking to or from the work site, slowing his steps to match hers even though they weren't allowed to talk.

Anatoly had, for some reason, singled her out for persecution, hitting her, threatening her, yelling at her about norms—but only when Georgi was nowhere near.

The camp director had commanded Anatoly and the other brigadiers that the prisoners were to get no less than a thirty-minute break for supper each day, so the ten-minute break was reluctantly extended. There was no such command to return the smoke breaks they used to get throughout the day, though.

Sitting on a tree stump overlooking the river and loading platform down the hill, Anna listened to Georgi talk about his time in the war and the POW camp. His smooth voice soothed her, and she found herself wishing to hear him sing again but didn't want to admit to listening to him when he was in the pit.

She snuck a glance at him, moving her gaze from his long eyelashes to his strong jaw covered with stubble. His kindness almost made her want to smile. Almost. The hunger gnawing away at her insides day and night made it impossible to fully focus on anything else. She wouldn't live long on these reduced rations.

"What are you thinking about, Anna?" Georgi pulled her from her thoughts of potatoes and sausage.

She shrugged, not really embarrassed to be caught with her mind wandering because the conditions they lived under merited it from time to time. "Food."

"Ahh, yes." He looked down at the last bite of his salted herring, then offered it up to her. "Hunger rules the world."

Anna shook her head. "No. I can't take your food. You need it as much as I do."

As much of a gentleman as he was, he still didn't offer twice. Food was too scarce and the need for it made one's convictions weak.

"What do you mean by 'hunger rules the world'?" Anna asked.

"Hunger rules every hungry human—unless you've made the decision to die. It forces an honest person to steal and an unselfish person to peer with envy into another's bowl. It invades the brain, refusing to allow it to be distracted by anything else or to think about anything else. It invades our dreams on the rare occasions it allows us to sleep." He stopped and looked at her. "I'm sorry about going on like that. Hunger has me in its grasp too."

"You sound like a poet." She glanced up in time to see a smile part his lips.

"Ahh. I used to really love words. Now I would trade them all for a half-eaten potato!"

This time Anna did smile, only slightly, as she shook her head.

38

Traipsing through the clay-like mud to the latrines was difficult, especially after a fourteen-hour workday, but still much better than in the midst of winter, when the temperature was fifty below zero and there was snow up to her knees. Anna pushed open the rickety door when she'd finished her business and stepped out of the foul little building.

"Ahh, I've been looking all over for you, citizen."

Anna turned to run from the trusty who had propositioned her a few weeks ago, but he was much quicker than her. He grabbed her arm and yanked her behind the latrine. He wrapped both arms around her and crushed her to his chest. His mouth next to her ear, he said, "This time, I'm not asking." His hands roved, and she struggled to get out of his grasp. "It's more fun this way, anyway."

He slammed her to the ground and slapped her when she called out for help—knowing there would be no one to save her. He straddled her and worked to unbutton his pants as she tried to push out from under him.

A blur of motion came around the corner of the latrine, followed by a heavy *thunk* and the would-be rapist slumping to the ground beside Anna. She pushed herself out from under his leg that lay limp across her, crying and ready to run.

"Anna."

Georgi's voice brought her back from panic. She wrapped her arms around herself, heaving breaths as she tried to gain control of the sobs. Looking from Georgi's gentle face down to the twitching body of the trusty, blood oozing from the back of his head, Anna was suddenly afraid for Georgi. She looked up at him and whispered through tears. "What are we going to do?"

"Leave him to rot in the mud as he deserves." Georgi took a step closer to her, still keeping a distance of several feet. "Are you okay?"

She nodded, but her continuing tears and now trembling body betrayed the truth. She wasn't okay. She would never be okay in this cesspit of humanity.

"Let me walk you back to your barracks."

Forcing one foot in front of the other as she wiped the moisture from her cheeks, she walked with Georgi back to the women's barracks, searching their surroundings for anyone who might have seen them leaving the scene.

Georgi talked quietly as they made their way across the compound. "I would never force myself upon a woman, Anna. I want you to know that about me. Any man who does that is not a man but an animal."

Anna took one last swipe at the tears and squared her shoulders. Still too shaky to speak, she just nodded her head, knowing she could trust this man. This soldier. Couldn't she?

When they reached her barracks, he bid her goodnight and went on his way.

The heat from all the bodies pressed together in the building was becoming unbearable—and it was only early May. Anna removed her jacket and laid it on her bunk before sitting on it. She stared up at Stalin's picture, a deep frown creasing her forehead.

"Isn't he wonderful?" gushed a woman, Sasha, from the next bunk over.

At first Anna, thoughts still on Georgi and the trusty, was confused. How did Sasha know Georgi?

"We're so lucky to have such a man as our Supreme Leader."

Anna whipped her head around. "What?"

"I don't expect an anti-Soviet such as yourself to understand. But I am a Loyalist! I served the Party on the outside, and I serve the Party here in camp! My long sentence has not broken my will in the struggle for the Soviet government, for Soviet industry."

Anna looked at the red scarf tied around the woman's head and clamped her mouth shut on any further conversation with her.

"Sasha, really, your own husband was executed by *the Party*," said an old woman named Maria. She was a nun, serving her second sentence for refusing to denounce her religion.

"I hold no grudge for that or for my own imprisonment, and if I leave here someday, I am going to live as if none of this had happened." Sasha spread her hands as if to encompass the entirety of the prison compound.

"If the Party is always so right, then what were you imprisoned for?" Maria asked.

Sasha's eyes widened, and she choked on her own inhaled spit for a moment. Anna had learned that Party members did not like it when asked that question, and Sasha was certainly having a hard time answering it.

"Why, nothing at all." She looked away from the old nun, up at Stalin's picture. "It wasn't the Party that arrested me. I was slandered, and here I sit among enemies of the people." She shook her head. "And so many of my acquaintances, so many loyal Communists..."

Maria laughed, a cynical, cold laugh. "So *you* are innocent, Comrade Sasha, but the rest of us have been imprisoned for good cause. In other words, you all remained calm when society was being imprisoned, but when those in your inner circle began to be imprisoned, your outrage boiled over!"

"Of course I don't expect you to understand."

"Oh, I understand," Maria said. "This is the price a person pays for entrusting your God-given soul to *human* dogma. I understand, also, that you must keep repeating your ideological arguments in order to hold on to a sense of your own *rightness*—otherwise you would go insane."

"And what of your daughter?" another woman asked Sasha. "Would you have her follow the same path as you and your husband?"

Sasha sat stiffly on her bunk, nose pushed into the air. "My daughter? I will tell you how my daughter will live. Only fifteen, she sent me a letter when I was first sentenced asking me if I was guilty. She said that if I told her I wasn't, then she would not join the Komsomol and would never forgive the Party for imprisoning me. But, she said, 'if you are guilty, I won't write to you anymore and I will hate you.' And," she wrung her hands, "how could she live without the Komsomol? How could I permit her to hate Soviet power? Better that she should hate me. So I wrote back simply *I am guilty. Enter the Komsomol.*" She wiped her eyes and again stared devotedly at Stalin.

"Ahh," Maria nodded, "it must be so hard for you to bear: having fallen beneath your beloved axe, and now having to justify its wisdom."

Anna had heard the Loyalist arguments before—so many of their own Party had been imprisoned in 1937 and '38—but she would never understand how so many human beings could believe the garbage that came from their own mouths. She laid down and wrapped her jacket around her head to muffle the sounds of chatter around her. She fell asleep thinking about Georgi, praying no one connected him to the likely dead thief trusty behind the latrine.

Morning headcount took hours because of the "missing" trusty. The guards counted over and over, never coming up with the right number.

As Anna stood in the brisk morning air, her thoughts tossed about in her head. Georgi. His smile and kindness and bravery. He'd found her as she was being attacked and didn't even hesitate to step in. So many times since her arrest she'd seen men watch the horrors committed against women and never attempt to help. Men who would never commit such acts, but were just as guilty for not trying to stop them. Cowering in the corner of a Black Mariah; watching from the safety of their bunks; averting their eyes and walking away out in the open compound.

But not Georgi. He'd come to her defense twice now. What made him so different from the rest?

Dark memories crowded in, intruding on her thoughts of gratitude toward Georgi. Kissing Nikolai in the alley just before his murder at the hands of the NKVD. How his body twitched as it was riddled by bullets there on the sidewalk.

The Black Mariah.

A strangled sound issued from her throat and she squeezed her eyes shut and shook her head to dispel the images. In its place, she saw the twitching trusty, blood oozing from his head, a blood-stained brick laying nearby. The act Georgi committed was justified. The man deserved it. Guilt crept in, though, battling with thoughts of justice.

"Woman!" a guard with a clipboard yelled in her face. "Name, crime, sentence!"

Anna rattled off the words she'd said every day, twice a day since arriving at the transit prison. Then, finally, after the sun had already risen, Anna's brigade was released to march an hour to their logging site.

It wasn't a conscious decision, but some of Anna's walls had been breached when Georgi saved her from the rapist trusty. At supper break, as they sat next to each other on two separate tree stumps,

Anna, for the first time, started the conversation. "Tell me about being a prisoner of war. Was it as terrible as this?"

He sat for a moment, chewing on the tough black bread.

Anna glanced at his uniform, where the insignia had been ripped off, and wondered what rank he had held.

Georgi swallowed and looked at her. "In some ways it was better, others worse."

She looked down at the crumb of bread left in her hand. "At least they fed you better, right?"

Shaking his head, he replied, "Not for the Soviets. There were a few POWs from other nations, and they got rations from the Red Cross. But not us. The USSR does not recognize the International Red Cross—hell, it doesn't recognize its own soldiers from the day before—so, we got no packages from them and had to survive off the war rations the Finns gave us."

"Why did they arrest you when you were released? Why weren't they happy for your safe return after fighting for the Motherland?" Anna shook her head. "I don't understand it."

Georgi sat in silent thought before answering. "I've spent many hours considering that question. And I've come up with multiple scenarios to try to make sense of it. But they all boil down to this for me: A Motherland that betrays its soldiers—is that really a Motherland? If your mother throws you to the dogs, is she still your mother?"

Anna nodded. She agreed with his sentiment, but still questioned why?

As if reading her mind, he continued. "I think that much of it comes from the idea that anyone—even a POW—who experiences the way people in other European countries live, will come back to the Soviet Union and spill his guts. Talk about how grand people live there—with white bread and no endless lines to get scarce food. Their own homes or apartments. A free press! But also, Anna, one must remember that our government never imprisons and executes people for having *done* something. They imprison and execute them to *keep them from* doing something. They imprisoned us POWs not for treason to the Motherland, but to keep us from telling our fellow villagers about Europe."

The shrill whistle of the guard roused Anna from the trance Georgi's voice and words had put her in. She sighed, nearly crying because of her bone-deep weariness.

Before parting ways back to their work assignments, Georgi said, "Can we continue our conversation tonight back at camp...if you'd like? We can meet up outside the kitchen."

Anna nodded. "Okay."

Georgi smiled. "See you then."

They met up and wandered over to the rocks where Anna and Pyotr used to sit and talk when the temperatures allowed. They'd miraculously returned from work detail before the sun had set, and they watched in silence as it drifted below the tree line in the distance.

Then they talked. And for the first time, Anna found herself telling someone what happened the night of her arrest. Georgi's fists curled up as she sobbed out the story while she looked at the ground, embarrassed and wondering why she was telling him, yet unable to stop. She didn't realize until she'd finished, that sometime during the torturous disgorgement of her soul, her soldier had taken her hand in his. And she allowed his warmth and kindness to thaw a little of her frozen heart.

39

Summer in the Kolyma was no more bearable than winter. Work hours increased to fourteen hours a day, with no increase in rations or days off. Anna strained to drag a large log through the thick, clay-like mud, sinking to her calves with almost every step. The effort it took to pull her feet from the sucking mud was more than it took to slog through the snow in winter.

She dropped the log next to the pile and swatted at the gray cloud of noisy mosquitoes buzzing about her. It was better not to swat at them, she'd learned, because the more she waved them away, the more they seemed to attack. But her face was a mass of swollen mosquito bites, and they crawled up her sleeves and got inside her scarf.

Anna's inflamed face flushed even deeper as her slog back to her assigned work area brought her near a naked man tied to a tree. Earlier that day, just after arriving at the logging camp, the prisoner had been caught nosing around the bag of rations the guards had brought for supper break. They'd stripped him of all of his clothing and tied him, hands bound, to the tree, where the mosquitoes had swarmed him relentlessly, crawling in his mouth when he cried out, climbing up his nose and into his ears. His skin was raw and swollen. Anna wondered how much blood so many mosquitoes could suck out of a man. Would he be dead before they were allowed to head back to camp? Drained of blood or too weak to make the trek back?

Trying not to dwell on the poor man, Anna thought about Georgi —until the shaking of her muscles with each lift of the axe drove all thoughts from her mind. She wasn't going to make it another eight years here.

Anna entered the barracks just as the guard snatched their lantern for lights-out and made her way to her shared bunk where Eva sat in the dark. They hadn't been shipping as many prisoners in, and with the dead bodies they foisted out each day, the executions, and transfers, there was sometimes actually room to breathe.

"You've been spending a lot of time with soldier boy lately," Eva said, her voice teasing.

Anna half-smiled in the dark. "He's very sweet."

"Well, I'm happy for you, kid." Her voice turned serious. "Just don't get too attached."

Anna knew she shouldn't. Their lives weren't theirs, and they could be separated by a transfer—or death—at any time. But dammit! She deserved just a spark of happiness, didn't she? And Georgi made her happy. He'd sung to her tonight, the first time she'd heard him sing since he'd been in the pit for standing up for her with the brigadier. And singing wasn't the only talent he possessed. He told her he was an artist—one of his paintings had even won a prize once.

Anna drifted off to sleep with thoughts of Georgi's sweet voice and honey-brown eyes in her head.

Walking hand-in-hand, Anna and Georgi enjoyed their rare day off—they hadn't gotten one in several months. They were always careful not to go off anywhere by themselves, that wasn't allowed for the *zeks*, but she had allowed him to hug her when they knew no one was watching except maybe the tower guard, and he had other things to watch out for.

"Anna, I've been thinking about the future," he swatted at a mosquito, "I know, it's a stupid thing to think about in our predicament, but I can't help it."

"Tell me about your dreams of the future, I want to hear them," Anna squeezed his hand.

Georgi looked down at her, his cracked lips forming a smile on his dirty face. "When you're released...will you wait for me? I know it's a lot to ask, I'm here for much longer than you, but maybe I'll be one of the lucky ones to get amnestied. I've heard of it happening."

She'd heard of it too, but had yet to see it with her own eyes. She thought it was probably just a cruel rumor someone had started to give them false hope. "I will wait for you, my soldier. Tell me of your plans for us." She didn't tell him she knew she'd never make it out of there. Eight more years was just too long for her body to endure the conditions. *Let him dream,* she thought. *And I'll dream with him.*

"Oh, you can come with me to my village, or I can go to you in Moscow so you can stay close to your mother." A touch of excitement sounded in his voice. "Or she can come with us to my village!"

Anna smiled, just short of a laugh, and stopped walking, turning him to face her. "My mama would love you, Georgi."

He pulled her to him and planted a quick kiss on her lips—their first, even though they'd spent every spare moment with each other for weeks—then pulled her to him and whispered, "I love you, Anna."

Anna's heart leapt and her pulse quickened. Her thoughts briefly flashed upon Nikolai before returning to the present. "And I love you, Georgi." She knew it was absurd and even dangerous. She'd seen other *zek* couples get caught sneaking off together to find some seclusion from the eyes of the camp—and none had ended well. The best outcome was a stint in the punishment cells; the worst... She couldn't think about that. She resolved that she and Georgi would never "be alone" together. They deserved to have this small bit of happiness among the crushing fear, hunger, and savagery brought upon them.

The guards and trusties had left her alone since she and Georgi had become a couple. There was, apparently, some unspoken rule amongst the prisoners not to mess with another's "camp wife."

She looked up at him, hoping for another kiss—this time maybe not such a quick one—and tried to envision what a normal life with him might be like. A married life. And she wondered what that would have been like with Nikolai had none of this horror ever happened.

PART IV

Winter 1940-1941

40

"I'm not going to make it through this winter, Georgi," Anna said through chattering teeth as they stood in the tramped down snow for supper break in the logging camp. "I can't do this work anymore." She looked down at her rag-covered hands, the mittens Zoya had given her had disintegrated months ago.

The sadness in Georgi's eyes almost made her sorry she'd said it. But she needed to prepare him for the inevitable. She was skin and bones, a walking skeleton. Her muscles had diminished to nothing but strings holding her bones together. She could no longer swing an axe or grip a saw, much less drag heavy logs into piles. Every time they slogged through the snow to or from the logging site, she wondered if she would make it. Wondered how it would feel to just lie down in the snow and never get up.

Georgi reached for her frozen hand and pled, "Please just hold on a little longer, my Anna. I'll find a way to get you off general labor."

Looking into his earnest eyes, she couldn't deny him. "I'll try."

Back to work after the break, Anna tried to lift her axe but did little more than lift the handle from the ground. The one-person saw was lighter, so she gripped it with both hands and went to work with her rebelling muscles to saw the limbs off of a felled tree.

On the way back to camp, Georgi trudged beside her, the two of them at the back of the column, with the only other person behind them besides a guard and his dog being an old man with yellow skin and sunken eyes, sores around his toothless mouth. Anna glanced back at him and thought, *last-legger. That's what I am now.*

That evening, after dinner at which Georgi insisted that Anna take his soup and a portion of his bread, he walked her back to her barracks, telling her he had something to do and would see her in the morning.

Anna curled up on her bunk, shivering, only getting up once before lights-out to empty her bowels of the food Georgi had so selflessly given her.

☭

Dragging her feet over the icy snow, Anna made her way toward the mess hall for breakfast, not looking up until she reached the serving window and held out her can for some gruel. Her memories flashed back to the warm, thick kashi she used to eat as a child. It was nothing like the watered-down version being ladled into her can.

Georgi caught up to her, the glint of a smile shining through the worry on his face. "Anna, I have some great news to tell you. After headcount, we won't be going out to the forest today—or ever again, I hope."

Anna frowned. "What do you mean?" She couldn't begin to comprehend how that could be possible—unless they were slated for execution.

"Well...do you remember a few weeks ago when the new camp commander asked at headcount for anyone who could paint to raise their hand?"

"Yes, and you didn't raise yours. You said you didn't want to paint for *them.*"

He shrugged. "I changed my mind. Last night I showed him a little of what I can do and told him I'd paint whatever he wants in exchange for moving you to a better job."

The heavy weight on Anna's shoulders seemed to lighten just a bit. "And he agreed to that?"

"He did! Today, I will start painting, and you will start doing laundry for the camp commander and his wife. No more general labor for either of us." He looked down at his dirty hands. "First, we need to clean up a little."

Tears sprang to Anna's sunken eyes, and she threw herself at him, hugging him without caring who saw. "Maybe I'll survive after all," she whispered in his ear.

The laundry for the camp commander and other camp officials was located in a separate shack from the general prisoners' laundry. The first thing Anna noticed was how warm it was inside, and she relished the warmth. It would be miserable in the summer, but she'd deal with that when the time came. For the first time in months, she had hope that she'd see summer again.

When Anna took the first load of freshly cleaned and pressed laundry to the camp commander's quarters, his wife opened the door and gasped. "Oh dear! You look like a walking corpse!" The chubby woman shook her head then pasted a fake smile on her face. "Well, you must be Anna. Joseph told me you'd be by today. Follow me, I'll show you where to put them."

After instructing her on precisely what to do with each different type of clothing and other laundry, she left Anna to finish up the job.

After doing a couple more loads and returning to the quarters to put them away, Anna found herself with nothing left to do. She found the commander's wife sitting by the fire flipping through a book. "Ma'am?" Anna whispered.

The woman startled and put her hand on her chest. "You scared me, Anna." Looking on her with pity as she'd done each time Anna had entered her home that day, she asked, "What do you want?"

Anna bowed her head to look at her pieced-together footwear

that somewhat resembled boots. "I...I'm finished with the laundry. Is there something else you'd like me to do?"

"No." She pursed her lips. "You've done enough for today. But don't expect me to take it easy on you every day."

Anna nodded and backed out of the warm room, not sure what to do with herself for the remainder of the day. She'd gotten full rations for supper break, and her stomach, not used to the increase in food, was a little irritable. So she bundled up and headed to the latrine on the other side of the compound. Each time she went there, the memory of the trusty's smashed-in head haunted her. They'd found his body a few days after the incident, but nothing had come of it. Nobody had seen her and Georgi leaving the area.

Afterword, she couldn't decide whether to go back to the barracks and rest—if the fire was going in the stove—or to go find Georgi. After remembering stories of what went on in the barracks before all the general labor workers returned, Anna decided to stay out in the freezing temperatures just a bit longer as she searched for the building Georgi had told her he'd be working in.

The only building in the area that had smoke coming from the stovepipe had to be it. Anna knocked before hearing Georgi's sweet voice, "Yes? Come in."

There stood her soldier, wearing a paint-stained apron, his brush stroking across a large canvas set on an easel before him. A small postcard was tacked to the easel above the canvas. Anna stood in awe as she studied the half-finished painting, comparing it to the much inferior picture on the card.

"Georgi, that's amazing!"

He stood and set his brush on a tray before taking her in his arms and giving her the longest kiss they'd ever shared. "How are you feeling today, my love?"

Anna leaned into his chest, taking advantage of being alone with him. "Like I might actually survive this. At least for a while longer."

She stepped back and stared at the painting again. "What are these for? These paintings?"

"Mostly they're for the camp leaders' apartments. They'll either hang them for their own enjoyment or sell them. They also have me painting rugs." He gestured toward a pile of plain rugs in the corner. "Apparently they sell quite well at the markets, making the citizen chiefs a good amount of extra money."

☭

Life drastically improved for both Anna and Georgi. Even full rations wasn't enough food, but it was a feast compared to what Anna had been getting. She even snuck bread and meat back to the barracks for Eva once in a while. Her friend and former logging-mate's health was declining fast. Anna worried she wouldn't make it through the winter, and she vowed to help where she could.

The camp commander and his wife were decent enough to Anna. She avoided going anywhere near the commander when he'd been drinking, though. He became more handsy the more vodka he drank—even in the presence of his wife.

Georgi's paintings and rugs were a huge hit, bringing the highest prices at the markets in the nearest towns. This allowed them to have a bit of breathing space from the camp rules—mostly that he and Anna were able to spend time alone in either his paint building or the laundry, while the commander and other camp leaders turned a blind eye.

The two lovebirds snuck in a few kisses when they had time alone together but their physical affection never went beyond that. They mostly just enjoyed the time together and talked while the other worked.

They both regained some health with the easy work and full rations, but the sequalae from three years of torture, hard labor, and the effects of being out day after day in the sub-zero temperatures had done a number on Anna. Her joints always ached like she was an old woman instead of a twenty-four-year-old. Her fingers and toes were always numb from the damage done by frostbite. Her back was permanently damaged from the smack of truncheons against it.

But life in the camp was finally bearable.

Anna sat on a crate in Georgi's paint building—they'd started calling it his "studio" as a joke. It was less a studio and more of a cramped room where the camp leaders stored stuff, including items they'd "confiscated" from the political prisoners to sell or keep for themselves.

"Maybe when we are both finally free, you can make a living with your beautiful painting," Anna said. "Then you can paint what you want instead of painting what they tell you to."

His smile didn't reach his eyes. "I'll still have to paint what they want. Just like everything else in the Soviet Union, you can't take a step before asking permission, first pledging your undying allegiance to the Supreme Leader and the Communist Party, and ensuring your steps are in-line with the current decrees—which change on a daily basis."

It wasn't like him to be so morose. Anna rubbed the soreness from her hands after a full day of stirring laundry in the big vats. "What would you paint, if you could paint whatever you wanted?"

Without hesitation he replied, "You, Anna, though I'd worry I could never capture the beauty of your soul just right."

She stood and took his paint brush and tray from him, setting it aside, then wrapped him in her arms and offered her lips up for his kiss. He'd always been so careful not to overstep with her, knowing her past abuses and fear of affection. But this time, he kissed her deeper, pulled her closer, curled his fingers in her hair.

"Anna," he panted as he pulled away from the kiss, his eyes glossy and lips red. "I'm sorry. I—"

Fear didn't take over as it had before when she'd thought about giving herself to him. This time, her body stirred, wanting more. She cut his words off with kiss, then took a step back from him and looked into his eyes as she untied the twine that held her skirt up around her waist.

"Anna," he looked at her questioningly, "are you sure?"

She nodded, afraid that if she spoke out loud her voice would betray her. She pushed thoughts of Nikolai and the Black Mariah and Isaak out of her head, replacing them with her soldier's honey-colored eyes and long eyelashes and kind words and actions.

They lay in each other's arms after, wrapped up in a painter's tarp near the stove. Georgi traced his finger along Anna's jaw, staring into her eyes, reluctant to bring an end to the moment. He kissed the tip of her nose and sighed. "We'd better get dressed before the dinner siren sounds."

They weren't worried about being interrupted, no one had ever walked in on them before. Georgi always went to the camp leaders to get his assignments, they didn't come to him.

The door rattled, and Georgi sat up, alarm written on his face. He stood and reached for his pants, getting one leg in them before the door opened with a whoosh of cold air.

There stood the camp commander and another, official-looking man. They looked from the naked Georgi to the dirty tarp covering Anna.

"Get dressed," the commander said, steel in his voice, "both of you."

As they scrambled to get their clothes on, the official sneered at the commander. "How long has this been going on?"

"I...I have no idea, inspector," the camp commander stuttered. "This is the first time I've seen them together...like this."

"Bullshit, comrade. Either this has been going on under your nose —in which case you aren't paying attention—or you've known about it and have been letting it happen."

Anger boiled in the commander's face as he whipped around to look at Anna and Georgi. "You two will spend two weeks in the penalty cells!"

Anna darted her eyes to Georgi, dread filling her chest. Two weeks! In sub-zero temperatures...

The commander's wife took pity on Anna and snuck her a thin blanket through one of the guards, but it did little to assuage the bone-deep freezing. At least they were put in cells with roofs this time, but no source of heat.

As she shivered in the darkness, Anna filled her head with memories of Georgi, and at times, she thought she could hear his voice, singing, sifting through the log walls.

At the end of the two weeks, she'd lost all the weight she'd been able to put on while getting full rations. Her bones ached and her skin sagged. Her hair had frozen a couple of times to the wall and the bench where she tried to sleep, and it had broken off in chunks when she sat up. As the guard escorted her back to the women's barracks mid-morning the day of her release from the punishment cell, she craned her neck to see if she could catch a glimpse of Georgi, but she didn't see him among the few prisoners hurrying about in the cold.

Nearing the barracks, Anna stopped and stared. They'd been busy in the last two weeks. Where there used to be an open area between the women's barracks and the men's barracks, now stood a six-foot tall barbed-wire fence.

"Yep," the guard said, "no more fraternizing between male and female prisoners. The inspector ordered it. He said something about not wanting enemies of the people to procreate or waste their energy on fornicating. You're here to pay a debt to the Soviet Union, not to enjoy yourselves like a bunch of horny teenagers."

He pushed her forward. "Come on."

Anna bit her lip. Besides warmth and food, the only thing she'd thought about for the last two weeks was being with Georgi. Thinking of ways they would be more careful so as not to get caught again. Even if they were both put back out on general labor details—they could have found a way. But now...Anna glanced at the fence again before the guard shoved her into the barracks. Now, how would they see each other?

Crying was a waste of time. Anger took the place of her tears as she stood in a mostly empty barracks with the last-leggers slowly dying on the wooden bunks, and the crackling camp radio playing soft music. She shouldn't have let herself be almost happy, because she knew they would take it from her, to take *him* from her like they had everything else that mattered in her pitiful life.

She faced the guard as he was turning to leave. "What am I supposed to do now?" She braced herself to hear the words she'd been dreading since being caught—*you're going back to the logging camp.*

Instead, he said, "The commander's wife somehow convinced him to keep you on as her laundress. She said for you to get your rations when the siren signals supper break, then head to the laundry —you have a lot of work to catch up on."

This news was unexpected and lifted her tired spirits just a little. Did she dare ask... "What about Georgi?"

The guard laughed. "Your camp husband isn't so lucky. He was sent out to general labor before the sun even thought about rising this morning."

Any smallest bit of hope she'd had was squashed to the frozen ground. *Georgi.* She didn't even notice the guard had left as thoughts stormed through her mind. How unfair this all was. They'd only been doing what men and women had been doing since Adam and Eve. What every trusty and guard did with whatever woman caught their eye. She would never understand why the criminals received so much more respect than the Fifty-eights. The horrible acts they committed seemed to be so easily forgiven by the Soviet powers, while the regular, hard-working citizens were the ones to suffer so many atrocities.

The supper break siren sounded, and Anna readjusted her scarf to cover her head and face, then stepped out into the cold of the tundra. She stood for a moment, looking at the new fence. Guards were posted on each side, rifles slung over their shoulders.

41

Stomping her feet and hugging herself, Anna looked around at the rows of male prisoners—they'd even separated them by sex for headcount now. She frowned beneath her threadbare scarf as she spotted Georgi on the other side of the fence, the spotlights glaring down on the section where he stood, shoulders slumped. He was gaunt and sickly looking, paler than usual with sunken eyes, dark circles beneath them. Anna wondered how they were planning to keep the men and women apart out on the general work assignments, almost wishing she'd been put back to logging too, just so she'd have a chance to talk to him.

But as she stood in the freezing cold, listening to the brigadiers and guards report the number of prisoners who'd died that day—from starvation, illness, freezing, or execution, it didn't matter, they were all just numbers to the camp chiefs—she was grateful she'd been allowed to keep her "easy" work assignment. Guilt flooded her for that thought as her eyes drifted back to Georgi.

After headcount, Anna wandered as close to the new fence as she dared, gazing through the barbed-wire, hoping to get a glimpse of him. Just when she could stand the cold no more and decided to return to the barracks, she spotted him at the same time as he found her. He pulled his scarf down briefly so she could see him smile, then he gave a thumbs-up and a cautious wave.

Anna smiled and waved back, longing to speak to him, to touch him—even if only through the wires. But the guard on her side spotted her wave and stepped toward her.

It went on like this each evening after headcount, both of them trying to avoid being seen by the guards as they gestured to each other.

Anna was falling. Where before, when she'd had Georgi and his company to look forward to each day, now she had nothing but to see him from afar and watch as his health continued to deteriorate.

Spotting him several yards from the fence, she tried to smile as she crossed her arms over her chest, hoping he understood her meaning—wanting so badly to hug him, to feel his body pressed against hers, or even just his hand wrapped around her icy fingers.

The guard on Georgi's side of the fence looked right at her and then turned to him. Anna's pulse raced when the guard stepped toward Georgi, the word "no" stuck in her throat. But the guard hadn't moved to reposition his rifle from his back where it hung, and he put a hand up in what appeared to be a goodwill gesture. So Anna swallowed the "no" and stood watching, shifting from one foot to the other in the cold.

The guard talked quietly, puffs of breath floating in the air in front of him, and Georgi nodded. They both twisted their heads to look at the guard on the women's side, standing at the opposite end of the fence. Georgi's guard jerked his head in the other direction, then headed toward his counterpart. Georgi pointed for Anna to go down the fence line where an outhouse partially blocked the view.

She followed him on the opposing side of the fence, looking back every few steps to ensure the guards weren't coming after them. They stopped, Georgi standing close to the fence and Anna a few steps away.

"Come closer, my Anna. It's okay."

With another look at the guards, both now smoking and talking, facing away from them, she stepped closer. Close enough to reach through the gaps in the barbed-wire and touch Georgi—but she didn't. She was scared.

"Anna," he whispered, "how have you been?"

"Worried about *you*," she responded.

His smiled warmed her heart, if not the rest of her body. "I'm just fine. Better, now that I can talk to you."

"Are you sure it's safe? What did your guard say?"

"It's safe as long as he can keep the other guard distracted. He's a soldier, like me. He served in the Winter War with a different battalion than me, but he holds some sympathy for those of us who were taken captive by the Finns and who are now imprisoned."

Anna looked down the fence line then back at her soldier. "So he's allowing us to talk?"

Georgi nodded, his eyes furrowed into a frown. "But no touching. He wouldn't go so far as to give us that little pleasure."

Oh, how she'd wanted to touch his face, hold his hand. But this was enough. Hearing his whispered voice and being close enough to see the lone freckle on the side of his nose, near his eye. "I've missed you so, Georgi."

"And I, you." His eyes took on a look of remorse. "I'm so sorry about what happened. I never would have—"

She stopped him by putting up her hand, palm toward him, and shaking her head. "No apologies. I just remember that night as beautiful before it turned terrible—and only the beautiful part was your doing, Georgi. Let's just remember that part and let go of the guilt."

He narrowed his eyes in determination. "We'll be together again, Anna. I have to believe that."

"And so we will," Anna said.

Any time that particular guard was stationed at the fence, Anna and Georgi were able to steal a few minutes to talk. She longed to touch him, but didn't dare take that chance.

The winter seemed like it would never end.

PART V

Summer 1941

42

The summer sun set on another day in the Kolyma. The only difference between this one and the dozen before it was that Anna had been allowed to shower and wash her own clothes that were shredded around the edges and falling apart. The camp commander's wife had insisted that, if Anna was to enter her house to gather and put away the laundry, she would have to bathe or shower at least every two weeks.

Anna watched for Georgi through the barbed-wire. Their soldier-guard was on duty tonight, and Anna was excited to get to talk to Georgi. He'd narrowly survived winter, and was just starting to regain some strength after being ill for a couple of weeks.

As soon as the guard signaled them to go to their meeting place, Anna hurried down the fence toward the outhouse. To her surprise, Georgi reached his hand through one of the gaps in the barbed-wire and touched her face with his calloused fingers.

She flicked her eyes down to where the guards were smoking, backs turned to them, then leaned into his touch and brought her hand up to cup his.

"My Anna," he breathed. "Promise me, Anna, that you will fight to survive, do what is necessary to live, even if I'm gone."

"Georgi, why are you saying this? What's going on?"

He shook his head and stared into her eyes. "Nothing. I just need you to promise me, just in case something happens. You shouldn't give up on life—not for me, not for anyone. Don't let them win. Find your way back to your mama."

Knitting her brow, Anna squeezed his hand. "I promise. But you're worrying me. You need to promise me back. Remember our plans? Remember how I'm to wait for you after I'm released so we can be together?"

A sad smile crossed his face. "I remember, my Anna. It's all I think about. And I do promise. I'll keep fighting until the end."

Movement down by the guards caught his attention, and he pulled his hand back through the fence as he swiveled his head in that direction. He hurriedly looked back at her and said, "I love you, Anna."

She was barely able to respond in kind before he hurried away. Anna turned and headed toward the barracks, resisting the urge to look back at Georgi or the guards.

Lying on her and Eva's shared bunk, she fell asleep thinking about his touch and his words of love, but underlying that was a gnawing worry that he knew something he didn't want to tell her.

☭

Anna was relieved to see Georgi across camp on the other side of the fence when they all lined up for headcount the next morning. She wasn't sure what had prompted his earnest words the night before, but she worried about him all day, relieved again at that evening's headcount to see him among the other exhausted loggers of his and Eva's brigade. She smiled—maybe they'd be lucky and their special guard would be on duty again tonight.

The camp chief was in attendance at headcount this evening,

Anna spotted him up front in the waning daylight. After assuring all prisoners were accounted for, he strode over to the fence, standing between the lines of women on one side and men on the other, and shouted, "The logging brigade of Anatoly Andreyevich, come forward. Line up in rows of ten in front of the gate!"

Anna's stomach dropped. She'd seen this before, the year she'd first arrived there. And—

She turned to Eva, whose sunken eyes were wide with fear. As Eva and the other women in the brigade made their way to the front, Anna searched frantically for Georgi through the barbed-wire. He was taller than most of the others, and usually easy to find in a crowd, but when she finally locked eyes with him, he was standing with shoulders slumped and a resigned, sad look on his face.

"This logging brigade," the camp chief shouted loud enough for the whole camp to hear, "is full of shirkers of the worst kind. They have failed to meet the norms assigned to them by our benevolent leaders time and time again." He turned to face the brigade. "Now, you will face your punishment."

A line of soldiers marched out, rifles and pistols aimed at the logging brigade.

Before a cry of distress and protest could build up any steam in Anna's throat, the camp chief shouted, "Fire at will!"

Anna covered her ears as the loud reports from all the guns rang through the warm air. She wanted so desperately to look away, but she couldn't. Her eyes found Georgi's, he kissed his fingertips and held them out toward her just seconds before one of the bullets blew through his chest. Only then could she avert her eyes, as sobs tore through her body, and it took every ounce of strength she had to remain standing.

When the shooting was done, not every member of Anna's former logging brigade lay dead—just most of them, including Georgi and Eva. The remaining members were tasked with loading the bodies onto a sledge and dragging them through the mud to a place outside the camp walls to bury them in a mass grave. A chill ran up

Anna's spine as the chief added, "Dig it deep and wide...and leave it open."

☭

The stench from the rotting bodies reached camp a few days later. Anna had cried every tear she had left until she straightened her shoulders and declared to herself that this horror of a place would not force one more from her. She placed a heavy lock on her heart, determined to survive as she'd promised Georgi.

As the summer wore on, Anna continued her job doing laundry and sometimes sewing and other things for the camp commander and his wife. She brushed off the commander's repeated and increasing attempts to bed her whenever he was drunk and his wife wasn't around. But he was becoming more insistent—and had even started making lewd comments to her when he was sober.

She sat on her bunk, now shared with two other women she'd not bothered to get to know, sewing a tear in the shirt the commander's wife had given her. The camp radio played as other women stripped down to their bras and underwear and fanned themselves with whatever objects they could find. Suddenly the music stopped and the voice of the Commissar of Foreign Affairs, Vyacheslav Molotov, replaced it. The entire barracks sat in silence and listened.

"Citizens of the Soviet Union.

"The Soviet government and its head, Comrade Stalin, have ordered me to make the following announcement:

"Today, at four o'clock in the morning, German troops have entered our country, without making any demands on the Soviet Union and without a declaration of war. They have attacked our borders in many places and have subjected our towns—Zhitomir, Kiev, Sevastopol, Kaunas, and some others—to aerial bombardments during which more than two hundred people have been killed or wounded. Hostile aerial attacks and artillery barrages have also taken place on Romanian and Finnish territory.

"This attack is unheard of and is a treacherous act that has no equal in the history of civilized peoples. The attack on our country was launched despite the fact that a non-aggression treaty between the USSR and Germany has been signed and that the Soviet Union has observed all conditions of this treaty in full honesty. The attack on our country was launched despite the fact that during the whole period this treaty has been in force, the German government has never once been able to dispute our observance of this treaty. The whole responsibility for this raid on the Soviet Union lies in its entirety in the hands of the Fascist German government.

"Only after the attack was launched, the German Ambassador in Moscow, Von der Schulenburg, informed me as People's Commissioner of Foreign Affairs at 5:30 in the morning on behalf of his government of the fact that the German government has decided to go to war against the USSR because of the concentration of Red Army units near the German eastern frontier.

"In answer to this I have informed him on behalf of the Soviet government that the German government has not made a single demand on the Soviet government up until the last moment and that the German government has launched the attack on the Soviet Union despite the peace loving attitude of the Soviet Union which makes Fascist Germany the offending party.

"Ordered by the government of the Soviet Union, I must also state that our troops and aircraft have not violated the border anywhere and that the announcement, to the effect that Soviet aircraft have allegedly fired at Romanian airfields, which was transmitted on Romanian radio this morning, is an outright lie and a provocation. A similar lie and provocation is Hitler's statement of today in which he attempted to fabricate incriminating evidence as to the non-observance of the Soviet-German treaty by the Soviet Union in the past.

"Now that the attack on the Soviet Union has been launched, the Soviet government has ordered our troops to repulse the raid and to drive the German forces off the territory of our homeland. This war has not been forced on us by the German population, nor by the German workers, farmers, and the intelligentsia, whose suffering we understand very well, but by a clique of blood thirsty, Fascist German rulers who have suppressed the French, Czechs, Poles, Serbs, Norwegians, Belgians, Danish, Dutch, Greeks, and other peoples.

"The government of the Soviet Union is unshakably convinced that our courageous army and navy and the gallant falcons of the Soviet Air Force shall do their duty towards their Motherland and the Soviet people in an honorable fashion and deliver a crushing blow to the aggressor.

"It is not the first time that our people face an arrogant aggressor. During Napoleon's Russian campaign, our people reacted with the War of the Fatherland; Napoleon suffered a defeat and went down. That shall also happen to the arrogant Hitler who has unleashed a new campaign against our country. The Red Army and our population shall once more wage a triumphant War of the Fatherland for our homeland, for honor and for freedom.

"The government of the Soviet Union is firmly convinced that the entire population of our nation, all workers, farmers, and the intelligentsia, men and women, shall meet their obligations and devote themselves to their work with the necessary conviction. Our entire population must now be staunch and unified as never before. Each of us must demand discipline, order, and self-sacrifice from themselves and others, worthy of a real Soviet Patriot, in order to attend to all needs of the Red Army, the Navy, and the Air Force in order to guarantee victory over the enemy.

"The government calls on you, citizens of the Soviet Union, to close the ranks around our triumphant Bolshevist party, around our Soviet government, and around our great leader, Comrade Stalin even further.

"Our cause is just. The enemy shall be defeated. Victory shall be ours."

As the radio went back to playing music, one of the prisoners shut it off and said, "Well, it's all over for us now."

"What do you mean?" asked a newer prisoner, who had just arrived on transport that week.

"Didn't you hear what he said?" The woman gestured agitatedly at the radio. "What do you think it means for *us* when he demands 'discipline, order, and *self-sacrifice*' from everyone? To 'attend to the needs of the Red Army'?"

"Well," the younger woman said, "they can't work us any harder than they already are, can they? It isn't possible."

"Just wait and see, citizen. Just wait and see."

The next day, the woman's prediction began to play out as the already paltry food rations were cut. The prisoners complained as the mess hall workers told them they would receive no more sugar, and other rations would be cut.

Anna stirred the commander's laundry in the large tub of heated water and wondered what else would come of this, and why Germany would invade Russia. Weren't they allies?

On day three of the war, all the foreign prisoners were rounded up and removed from camp. Anna didn't want to know what had happened to them, some of them had been her friends. That same day, the camp commander announced that political prisoners would no longer be allowed to receive letters or newspapers, and they took away all camp radios.

After dinner that night, Anna stopped where a crowd of women were huddled around someone who was howling like an animal.

"What's wrong with her?" she asked.

"She was set to be released today, but she was told that an order was passed down on June 22 forbidding all prisoners convicted of betrayal of the Motherland—so all us Fifty-eights—from leaving camp."

Anna picked up a crumpled piece of paper near the woman's prostrate body and glanced over it, stopping at the part that stated the prisoner was ordered to stay in the prison camp "for the duration of the war."

The woman crying on the ground, Anna remembered, had a baby that was being kept in a nursery outside of camp. She'd talked only about that baby whenever Anna heard her speak, about getting him back.

In the coming days, there were many such anguished cries and rantings from prisoners whose release dates came and went, and they remained just as they'd been the last five, ten, or fifteen years or more. Prisoners.

Longer work days were established, tacking more hours onto people who were receiving less food. The death rate climbed as the summer wore on, and Anna knew it would only get worse when the cold weather set in.

The camp commander cornered her in his house as she was putting away the laundry. His wife had left for Magadan and wouldn't be back for a week. He rubbed up against Anna as she bent over to place some towels in a drawer. She shot up, but was trapped between him and the sideboard. He held her around the waist, his alcohol-tainted breath blowing on her face, and he pulled her back against him. "You know, Anna Levitskaya, I'm a man of honor. I've never taken a woman by force—and I never will." He squeezed her tighter. "But I'm tired of your rejections. You aren't even that pretty anymore in your worn and sagging body. I'll give you a choice. Either you let me have my way with you—whenever I wish—or I'll send you back out to general work. I heard they need more loggers out there."

Anna's heart was dead. She couldn't remember why she'd so adamantly resisted in the first place. She just didn't care anymore. She wouldn't survive going back to logging, back to reduced rations. And she wanted to survive. So, she screwed her eyes shut, bit her lip until it bled, and let the commander have his way with her.

PART VI

Winter 1942-1943

43

Anna's twenty-fifth birthday came and went. She stared down at her withered body as she hurried through the bath house in the cold. She didn't look or feel like she was still in her twenties—more like what it should feel like to be in her sixties or seventies.

She dressed in her tattered clothing, buttoning up her "quilted" jacket that had lost all its warmth. The clothing allotment had been awful to begin with, but since the war started, it had grown even worse. Why would they waste the good stuff on enemies of the people when the boys fighting at the front needed it instead? The last year-and-a-half had hardened the Gulag even further—a thing Anna hadn't thought possible before the war started. They were receiving less food and expected to work longer hours and produce more from that work. The discipline had become even more ferocious and the punishments more severe. And slapping on a second term to anyone getting close to their release date was now expected—without a trial or even being given a reason at all—these *second terms* hung over the prisoners' heads like an axe. Anna guessed it was easier to keep them there than to arrest, try, and transport new people to take their places. And, after all, the Red Army needed their labor!

Snow easily infiltrated the layers of felt Anna had wrapped around her disintegrating boots, and once again, she was grateful for her assigned job. Grateful for what Georgi had done for her. She pushed his memory from her mind—she only allowed herself to think of him at night, after lights-out when the chances of being interrupted were less.

She hurried to the laundry building and started a fire in the stove to heat the tubs of water. While she waited, she took down and folded the laundry she'd hung from lines crisscrossing about the room the night before. She'd take it to the commander's house and pick up his wife's dirty clothing from the trip she'd returned from last night. It should be safe for Anna to go there now that she was home.

Able to avoid the commander the entire day, Anna watched from the mess hall as the loggers and other general laborers trudged into camp. They died by the dozens each day, their bodies dragged out of the way and left along the side of the road or just outside the logging camp, to be buried under the snow and ice. Those who died while in camp were piled alongside the barracks until the spring thaw when the stench grew unbearable and graves could be dug. She knew she would have been one of them long ago had Georgi not secured an easier job for her in camp.

Wrapping her scarf around her head and face, she readied herself for evening headcount in the sub-zero temperatures.

Every day was the same for the prisoners, with little variation. Anna stood amongst the other women, all stamping their feet and beating their hands against their arms to keep from freezing at morning headcount.

The camp chief joined them this morning, and wasted no time calling out dozens of names, separating those prisoners from the ranks. That meant one of two things, either those being moved to the side were going to get transferred...or they were going to get executed.

Both things had been happening with varying frequency since Anna had arrived.

"Anna Levitskaya…" the guard rattled off her prisoner number, but the shock running through her at hearing her name caused a thick fog to envelop her brain and she didn't hear it.

In a daze, Anna joined the others whose names had been called. A small amount of relief spread through her as a convoy of transport trucks pulled up outside the gates. *Transport then*, she thought. *Not execution.*

The large group of prisoners, both men and women, were forced into the beds of the trucks with only a light canvas covering the rails and top of the cattle truck. Anna was pushed up against one of the sides, too crushed by the other bodies to do anything but stand with her arms at her sides. As the trucks rumbled down the road, a man mumbled as his steaming breath joined everyone else's floating above them, "Not surprised. The Red Army has no need for lumber. They need our labor somewhere else."

They traveled in the miserable truck for hours, packed in like frozen fish. By the time they reached the railway cars waiting for them, at least a half-dozen of the prisoners in Anna's truck alone had perished—from cold, from illness, from starvation, or from being crushed together, who knew? And…who cared? Not the NKVD or the Soviet government.

Now packed into railcars, just as cold and just as crowded, the prisoners were on their way again. Only one of the guards deigned to answer the multiple questions about *where* they were going.

"Gold mines. Now shut your mouths."

Ahh, yes, Anna thought, *the guy in the truck was right. The army has no need for lumber—but* gold, *now that is something else entirely.*

Anna figured it took them just over twenty-four hours to reach the gold mine labor camp—and of course no food or water was given them during that time. Also, no bathroom breaks, so the train car smelled of urine and feces by the time it pulled to a stop.

They unloaded, and everything started all over again for Anna.

The arriving prisoners were sent directly to the bath house and made to strip. After a cold dip in the water without soap, she stood in front of a camp physician. This time was much different from when she's arrived at the logging camp. None of the guards ogled her or made lewd remarks. Instead, they looked right through her as if she wasn't even there. And no wonder: her shoulders stuck out at sharp angles, her breasts hung down like little dried-out prunes, folds of skin formed wrinkles on her flat butt. The gap between her thighs was so large from loss of muscle that a soccer ball could have fit there. Her voice was no longer that of a young woman, instead it was hoarse and rough, and her face was darkened with spots from pellagra. Such were the results of hard labor and starvation.

In the barracks, she found a spot on the floor to sleep before being sent out into the harsh elements for general labor early in the morning.

At the five AM headcount, Anna was assigned to a brigade. She looked around as they marched the short distance to the mine. The landscape was similar in this new camp, but with fewer trees. There wasn't much snow on the ground when they reached the work site; it had all been trampled down by boots and wheelbarrows. Piles of frozen dirt, haphazard bridges made only of lengths of rough boards spanning from one hill to another or over a deep dip in the ground, and dozens of wheelbarrows, shovels, pick-axes and other tools littered the area, with a river running through the middle.

The brigadier handed out assignments to the new arrivals as the others went to work. Separating them into groups of ten or twelve, he pointed to Anna's group. "You will each sift through one-hundred-fifty wheelbarrows a day for gold. Those who do not finish with that amount by the end of the workday will remain until you have."

Anna was there until midnight. At least they gave her some soup when she returned to the main camp. Five AM came early that morning.

As she sifted through the frozen silt and rocks in the wheelbarrow before her, she thought about the warmth of the laundry hut and the shorter work days. How she ended each day tired, but not exhausted to her core. She wiped a splotch of mud that had splashed on her face, using her shoulder, and thought about her disgust at giving in to the sexual advances of the camp commander. She was ashamed at what she'd done, but...she'd probably do it again if given the chance. It was, as Zoya had so often told her, a matter of survival.

44

After being at the goldmine camp for a couple of months, Anna still hadn't been able to finish sifting her one-hundred-fifty wheelbarrows a day before the end of the shift, often staying at the mining site until ten PM or later. But she wasn't alone. There were several other women and a few older men who regularly worked into the darkness with her. They jokingly dubbed themselves the "night owls."

The work wasn't as hard as in the logging camp, but the sub-zero temperatures weren't any better, and her boots were always soggy with icy water as she stood near the partially frozen river, sifting through the sludge to find gold.

Their brigadier was a Fifty-eight, not a trusty, and he made sure they all got fed, even if the portions were smaller, no matter what time they returned to the main camp area.

But even with the slightly easier work and the assurance of three meals a day, measly as they were, Anna's body was giving out. The late nights and early mornings and seventeen hour plus work days, were taking their toll. She rubbed her aching fingers as she waited in line for a bowl of dishwater soup.

She looked around the mess hall, noticing the new arrivals sitting at the long tables sipping their soup. The transport train had lumbered past the mining site a couple of hours ago, and some of the transferred prisoners were getting what she figured was their first meal in a day or two, depending on how far they'd traveled.

Soup in hand, Anna found a seat away from the new arrivals where she could observe them without it being too obvious. They got a lot of transfers, Russia needed the gold to support the war effort. She'd made a habit of searching the faces of the arriving prisoners, hoping to find Zoya or another familiar face. So far, none of the transports had come from the logging Gulag she'd been at.

She took a sip of her soup, then inhaled, coughing and spluttering as she breathed some down her windpipe. Shoulders slumped, eyes staring down at the table, sat none other than her former camp commander, insignias and shoulder boards ripped from his uniform. She narrowed her eyes at him and thought, *Oh, how the mighty have fallen.* It had always been true—at least since 1937—that even those who thought they were untouchable, those in power, Party members could be swept up into the cogs of the Soviet Gulag system. Anyone could be a spy or an anti-Soviet agitator. Anyone—except the true criminals, of course—could be a Fifty-eight.

Though she despised him and what he'd forced her to do, she couldn't feel any joy at seeing him brought down to the level of those he'd repressed. If anything, his arrest just proved the system was broken. Or was it working exactly as designed? She didn't know and didn't care. Anna finished her soup and wrapped her scarf around her face before sneaking out the door. She didn't want him to see her. She had nothing to say to him.

Hobbling back to the barracks on frozen, painful feet, Anna met up with Ada, a woman on the same work detail, and her current bunkmate.

They walked side by side until entering the barracks, and both headed for the stove, which was, of course, cold.

"Do the soldiers at the front really need *all* the firewood and coal?" Ada plopped down on their bunk.

"All of that and most of the food and warm clothing, apparently." Anna pulled her worn gloves from her pocket and put them on. She didn't wear them while working, they wouldn't do her any good in the wet and muddy conditions, but she wore them when she slept, for the small amount of warmth they added.

The former camp commander was assigned to shovel silt from the river bottom and nearby shore. His portly physique shrank at a visible rate until the skin of his face hung like a basset hound's. Within a couple of weeks one would never have known he'd come from high status in the Soviet government. Again, it gave Anna no joy to see his difficulties—the same as she and all the other general laborers bore. But there were others who knew who he was and made sure to make his pitiful existence even more difficult every chance they got.

They'd locked eyes a couple of times, but it seemed as though he didn't want to talk to her any more than she him.

Joseph, the former camp commander, met his demise the way so many others did—he became ill and died covered in his own feces and vomit, too weak to crawl to the bucket in the men's barracks. He hadn't lasted long as a victim of the Kolyma.

PART VII

Summer-Fall 1943

45

Miraculously, Anna had made it through another harsh winter. Spring had been hard, as the ground thawed and the wheelbarrows sunk in the mud, forming deep ruts. And the stench from the bodies that had been left where they'd fallen all winter, and now decomposed with the warming temperatures, was overwhelming.

Anna's legs and hands, any place her skin was exposed or easy to get to, were covered with irritated welts from the hordes of mosquitoes that were particularly bad down by the river.

She paused and looked back at the bloody corpse of a prisoner who'd been shot earlier in the day for hiding gold dust in the hems of his pants. She was so used to seeing death all around her, that she couldn't even find a touch of humanity to mourn his loss. Just another day in the Gulag.

Rations had improved slightly, but that didn't seem to be helping with all the illness and starvation. One in four prisoners died that spring and summer, overwhelming the camp hospital and any surrounding hospitals.

"Anna Levitskaya!" the guard holding a clipboard called her

name, followed by three others in the women's barracks. "You four come with me."

Anna looked at the other women, fear showing on their hardened faces. The executions had decreased, but they were still happening. Is that what this was? Were they being led to the shooting field where a mass grave lay open, waiting for more bodies to fall?

The guard escorted them, not to the killing field, but to the hospital. It was housed in a building only slightly better than the barracks, but smoke could always be seen floating up from the chimney. He stopped at the door and turned to face them. "You've been reassigned to help out with the sick. Go inside and find the doctor for instructions." He looked at the door as if, on the other side, the *Babayka* waited to spring out at him.

Anna stepped past him and entered the building, followed by the other women. The welcomed warmth hit her first, but then the overpowering stench of sickness smacked her in the face. The women stood in the small reception room as the door shut behind them. Anna looked at the others and shrugged. "I guess we should go find the doctor."

Covering her mouth with her hand, Anna stepped through the door on the other end of the reception room, where the full force of the odor hit. She retched, but was able to hold down her breakfast. A couple of harried looking orderlies ran from bed to bed as a man wearing a lab coat made rounds among the beds. Anna made her way to him, looking at the chaos around her, careful not to step on the feet of the men and women lying on the floor between the cots that held two patients each.

She closed in on the man in the dirty lab coat, noting that he was younger than she'd first thought. "Doctor?" she asked.

"Yes. What do you want?" He continued to stare down at his clipboard.

"We were sent here to help."

At last he looked up. "Oh, yes, right. Well, get to work then."

"Umm," one of the women behind Anna spoke up. "Get to work doing *what* exactly?"

"I don't have time to babysit you! If you can't figure out what needs to be done and do it, then go back to the mines!" He whirled around and hurried over to where an orderly held down a convulsing patient.

Anna took an inventory of their surroundings and quickly prioritized. A stack of bowls sat near a pot of gruel. "Hey!" she called to the nearest orderly. "Have these patients had breakfast?"

"Not yet."

"Let's dish up some gruel and hand it out to the patients that can feed themselves," Anna said to the others.

From there they started cleaning up the patients who had grown too weak to get themselves to the single, stinking toilet and had evacuated their bowels where they lay. There were no linens, and the cots were crusted with bodily fluids. Buckets full of vomit sloshed as the women carried them out to dump them behind the hospital building.

There were no medications, so the best they could do was to get cups of salted water into the patients that could hold it down and give small sips to the others in hopes they could retain some of it.

Of the fifty patients Anna counted in the small hospital room, ten of them were hauled out and dumped onto the sledge destined for the mass graves outside of camp by the end of the grueling day. They were quickly replaced with ten more ill men and women.

The doctor, whom Anna learned was really just a third-year medical student and was also a Fifty-eight, spent most of his day triaging new arrivals, sending most of them away, back out to their general labor assignments. The requirements to be admitted to the hospital were strict during these days of epidemic illness: the diarrhea had to come every half-hour, and it had to be bloody. Everyone else was deemed fit to work.

Summer wore on, and they finally got a hold on the illness. The other women were sent back to general labor, but the doctor asked to keep Anna, as she'd proven herself to be invaluable during the outbreak.

As the chill in the air turned to freezing in the fall, Anna saw a side of camp life she'd only heard about: prisoners who mutilated or maimed themselves to get out of doing heavy labor. The first was a man who had blown off his fingers with a dynamite cap. The torn flesh and bleeding stumps made her cringe inwardly. As she ran to get some rags to bandage the wound, the doctor stopped her. "No bandages for him. We aren't to treat 'shirkers' who purposefully injure themselves. It is an administrative order."

Anna frowned and had to look away from the man's pleading eyes as the doctor told him to leave.

Another duty that Anna abhorred was the "requirement" that one of the medical workers sign off on the camp chief's decrees for imprisonment in the punishment block. The doctor, scared to be sent out to general labor, signed every one brought to him, but Anna refused. No one, not even an animal, should be put in the horrible punishment block. It didn't matter in the end, though, the prisoners were sent there with or without a signature.

The work in the hospital was hard, sometimes nasty, and often entailed long hours—but it was better than general labor by far. If her luck held out, Anna just might survive the next five years and see her mama again.

PART VIII

Spring-Fall 1945

46

The prisoner amnesties brought on by the war—mostly men of fighting age and almost never a political prisoner—to bolster the Red Army, had slowed to a trickle. But as the ground thawed and the camp compound turned to mud, the prisoners' hopes were again raised that there might be another large amnesty. Anna tried not to get her hopes up, knowing the Fifty-eights were never included in such things. But other prisoners went about talking about "another big amnesty" they'd heard about. "It's coming. That new guy that just came from Moscow said he'd heard it from a reliable source," and other such comments gave hope where, as far as Anna was concerned, there shouldn't be any.

Some of the women in her barracks pointed to the general amnesty that had been announced in January—for women who were pregnant or had small children—and the large numbers that had already been released. At first, Anna thought that maybe the regime was softening, maybe the years of war had relaxed their malevolent ways. But another woman, newly arrived, suggested that this amnesty for women—political prisoners excluded, of course—did not represent a change of heart, but was a response to the shocking increase in the number of orphans, homeless children, hooliganism, and children's criminal gangs all across the USSR. The authorities had to grudgingly admit that mothers were part of the solution to these problems.

The wartime restrictions had been eased, allowing prisoners to again receive packages from home. It was widely thought to be because of the wartime famines and the camps being increasingly unable to feed the prisoners. This placed some of that burden on the families. Many prisoners drew hope from these decrees, hoping they meant a new, more relaxed era was beginning.

Anna received no such packages, and worried about what that might mean concerning her mama. As she gave a bed-bath to an unconscious last-legger, she wondered where her mama might be and hoped her sister was taking care of her—hoped she was still alive and well.

The camp radio, just recently allowed again, played in the background. It moved to the forefront of her thoughts as the music stopped mid-song and the announcer came on: "Shortly before midnight on this day, May 8th, 1945, in Berlin, Field Marshal Wilhelm Keitel and other German representatives of the Armed Forces High Command, signed a document of unconditional surrender to all Allied forces..."

"Japan won't be far behind." The doctor said from behind her.

Anna jumped a little at his voice, not expecting him to be in this early. She thought for a moment, then shrugged. "Doesn't make a difference to me. But I'm happy our boys won't be at war anymore...for a while." Her thoughts went to Georgi, and she wondered how many of "our boys" would be accused of spying or other anti-Soviet activities and executed or sent to the Gulags when they returned home.

"Well, it doesn't really change things for me either, except that perhaps we'll be able to get medication and other supplies a little easier."

"That would be good." Anna nodded and went back to the bed-bath.

"And, maybe those whose release dates came and went during the war will finally be allowed to leave."

She hadn't thought about that because her release date was still three years away, but she knew many who had been forced to stay past theirs—after all, the great Soviet Union *needed* their forced labor to supply the war, they couldn't force *free* people to work under such deadly conditions.

Any hopes that the arrests would decrease and the working conditions improve after the war were quickly quashed. As Anna helped with the medical examinations of a trainload of new arrivals to camp, she heard the murmurings of the prisoners. Indeed, it seemed, instead of relaxing the repression after the war, the Soviet leadership began a whole new series of arrests—focusing on the returning soldiers as well as select ethnic minorities, including Soviet Jews.

One young prisoner, he stated his age as fourteen, said, "Me and a bunch of other boys, dozens of us, were accused of being part of an anti-Stalinist youth conspiracy group. Met a bunch more from other cities in the transit prison." He shook his shaved head. "Not a one of us is guilty of that. Not a one."

"On the outside," a prisoner still wearing his Red Army uniform said, "the newspaper and radio all say the new directive is that the Soviet economy must devote itself wholeheartedly to military and industrial production."

"So, of course," an older prisoner said with a frown, "that means they must make as much use of forced labor as they possibly can." He looked around. "And they seem to have perfected that—at least as far as how to procure such forced labor."

"But the war is over," Anna said as she threw anti-lice powder on the genitals of a naked man, "what's the need for more military production?"

"Ah," the man said, "the Americans have superior power—the atom bomb—and that is just unacceptable to the Soviet leadership."

And so the cogs of the Gulag machine continued to turn.

PART IX

1946

47

The prisoners lined up in rows for the morning headcount. An extra buzz ran through the ranks of both prisoners and guards. Anna looked around at the extra guards with their dogs and rifles on duty around them. At least twice as many as usual. Her eyes were drawn to the train cars pulled up just outside the camp. That was unusual for this time of day.

"If I read off your name, assemble in rows of five at the gate!" shouted the camp chief. At least a quarter of the women prisoners' names were called. Anna's was not one of them.

The women were led to the train cars and crowded inside, more than a few of them crying out goodbyes to friends or lovers as those who remained at camp were excused to go to their work assignments.

When she reached the camp hospital, Anna asked the doctor, "Do you know what that was all about?"

He looked up at her and frowned. "I heard from one of the guards last night that a new decree has been set forth. The government has called for the complete separation of women from men in the Gulags. He said they figured it would take a couple of years to complete, but it looks like this camp will be one of the first."

The doctor seemed quite put-out by the new rule—one that made complete sense to Anna. If only that had always been the way of things, it would have saved her from much pain and heartache. She thought of Georgi then—it would have kept her from finding love again among the horrors of the camps. Would she, given the choice, have given that up to avoid the rest—the rapes and many other degrading episodes she'd been forced to endure this past eight years?

Yes. She would give it up. She would never have known about Georgi and would have just remembered Nikolai as her one and only true love. She wouldn't have had to witness Georgi's death after already having been only steps away when Nikolai was murdered by the NKVD. Was she horrible to think that—to be willing to sacrifice Georgi's part in her life for a life without rape and the almost constant threat of it? No matter. It had all happened and there was no going back to the beginning.

The next morning at headcount, Anna's name was called among the dozens of other women, and they were forced into the train car so tightly it was hard to breathe. She'd said her goodbyes to the doctor the night before, anticipating she'd soon be gone. She'd also emptied her bowels and bladder and only drank a few sips of watered-down tea. Her morning bread ration was tucked away in her jacket for later. She wouldn't be able to even get to it until they were released from the train car, as her arms were pinned at her sides. But she was used to being hungry. She'd endure that, so she didn't have to degrade herself with incontinence of urine or stool. At least for as long as possible, not knowing how many hours or days this train ride would be.

Anna had no idea how long they'd been packed into the train cars— she just knew that they'd left in the morning and weren't allowed to disembark until well after the sun had set and the stars came out to fill the black sky. Her legs and hands had lost all feeling hours ago. As she moved toward the door amidst the crowd, she tried stomping her feet to get some of the circulation moving again. She stumbled as she stepped out of the train car, but caught herself before falling to the ground. The girl next to her wasn't so lucky and was roughly yanked up by the arm and shoved in the back with the butt of a rifle.

The women were pushed inside a mostly empty barracks that smelled of men and illness, rot and decay. They weren't afforded a light, so they all stumbled their way in the dark to find an open bunk. It would be the first time since entering the Soviet prison system that Anna had a bunk to herself. She enjoyed it while she could, as she knew it wouldn't last.

Things were a little different in this camp. After a breakfast at the mess hall that consisted of a cup of a black, unsalted infusion of nettle leaves and a fifteen-ounce slice of bread that was to be the only bread they got that day, the women lined up for "interviews."

Anna worried as she stood in line that an "interview" was code for another "interrogation," and she had to force herself not to run, screaming, toward the guard tower—as she'd rather be shot than go through that again.

But it turned out to be a way to determine who was to be sent where for work detail. The masculine woman who sat at the desk Anna stood in front of asked only three questions. "Anna Levitskaya, enemy of the people, what did you do before your arrest?"

"I...I worked at a garment factory. I sewed."

The woman grunted and mumbled, "That'll be no help here." She looked up with a scowl. "And what have you done since your arrest? What work assignments have you had?"

How she answered this question could mean life or death—an easy assignment or general labor. But she couldn't lie, the woman had her file right in front of her. She had to make herself look invaluable to the camp. "I...umm...started out as a logger, but then I was assigned to the camp commander and his wife's house to do their laundry and mend their clothing. When I was...transferred to the mining camp, I was assigned as a sifter at first but then moved to the hospital as a hospital attendant during an outbreak of typhus and dysentery. I was the only assistant they kept on after the outbreak ended. That's what I was doing before being transferred here."

"*Hmf.* Well, we have plenty of hospital workers and more than enough launderers." She glared up at Anna. "Are you a Party member?"

"I...I'm..." Anna closed her eyes and sighed. She couldn't lie about that either. She'd be found out and likely executed. "No. I'm not a Party member."

"As I presumed. You're assigned to work in the clay pits. We have three shifts, you'll work the morning shift from six to two. Go find the brigadier, she'll tell you what the norms are."

And that was that. Anna was sent back to the slow death of general labor.

She found her way to the wet-pressing plant of the brickyard, trying to get her bearings. It looked like they hadn't completely separated the men from the women, as there was a men's compound on the other side of a twelve-foot tall barbed-wire fence, where the dry-pressing plant was. She found a woman who had the appearance of someone in charge and, after getting her attention, asked, "Are you the brigadier?"

"Yes. I'm Olga. Who are you?"

"I'm Anna. I've been assigned to work in the clay pits, morning shift." She'd never done a general labor job that had "shifts" before, and working only eight hours a day sounded like a good thing...

"Good. We need more clay-diggers. Many more."

Olga pointed her toward a distant corner of the compound where a large piece of rickety machinery stood. "Follow the trolley track to the windlass and meet up with the foreman. She'll tell you what to do."

Anna stepped carefully across the torn-up ground, avoiding deep ravines that looked like cave-ins. The foreman saw her coming and hurried over to her. "Have you been assigned to work in the clay pits?"

"Yes, I—"

"That's all I need to know. Grab a shovel and follow me." As she walked at a brisk pace, she said, mostly to herself, "I don't know whose idea it was to separate the men and women, but we definitely don't have enough women here to get the job done." She led Anna down an incline and stopped at a pit in which a woman worked alone. "You two work together. The norm for two sloggers working together is sixteen cars full of clay per shift."

"And it's flaming impossible, of course," the woman in the pit said.

The foreman shrugged like she agreed but knew there was nothing to be done about it.

Anna climbed down into the pit. They managed to fill and transport four and a half cars before the next shift arrived at 2:00. The trolley cars were heavy and the tracks not at all even over the ravine filled terrain. The windlass was only used to pull the full cars up out of the pit area, and the two women had to push them the rest of the way to the wet-press plant.

Anna trudged back to the center of the compound, muscles spent and more tired than she'd been since working in the logging camp. She found a water spigot and tried to wash some of the sticky clay off her hands and legs, splashing some water on her face. Then she went to the barracks to get some rest before the dinner siren sounded.

Another trainload of women prisoners arrived late that night.

The next morning, as Anna and Liliya, her new workmate, pushed two trolley cars down into the pit, an autumn drizzle began to fall. As the clay became wetter, it stuck to the shovels and became heavier and heavier. Anna could barely lift each shovelful up to the edge of the car. Of course they didn't make the impossibly set norms, but they didn't even come close to digging as much clay as they had the day before.

"We'll just have to live with having a penalty ration for dinner tonight," Liliya said. "I can't lift another shovelful of this sticky shit."

The two women meandered their way back to camp and slept in their wet clothes, shivering because the camp chiefs weren't yet wasting wood or coal to heat the barracks.

The next day was no better, as the slow drizzle hadn't ceased and the clay pit was now drenched. No matter how much clay Anna was able to get on her shovel, it wouldn't drop off into the car—even after banging it against the side repeatedly. Frustrated at having to reach over the trolley and push the clay off into it every time, Anna threw her shovel to the side and started scooping up the squelching clay from beneath her feet and tossing it into the car. Liliya followed suit, ditching the shovel for her hands.

And the rain kept coming.

Anna and the others had to be pulled from the pit at the end of their shift, the incline was too slippery to climb out on their own.

The third day of the incessant rain, Anna felt like crying. When would it stop? Her coat and skirt and very *skin* were soaked to where she felt she'd never be dry again. She was hungry and exhausted and yearned to be back in her former camp's hospital or laundering the camp commander's clothes.

Anna, Liliya, and all the other women kept at it, nonetheless. But when it neared the end of their shift, Olga stood over the pit, head covered with a dark shawl, and gestured her hands to the near and far ends of the pit, talking to the foreman. Word spread that they weren't going to pull the brigade of workers out at 2:00, but would keep them all in the clay pit until norms were fulfilled. And...only then would they get both lunch and dinner.

Olga left, and the rain fell harder. Red puddles formed everywhere in the clay, including in the cars.

Anna's hands were already numb from scooping up the cold clay, and neither she nor Liliya were making any progress in filling up the car.

"I'm done," Anna said. "Help me up out of here."

"What do you mean you're 'done'?" Even with the question Liliya laced her frozen fingers together and bent down, prepared to boost Anna up.

"This is asinine. If Moscow needs bricks so badly, they can wait for this blasted rain to stop." Anna put her foot in Liliya's hands and scrabbled out of the pit.

Liliya handed up their shovels and then Anna offered her a hand.

Once out of the pit, Liliya looked around. "Where will we go? We can't go back to camp."

"Somewhere without this nasty, red mud." Anna gestured for her to follow and climbed up the hill to where there was an area of grass. She sat down and pulled the collar of her red-stained coat up to cover her neck.

Liliya joined her without a word.

The rain tapped on the backs of their bowed heads and a chill ran up Anna's spine. She took a moment to look about them. Half-loaded cars lay overturned in the mud. She didn't spot a single prisoner in the entire clay pit. "No sense sitting out in the rain. Let's find somewhere a little drier."

They grabbed their shovels and splashed their way to a shed near the plant, where they found others huddling in the drafty building.

The clay pit did not fulfill its norm. Olga ordered that the prisoners should be left out there all night. But when the power went out, the camp chief called for everyone to return to the compound. In the pitch black, the prisoners linked arms and moved toward camp with a group of convoy guards and their barking dogs.

Back in the barracks, Anna lay on her bunk next to a girl who had arrived just the night before, still dressed in her wet clothes as it seemed it would be warmer that way rather than taking them off.

Anna's last thought before drifting to sleep was, *Tomorrow will be the same. And every day after that. Six cars of red clay, a ladleful of black gruel, a small portion of black bread. Every day the same.*

PART X

Summer-Fall 1948

48

Summer in the clay pits was every bit as awful as winter. Instead of forcing a shovel through frozen clay, Anna had to scoop up the sticky, wet, heavy stuff and struggle to get it off the shovel and into the car. All while mosquitoes dive-bombed her and the sun beat down on the back of her neck.

The palms of her hands were covered with callouses, and her skin hung loosely over her bones and joints. But she'd had a renewal of hope lately as she'd seen other prisoners released after their sentence was up. And her sentence would be up in a couple of months.

Ten years.

She'd been imprisoned by the most sadistic, inhumane, power-hungry government for a third of her life. She was now thirty-one years old—with the body of an elderly woman.

Ten years.

For nothing. She'd done *nothing* wrong. But, as she'd come to understand quite early on, neither had most of the other thousands—maybe millions—of political prisoners. And maybe, just maybe—if she made it through the next couple of months—she could go home, wherever that may be. Her sister had denounced her. She hadn't heard from her mama since leaving the Lubyanka—and she worried about what that could mean. Had she died? Had Nadya turned their mama against her? Had she been arrested? Anna shook her head at the thought. She didn't want to imagine her mama in a place such as this. But...she had encountered women even older than Mama, sentenced to ten years, sometimes more.

A new transport of prisoners came in that night after dinner. Anna watched without much interest as the women entered the barracks in the dim light. Her eyes lingered on one woman whose face seemed familiar, and she wracked her brain to figure out why. Had she been someone she'd known from another gulag or the Lubyanka? She couldn't remember and soon moved on to other thoughts.

But the woman stopped in front of her as she sat at one of the two tables amidst the bunks. Anna looked up, still not realizing why the woman seemed so familiar.

"Anna?" the woman said. "Anna Levitskaya?"

Anna squinted up at her. "Yes? How do you know me?"

"It's me, Lena. I lived in your building."

"Ahh. Yes. That's why you look so familiar." Anna stood abruptly as her thoughts narrowed in on that information. "When were you last there? In Moscow? Have you seen my mama?"

Nodding, Lena said, "Yes. I was there only a few months ago, before..." She shook her head. It needn't be said. Before her arrest. "Your mama was sick, then, Anna. I'm not sure with what. But your sister was worried about her."

The next two months seemed like they comprised more time than the whole ten years since Anna's arrest. Constant worry about Mama invaded her every thought.

On the morning of November 5, 1948, Anna was called to the camp administrator's office. Nerves made her stomach churn, as she knew this could go either way. She'd known many prisoners who had been called in thinking they were being released, only to be given a second sentence. She thought her mind might just crack if that were the case. And then there were the prisoners who were released—but exiled for three, five, or eight years...

The guard led her into an office, nicely furnished and well lit. A camp administrator sat at his desk, flipping through papers in a worn folder.

Anna stood in front of the desk.

After several minutes, the man looked up with a bored expression. "Anna Levitskaya?"

"Yes, citizen chief."

He read from a form in front of him. "On this day, November 5, 1948, you are hereby released from your imprisonment in a Soviet Labor Camp." He pushed a folded document toward her. "This is your residence permit. You are to return to Moscow and may not leave the city's limits without permission. You will need to show this in order to find employment."

Anna took the papers he pushed toward her. And that was it. She was escorted outside the gates of the Gulag and told she was on her own. Without food or money, in just the tattered prison-issued clothing she wore on her back.

After walking most of the day, she hitched a ride with a free man and woman delivering goods to Magadan. She sat in the back of the bumpy truck with a variety of livestock and crates.

They reached Magadan late at night and dropped Anna off at the docks, where she hoped to find passage back to Moscow.

It took five days and nearly starving to death before she bargained for passage on a cargo ship that needed to quickly replace their cook who had become ill and died just before their arrival. They would allow her passage to Moscow and three meals a day to cook for the crew.

The trip back over the ocean and down the rivers to Moscow took two weeks—and even with the occasional haranguing by the crew, it was the best and safest Anna had felt in over ten years. She was even able to put on a little weight, enjoying the potatoes, cabbage, and sometimes even sausage she cooked and served to the crew along with thick gruel and stew with actual chunks of fish in it.

When they finally docked in Moscow, the captain of the barge slipped her five rubles and a sack of cooked potatoes, and wished her luck, whispering to her that his sister had died in the Gulags.

Anna rushed through the streets to her family's old apartment. It winded her to climb the stairs, but she knocked on the door where she'd once lived, gasping like she'd run a hundred miles.

A man opened the door, frowning and eyes wide with fear. "Who are you? What do you want?" he whispered as he searched behind and to the sides of her.

Disappointment beat in time to the rhythm of her heart. "I'm Anna Levitskaya. I...my family used to live here. Do you know where they've been moved to?"

"No. Now go away." He shut the door in her face.

Anna found shelter in the doorway of an abandoned store, where she sat and ate one of the potatoes from her bag while she pondered her next steps. She needed to check in with the local authorities, get a work permit, and find a job. But before she could think about all that, she needed to find her mama and let her know she'd survived, just as Mama had asked.

She started by going to nearby state-run stores and the tailor Mama had done odd jobs for right after Papa had died. She didn't recognize any of the workers, but decided to ask, just in case someone knew Nadya or Mikhail. The sun had set a couple of hours ago, always slipping behind the buildings early this time of year. Anna decided to try one more place before checking in with the authorities and hopefully being given a place to stay.

The butcher shop. Anna had been avoiding this area—this was where Nikolai had come to get the sausage for Mama's birthday that fateful night when he'd drunk too much and told a joke...

The old butcher looked up as the bell above the door jangled. He tilted his head, as if trying to place her weathered face. "Anna?" he finally asked.

She nodded, tears close to the surface at seeing someone who finally recognized her.

"You made it. It's so good to see you."

"Don't say that too loud, you don't want to be seen sympathizing with—"

"Bah! I'm too old to worry about who is listening. Let them haul me behind the Lubyanka and shoot me." He glanced around quickly, belying his devil-may-care attitude. "What can I do for you?"

"Do you know where they are? Where Mama and Nadya are? I went to the old apartment, but someone else is living there now."

"Ah, yes. That bastard of a brother-in-law of yours was in here just last week and asked for a delivery to be sent to his residence when I get my meat order in." He flipped through a notebook at the counter. "Ah, here it is." He turned the page to Anna.

She read and memorized the address. It wasn't far, she should be able to make it there to check on Mama and then back to the government offices before they closed at six.

☭

Her limbs shook as she lifted her hand to knock on door number twelve in the apartment building in a better part of town. Nadya had denounced her, Mikhail had turned Nikolai in—but she wasn't there to see them.

She knocked, then stepped back with her shoulders straight and head up.

Her sister opened the door just a crack then gasped and shook her head. "Anna. You aren't welcome here." Nadya spit at her. "Leave. Now. Mikhail has moved up in the Party and can't afford for anyone to see *you* here."

"I want to see Mama. Where is she?" Anna tried to see around her sister, into the apartment.

Scowling, Nadya said, "You just missed her..."

The dread Anna had been feeling all day turned to hope. She'd just missed her...

"She died three days ago. We buried her yesterday." There was no sign of love or remorse in Nadya's voice, just disgust and...maybe fear? "Now leave. And never come back here." She shut the door, locks clicking on the other side.

49

Anna stood at the conveyor belt, bundling the bullets into packages at the small arms munitions factory where she'd finally found work after searching, homeless, for three long weeks.

The government officials had been no help, only telling her she wouldn't be assigned living quarters or a food ration card until she had a job. And that was left up to her. Now she lived in a crowded dormitory with a shared kitchen and one bathroom for over a hundred residents.

Life out in "freedom" wasn't much better than life inside the Gulag—except a little more food, a warm place to sleep, and less chance of being sexually assaulted. But she had no friends. People were afraid to befriend an "enemy of the people," even if she had been supposedly rehabilitated. Even others who'd by some miracle made it out of the deadly camps were reluctant to talk to each other.

They were required to work long shifts in the factories, and Anna glanced at the clock, counting down the last hour of her fourteen-hour shift so she could go back to the dormitory, eat, and get some sleep before starting all over again in the morning.

She let her mind wander, only allowing the good memories to

flow freely past the hidden horrors of the past ten-plus years. Her younger years with Mama, Papa, and Nadya—before she turned against Anna. Nikolai and stolen kisses, innocent and sweet—how he'd gotten down on one knee to propose to her. Zoya—always her ill-tempered protector. Pyotr's kindness and knowledge. Georgi and their one, precious evening of love together.

"Anna!" the plant manager yelled from his office. "I need you in here, now!"

She finished up the bundle of bullets she was working on then turned toward his office behind her. Her blood turned to ice, and she stopped, frozen mid-step. Two NKVD officers stood beside the manager.

They approached her where she stood, leaving the manager to stare from his open doorway. "Anna Levitskaya," the taller of the two officers said, "you've been sentenced to a second term in a corrective labor camp. We're here to take you to the transit prison to await transport back to the Kolyma."

"Why?" Anna choked on the word, knowing they didn't need a reason.

"There was a mistake made when you were released. The administrator overlooked an order for you to be resentenced while still in camp. Ten more years." He grabbed her by the arm. "Let's go."

She glanced at the gun hanging at the officer's side. Nikolai had had the right idea all along. But before she could act on the impulse, her vision darkened and her knees buckled as her shocked mind shut down, taking her body with it.

AFTERWORD

Numbers:

The precise number of victims killed during the reigns of Lenin and Stalin in the USSR will likely never be known. At best, the numbers come from educated guesswork. If you want to read up on why drilling down on exact numbers has been so difficult, I recommend reading Gulag A History by Anne Applebaum, pages 578-586.

Here are a few of the compiled numbers from experts:

1. In Gulag A History, Anne Applebaum states: *...we have to rely upon what we have: a year-by-year account of Gulag death rates, based on the archives of the Department of Prisoner Registration. This account seems to exclude deaths in prisons and deaths during transport. It has been compiled using overall NKVD reports, not the records of individual camps. It does not include special exiles at all.*

1930: 7,980 (4.2%)
1931: 7,283 (2.9%)
1932: 13,197 (4.81%)

1933: 67,297 (15.3%)
1934: 25,187 (4.28%)
1935: 31,636 (2.75%)
1936: 24,933 (2.11%)
1937: 31,056 (2.42%)
1938: 108,654 (5.35%)
1939: 44,750 (3.1%)
1940: 41,275 (2.72%)
1941: 115,484 (6.1%)
1942: 352,560 (24.9%)
1943: 267,826 (22.4%)
1944: 114,481 (9.2%)
1945: 81,917 (5.95%)
1946: 30,715 (2.2%)
1947: 66,830 (3.59%)
1948: 50,659 (2.28%)
1949: 29,350 (1.21%)
1950: 24,511 (0.95%)
1951: 22,466 (0.92%)
1952: 20,643 (0.84%)
1953: 9,628 (0.67%)

These numbers are based on information available to Ms. Applebaum in the 1960s when she published her book.

--Anne Applebaum, Gulag A History, pages 582-583

2. "The victims include:

- 200,000 killed during the Red Terror (1918-22)
- 11 million dead from famine and dekulakization
- 700,000 executed during the Great Terror (1937-38)
- 400,000 more executed between 1929 and 1953
- 1.6 million dead during forced population transfers

- and a minimum 2.7 million dead in the Gulag, labor colonies, and special settlements.

"To this list should be added nearly a million Gulag prisoners released during World War II into Red Army penal battalions, where they faced almost certain death; the partisans and civilians killed in the postwar revolts against Soviet rule in Ukraine and the Baltics; and dying Gulag inmates freed so that their deaths would not count in official statistics.

"If we add to this list the deaths caused by communist regimes that the Soviet Union created and supported—including those in Eastern Europe, China, Cuba, North Korea, Vietnam and Cambodia—the total number of victims is closer to **100 million**. That makes communism the greatest catastrophe in human history."

--https://www.hudson.org/national-security-defense/100-years-of-communism-and-100-million-dead

3. "Under a headline proclaiming 'The Number of Victims of Stalinism Is About 40 Million People,' in a terse, question-and-answer format, Mr. Medvedev cited the human cost of Stalin's leadership year by year, leaving it to the reader to complete the arithmetic.

Mr. Medevedev's accounting included these victims:

- One million imprisoned or exiled from 1927 to 1929, falsely accused of being saboteurs or members of opposition parties.
- Nine million to eleven million of the more prosperous peasants driven from their lands and another two million to three million arrested or exiled in the early 1930's campaign of forced farm collectivization. Many of these were believed to have been killed.

- Six million to seven million killed in the punitive famine inflicted on peasants in 1932 and 1933.
- One million exiled from Moscow and Leningrad in 1935 for belonging to families of former nobility, merchants, capitalists, and officials.
- About one million executed in the 'great terror' of 1937-38, and another four million to six million sent to forced labor camps from which most, including Mr. Medvedev's father, did not return.
- Two million to three million sent to camps for violating absurdly strict labor laws imposed in 1940.
- At least ten million to twelve million 'repressed' in World War II, including millions of Soviet-Germans and other ethnic minorities forcibly relocated.
- More than one million arrested on political grounds from 1946 to Stalin's death in 1953."

--https://www.nytimes.com/1989/02/04/world/major-soviet-paper-says-20-million-died-as-victims-of-stalin.html

SUMMARIZING QUOTES

"We have to exterminate the useless classes. You do not have to look for proof that an accused person acted against the Soviets with the help of a word or a deed. The first question is to what class he belongs, what his origins are, what his upbringing, education, and profession are? These questions will define the accused's fate. This is the sense and essence of the Red Terror." ~ Martin Latsis, an influential security apparatus official.

"The problem with Soviet power is the fact that it gives rise to the vilest type of official—one that scrupulously carries out the general designs of the supreme authority... This official never tells the truth, because he doesn't want to distress the leadership. He gloats about famine and pestilence in the district or ward controlled by his rival. He won't lift a finger to help his neighbor... All I see around me is loathsome politicizing, dirty tricks and people being destroyed for slips of the tongue. There's no end to the denunciations. You can't spit without hitting some revolting denouncer or liar. What have we come

to? It's impossible to breathe. The less gifted a bastard, the meaner his slander. Of course the purge of your Party is none of my business, but I think that as a result of it, decent elements still remaining will be cleaned out." ~ A manager at Transmashtekh (a vast industrial conglomerate), in a letter to Soviet President Mikhail Kalinin (1932). From The Whisperers: Private Life in Stalin's Russia by *Orlando Figes*, pages 156-157.

Stalin must have known that the vast majority of these victims were entirely innocent. But since it only took a small handful of "hidden enemies" to make a Revolution while the country was at war, it was fully justified, in his view, to arrest millions to root these out. As Stalin said in June 1937, if just five per cent of the people who had been arrested turned out to be actual enemies, "that would be a good result." Evidence was a minor consideration. According to Nikita Khrushchev, then the head of the Moscow Party Committee, Stalin "used to say that if a report (denunciation) was ten per cent true, we should regard the entire report as fact." From The Whisperers: Private Life in Stalin's Russa by *Orlando Figes*, page 239.

"To be honest about those times, it is not only Stalin that you cannot forgive, but you yourself. It is not that you did something bad—maybe you did nothing wrong, at least on the face of it—but that you became accustomed to evil. The events that took place in 1937-8 now appear extraordinary, diabolical, but to you, then a young man of 22 or 24, they became a kind of norm, almost ordinary. You lived in the midst of these events, blind and deaf to everything, you saw, and heard nothing when people all around you were shot and killed, when people all around you disappeared." ~ Kirill Simonov

"They thought I had got what I deserved because I was critical of the excesses. Yet when the same happened to them, they thought it was a mistake that would be fixed—because they had never had any doubts whatsoever, and whatever instructions had come down from the top, they had always cheered and carried them out... And when they were being expelled from the Party, none of them stood up for each other; they all kept quiet or raised their hands in support of the expulsion. It was some kind of universal psychosis." ~ Nadezhda Grankina

That was the way it was in those years: people lived and breathed and then suddenly found out that their existence was inexpedient.

And it must also be kept in mind that it was not what he had done that constituted the defendant's burden, but what he might *do if he were not shot now. "We protect ourselves not only against the past but also against the future."* ~ Aleksandr Solzhenitsyn

Orachevsky had been given only five years. He had been imprisoned for a facial *crime (really out of Orwell)—for a smile! He had been an instructor in a field engineers' school. While showing another teacher in the classroom something in* Pravda, *he had smiled! The other teacher was killed soon after so no one ever found out what Orachevsky had been smiling at. But the smile had been observed, and the act of smiling at the central organ of the Party was in itself sacrilege!* ~ From The Gulag Archipelago Volume 2, page 283, *Aleksandr Solzhenitsyn.*

The best of the writers suppressed the best within themselves and turned their back on truth—and only that way did they and their books survive. And those who could not renounce profundity, individuality, and directness... inevitably had to lay down their heads during those decades, most often through camp, though some lost theirs through reckless courage at the front. ~ Aleksandr Solzhenitsyn

Unlimited power in the hands of limited people always leads to cruelty. ~ Aleksandr Solzhenitsyn

The permanent lie becomes the only safe form of existence, in the same way as betrayal. Every wag of the tongue can be overheard by someone, every facial expression observed by someone. Therefore every word, if it does not have to be a direct lie, is nonetheless obliged not to contradict the general, common lie. There exists a collection of ready-made phrases, of labels, a selection of ready-made lies. And not one single speech nor one single essay or article nor one single book—be it scientific, journalistic, critical, or "literary," so-called—can exist without the use of these primary clichés. In the most scientific of text it is required that someone's false authority or false priority be upheld somewhere, and that someone be cursed for telling the truth; without this lie even an academic work cannot see the light of day. And what can be said about those shrill meetings and trashy lunch-break gatherings where you are compelled to vote against your own opinion, to pretend to be glad over what distresses you, and to express the deepest anger in areas about which you couldn't care less. ~ Aleksandr Solzhenitsyn

One little note on eight-year-old Zoya Vlasova. She loved her father intensely. She could no longer go to school. (They teased her: "Your papa is a wrecker!" She would get in a fight: "My papa is good!") She lived only one year after the trial. Up to then she had never been ill. During that year she did not once smile: she went about with head hung low, and the old women prophesied: "She keeps looking at the earth; she is going to die soon." She died of inflammation of the brain, and as she was dying she kept calling out: "Where is my papa? Give me my papa!" **When we count up the millions of those who perished in the camps, we forget to multiply them by two, by three.** ~Aleksandr Solzhenitsyn

BIBLIOGRAPHY

-Black Mariahs: *Aleksandr Solzhenitsyn*, The Gulag Archipelago, Volume 1, pages 527-529.

-Fifty-eights (Article 58 of the Criminal Code): *Aleksandr Solzhenitsyn*, The Gulag Archipelago, Volume 1, pages 60-67

-Arrests of *Intelligentsia*: *Aleksandr Solzhenitsyn*, The Gulag Archipelago, Volume 1, Pages 72-73

-Housing: *Orlando Figes*, The Whisperers: Private Life in Stalin's Russia, pages 174-175

-Propaganda posters: https://www.sovietposters.com/periods/1930

-Nighttime Arrests: *Anne Applebaum*, Gulag A History, pages 127-128

-Arrests: *Aleksandr Solzhenitsyn*, The Gulag Archipelago, Volume 1, pages 4-6

-The Young Pioneers: https://en.wikipedia.org/wiki/Young_Pioneers_(Soviet_Union)

-Arrests of 1937-38: *Aleksandr Solzhenitsyn*, The Gulag Archipelago, Volume 1, pages 24-25

-Arrests of 1937-38: *Anne Applebaum*, Gulag A History, page 135

-Reasons for Arrests: *Aleksandr Solzhenitsyn*, The Gulag Archipelago, Volume 2, pages 292-301

-Arrest over a spool of thread: *Aleksandr Solzhenitsyn*, The Gulag Archipelago, Volume 2, page 149

-Jokes/Arrests: https://aeon.co/ideas/the-jokes-always-saved-us-humour-in-the-time-of-stalin

-https://www.calvertjournal.com/articles/show/11965/humour-under-stalin-book-jonathan-waterlow

-Arrest Quotas: *Aleksandr Solzhenitsyn*, The Gulag Archipelago, Volume 1, page 71

-Rape in Black Mariah: *Aleksandr Solzhenitsyn*, The Gulag Archipelago, Volume 1, page 530

-Thieves trading with guards: *Aleksandr Solzhenitsyn*, The Gulag Archipelago, Volume 1, page 506 and page 530

-Process upon entering prison: *Anne Applebaum*, Gulag A History, page 131-134

-Torture, testicles: *Aleksandr Solzhenitsyn*, The Gulag Archipelago, Volume 1, page 128

-The box, bedbugs: *Aleksandr Solzhenitsyn*, The Gulag Archipelago, Volume 1, page 109 & 113

-Locked in where unable to change position, *Aleksandr Solzhenitsyn*, The Gulag Archipelago, Volume 1, page 114

-Feelings after bedbugs and the box: *Aleksandr Solzhenitsyn*, The Gulag Archipelago, Volume 1, page 112

-The use of torture by interrogators in 1938: *Aleksandr Solzhenitsyn*, The Gulag Archipelago, Volume 1, page 99

-Forced standing: *Aleksandr Solzhenitsyn*, The Gulag Archipelago, Volume 1, page 111 and 182; *Anne Applebaum*, Gulag A History, page 143

-"We never arrest anyone who is not guilty...": *Anne Applebaum*, Gulag A History, page 137

-Rubber truncheon, beatings: *Aleksandr Solzhenitsyn*, The Gulag Archipelago, Volume 1, page 116 AND *Anne Applebaum*, Gulag A History, page 140-142

-Sleeplessness: *Aleksandr Solzhenitsyn*, The Gulag Archipelago, Volume 1, pages 111-113 AND *Anne Applebaum*, Gulag A History, page 143

-Forced "depositions": *Aleksandr Solzhenitsyn*, The Gulag Archipelago, Volume 1, page 117-118.

-Denouncing of others: *Aleksandr Solzhenitsyn*, The Gulag Archipelago, Volume 1, pages 117-119

-Denouncing of others: *Anne Applebaum*, Gulag A History, page 138

-Stalin, Central Committee allowing torture of prisoners: *Anne Applebaum*, Gulag A History, page 140-141

-Vise to hold hands to desk: *Aleksandr Solzhenitsyn*, The Gulag Archipelago, Volume 1, page 116

-Needles pushed under nails: *Aleksandr Solzhenitsyn*, The Gulag Archipelago, Volume 1, page 126.

-Salt-water douche in the throat: *Aleksandr Solzhenitsyn*, The Gulag Archipelago, Volume 1, page 126

-Hot/cold punishment cell: *Aleksandr Solzhenitsyn*, The Gulag Archipelago, Volume 1, page 98

-Punishment cells: *Aleksandr Solzhenitsyn*, The Gulag Archipelago, Volume 1, page 113; and *Anne Applebaum*, Gulag A History, page 142

-Starvation: *Aleksandr Solzhenitsyn*, The Gulag Archipelago, Volume 1, page 114-115

-Suspicion of Espionage: *Aleksandr Solzhenitsyn*, The Gulag Archipelago, Volume 1, page 64

-Wrecking: *Aleksandr Solzhenitsyn*, The Gulag Archipelago, Volume 1, page 64

-Rubber strap, beating back, soles of feet: *Anne Applebaum*, Gulag A History, page 141

-Smelling salts/Ammonia: *Aleksandr Solzhenitsyn*, The Gulag Archipelago, Volume 1, page 114

-Stool in corridor: *Aleksandr Solzhenitsyn*, The Gulag Archipelago, Volume 1, page 109

-Sleep deprivation – periods of no recollection: *Anne Applebaum*, Gulag A History, page 143

-Standing on knees: *Aleksandr Solzhenitsyn*, The Gulag Archipelago, Volume 1, page 111

-Starosta (Elder): *Anne Applebaum*, Gulag A History, pages 154-155

-Crowding in cells: *Aleksandr Solzhenitsyn*, The Gulag Archipelago, Volume 1, pages 124-125; *Anne Applebaum*, Gulag A History, pages 149-150

-Breakfast: *Anne Applebaum*, Gulag A History, pages 151-152

-"Judas hole"/ peephole: *Anne Applebaum*, Gulag A History, page 152

-Not allowed to talk to each other: *Anne Applebaum*, Gulag A History, page 152

-Informers/stool pigeons: *Anne Applebaum*, Gulag A History, page 153; *Aleksandr Solzhenitsyn*, The Gulag Archipelago, Volume 1, pages 185-186

-Questioning by the prosecutor: *Aleksandr Solzhenitsyn*, The Gulag Archipelago, Volume 1, pages 140-141

-Article 58: *Aleksandr Solzhenitsyn*, The Gulag Archipelago, Volume 1, pages 60-67

-206 procedure: *Aleksandr Solzhenitsyn*, The Gulag Archipelago, Volume 1, page 141

-Food parcels: *Aleksandr Solzhenitsyn*, The Gulag Archipelago, Volume 1, page 195.

-Bath before sentencing, *Aleksandr Solzhenitsyn*, The Gulag Archipelago, Volume 1, page 274

-Sentencing: *Aleksandr Solzhenitsyn*, The Gulag Archipelago, Volume 1, pages 277-279.

-Trucks/transport to railway cars: *Anne Applebaum*, Gulag A History, page 161

-Railway station, knees, guards: *Anne Applebaum*, Gulag A History, page 162-163

-Stolypin cars: *Aleksandr Solzhenitsyn*, The Gulag Archipelago, Volume 1, pages 491-493; and *Anne Applebaum*, Gulag A History, page 162-163

-Thieves and murderers, better treatment, tormenting politicals: *Aleksandr Solzhenitsyn*, The Gulag Archipelago, Volume 1, pages 500-506

-Food and water, trips to bathroom in Stolypin car: *Aleksandr Solzhenitsyn*, The Gulag Archipelago, Volume 1, pages 494-498

-Crowded train compartment, feet not touching floor, suspended: *Aleksandr Solzhenitsyn*, The Gulag Archipelago, Volume 1, page 493

-*Vtoraya Rechka, Anne Applebaum*, Gulag A History, page 168

-Feed only those who work: *Anne Applebaum*, Gulag A History, page 168

-Keeping dead in barracks to get their rations: *Aleksandr Solzhenitsyn*, The Gulag Archipelago, Volume 1, page 535

-Osip Mandelstam, poet: https://www.rbth.com/literature/2014/07/16/the_final_days_of_russian_writers_osip_mandelstam_38249.html ; and *Anne Applebaum*, Gulag A History, pages 3, 125, and 168

-Crowding in transit prison and quarantine barracks: *Aleksandr Solzhenitsyn*, The Gulag Archipelago, Volume 1, page 535 and 536

-Typhus: *Aleksandr Solzhenitsyn*, The Gulag Archipelago, Volume 1, page 535; *Aleksandr Solzhenitsyn*, The Gulag Archipelago, Volume 2, page 125

-Standing naked while clothes were treated: https://www.rbth.com/literature/2014/07/16/the_final_days_of_russian_writers_osip_mandelstam_38249.html

-Prison ships/steamships: https://en.wikipedia.org/wiki/SS_Indigirka

-Dalstroi Fleet: https://en.wikipedia.org/wiki/Dalstroy

-Transport on cargo ships: *Anne Applebaum*, Gulag A History, pages 169-172

-Toilets built off side of ship: *Anne Applebaum*, Gulag A History, page 170

-The "Kolyma Tram" - *Anne Applebaum*, Gulag A History, pages 171-172

-Slogans on the gate - *Anne Applebaum*, Gulag A History, page 175

-Baths, shaving, clothing, arrival at camp - *Anne Applebaum*, Gulag A History, pages 176-177; *Aleksandr Solzhenitsyn*, The Gulag Archipelago, Volume 2, page 229;

Aleksandr Solzhenitsyn, The Gulag Archipelago, Volume 1, page 542; and https://gulaghistory.org/nps/onlineexhibit/stalin/women.php.html

-Barracks - *Anne Applebaum*, Gulag A History, pages 195-196

-Trusties "choosing" women to "visit" them - *Aleksandr Solzhenitsyn*, The Gulag Archipelago, Volume 2, page 230

-What general labor does to a woman's body - *Aleksandr Solzhenitsyn*, The Gulag Archipelago, Volume 2, page 236

-Logging, dry execution - *Aleksandr Solzhenitsyn*, The Gulag Archipelago, Volume 2, pages 199-201

-Roll call, meals, routines - *Anne Applebaum*, Gulag A History, pages 191-195

-Priests in the gulag - *Aleksandr Solzhenitsyn*, The Gulag Archipelago, Volume 2, pages 310-311

-Priests and other Christians in the gulags: *Aleksandr Solzhenitsyn*, The Gulag Archipelago, Volume 1, pages 36 & 37

-Women, logging, sawing down trees: *Anne Applebaum*, Gulag A History, page 222

-Large-scale arrests of clergy, closing down churches: *Aleksandr Solzhenitsyn*, The Gulag Archipelago, Volume 1, page 51

-Words and the Soviet government: *Aleksandr Solzhenitsyn*, The Gulag Archipelago, Volume 1, page 66

-Work norms and food rations: *Anne Applebaum*, Gulag A History, page 222

-Days off for prisoners: *Anne Applebaum*, Gulag A History, page 194

-Waste buckets, urine "pyramids": *Anne Applebaum*, Gulag A History, page 199

-Family renouncements: *Varlam Shalamov*, Kolyma Tales, page 55

-Work in below zero temperatures: *Aleksandr Solzhenitsyn*, The Gulag Archipelago, Volume 2, page 201; and *Anne Applebaum*, Gulag A History, pages 224-228

-Escaped prisoner, woman forced to stand out in cold: *Aleksandr Solzhenitsyn*, The Gulag Archipelago, Volume 2, pages 148 and 149

-Winter storm: *Anne Applebaum*, Gulag A History, pages 224-225

-Soup in camp: *Anne Applebaum*, Gulag A History, page 206

-Piling corpses outside barracks: *Aleksandr Solzhenitsyn*, The Gulag Archipelago, Volume 2, page 384

-Sickness: *Anne Applebaum*, Gulag A History, page 369+

-Hospital: *Anne Applebaum*, Gulag A History, pages 370-371

-Children in orphanages rejecting parents: *Anne Applebaum*, Gulag A History, pages 326-327

-Logs crushing a man: *Anne Applebaum*, Gulag A History, pages 227-228

-Woman making "norms" cutting down trees: *Anne Applebaum*, Gulag A History, page 356

-Pictures and posters in barracks: https://allthatsinteresting.com/wordpress/wp-content/uploads/2021/05/gulag-with-communist-posters.jpeg

-Arrests and Quotas: *Aleksandr Solzhenitsyn*, The Gulag Archipelago, Volume 1, page 11

-Collectivization, dekulakization of agriculture, famine: https://www.loc.gov/resource/gdclccn.96024752/?sp=400&st=image&r=-0.01,0.658,1.089,0.586,0

-Ideology and evil: *Aleksandr Solzhenitsyn*, The Gulag Archipelago, Volume 1, pages 173 and 174

-Punishment cells: *Aleksandr Solzhenitsyn*, The Gulag Archipelago, Volume 2, page 416; and *Anne Applebaum*, Gulag A History, pages 244-247.

- Russo-Finnish War, prisoners https://en.wikipedia.org/wiki/Soviet_prisoners_of_war_in_Finland

-Open pit punishment cells: *Aleksandr Solzhenitsyn*, The Gulag Archipelago, Volume 2, page 416

-Winter War (Russo-Finnish War): https://en.wikipedia.org/wiki/Winter_War

-Communist Loyalists in prison camps: *Aleksandr Solzhenitsyn*, The Gulag Archipelago, Volume 2, pages 180, 181, 327-328.

-Soldiers/POWs imprisonment and execution: *Aleksandr Solzhenitsyn*, The Gulag Archipelago, Volume 2, pages 219-220, 243-245.

-Summer in the tundra, mud, mosquitoes: *Anne Applebaum*, Gulag A History, page 223

-Punishment – tied to tree – mosquitoes: *Aleksandr Solzhenitsyn*, The Gulag Archipelago, Volume 2, page 38 and 127.

-Relationships between male and female prisoners; "not of the flesh": *Aleksandr Solzhenitsyn*, The Gulag Archipelago, Volume 2, pages 153 and 239.

-Artists in camp: *Aleksandr Solzhenitsyn*, The Gulag Archipelago, Volume 2, pages 477, 486 & 487.

-Mass Executions in Gulags: *Aleksandr Solzhenitsyn*, The Gulag Archipelago, Volume 2, pages 128-129, 305, 386-390

-Announcement of Germany's invasion of Russia: *Anne Applebaum*, Gulag A History, page 412

-Effects of WWII on political prisoners: *Anne Applebaum*, Gulag A History, pages 412-419.

-Conditions at gulag during war: *Aleksandr Solzhenitsyn*, The Gulag Archipelago, Volume 2, pages 133-137.

-Second Terms: *Aleksandr Solzhenitsyn*, The Gulag Archipelago, Volume 2, page 376

-Working at gold mine: *Anne Applebaum*, Gulag A History, page 193

-Effects of hard labor on the body: *Aleksandr Solzhenitsyn*, The Gulag Archipelago, Volume 2, page 236.

-Camp hospitals: *Aleksandr Solzhenitsyn*, The Gulag Archipelago, Volume 2, pages 215-219.

-Self-mutilation to get out of heavy labor: *Aleksandr Solzhenitsyn*, The Gulag Archipelago, Volume 2, page 214

-One in four or one in five prisoners dying: *Anne Applebaum*, Gulag A History, page 414

-Signing decrees for imprisonment in punishment block: *Aleksandr Solzhenitsyn*, The Gulag Archipelago, Volume 2, page 215

-Amnesty for pregnant women and mothers of small children: *Anne Applebaum*, Gulag A History, page 461

-Conditions and new round of arrests after the war: *Anne Applebaum,* Gulag A History, page 462

-Separation of women from men 1946-47: *Aleksandr Solzhenitsyn,* The Gulag Archipelago, Volume 2, page 246

-Working in a clay pit: *Aleksandr Solzhenitsyn,* The Gulag Archipelago, Volume 2, pages 178 and 192-195.

-Release: *Aleksandr Solzhenitsyn,* The Gulag Archipelago, Volume 3, Pages 445-451.

-Second terms (1948-1949): *Aleksandr Solzhenitsyn,* The Gulag Archipelago, Volume 2, page 376

ABOUT THE AUTHOR

H. L. Anderson has a Bachelor's Degree in Nursing—which has nothing to do with writing, except maybe by adding some pretty descriptive injury and vomit scenes to her books. She discovered her joy of writing during a very trying period in her life when escaping into make-believe saved her. She enjoys reading any book she gets her hands on.

Along with her husband, Steve, and their four sons, she lives in Grantsville, Utah—the same small town in which she grew up.